"*The Fuck-Up* is *Trainspotting* without drugs, New York style."
—Hal Sirowitz, author of *Mother Said*

"Fantastically alluring! I cannot recommend this book highly enough!"
—*Flipside*

"Combining moments of brilliant black humor with flashes of devastating pain, [it] reads like a roller coaster ride . . . A wonderful book."
—*Alternative Press*

"Touted as the bottled essence of early eighties East Village living, *The Fuck-Up* is, refreshingly, nothing nearly so limited . . . A cult favorite since its first, obscure printing in 1991, I'd say it's ready to become a legitimate religion."
—*Smug Magazine*

"Not since *The Catcher in the Rye,* or John Knowles's *A Separate Peace,* have I read such a beautifully written book . . . Nersesian's powerful, sure-footed narrative alone is so believably human in its poignancy . . . I couldn't put this book down."
—*Grid Magazine*

For *MANHATTAN LOVERBOY*

"Best Book for the Beach, Summer 2000." —*Jane Magazine*

"Best Indie Novel of 2000." —*Montreal Mirror*

"Part Lewis Carroll, part Franz Kafka, Nersesian takes us down a maze of false leads and dead ends . . . told with wit and compassion, drawing the reader into a world of paranoia and coincidence while illuminating questions of free will and destiny. Highly recommended."
—*Library Journal*

"A tawdry and fantastic tale . . . Nersesian renders Gotham's unique cocktail of wealth, poverty, crime, glamour, and brutality spectacularly. This book is full of lies, and the author makes deception seem like the subtext of modern life, or at least America's real pastime . . . Love, hate, and falsehood commingle. But in the end, it is [protagonist] Joey's search for his own identity that makes this book a winner."
—*Rain Taxi Review of Books*

"Funny and darkly surreal." —*New York Press*

"... a hilarious and warped passion play ... the dense story surges with survivalist instinct, capturing everyman's quest for a sense of individuality."
—*Smug Magazine*

"*MLB* sits somewhere between Kafka, DeLillo, and Lovecraft—a terribly frightening, funny, and all too possible place."
—*Literary Review of Canada*

"Nersesian's literary progress between *The Fuck-Up* and *Manhattan Loverboy* is like Beckett's between *Happy Days* and *Not I* ... *MLB* is about how distance from power and decision-making can skew our reality, can leave us feeling like pawns in an incomprehensible game."
—*The Toronto Star*

For *CHINESE TAKEOUT*

"Not since Henry Miller has a writer so successfully captured the ... tribulations of a struggling artist ... A masterly image."
—*Library Journal* (starred review)

"One of the best [books] I've read about the artist's life. Nersesian captures the obsession one needs to keep going under tough odds ... trying to stay true to himself, and his struggle against the odds makes for a compelling read."
—*Village Voice*

"... a heartfelt, tragicomic bohemian romance with echoes of the myth of Orpheus and Eurydice ... Infused with the symbolism of Greek legend, the hip squalor of this milieu takes on a mythic charge that energizes Nersesian's lyrical celebration of an evanescent moment in the life of the city."
—*Publishers Weekly*

"Magnificent ... Nersesian's story of a man on a search for authenticity won't leave you hungry ... Nersesian is this generation's Mark Twain and the East River is his Mississippi."
—Jennifer Belle, author of *High Maintenance*

"Nersesian's writing is fun and gritty. He'll give you a glimpse of a world that may be very different from your own. He'll enable you to identify with people you may have little in common with. As a result, your perception of reality may be affected."
—Amanda Filipacchi, author of *Nude Men* and *Vapor*

"When the protagonist of *Chinese Takeout* falls hopelessly in love with a mysterious I.V. user, a powerful metaphor is made—not only is love an addiction, but so is art, as we witness a young man's compulsion to paint to the sacrifice of nearly all else. By the final crescendo this is confirmed, when the young artist risks everything in pursuit of what he perceives as greatness. Nersesian's book examines these themes more dramatically than any other novel I can think of."
—Dr. Lisa M. Najavits, author of *A Woman's Addiction Workbook*

For *dogrun,*

"Darkly comic . . . It's Nersesian's love affair with lower Manhattan that sets these pages afire."
—*Entertainment Weekly*

"A rich parody of the all-girl punk band."
—*New York Times Book Review*

"Nersesian's blackly comic urban coming-of-angst tale offers a laugh in every paragraph."
—*Glamour*

For *UNLUBRICATED*

"Nersesian's raw, smutty sensibility is perfect for capturing the gritty city artistic life, but this novel has as much substance as style . . . Nersesian continuously ratchets up the suspense, always keeping the fate of the production uncertain—and at the last minute he throws a curveball that makes the previous chaos calm by comparison. Nersesian is a first-rate observer of his native New York . . ."
—*Publishers Weekly*

"A real delight—fast and funny and pure New York. *Unlubricated* has only one flaw: It ends."
—Steve Kluger, author of *Last Days of Summer*

DELPHI BASILICATO

ARTHUR BURKE NERSESIAN, a fifth-generation New Yorker, was raised on Fiftieth Street and Third Avenue, until he was evicted. Soon after, he moved down to Sixteenth and Third Avenue, but lost that apartment too. Eventually, he went north again, stopping at Eighty-eighth and Amsterdam, until he was once again compelled to leave. He then relocated to Forty-fifth and Eighth Avenue; he lived there until a second eviction notice was served. Soon after, he again found himself on Sixteenth Street, this time closer to Sixth Avenue. Now he lives and writes in the East Village.

His only true home is New York City.

Suicide
Casanova

ARTHUR NERSESIAN

AKASHIC BOOKS
NEW YORK

Other novels by Arthur Nersesian

The Fuck-Up
Akashic Books, 1997
MTV Books, 1999

Manhattan Loverboy
Akashic Books, 2000

Unlubricated
HarperCollins, 2004

Chinese Takeout
HarperCollins, 2003

dogrun,
MTV Books, 2000

Published by Akashic Books
©2002, 2005 Arthur Nersesian

ISBN: 1-888451-66-1
Library of Congress Control Number: 2004106239
All rights reserved
First paperback printing

Printed in Canada

Akashic Books
PO Box 1456
New York, NY 10009
Akashic7@aol.com
www.akashicbooks.com

To Delphi Basilicato

PART ONE: REWIND

EXCEPT FOR THE FACT THAT IT TERMINATES LIFE, DEATH IS such a little thing. Muscles cease to twitch, cells fail to regenerate, the body rots. Accidents are the perfect murder. Even the murderer doesn't know he's committing them. Until he finds the little gag ball of guilt somewhere inside himself. Opportunity was obvious, but I'm still trying to ascertain motive.

Dead skin—that's the primary ingredient of dust. My dearly departed would never have tolerated the fine skin of dust that now veils her room. Two cheesy paperbacks on her desktop say it all—*The Disciplined Gentlemen* and *Love Bound*—pop psychology attempts at explaining the phenomenon that my wife had turned into her deadlihood. She was forever curious about what drove sensitive, educated, wealthy men to her velvet rack.

In the two months since she died, I haven't once stepped inside her chamber—a spacious kitchen until she had the stove, sink, and fridge removed and it was converted into her office. We always ate out. Although she had impeccable taste, she always kept the room bare and functional: a large mission-style desk, two four-drawer filing cabinets against the far wall, a color TV with a VCR. No paintings, lamps, or knickknacks. A stack of boxes held the paraphernalia from her now-defunct dungeon.

For the first time, I am recalling her beautiful face, minutes dead, with Lana's drool and lipstick still slobbered around her mouth. Her blue lips, that red flush rising up from the black leather neck collar which was still dug deep into her throat. Her eyes, shocked, bulging up from death, eternally astounded as she gagged on that little red ball.

I draw the drapes in her office just a bit so that a poker of sunlight stabs across the wall, illuminating her oak bookshelf. Early editions in Mylar covers and boxed sets that she ordered over the Internet. Collectors copies of DeSade, de Maupassant, Flaubert, Zola, Jarry, Artaud—toward the last months she was buying up French Naturalists, working her way to the Surrealists. The bottom shelf is lined with videotapes, boxed and labeled.

When the phone rings in the next room, I can hear Beckwith's combed-over voice on the answering machine asking how the new medication is working.

Fine, that's why I'm not speaking to you, asshole.

Her videos are mainly old Hollywood flicks; Preston Sturges and John Huston films are among her favorites. There are some documentaries: *Chicken Hawk*, about NAMBLA, and Ken Burns's *Civil War* series. Yes, she was a dues-paying member of PBS. A lot of the tapes are TV shows she used to pull herself out of her moods. *Seinfeld, The Simpsons*. That sort of thing. There are roughly half a dozen porn films, mainly S&M, some starring friends and associates. She used to say that they gave her ideas for work.

In the late seventies, I used to be addicted to these films. Each one was a little amyl nitrite rush. Back then, watching hours of grainy porn in filthy, alkaline-smelling booths for about a quarter per minute, it would only cost about a buck before I would cum. On a horny afternoon I could even do it for fifty cents. Nowadays, I'd go broke having to pay by the minute, and with video technology, a sultan's orgy can be copied for peanuts.

Beckwith is still whining on my answering machine, pleading for me to return his calls. Did the court appoint me to look after him, or vice versa? I have a theory about these latter-day priests: to appease their own guilt they search out their confessions in the mouths of their patients. Why else would Beckwith be so insistent? *". . . you need help, Leslie, please!"*

Well, he's not getting shit out of me.

Hidden sideways behind the videos, I see it — *Teacher's Pet*, a porn flick starring the great seventies diva, Sky Pacifica. My wife knew that I was once involved with Sky. After we got married, though, we never talked much about it. All she ever knew was that I had had a relationship with her and that it had gone sour. I feel badly that she had apparently gone out of her way to inspect my former fuck. In truth, Sky was a lot of things — con woman, charity case, object of idolatry — but I can barely remember ever making love to her.

With her firmly balanced breasts only eclipsed by her perfectly looped thighs, her holy body seemed the product of a salacious cosmetic surgeon's fantasy. But it was her face that stole the show — I simply couldn't get enough of it. For that matter, I couldn't get a fix on it. It seemed to change constantly, reflecting and refracting at various angles as if made of fleshy sequins. Sky epitomized pornography by being not just *one* drop-dead knockout but, at different angles, reminiscent of all of them. Early in her career she was thin, later she grew curvaceous. She was brunette, but at times would go blond.

Despite what legally had to be called wild infidelities on my dear wife's part, I never doubted her loyalties for an instant. And I never sensed a hint of her jealousy of me.

Well, maybe just a hint. Toward the end—on that final night, anyway. The M.E. said the mouthpiece was loose enough, she should've been able to spit the ball out. There's only one reason she didn't stop it—she died to spite me.

In every relationship, to paraphrase Auden, doesn't one partner love the other just a bit more? Through the course of our relationship, I wondered if I was the one more or less loved. I was always testing her. If I had found this tape of Sky earlier, well, this is the pigeon feather that imbalanced the wings of our affection.

During our marriage, it had never occurred to me to reconnect with Sky. But now, the thought of seeing her sensuously penetrated makes me catch my breath. They try to teach sex offenders to avoid those pesky erotic triggers. And this tape is the button to a nuclear warhead.

In the kitchen I locate a can opener and a can—tuna fish. Lunch. I frantically start hooking and twisting.

My obsession with Sky started when I purchased every loop of hers I could get my sticky hands on, and there were plenty. Sky used three separate professional identities early in her career. I located four films in which she acted under the name Blue June. As Blue she was at her youngest, undoubtedly a minor. She had more of a girlish body: puffy breasts, a mischievous smile, gangly limbs, a torso not yet developed enough for its final erotic destiny. Her next *nom de frame* was Sarah Moreau; she was more self-conscious as an actress, her style more aggressive; less content to lie still and be done unto. Under this identity her physique was a bit more mature. Her breasts were still filling out, but the bony edges of her shoulders, rib cage, and knees contrasted with the spring baby-fat padded over all else.

One film called *Missy's Tizzy* featured young Sky under the playful pseudonym Sue De Grace. She appeared adolescent and smutty, like a naughty little girl who had been playing with her mother's cosmetics—there's a familiar fantasy. She confused trashiness with promiscuity and promiscuity with sophistication.

Trying to open the tuna fish, my fingers start trembling. Fuck tuna. Returning to the fresh dust of Cecilia's room, I look on her desktop blotter: bills to late-middle-aged men whose flabby asses she'd whip raw, lucky lads; an unmailed warranty for a cellular phone she'd never use. I spot a photograph of Britney Spears clipped out of some magazine, a reminder of youth eternal.

Able to resist no longer, I pop *Teacher's Pet* into the VCR and barely touch the play button.

There she is, or was: young Sky Pacifica. Not much more than sixteen years old, but easily passing for eighteen, pre–Tracy Lords. *Teacher's Pet* is about a student who needs an after-school tutorial. *Sure she does*. Right away she establishes a puppy crush on her much older teacher. Her red and white striped panties peek out whenever she bends over for a pencil. We know where she's heading. Too bad the adult entertainment industry only uses plot as a shield—the old First Amendment defense.

Back in the golden age, most porn sagged toward satire or campy dramatic. If the scenarios were just slightly credible, instead of opening around attractive, overly coiffed couples who happened to be sitting naked in hot tubs, and if the sex started out a bit awkwardly, even begrudgingly, instead of reducing the sacred act into something as blasé as a handshake, the orgasm would have spurted so much further.

Over the past ten years, the closest device the industry has come up with has been the straightforward interview, dropping all pretense and artifice, which has actually been quite an innovation since the actors speaking off the cuff are usually brighter and more interesting than the characters that were formerly scripted. On the other hand, porn actresses nowadays—with their dyed-blond bouffants, phony tits, collagen lips, plucked eyebrows, and shaved pubes—usually look alike, and can't get me hard.

In *Teacher's Pet*, the young and hairless Sky is chitchatting for far too long with the older teacher. The fast-forward button cuts through all that tedious exposition. Then *play*: Her pink little tongue is licking the salt off the droopy goat-like testicles of a man more than twice her age. Hairy, fat, and lecherous, he probably smells like a colostomy bag. The divining rod in my pants is my first erection in some time, and it's pointing to the past.

DECEMBER 2, 1979, NYC

A DISTANT AND SPORADIC TWEAKING ON THE VERY brink of her still consciousness grew louder and more intrusive, until Sky finally opened her eyes. It was the repeated honking and screeching of traffic. Where the fuck am I? she thought. She sat up, filled with dread. Seeing a guy sleeping next to her, she wondered if another horny bastard had got a free fuck while she was under. She reached down and was glad to find that her panties were still on.

Regardless, her self-disgust turned to self-loathing and suddenly erupted as she slapped herself hard across the face. Why was she always doing this shit? She scratched her fingers down her face just short of tearing the skin, and finally boiled out, "What the fuck am I doing here?"

The guy next to her bolted up; she had now compounded her fuck-up. He swiveled his legs down and sat at the bed's edge. She could have rooted around while he was still asleep. He might've had some cash, then she could have just taken it and split.

"What's the matter?" he said, still half-asleep.

"My fucking life."

"Come on, you're only twenty-three."

"Twenty-two, asshole!" That was her second mistake. Don't insult strangers. She still had a scar on her chin from the time she had blithely insulted a Turkish importer with a callous cock. As a pressure built up behind Sky's eyes, she tried to push it back, but it was too much. All at once she seemed to give birth to woe. Tears flowed through her hands. She knew she was making her third mistake by crying, but she couldn't stop. When he opened the blinds, revealing a sunny new day, she restrained herself from shouting at him to leave them closed. The grief was turning her ugly, making her face splotchy red, diminishing her beauty and therefore her power. But in another moment the room began to feel humid with her tears. All self-consciousness was washed away and she stared starkly at the question, what am I going to do?

"Maybe you need to eat something," he said, responding to his own hunger.

"I'm never hungry in the morning, asshole!" she shot back.

"So now I know," he replied meekly.

She muttered, "Sorry," and remembered all the sleeping pills. That was why she felt particularly lousy. The man prepared and slid a cup of coffee next to her. She rose to the wooden cabinet, grabbed a bottle of Jack Daniels, spun open the black top so that it fell to the floor, and took a hard gulp before the guy pulled the bottle away. Finally she recognized him: It was the geek with the girl's name. He had met her by pretending to be a photographer. Harmless.

"Why does my head hurt so much?" she asked, feeling a sensitive rise in her scalp. The hot glow of Jack inside of her immediately did its job.

"You probably have a hangover," he said stiffly.

"Why do I have a bump?" She wondered what he had done with her last night. She remembered boarding a plane with him in California, but she didn't remember landing.

"Look," the guy replied, "do you recall what we discussed in LA? You said that at the end of this year you wanted a second chance." She sat perfectly still like a child being scolded. "You said you wanted to do something more with your life in 1980 than just fucking, coking, and partying."

She sighed. Yesterday morning she'd fled the West Coast. She remembered that he had proposed helping her get her life back on track. At the time it had sounded like a good idea. Now, she silently thought, okay. Things aren't so bad. I can call Janine. She lives here somewhere. I can get a dance gig, save some money, and within the month get my own place and be free of this geek.

She shook her head in contrite agreement, mumbled a brief apology, and said, "Look, I'm really embarrassed to be asking this, but I forgot your name."

"Leslie," he replied.

APRIL 13, 2001, NYC
WITH THE HELP OF THE PORN VIDEO I REMEMBER SKY'S beautiful lips. Her jaws seemed to dislocate like a snake's when she swallowed. When my reddened member spurts further and hotter than it has since I was a teen, I realize — hallelujah — I'm cured!

At that moment, at that place deep inside where primal

decisions aren't so much figured out as recognized, I know that I have to locate her. Checking my wife's old Rolodex, flipping through her slap 'n tickle clientele, I locate Ron Marauder, the sole proprietor of a private investigation agency he calls The Dogs of War.

Beyond all the clandestine information Ronny has gathered in his lifetime, it's ironic that I know his one big secret. Strong and quiet by day, he is a whining, diaper-wetting infantilist in the wee hours of the night.

I dial his beeper and get a return call within fifteen minutes.

"Leslie, is everything okay?" Ron says nervously.

"Sure."

"Before I forget, I gave Cecilia an unlicensed handgun. Can you look through her things and give it back?"

"I packed up all her stuff and I don't recall seeing any handgun," I respond peacefully.

"If you find it, hold it for me," he replies, and returns to square one. "So, why'd you beep?"

"Ron, I have another job for you."

"No way. I don't do shit like that. The only reason I did the last one was for Cecilia."

"It's nothing like that. I'm just trying to locate an old friend."

"I am trying my best not to hold you responsible for Cecilia's death. I think you know that I loved your wife. Twice I asked her to leave you and marry me."

"I don't know what to say," I reply flatly.

"I gave her the gun to blow your brains out!" he shouts. "No half-decent husband would have allowed her to do what she did. You obviously didn't give a shit about her."

"Maybe so," I respond with dejection.

Perhaps it was due to the furious devotion of slaves like Ron that Cecilia was always attracted to my cool ambivalence.

"Truth of the matter is," he finally resumes, "I have been walking around like a zombie since she died." Silence, and then I hear him crying.

"Ron," I interrupt, "if it's of any consolation, I would gladly have traded my life for hers."

"If I didn't believe that, I'd stab your eyes out," he says sincerely, and then adds, "motherfucker!"

All that out of the way, we arrange a time—later that week—and a place—a macrobiotic restaurant—to discuss my case.

◄◄

Over herbal teas, I give Ron some old photos and all the information I know about Sky Pacifica. Her real name is Jeane. I last remember that she was married to a guy named Eddie Lindemeyer and had given birth to a baby girl named Kate.

"Have you checked the Internet?" Ron asks.

"No." I warm my hands against the tea mug.

"You know, I must've earned ten thousand dollars alone just going through the Net," he reflects.

"You don't say," I feign fascination.

"Leslie, was that Shirley Temple guy someone important?"

"Not really. If it makes you feel better, nothing came of it."

"You've got to promise me something up front: There's no hanky panky in this case. I'm not going to jeopardize losing my permit."

"It's nothing like the last case."

"It's personal," he clarifies, "not business."

"Exactly." Keeping a business tone is a safe bet when dealing with this nut.

Ron shakes my hand and leaves, refusing to commit to how long this will take.

Once, years ago, someone from LA, a cancerous porn producer named Fillip, hunted me down. He was like an incestuous father to Sky and he wanted his little girl back. It took him several months to track me. By then, Sky was gone. A few months later, Fillip was dead.

DECEMBER 16, 1998, NYC

STANDING OUTSIDE THE PLAYROOM AT HER DUNGEON, Excaliber's, Mistress Guinevere, a.k.a. Cecilia, kept reminding herself that the Camcorder was hidden in the closet on the upper shelf. Her frame was to the right of the wall cuff and left of the rack. She had to keep him within this range. She checked her wristwatch and listened. When she heard the tinkling of her beauty aids she opened the door violently, just as he liked, and looked at him sitting before the antique vanity, staring into the large beveled mirror. Sure enough, he had taken out her mascara and left it scattered over the quilted lace on top—as he had done every second week since 1982. He had even managed to apply some of the lipstick.

"Who made this fucking mess?" she said right on cue, slapping his hand and tossing the lipstick, eyeliner, and nail polish back into the cosmetic bag.

"Honey's sorry, Mommy," he began slowly, in his high-pitched falsetto. "She's so-o-o sorry. Please don't hit your honey bunny." The prick was deliberately slowing the pace to annoy her.

"Every fucking time I turn around, you make a mess!" She delivered her line with authentic rage while wiping his face, smearing the lipstick on his cheek.

"Honey's so sorry. Honey will never ever make a naughty mess again."

She hated this. The Honorable Peter Sanders, Administrative Judge of the Southern District of New York, Bankruptcy Court, had been her unwanted slave for over fifteen years. Finally, after so long, she had turned the tables — she was planning to extort him with the hidden camera.

In 1984, when she had first opened up her own dungeon, she informed him that she was slimming down her clientele. She politely offered to set him up with another mistress. But Judge Sanders grew livid, he would have none of it. When she explained that she simply couldn't see him any longer, he threatened to shut her down, and she knew he had the clout.

"Honey's going to have a seriously sore ass this time," she said, and cursed herself for adding the word "seriously," which was not in the script. Whether it was due to boredom or nervousness she would usually slip in an extemporaneous word. She quickly added, "Put your hands behind your back, right now!"

"Yes, Mommy."

She took a long leather sash, roped it around his wrists several times, making hard knots the way he liked it.

"Now bend over," she commanded.

No sooner had he bent over the usual chair than she heard him mutter, "Oh shit! My bifocals!"

She was waiting for that. Last week it was a runny nose. The week before, the sash was too tight.

"Screw your glasses!" she replied. Each week he deliberately needled her, always in different ways.

"No," he said softly. "Mercy."

She slumped when he said the safe word.

"I have to have my glasses on or I can't see what's going on. Now untie my hands."

"I'll put them on for you." She reached down and was about to place them on the bridge of his narrow, fleshless nose.

"Mercy! I fucking said mercy! Are you an idiot?"

She leaned her head down and sighed.

"I asked you if you are an idiot!" he barked.

"No," she said, demurring to him.

"Untie my hands and be quick about it then."

"I'm only trying to save you time and money," she mumbled contritely, as she untied the sash around his wrists.

Under his breath he whispered, "Idiot."

Initially he was the perfect slave: on time, reticent, not too weird, predictable. Over the years he had slowly grown contrary. Gradually she lost control and slipped into this groove. She felt a twinge of embarrassment that this was being filmed. Once every two weeks, in the strangest of ways, she was unintentionally being victimized by this knobby little man. And now she wanted out.

Her husband Leslie had known all along that the bankruptcy judge was her client. He had listened to her repeated gripes about the slave who was holding her captive. But not until the last few months had he taken an interest in the man. When he finally sat down and proposed the plan of extortion, she jumped at it. Not for the money, but in hope of being free of Sanders.

"The sooner I get my glasses on, the sooner we can get back to the business at hand," he said very properly, as Cecilia finished untying the sash. The old man fetched his eyeglasses and planted them on his nose. Resuming his former posture, he refitted the curly Goldilocks wig on his balding scalp and lifted his ridiculously short, red polka-dot skirt above his flaccid hairless ass.

"Ready," he said, and crossed his wrists again behind his back. She retied the sash tightly.

"Someone's going have a sore ass," she continued.

"Please don't hurt Honey too badly," he said in a plaintive tone.

Cecilia spanked the judge across his bare bony bottom with the hairbrush and wondered if her stance was casting a shadow, obscuring the light. Was Ron getting all this on the videotape?

APRIL 22, 2001, NYC

TIMES SQUARE WAS FORMERLY LONGACRE SQUARE, around a hundred years ago, when the theater district was on Fourteenth Street and the *New York Times* offices were who remembers where. This section of town was empty.

My law firm, which occupied the top floor of the old Longacre Building, 1472 Broadway, right at Forty-second and Seventh, was one of the first casualties of the neighborhood's overhaul. Now we are housed in the city's hottest new skyscraper—the Condé Nast Building at 4 Times Square, a shiny silver missile silo that looks out over other shiny silver missile silos.

Maybe it's no coincidence that right in the center of Times Square is "the zipper." The neighborhood for years was one thinly concealed erection. Although everything else has been replaced, the zipper is still there. Before the "New Times Square," Forty-second Street had about fifty "sex parlors" between Seventh and Eighth Avenues. With a Warner Brothers store where my dick used to be—at the front of the old Allied Chemical building—and a Disney store in my balls—where my favorite porn arcade was—I feel as though I've had a concrete and steel vasectomy. I, like most of the old-timers, still prefer my petri dish out in the open—quintessential New York City.

Ironically, if old Times Square has gone anywhere, it has transcyberized onto the Internet. It unites Bangkok, Thailand to Blue Balls, Pennsylvania through a byzantine funhouse of "boutique" websites and transvestite chatrooms. Anyone at any age can anonymously log on in the privacy of his or her living room. In all my most perverted dreams I would never have imagined such a wonderful and wicked creation. Vulgar old Times Square with its sticky porn shops and infected whores would never have allowed the sick shit that I've downloaded to my computer screen. Fetishes aren't merely catered to, with all the sexual specialties, they are encouraged. Think I'm kidding? Start your search engine and type, "hairy+Asian+grannies." Something will pop up; even in its vilest most medieval days, you couldn't get that service on Forty-second Street.

People need their dirty habits, if only to shame them into their clean habits. I regard the sanitizing of Times Square — and, for that matter, the censoring of municipal art — as not much more than the kinkiest fetish of Mr. Giuliani and his loveable cronies.

Still, you can cut the leaves and even the branches, but the roots are still down there. The once bushy center of New York has now been entirely defoliated. They've installed a series of windows: an outdoor MTV window, the ESPN Zone, backdrops for ABC's *Good Morning America* and various other live-TV soundstages. Fresh-faced youngsters fill the street with banners of encouragement and greetings. Twenty years ago, they would've been shanghaied by pimps and chickenhawks. This city reinvents itself every thirty years or so. If the juvenile crap cross-pollinates with the old sleaze, this place might become the kiddie porn capital by 2030.

◄◄

The metallic aerial at the top of the Empire State Building looks like a big syringe and I feel it in my system. The commotion and distraction of New York is my heroin addiction.

I don't remember not being strung-out on stomach-turning anxiety, and though I initially found it thrilling, I subsequently hated it. Now I can't live without it.

The crowd. My eyes flip from face to ephemeral face. They part like a fleshy oriental fan dance. Old faces move aside, revealing new faces behind. Beauty turns, blends, bleeds into different types of prettiness.

I think of them like word groups: homonym faces that sound like other faces but mean something else; synonym faces that nuance into similar faces; antonym faces that starkly contrast; new anagram faces that rearrange into former faces. Soon, such subtleties fall away: a deck shuffle of polar faces—young, old; black, white; masculine, feminine; blemished, clear; shadowing, light-emitting. I collect a pair of eyes here, a set of lips there.

Finally feeling that rumble below my feet, I dash down the stairs and catch a crowded subway to Seventy-second. A bottleneck of bodies crowds around one of the narrow stairways on the Seventy-second Street station. There's blockage. People are creeping up single file. A homeless man is obstructing passage, leaning against the banister. I study his pitted face. He definitely looks like a Wilbur.

His eyes are reddening, his breathing is growing more labored by the second. It's hypnotic watching him become unWilbured; an invisible noose is slowly tightening around this man's wretched neck. As he makes it up just the first few steps, a local train pours into the station. Several large men lumber down the stairs, pushing him back onto the platform. Within seconds, waves of people are shoving their way out of the disemboweling train, forcing him upward. He's trying to resist. His swollen hands are like the aged suctions of some sea creature. He's trying to hold on to the banister. I can hear him emitting a phlegmy rasp.

He gasps dramatically for several minutes. He knows he's

being watched. Finally he stumbles downward and lowers himself to the filthy concrete platform, leaning up against a blue post. He closes his eyes. In another moment he topples to his side. A small crowd forms.

"Call an ambulance!" someone barks.

An Indian lady in an indigo suit flies up the steps to the street-level token booth. I've seen these histrionics before on the part of the homeless and their ongoing drive to waste the time of others. But inspecting Wilbur's countenance—a series of sharp jerky twitches, bright redness draining into pale, drool unspooling onto the ground—I see that he truly is unconscious.

"He's having an asthma attack," I say, and strictly for appearances, I call out, "Does anyone have any Primatine Mist?!"

Of course they don't.

A young lady in distressed denim and cheap perfume unclips a small compact and holds the mirror to Wilbur's scraggy mouth.

"His breathing is shallow!" she hoots.

"An ambulance is on its way," some voice consoles.

"Are you kidding?" a more realistic perspective cries out. "In this city, with the average response time during rush hour—forget it!"

I take a deep gulp of air, lean over, and lift Wilbur.

"You can get sued for that!" some ancillary voice chides.

"An ambulance is on its way!" someone else pipes up as I steal away everyone's opportunity for cheap heroics.

He is one heavy load. Struggling to haul the body up the stairs, I feel someone helping. It is the cheaply perfumed lady with the compact. She grabs one of Wilbur's crooked legs. By the time we are halfway up the steps, clinging to the unpainted wooden banister, another man joins in. When we get to the sidewalk, the three of us are panting.

"This way!" I yell, pushing through inpouring commuters moving along the curb and sidewalk.

We stumble, walk, run in unsynchronized steps, pulling and thrusting the inert man held out before us.

Suddenly, right behind us, a car honks.

"Fuck you!" I yell as reflex. He honks again. It is a yellow cab. The vehicle is driven by a bearded Pakistani in a tan turban, hollering for us to get in the back. All three of us pile in with our stinky body.

Once inside Roosevelt Hospital, through the waiting room, my two compadres and I start screaming for help. Two hefty attendants center Wilbur on a gurney. Without words my posse vanishes.

"He's having an asthma attack," I diagnose aloud, before I too evaporate into the crowd.

◄◄

When I eventually meander into the lobby of my apartment building, I find my charity has been rewarded. A manila envelope sits in the mailbox with an invoice for three hundred and fifty dollars. Ron has located Sky Pacifica in Suffolk County, Long Island, in the small town of Borden, closer to south-shore crass than north-shore attitude. It has taken Ron just over a week. An information form lists her home address, home phone number, work address, a short profile of her husband Eddie, and several details about his business. Subsequent pages give a brief description of the two children along with where they go to school. Just like Sky, her daughter Kate has exhibited little penchant for formal education. At age nineteen, she has flunked two grades and remains a pouty, sullen high-schooler. Several long shots of her and the family are included. The best photo shows Sky Pacifica getting into her car. It's the first time I've seen her in fifteen years. Now Jeane Lindemeyer, soccer mom, is flav of the day. Poor dear Sky, porn queen, has melted away.

I stare at the photos. Vigor, intelligence, style are qualities that crystallized in place of the youthful filament of innocence that once glowed from her skin. Her daughter Kate is equally remarkable: Jeane's pageant-perfect bone structure beneath a smoky brown skin. I keep staring at the photos as I take the elevator up to my apartment. Once inside, I lock the door and play my machine. Bill Holtov, an old friend and fellow law partner, is going nuts over the Sanders ruling. I turn off my machine and without thinking, I dial Sky's number. As I hear her phone ringing, I figure I'll invite her for a coffee.

With closed eyes I listen to her recorded voice: *"This is the Lindemeyer Family — we're not home right now . . ."* When the machine beeps, I hang up. I know that I will not be able to control myself in the future. I tear the phone number out of the investigator's information sheet, rip it into little pieces, and throw it out the window.

All I need is a simple surveillance job. I ponder hiring Ron for the task, just a slice-of-life tape. But I realize that only I can find the three-hundred-and-sixty degrees of her character. Only I would know what to look for; the glimmer in her smile, the twinkle in her eye.

Her work address says Mercy Hospital in Franklin Square Township. Instead of driving, I call Long Island Railroad. They give me a schedule of trains leaving tomorrow for West Hempstead. I pop a couple of sleeping pills, fold my arms across my chest, and move into my coffin.

To die, to sleep.

◄◄

Upon waking up, washing, and dressing the next morning, I grab my Sony Camcorder, my CD Walkman playing Eminem—a break from opera. I subway it downtown to Prozac Station, where I purchase a ticket for the Huntington train. I take a seat on the 10:28 from track 17 and put on my headphones. A little blond girl not much older than eight is seated in front of me. She looks timidly at a middle-aged lawyer across from her reading the *New York Times*. That man, bland in appearance, diabolic in intent, is me. Her mother turns her away. Fifteen years from now, who will that girl be? If she develops a shapely body and becomes Sky when she turns eighteen, will she become Jeane Lindemeyer fifteen years later?

People assume that just because one is out of control they are also unaware of it. Before grief, lechery, and even courage broke me out of my maximum security of reason, what was I? In 1979, I was someone who believed pursuing Sky was an artistic, even redemptive endeavor; I was someone who believed what he saw.

A nice conductor is handing the little girl a lollipop; noticing me, he winks. I give the fellow scumbag a wink back.

DECEMBER 12, 1979, NYC

"IT FEELS . . . IT FEELS LIKE MY ARM HAS BEEN ripped off and all this energy is just . . . just gushing out of me," Sky thought, and realized she was muttering her thoughts aloud. She could no longer dance to the music. She was smiling, topless, struggling to keep her lids open and hold onto the metal pole that served as her dance partner.

"Oh shit! Hymie! Look at this!" Laughter.

"Can you fucking believe this?" It was Hymie's voice. He was the manager of the club. She wanted to inform him that she was okay. She just needed a minute to collect herself, but she felt herself weakening even further and she was sliding down the shiny bar as men hooted and screamed.

"What's under here?" she heard. A hand reached out of the darkness and yanked her G-string down past her knees and ankles. Fingers like a frenzy of sand crabs dashed through her bristles. It was turning out like the other times.

"Fuck off!" she hollered, as if breaking out of a shell of exhaustion. She stumbled several steps forward before her eyes started sinking and her head started drooping.

"Hey, this chick is the perfect date," she heard. "Give me ten minutes with her, will you, Hym?" She felt a large hand scoop up her naked breast.

Finally, an iron-clasp spun her around like a fleshy duffel bag. Her eyes popped open and she could see the strip club in the darkness slipping away behind her. Hymie was dragging her downstairs to the changing room.

"You are one dumb fucking cunt!" he said angrily, smiling. "Never, never had a dumb cunt OD on me in the middle of a show."

I'm banned in LA, she thought, now I'm fucked here, too. Sky could feel her knees and elbows banging along the ground and walls. She wanted to get up, but her neck and arms, everything, felt under water. She couldn't even lift her head. Just the wonderful, wonderful falling. Always conscious, always drained of consciousness. Every coiled second was a separate wonderful.

"HEY!" She was lying down on something and it felt so, so good.

"HEY!" She could hear some of the other girls dressing.

"HEY!" She felt a slap across the face, waking her, stealing the falling.

"Fuck . . ." she mumbled.

"Who's this girl's pimp?" Hymie was speaking to the other girls.

"I don't know. Look in her purse for a number."

"Where's her clothes?"

"In the closet," said one of them.

"Fucking junkie passes out right on the fucking stage."

"That's what you get for looking at their tits instead of their veins," one of the light-chested girls replied.

"Hey, this is Sky Pacifica," a voice wobbled.

"Who the hell's that?" an echo returned.

"She's a big-time cocksucker porn actress. Figured you had to be sober for that. See her at work. Fucks like a bunny. Look at that ass." Hymie gave her a hard slap across her naked buttocks.

"HEY!"

"Well, she's a dead bunny now."

"Fucking embarrassing up there. Zonking out in front of everyone. What am I running, the Betty fucking Ford clinic? Where's the bitch's locker? I'm taking her clothes." One of the girls pointed. Hymie reached in and grabbed her garments in a ball. "Where's her cash?"

"Christ, Hym, leave her something."

"I'll leave her the singles."

"Stay out of . . ." Sky tried to respond, but wasn't sure if she was actually talking or just wanting to talk.

She fell asleep, to reawaken some time later, hearing him calling: "Sky!"

She opened her eyes a woozy slice, enough to see the geek staring back at her and think, Oh shit. He didn't know I was doing this. Doesn't got a forgiving bone in his spindly body.

Leslie was in his business suit. As Sky slid back into herself, she thought, Fucking Hymie went and ratted me out. Leslie stared at her silently. In a moment she was snoring, out cold.

Biting his lip, he wondered if she was drunk or had taken too many pills, like on the plane. Secretly stripping in this dive was bad enough. But the fact that she had been doing drugs as well instantly destroyed all the trust she had gradually built up these past few weeks.

Another girl behind Sky pursed her lips in front of a white plastic mirror circled with small burnt-out bulbs. Leslie stole a glance at the slim redhead with a narrow face and nipples like chocolate kisses.

"Hey, Marla, if you can get off your coked-up ass and not break your neck, I need someone up there," the manager said to the redhead. Marla rolled a glossy lipstick on her lips and nips, checked her hair, and departed.

As Leslie examined Sky, he could hear the rising volume of two girls brawling in the hallway:

"You are a fucking slut!" shot a husky-voiced entertainer.

"Look who's talking!" rejoined the other. "Every filthy cunt at the Cubby Hole winds up under your sponge!"

"At least I don't suck cock as well!"

"Shut up, the both of you!" the manager snorted,

reappearing. Leslie held Sky's slack face in his palms and stared despondently into her liquidy pupils.

"What the hell is the matter with her?" Leslie asked.

Sky heard his grating voice again, and thought, Ignore asshole and he'll go away.

"She was dancing up a storm earlier and then . . . Check her arm," the manager said out of the corner of his mouth.

Inspecting the crook of her right elbow, Leslie spotted small yellow-speckled bruises.

"What have you done?" he yelled, appalled.

She felt herself curl up like a froggie's tongue.

Out of nowhere, a sexy young woman who Leslie thought looked like an NYU coed took a seat in front of a mirror. Without noticing him, she tossed down her shoulder bag, removed a can of air freshener, and sprayed the small room. When she saw Leslie looking woefully at Sky's needle marks, she responded, "A little Preparation H closes 'em right up."

Leslie noticed her book, *Memories, Dreams and Reflections* by C.G. Jung, and was about to comment, when Sky began flopping her arms.

Leslie dashed upstairs and located the manager among a group of blunt-edged men demonstrating jabs from a recent boxing match.

"I need an ambulance!" Leslie exclaimed.

"Your porn star's a junky, pal," the manager replied, with his fists still frozen in the air. One of the guys chuckled. For amusement, the manager added, "And she was that way long before she stepped in here."

"Will you please call an ambulance? She could be ODing!" Leslie said angrily.

"She ain't ODing, and I'm not handing out excuses to

lose my liquor license. I did you a favor by calling you here. I'd just as soon drag her ass out onto the sidewalk and let the Mau Maus eat her."

"What am I going to do?" Leslie nervously looked about.

"You want my advice? Take her home. Let her sleep it off. When she wakes up, give her walking papers."

Leslie scrambled back downstairs. The coed was now in panties and bra; her hair had been teased and her face was made up so that she looked cheap and theatric like the others. Sky was deep asleep. A thread of drool connected her to the dresser she was leaning over. He put his jacket around her shoulders.

"Do you know where her clothes might be?" Leslie asked the curly-wigged blonde who had just finished a rotation. She pointed to a locker but it was empty.

"Anyone know where her clothes are?" he howled.

"She hid them," one of the two fighting lesbians replied. "Moon or Air, or whatever her bullshit name is, she kept saying we were all thieves."

One of the girls gave Leslie an old pair of bloodstained panties that he slid up around Sky's crotch. The manager reappeared and offered Leslie a squeezed wad of dollar bills.

"What's this?" Leslie asked.

"Tips. She earned them," the manager said.

Buttoning his jacket around her chest, Leslie helped Sky to her feet and half-walked, half-dragged her up the stairs.

"Take her money," the manager called out.

"Keep it," he cried back, disgusted.

"One beer bottle, sure, but I never saw a girl do that with two," Leslie overheard the manager say to one of the girls.

"Said she's a big-time actress," the portly blonde replied. "Big-time phoney!"

Once they were up the stairs, Leslie helped Sky through the bar and made it fifty feet down the street before his arms gave way with fatigue. He laid her down on the hood of an unwashed Pontiac and hailed a cab.

"Saint Vincent's Hospital," Leslie said, pulling her into the backseat.

As they slowly weaved their way through the traffic, Leslie inspected Sky carefully and decided the manager was right. She just needed a long, detoxifying sleep. He redirected the cab to his place on the Upper West Side and sat furious throughout the entire ride.

Inside his apartment, sweating from having carried her up the stairs, Leslie tossed Sky on the bed and stared at her, seething as his blood boiled. He grabbed a large pair of sewing scissors and snipped the filthy panties off of her dirt-streaked body. Glaring at them a moment, he angrily began cutting into the blood-stained underwear, tearing them apart. Looking at Sky naked before him, he had to restrain himself from hitting her.

He spread her out flat on her back. Trembling, he caught his breath and grabbed a magnifying glass from his desk. Like a detective looking for fingerprints, he carefully examined each pore of her limbs. After five minutes, he isolated three needle marks in her right forearm. He went into the kitchen, opened a can of seltzer. He wished it were a beer, but chugged it down anyway.

In the shower, it occurred to Leslie that Sky had recently been dressing differently. Her sexy new garb must have been the result of her secret profession.

Jumping out of the shower, naked, tracking puddles of water through the house, he headed to her closet. Leslie hastily tore through Sky's recent stockpile of gaudy belongings—hot pants, miniskirts, tank tops, leather vests, glittery G-strings, fishnets. As he pieced through them, a small snuffbox fell from a garment. He opened it and guessed the cellophane bag of white powder to be heroin. He flushed it down the toilet, then twisted the tiny brass hinges of the box apart, breaking it in half. After his third can of seltzer, he lay next to Sky, tired and sweaty, and quickly drifted off.

◄◄

The next morning, slaps and punches whacked him from sleep.

"Where the fuck is it?!" Sky stood naked and sweaty before him.

"I flushed it," Leslie replied matter-of-factly. Sky screamed as she lunged, trying to scratch and bite him. He managed to keep her claws from his face, but she was able to run a long, deep scratch down his right shoulder. Soon he pinned her down and sat on top of her.

"Calm down and we'll talk," he stated crisply.

She spat up into his face. The phlegm oozed down his chin, dripping back onto her face. At the top of her lungs, she shrieked, "YOU COCKSUCKING FAGGOT!"

He quickly grabbed a pillow, put it over her softly so as not to suffocate her. He listened to her yell as she struggled to breathe. When she stopped screaming, he removed the cushion.

"What the fuck have you been doing for the past four weeks?" he accused.

"Fucking! I've been fucking guys! Stripping and fucking! With real men! You little shit!"

Leslie rose and stumbled into the bathroom. He thought back over the past two weeks. While he had been tediously researching the fine points of corporate law, she was teasing strange men, allowing them to slip tens and twenties into her G-string, meeting them later, exchanging money for hand- and blowjobs.

While she quickly packed her bags, he ran water loudly to mask his humiliation at being betrayed. He had actually thought she was starting to like him. He was beginning to hope that they could be together. Tears came to his eyes. When he heard the front door slam, he knew she was gone.

APRIL 23, 2001, LI

"FRANKLIN SQUARE!" SHOUTS THE NICE CONDUCTOR, who at best can't be pulling down more than twenty-five thousand. Last year, I earned my minimum wage: two hundred thousand dollars in salary, one hundred thousand more in distribution and bonuses, and about fifty thousand in the bear market. I know my life is half over because I peaked out in 1986. Between my salary, my private consultations, and my investments—largely through Cecilia's trading clients—I made about two dollars and seventy cents per minute, morning, noon, and night, for the entire year. That year I netted about a million four hundred thousand bucks. By '87 I had lost most of it during the Great Correction. That's how my fortune cookie crumbled.

I still have about three million bucks in this and that. This consoles me as I turn off my CD and grab my bag. Fuck! I don't even know if Jeane is working at the hospital today. I should have called ahead pretending to be a patient. Since

I'm here anyway, I get off the Long Island Railroad and ask for directions. A lady with a beehive hairdo and bee-stung lips explains that Mercy Hospital is a ten-minute walk down the main road.

"Like me," I comment, "you must have to resist the ongoing feeling of being out of sync. Well, fuck them, right?"

"Right," she blankly responds.

All I want to do is tape Jeane going from her office to her car. Nothing cheap or farfetched. Just a simple keepsake. I spot the red brick building nestled behind a dusty parking lot and bordered by unevenly maintained bushes. Jeane's office — according to Ronnie's nicely typed report — is on the second floor, room 209. I put on my magic sunglasses that make me invisible and head up the front steps.

The hospital lobby is tighter than it appears because of the long receptionist desk that crowds out the seating area. Noticing the gauge on my video camera, I see that I am low on tape. Before hunting for her office, I take a seat, pry out the old cartridge, and snap in a new one.

While doing this I look up, and there you are. From the pink marble of the ancient Greeks, through the Renaissance oil paints, to the Hollywood celluloid of today, I've tracked your beauty now pressed in living flesh. Between my restraining tension and your compelling splendor, I would gladly be vanquished.

"Hey! Out of my way." Some pill-popper pushes me aside.

You must have recently shed your skin; you moist, glistening Czarina. My feet flatten onto the linoleum tile. My head inflates and rises like a balloon. Slowly, you take off your wraparound pair of Foster Grants. My heart pumps up like a tetherball about to explode.

Although you are Jeane and forty-three now, the past twenty years collapse away like a chunk of corroded concrete. The power apparent in your very walk strikes me as ticklish. No longer the nervous and tentative cadence I had once known when you moved like a furtive feline entering new surroundings. You look through me as I lift the Camcorder to my eyes and push the assassin's trigger. Not twenty feet away from you, among the listless and waiting others in the seated area, I calmly tape you. You stroll to the elevator bank, oblivious, press the calico-colored button, and wait. Your dignity act only conjures up your past vulgarities; endless loops of strap-ons and hard-ons turning you into a female pin cushion.

I remember the time I had to carry you high as a kite when you collapsed at a striptease bar, twenty-two years ago, or even worse than that when you showed up at my house, a year later, knocked up, used up, tossed out, bottomed out, but here you are, re-phoenixed, and I'm on the bottom, film and film and filming, sucking it all up—time and place— through that little glass eye.

The aqua blue walls of the hospital inhale what little available light the cavernous lobby allows. Thank god your dress is stand-out red. Swathed in authority. The elevator doors open, you enter, slam—that's a cut.

Walking over to the elevator bank, I sniff the sweet air. I gently push the calico button, but not for the elevator. All I really want is to touch what you have just touched. When the elevator doors slide open, I have to fight that magnetic force pulling me up to thee.

To walk up to you and let you see me, a distant and terrifying mirror, and watch me watch you panic.

Prozac races through my middle-aged system and forbids the inhibition, but not the passion of the next bland thought: I could rape you in your office. It's what you expect from me and therefore, in an odd way, it's what you want. But it's not what I want.

I need more, a lot more. The proffering of a meager surveillance tape is an insult to my blood-thirsty, piranha-toothed appetite. I need more; a porn film of you that twines our bodies until they burst into one fiery, common pool.

I regain my equilibrium and slowly squirm through the suburban town of Franklin Square back to the train station from whence I uncoiled. I dream and scheme: numbers and dates and costs combine with delicious bite-size fantasies. Plan A is simply the legitimate approach. After all, even though I don't feel like it, I am worth millions. As the New York train pulls into the Long Island station, I make a point of walking toward the front and getting a seat next to the door. A school-age girl and boy sit across from me, bantering nonsense, punctuated with jolts of annoying, kill-me-quick laughter.

What are Sky's strengths? Who will fight for her? No one after Hot Dog Eddie, her geriatric husband.

"Ticket, please."

I give my ticket to the blue-cap, who punches it. Although the photos I have of old Ed show him still stringy and flexible as a piece of jerky, can his hips still rock? Can his weegee still squirt? Jeane liked to fuck. It fortified her. Soothed her nerves at night. Sped her up in the morn. A good, long hard one to remind her of what she really is. No way is he still up for that task. So what does that mean? Sky always broke things down to their replaceable parts. It means she must have a younger lover squirreled away somewhere.

Like a killer entering the mind of a detective, I assume Jeane's thoughts. Emotional fidelity is important, but habit too long has tied it to physicality. I love Ed, but I must fuck Rudy, the thick ponytailed wop who can't read a word, but watches my tight, aerobicized ass like a hawk and knows nothing but discretion—the saving grace of one who knows he's dumb. After a day of pushing a broom, Rudy wants to untie the apron, Rudy wants to dog someone who's cling-free. Here I am, cling-free Jeane: fuck, Rudy, fuck. See Rudy fuck!

We pull into Penn Station and I realize that if there is a Rudy, he's going to be my real obstacle. But any weapon can be turned into a tool. Maybe I can extort her with him. But the blackmail business is not as easy as it seems. Something I learned from the eminent Judge Sanders, who has been sent the merchandise, but is not coming up with the rulings. Besides, if there is a Rudy, Ron would have rooted him out.

Steering through the crowded mezzanine in Penn Station, I consider Jeane's weakest point — her past. She is now a professional social worker, a mother of two to boot, pinned down like a dissected frog in the waxboard of the suburbs.

The porn industry now generates over a hundred billion dollars annually; it has pushed Sky's cinematic works off the shelf. Unregimented, I march with others, through tunnels, sidewalks, down stairways, and along platforms, one member of life's defeated and retreating army.

What does pornography really come down to?

After finding an actor who might resemble someone we long for, or registering a dash of their personality, beyond the various facial expressions from cold stoicism to orgasmic tremors, studying the dominant flourishes of the guy, the submissive winces of the girl, upon checking the anatomical eccentricities, and finally settling on glandular turgidity and sphincteral resilience, what are we really left with? It's all essentially repetitive stress disorder caught on film. Pegs and holes.

The real drama was always going on in the mind. Porn was just a catalyst. One part of us comes in contact with another part, where the waves of shock erode the terra firma of innocence.

Wittgenstein once said of his philosophy that it's like a

ladder: After you climb over it, you no longer need it. I thought I had degenerated beyond pornography. In a way I have, and yet here I am hitting the old play button again.

I grab the uptown IRT local. The subway doors open. A tidal rush for seats as people swirl and spin. Losing the desperate game of musical chairs, I stand, rub the shiny pole, and stare at the blender-mix of ever-changing faces: Sexuality draws me toward the young ones; mortality, nobility, morbidity compel me to the older ones. Sentiment associates them with faces of my past. Yet common sense—or what naïve people would call cynicism—reminds me that salvation never never NEVER comes from other people.

Ultimately, insecurity cajoles me to impress myself with the parlor trick of my own intellect: There is an identicality to beautiful faces, whereas much more individuality to the ugly ones. Faces finally are labels of identity, age, and experience—the over-exercised muscles of grief, the baggy, red eyes from too much crying and too little sleep. Or fresh, round, uncreased faces of those who haven't peaked, their buds still unfolding.

Why do people doll themselves up in a million little ways for my humiliation? They do it to look beautiful. What is beauty? What is truth? Truth is the awfulness of being themselves, and beauty—as they perceive it with costumes and cosmetics—is a reprieve from that awfulness.

Since I can't ingratiate myself to Jeane, how else can I get her? I can edit together her raunchiest moments and duplicate the tape, then all I need to do is threaten to mail them to all her business associates and neighbors. I cross Seventy-second Street and sprint into the lobby of my building.

"Hello, Mr. Cauldwell!" When I don't respond, the doorman says it again and adds, "There's a package for you, Mr. Cauldwell." I take the package and thank Luis, the friendly doorman of the Deacon Arms.

It is an accordion of the Sewter case; inside are briefs and motions, as well as the original reorganization plan filed some years ago. Two boyish associates, Holtov's proteges David Polk and Irving Proskauer, have flagged different sections of the briefs, pelting me with dumb questions. One of the unwritten laws of gravity is that small brains are pulled in and willingly swallowed up by larger brains. Inside the elevator, I'm acutely aware of the image of power and responsibility I'm presenting to my neighbors as I peruse reorganization documents.

The irony of being able to extort Jeane with her own past causes me to chuckle. But I make it look like I'm amused by a legal point. This is the true nature of perversity, enjoying aberrant pleasures in the midst of others, where one can both blend with the bourgeois and stand exquisitely apart.

Inadvertently, I end up reading the corporate history of the case: Three generations of Sewters competently ran the enterprise. It had more than its share of government and military contracts through both world wars. After the Marshall Plan, it expanded with new divisions, collected holdings, and it vanquished competitors. Over the past twenty-five years, overseas competitors gouged into its market share. Unions refused give-backs. When the last Sewter sold off his controlling share, the real trouble began. There was a string of ill-equipped CEOs whose apparent folly — but probable embezzlement — brought this once proud institution to its knees. Debts accumulated, interests accrued, and many of its subsidiaries were either sold or liquidated.

One ambitious plan of reorganization was filed about seventeen years ago. As a young associate I had worked on it. For a while, in the kill-the-poor age of Reaganomics, the Sewter Company bounced back. They started expanding again. In the early nineties when the recession hit, the company scaled down once more. During the wonderful age of

Clinton, with the longest uninterrupted economic expansion in history, when all you had to do to get money was hold out a hat, these halfwits blew it. As of a few months ago, hundreds of millions of debt dollars later, with lawsuits pouring in from all directions, Big Bill Holtov and I tried to restructure this titanic company, dumping the deadwood and fusing the profit-generating parts together. We completed our complex proposal by Christmas just as the market started going south, then we eagerly awaited a ruling.

The fact that the Sewter Company already had a plan of reorganization over a decade earlier means that the judge has more discretion to refuse this second plan. A little more than two years ago, when I first heard that the Honorable Peter Sanders was handed our case, I was worried. I had argued before him in the past. The man had a reputation for being a creditor-friendly judge. Even so, Holtov felt we had a more than fair chance. For some reason, I was picked to guarantee the ruling.

For years I had known that Sanders was one of my wife's oldest slaves. This wasn't too unusual; her willful sufferers include a who's who of semi-recognizable dignitaries. She was always very respectful of their privacy. But Sanders was different. She couldn't stand the man, and hard as she tried, she couldn't unshackle him. So we nuptially negotiated an extortionist accord. We would videotape the jurist during one of his infantilist sessions and in exchange for our silence, he would rule in favor of the second reorganization. In addition to a ten-thousand fee for Cecilia, which would come from the Sewter Legal Emergency Fund, I was to inform Sanders that he had to seek new domination services. Ron Marauder received two grand for wiring and shooting the event. The film was made, and the tape was delivered to his chamber along with simple instructions of what was required of him.

Two months ago, just before my wife's strangulatory estrangement, Sanders rejected the reorg plan.

Bill, who doesn't know about the extortion, is still scratching his head. He's reexamining the reorganization, trying to come up with new ideas. But the ball's in my throat. Though I dread it, I've got to nail Sanders with the tape and start with the extortion process.

Jeane, where art thou?

It is late morning. There is a smell of freshly cut grass. Jeane's family has gone off to work and school. I ring her doorbell. A neighbor several houses down is backing his wood-paneled station wagon out of his bush-paneled driveway. He turns and drives off. Telegraph poles, front lawns, the far-off voices of playing children. A black bird lands, trills three notes, and flies again. Eventually she steps out.

"Would you mind?" I motion to her from the sidewalk.

There, scattered on her front lawn, would be the most lurid photos of her pornographic past. She snatches these photos up in terror and I calmly explain: just plain old-fashioned sex, or these photos will be everywhere, wheat-pasted to every lamppost, stuffed into every mailbox on her block.

Stepping out of the elevator, fingering my pocket for my apartment keys, I iron out the finer points. The entire rendezvous would be quite tasteful, I assure her. Civilized. Even romantic. Nothing freaky or humiliating. Very conventional. Indeed, it should be quite a lark for her. An expensive hotel. A tasty meal. A good Rothchild. Hell, we had sex before, back when we were younger. I lock my apartment door, throw my jacket on my leather couch, and decide that I'd even slip on a condom, which at my age is like lubricating myself with Novocain.

Behind the curtain in my study is a high-power telescope screwed to a tripod.

Scanning some of the apartment houses across the valley

of streets, I spot a redheaded flower in her twenties who looks to me like a Heather. Tall, shapely, and beautiful, she is one of the most perfectly sculpted works in today's telescopic statue garden.

She is walking around her apartment, not naked or even scantily dressed. Just to see her in her self-induced state of privacy is enough. She's swaying back and forth. Music must be on. I have time to either heat up a frozen TV dinner of Salmon Almondine in the microwave or fix the zoom lens to the Camcorder and screw it onto the tripod. Thereby I could tape Heather's impromptu dance of no veils. I have taped several voyeuristic delights of girls in the past, but I don't want to become obsessed with collecting tapes as I once was years earlier. Porn is a zoo of exotic animals that becomes boring upon ownership.

I warm up the salmon and open a Chardonnay. Heather flips off the lights and leaves her apartment. True visions of beauty cannot be captured. I take a pill and wait for sleep. Beckwith suspected that I was a serial murderer. He said individuals who don't properly learn about healthy sexual habits can have a traumatic imprinting at an early age. He sniffed my farty guilt. Sexual deviations are usually eroticized adolescent abuse. A foot fetish, for instance, might result from a mother chronically walking away, neglecting her child. Beckwith tried to wax a trauma out of me. But he got nothing because, sadly, I'm normal.

◄◄

The next morning, I awaken to the sound of cooing. A pigeon sits on my balcony. Naked, I grab my pellet rifle, take aim, and *poof,* the pigeon falls to its side. It beats its wings. With its red scaly feet it tries to upright itself. I race out and put another pellet into the bird's pointy head, blasting off its little scalp. After I kick the grime-gray interloper under the open space in the railing, down twenty-two floors below, all that remains are a few drips of blood. Although the pigeon slaughter seems cruel, it's actually good for mankind, purging the serial murderer in me.

Today the air tastes dusty and stale, as if it has been coughed up. I review the miniature golf course of my day: a shower, a basket of California strawberries, a jog in Mr. Olmstead's park, one hundred push-ups, and then the drive to Long Island, to you, my dear Jeane.

So on with the Nikes and the four laps around the reservoir, then back home to my exercises. In my bathroom, I shower. Twenty minutes in the mirror for face restoration, clipping the tiny hairs that creep out of my brain through my nose, ears, and eyebrows. My face, which used to be a tight quarter-inch snap of flesh stretched over cheeks and chin, is now three-quarters-of-an-inch loose, just beginning to sag. With less and less subcutaneous vitamin C production each day, it no longer glows.

I lay out what I think will blend with the suburbs—a pair of dark pants and a bone-white turtle neck? Too dashing. A pair of jeans and a red plaid lumberjack shirt? Too rustic. I grab my shoulder bag with the Camcorder and the Sewter file to review. Every second of life is billable, and every bill padable. I head down to a Banana Republic on Broadway. A tall blond salesclerk with big white teeth who exudes suburban styles and mannerisms nabs me at the door.

"I need something casual for, say, a barbecue," I evoke.

She points to a light-blue, short-sleeved button-up that is so perfect I can already see ketchup stains dotting the front. I put it on and charge it.

On my way to the parking lot behind my house, I purchase a single camellia which I crush in my palm and intermittently sniff when no one is looking. I put the white petals in the ashtray and drive to the Queensboro Bridge, heading for the Long Island Expressway. Passing the Calvary Cemetery, I incant, "Soon, Cecilia, I shall be with thee." Then I pop *La Boheme* into the CD player, one of her favorites. Life requires constant self-forgiving.

Exiting at Borden, Long Island, I pull over at Peninsula Boulevard and unfold a map. I tabulate the number of turns and traffic lights I'll have to pass before I am on Jeane's block. To keep my sanity, I count off blue hydrants and evenly spaced poplar trees. If the mind can't fly from thought to thought, it falls to the dirt of despair.

I slowly drive past the address — 287 Alder Street. Theirs is a light-brown, three-bedroom track house, constructed just after the war, à la Levittown. Through my rearview mirror I observe the front of the place with its mansard roof over a small enclosed porch. A single oak sprawls over their plastic green carport. A garden hose lies uncoiled on their poorly cut front lawn. Turning around, I drive past the waist-high shrubbery. Two old cars, one in front of the other, are sitting in the driveway.

I park at the end of the block, locate my Camcorder, then check to see that there is a sufficient amount of tape. My Presidential Rolex salutes 11:30.

I pass the surveillance time by working on the file I just received. I skim the riders and flags. Holtov is suggesting a re-revised plan, more generous to creditors, but I can see that this plan won't fly with shareholders either. I flip open my cellular and, pushing my speed dial, I call old buddy Bill Holtov.

"Hello," a winded male answers.

"Bill, I am holding your latest proposal before me."

"What do you think?" he asks nervously.

"The company can't afford it and Sanders knows it. The last plan was as close to the bone as we could go."

"He thinks we're not doing a full disclosure." He affects professional earnestness.

"Look, he's well known as a debtor's judge." How can I tell him the truth?

"I thought you said you could impress him!" Bill's beginning to lose it. Jeane suddenly exits her house, wearing black slacks and a burnt-orange pullover. Her hair is knotted up in a red scarf.

"It's not over till it's over." I flip the phone off. Time for 007 to make his move. I hold up the Camcorder.

Her daughter is wearing a *Sopranos* T-shirt. The two get into the lead car in the driveway, an old Honda hatchback. Kate puts on a loud rock station. Jeane switches it off. As soon as Jeane turns toward me, I lower my camera and start my ignition. When they pass, I U-turn and speed after them. I constantly keep them in view, but will not tail closer than a block. Fortunately, there's no traffic and the lights aren't angry today.

When I can see that they are heading for the freeway, I slow down, then catch up with them again on the L.I.E. where other cars hide my motives. Popping a mint in my mouth, I put on *Madame Butterfly* and sing along to the death scene as I keep behind their Honda. Puccini knew a thing or two about the sacrifices of love. That's why they keep regurgitating him on Broadway.

When they exit, I exit. When they turn into the Hill Valley Mall, so do I. They luck out finding an immediate parking spot. Like a vulture, I keep circling.

The mall is a landfill of weekend shoppers. I curse as I search slowly up and down rows of parked cars, unable to find an opening. If stalking is a psychological disability, I should be able to pull into the handicapped zone. A spot finally opens, and I zoom for it. But another, closer car is heading for it too.

"Hey, fucker!" a beefy kid with a baby face yells from behind the wheel of a beat-up Mazda. I ruthlessly shove the front end of my car into the spot. The Mazda has already entered just enough to block my passage.

"I got in first!" I yell back.

"The fuck you did." Baby Face guns his engine and yells, "You want to see what I can do to that Jag? Just stay there."

"All right," I say, after waiting a few moments in suspenseful silence, "I'll give you twenty bucks for the spot."

"What?"

"Twenty bucks." I take it from my wallet and wave it at him.

"Fuck your twenty, fucking dotcom sucker," the kid replies, pulling on the visor of his baseball cap as if ready for a demolition derby tournament.

"Thirty, then."

Without a word, the kid opens his car door. I throw the bills on the oil-splotched asphalt before he can snatch them from my hand. He scurries to collect, hops back into his vehicle, throws it into reverse, and pulls out for me.

Before the Mazda leaves, I shout, "I would have given you a hundred, asshole!"

"Fuck you!" the kid replies, and hits the accelerator, peeling rubber. I emerge through a plume of black smoke — victory in blue area, eighty-two.

Pushing through the outer and inner aluminum doors of a Stern's department store, I know I've lost them.

I check women's fashions; elegantly cheesy. I dash up the escalator and walk through the several aisles that contain "junior wear" and "casual wear." Rows of waist-high white-Formica monoliths hold folded sweaters and shirts. Gangs of embarrassed mannequins are forced to wear these tacky outfits with pride. Between racks of dresses, coats, gowns, and jackets, I see no sign of the Lindemeyer ladies.

Passing through to the interior of the store, I am in the nerve center of the leviathan mall. Although its pillars and vaulted roof look nothing to me like the inside of a whale, I feel swallowed up. At the base of the walkway, "The Pavilion" seems to be a miniature town square, complete with a large fountain that shoots out intermittent blasts of "dancing" waters. It takes ten minutes to walk the length of the promenade that ends at a gluttonous food court: a large zeppelin-like structure that troughs out every disgusting fast food.

Based upon my observations of people around me, I deduce that contemporary America is all about putting on unnecessary pounds. Beyond that, atrophy, water retention, osteoporosis — death.

Time to claim defeat and wait for them back at Alder Street. But turning around, I glance at some of the stores: Driving Impressions, Create a Potato, Victoria's Secret. Across the walkway, approximately seventy feet away up on the mezzanine level, I spot two leggy adolescent girls who slow down, stop, and start chatting to a third pair of legs. This tertiary female is Kate. When I see Jeane come up from behind, I focus my Camcorder and start filming.

After a few minutes, someone taps me on the back. "Excuse me, sir."

I peak as I keep filming. Some overweight kid with bad skin is sitting on a golf cart with a blue and white shirt and a Smoky the Bear hat.

"Videography is not permitted in the mall, sir." He's got a slight lisp that can be quickly remedied with a smack.

"What's your stand on holograms?" I ask, trying to trade time for free-associative sarcasm.

"Excuse me?" Stupid says, probably citing his most used phrase.

"What's the mall's stand on pentagrams?"

"I'm going to have to ask you to cease filming, pending a citizen's arrest," the youth says, sidestepping my ruse.

"Arrest me and I'll sue the dog shit out of this cruddy mall. Be warned, I'm a crack litigator. Ask the Disney Corporation." With one hand still filming, I quickly take my business card out of my pants pocket and hold it out to the pint-size insecurity guard.

"Alpha Blue calling Phi Beta, come in Phi Beta!" The adolescent despot is calling for backup over a walkie-talkie with a long cockroach-whiskered antenna.

Jeane's daughter Kate kisses one of her friends on her candy-apple cheek. The two groups separate. I follow the Lindemeyer ladies.

"Hold on!" the guard yells out.

"You're too much of a man for me," I reply as I walk away. "You've scared me into shopping."

He stands watching me move on. I could dismember him, then chuck his bloodied parts about the four corners of the ever-unfolding mall, but I might get my shirt dirty. When I finally cut my way through the tall grass of shoppers and exit through Freedman's Sporting Goods to the parking lot, Jeane and Kate are gone.

I drive onto the expressway, heading back to the city. Slowly, the speed of the surrounding cars turns into a dare. Drivers look at my Jag and their stares say, "*Come on, you rich faggot. Let's see you haul.*" Okay, fuckers! Flooring the pedal, I hold the steering wheel with both hands and weave between buses and trucks, blurring them as they come to life in my windshield and evaporate in my rearview mirror a moment later.

DECEMBER 29, 1979, NYC
THE YOUNG JOAN BAEZ AND BOB DYLAN WANNABES were collecting across the street from Penn Station

with knapsacks and peeled-stickered guitar cases. Although most were around Sky's age, she felt so much older than them and envied their innocence.

Two weeks after ODing on stage and leaving the geek, Sky got another stripping job around Times Square and located a one-bedroom apartment for one hundred and fifty dollars a month on Sixth and A, in a cruddy dump in the ratty East Village. Cabs would let her off at First Avenue, unwilling to go any further east.

Immediately, life got very loose and lonely. Her days seemed longer and every decent person in the city appeared to be shunning her. She felt like a skank who was only seen by other skanks. The West Coast was a lot friendlier. After guzzling down a quart of Absolut and missing three days of work, she was promptly fired from her second gig. She saw it as a sign and left the apartment before finishing out the month.

The Gray Tortoise, an illegal hippie bus line that ran cross-country, wasn't due to collect everyone for a half an hour. Sky went into the bagel shop and ordered a cup of coffee, light and sweet. She sipped it while staring out, watching the sleazebags and riff raff passing by. She hoped for a new start in the city by the bay, where even in the winter it was the summer of love.

As she considered her month in New York, she felt a twinge of guilt about what had happened. The geek had been decent to her. At nights they talked honestly and had sex only twice. He had never forced her or tried to take advantage. She considered calling him up and apologizing, but figured that the nicest thing she could do was leave him alone.

MARCH 22, 1980, NYC

A FEW MONTHS AFTER SKY OD'D AT THE STRIP JOINT and dumped him, Leslie met a girl at work, a paralegal named Cecilia. She was tall and slim with broad shoulders, long black hair, and a sleek, sexy neck. There was an unconfirmed rumor that she had had some kind of fling with one of the partners.

While working on a case together, Leslie managed to crack through her cold professional exterior and become friendly with her. Over the following months they'd have little conversations in his office. After work one evening they went for drinks. While walking Cecilia to her door, he kissed her. She kissed back and invited him upstairs.

"Really?" he asked.

"Well, you don't have to," she said coyly, as she opened her door and went in. He followed.

Upon entering her apartment, they both took off their coats. She hung them up as Leslie took a seat on the couch. Cecilia turned off the overhead light and flipped on a lamp. She was about to offer him either a juice or soda, when she noticed him staring at her. Thoughtlessly, she felt herself go limp with a smile. Without hesitation, he rose and began kissing her softly on the lips.

"Wait a sec," she said, and moved to the couch.

He sat next to her. Her sharp, dark beauty and the strange rumors around the water cooler allowed him to believe that once he got her started, she would go all the way.

She felt the tips of his fingers graze along her cheeks and neck. His right hand moved down her lean arm and breast. It felt as though her peach fuzz was swimming. His fingers finally stopped splayed out on her abdomen.

"Wait a second. I feel anxious." She pushed his hand off. "I want you to promise me you won't try anything."

"Like what?"

"What do you think?"

"I promise," Leslie replied urgently, and resumed kissing her. His minty mouth pulled back just far enough to make each flick of his tongue distinct. Slowly, he moved his hands up her back under her shirt and unsnapped her bra.

Is this too far? Cecilia asked herself. But when she felt him reaching around, cupping her breasts in his warm hands, the doubting ceased.

As he caressed her nipples, she kissed him harder on the mouth. In another moment, Leslie's fingers were slipping down along her ribs, down the hem of her dress, then softly onto her knee. She neither opened her legs nor closed them. She trembled as he stroked her inner thigh and gently edged the strip of fabric aside. He combed through her dark bristles and warm lips. Gradually, without intending it, she eased onto her back, making herself more accessible to him.

It was the softest of sensations, tingling throughout her entire body. She felt heat rising from the surface of her skin. When he slipped the tip of his middle finger into her, she issued a soft musical triad that sounded to Leslie like an angel wincing.

He freed one hand and, reaching down, unzipped his pants and liberated his stiff penis.

He continued fingering her while massaging himself gently. He rubbed the bulbous head of his penis between her legs, pushing against the promise he made to her.

"Careful," she whispered, as if not wanting to awaken from a hypnotic trance she was glowing in.

He rolled the tip of his cock around her outer edges and thought, That's it; that's enough. But she moaned again, urging him on. Shoving, withdrawing, shoving a bit more, then easing out, penetrating ever more deeply, running along those tender lips. He could only stop when he could go no further. In a moment he was locked in an ever-shortening rhythm.

It felt like red-hot marbles were shooting up, punching through the veins in his groin. He was spurting deep, deeper inside her.

"Oh, fuck!" she moaned, convulsively clamping her thighs solidly around his waist. They rocked together, then Leslie collapsed forward. They lay deathly still.

After what seemed like hours, he awoke, smelling a shampoo fragrance. He grabbed a handful of her thick beautiful curls, then slowly straightening them out, he tugged softly. She didn't utter a sound. But when he lowered his lips to hers, to gobble up her gorgeous, warm mouth, she came instantly alive, shoving him off of her.

"You bastard! I told you not to fuck me!" She was enraged, and concealing her nakedness.

"But . . ."

"Get the fuck out!"

"You never said no," Leslie uttered.

"Yes I did! Liar! I told you. You promised! GET THE FUCK OUT BEFORE MY BOYFRIEND COMES HOME!"

"Boyfriend?"

She jumped up and ran into the bathroom.

He hastily cleaned off and dressed. Before leaving, he called out that he was sorry. Heading down the stairs, through the pink hallway, he wondered if his apology implied guilt and could be used in a court of law.

◄◄

He didn't see her at work the next day. A few days later, he discovered that she was working while he slept, third shift, from midnight to eight. Leslie returned that night to see her.

The young associate in charge, William Holtov, spotted Leslie when he entered the conference room and called over to him, "What are you doing here, boy?"

"Passing by."

The two associates briefly complained about the cases each were assigned. When Leslie spotted Cecilia, he lost all his courage and left the large room.

Around three in the morning, Cecilia headed down an empty corridor on the twenty-fourth floor to the soda and candy machines.

She suddenly heard his voice behind her: "Cecilia."

She turned and snapped back, "It wasn't supposed to happen!"

"But you seemed so . . ." Leslie twisted his face into a look of sincere regret.

"I told you that you couldn't!" she scolded, refusing to be drawn in.

"But they all say no." He threw up his hands with a smile.

"I'm not just another one of your sleazy conquests!"

"What I'm trying to say is," he edged closer to her and lowered his voice, "if I felt more entitled than I should have, it was because I had very strong feelings toward you."

"I wonder how many rapists have used that excuse."

She vanished into the women's room, which was empty.

Leslie followed her in and appealed, "Look, this is ridiculous!"

"Get the hell out this instant!"

"Did you treat Tanen this way?" It was the rumor that had initially enticed him to ask Cecilia out.

She grabbed him by the lapel of his jacket. "Where'd you hear that?!"

"Nowhere, forget it." He turned to go.

She pushed him up against the wall. "Hold it! You're going to give me the respect of listening to what I have to say."

"Take it easy, there's no reason to get pushy."

She released him and could see him put on his lawyer mask. "If you think you can humiliate me because of what happened, you're mistaken!"

"Will you relax?" he muttered.

"I'll have Tanen fry your ass!" she said, louder. "You'll be the oldest associate in existence!"

"Get over it!" he fired back.

"Get over it?" she screamed. "You got me drunk and you . . . you fucked me!"

Leslie swiftly grabbed Cecilia with one hand and put his other hand over her mouth. For an instant, she thought, Christ, he's going to hit me!

When Cecilia heard an associate pass behind her, she broke free, silently realizing that they had both gone too far.

"Look," he said sympathetically, "you have nothing to worry about."

She exhaled, walked a few steps away, and took a seat at an empty secretary's desk. Leslie sat next to her patiently. She knew he wasn't a bad guy. He wouldn't be there in the middle of the night trying to mend things if he was. She was angry at herself for being so vulnerable and was taking it out on him.

"I don't know you," she said, now meekly. "We moved way too quickly and now I feel far too vulnerable. I have to resign."

"Give me a break. You're treating me like some asshole who humps and dumps women on a routine basis, and that's not me!"

"Then why did you, when I distinctly asked you not to?"

"You were beautiful. I was hard up. My girlfriend left me suddenly and I suppose I had to prove something to myself." Sky the porn actress was hardly a girlfriend, yet she was all he had.

Cecilia could see that look on his face—loss tinged with a bit of hurt. That was how he had looked when she was first attracted to him, watching him sitting at his desk day-in, day-out, so serious and sad.

"I didn't know you had a boyfriend," he replied contritely. "You probably feel like you cheated on him. You didn't . . ."

She had forgotten that she had told this lie and wished she hadn't. Now she wasn't merely promiscuous, she was also an infidel to some fictitious lover.

"I'm not going to be working here much longer," she replied, more to herself than to him.

"What will you be doing?" he asked softly.

"Counseling."

"Counseling what?"

"Long story," she said. She really did find him quite attractive. Probably due to sleepiness, she reached out and gently rubbed Leslie's face. Then, to hide the impropriety of her action, she announced, "You need a shave."

"You wouldn't be interested in joining me this weekend?" Leslie asked, explaining that he had an extra ticket to the opera. Although this wasn't true, he was pretty sure he could get one.

"Which opera?" she replied, and wondered if her lipstick and mascara had smudged in the emotional tumult.

"*Tristan and Isolde*," he pronounced with a slight affectation.

"Actually, my boyfriend is going to be out of town this week," she said, sustaining the lie, "if all you have in mind is the opera."

He assured her it would be the opera and nothing else. She accepted.

◄◄

Saturday night at 7 o'clock, Leslie picked Cecilia up in front of her apartment, and together they took a cab up to Lincoln Center.

Upon arriving, Leslie handed over the tickets and an usher showed them to their seats in the orchestra. Intent on proving himself a perfect gentleman, Leslie was careful to not so much as glance at her improperly. Since the production was wonderful, Leslie had no trouble ignoring Cecilia, seated next to him.

During the intermission, in the palatial lobby, they sipped glasses of complementary white wine. Initially, Leslie talked with superficialities and pleasantries, trying to sound genuine and interesting. When they heard the chime for the second act, Leslie and Cecilia headed back into the auditorium. Cecilia paused, searching through her purse.

"I thought I had some aspirin," she muttered.

"Headache?" he asked.

"Yeah. I think it's from the wine." She didn't want to be a pain in the ass, but her skull was throbbing.

He gently stroked her hair for a minute.

"Why don't you take a seat?" He led her to a bench. "There's a place up the block, I'll get it for you."

Lorenz would never have done that, she thought. She was going to say something nice to him, but, to his surprise, she kissed him gently on the lips. Leslie felt Cecilia's cold hands softly touch the sides of his body. He was about to hug her, but sensing that she wanted to be in control, he remained still. Everyone had already returned to their seats. Ushers were closing the doors. As her lips touched his, he could hear the alto tenor singing sublimely in the key of E. At that moment the passion of the opera and the eros of Cecilia blended ideally.

"Let's leave," he suggested.

With a nod of her head, she consented, still not mentioning her nonexistent boyfriend.

Outside, they grabbed a cab to his apartment, kissing in the backseat as they sped up Broadway with its lights and crowds.

Inside, Cecilia looked around his studio. It smelled slightly sulfuric. She was surprised that he lived there, what with his income. The furniture was shabby and the place seemed dingy.

"It wouldn't hurt to buy some new things," she hinted. "Maybe get a paint job."

"I know, I've just never been home much since I graduated from law school."

"I need something to drink," she said, nervous about the idea of making love in such a dump.

Leslie went to the fridge and offered her orange juice, seltzer, or vodka.

"Is the juice fresh?" she asked.

"Yes."

"Mix them half juice, half vodka," she instructed.

Leslie did so, and brought the glass over. She inspected it to make sure it was clean and only touched the liquid to her lips before putting it down and stating, "Sorry again for all the nonsense the other day."

Leslie let some time pass before he replied. "I really thought you were going to have Tanen fire me. I can't believe you said that." She kissed him and he returned the kiss. "You are so bad."

Kneeling on the edge of his sofa, she beamed a smile and replied, "Gee, I hope that doesn't mean a spanking."

Leslie reached up into her skirt and felt around for the elastic band of her panties, then slid them down.

"I beg your pardon, monsieur," she feigned surprise. "What do you think you're doing?"

He glared at her. She started giving him a series of tender kisses and he began to slip his fingers through her bristles. He heard a soft, barely traceable whimper stir out from the back of her throat. He located the nub of her clitoris, which he gently brushed with a fingertip.

"Take me out," he charged, softly.

What audacity, she thought with delight, and said, "No way."

When he gave her a slap on her rear, she looked at him with grinning disbelief. She unzipped his pants and slipped out his erection without touching it. Lowering her head playfully, she slowly opened her lips and paused just over his penis. Her mouth puckered, then softly exhaled down the shaft of his cock, before she pulled away, giggling.

"So help me, the next whack and you won't be able to sit for a week," he warned.

She closed her eyes, held her breath, and put her lips over the head of his cock. Breathing slowly, she ran the tip of her tongue over him, tasting his hot, cellophane-thin skin. When she took hold of the base of his cock, he slapped her rear again.

"I didn't say you could use your hands," he voiced in a raspy tone. She released him and slobbered on the head a while until she started getting into it. She gently took him with her lips. He caressed her hair and neck. At one point, her mouth fully embracing him, she looked up for approval. A solid stinger fell across her ass, which she knew would leave a red mark.

"I didn't tell you to look at me!" he scolded.

She closed her eyes and couldn't remember when she last felt so aroused. Focusing on the sharp tingly sensation on her thighs, she lowered her head and was able to envelop his entire prick without gagging. Then, measuring how much her mouth could comfortably handle, she wildly sucked him, just to show what an absolutely perfect whore she could be. He put his hands in the tangle of her hair, grabbing her locks in his fingers, and gently jerked her head up and down. She completely had him. She listened to his groaning and tried to breathe steadily through her nose. Soon, she could feel his spasms between her lips and then the hot spurts along the back of her tongue and top of her throat. She quietly gulped it all down. When he finally opened his eyes, she pretended to be holding the results in her mouth.

"Swallow," he commanded with a wily smile.

She dramatically appeared to comply, releasing a stiff quenching sigh. She leaned back tiredly. He kissed her hard on the mouth, gently massaging her breasts and stomach. He opened her legs, working one finger in at a time. When he finally had four fingers inside of her, he slid down and simultaneously tongued and flicked her. He was hard again. In a moment they were fucking on the couch. Several times, he had to grab her and hold her tightly against him, digging his fingers into her ass cheeks, to keep from coming. Finally, as she started coming, he slammed into her again and again, until the bedframe rocked so intensely that the downstairs neighbor responded with several clangs on the radiator.

After a nap, they held each other gently. Leslie finally asked, "Did you have some kind of an affair with Tanen?"

"Fuck you," she responded matter-of-factly.

"That day you first saw me," Leslie confided, "I had just gotten dumped by my girlfriend who was a former porn actress."

"Why are you telling me this?"

"'Cause I want you to understand that there is really nothing you can't tell me. You can trust me."

"Okay," she said, deciding to test him. "Remember I told you that I was quitting paralegaling. Well, it's because I have slowly been developing another skill that is actually very profitable."

"You told me—counseling kids," he said, and softly nipped her right nipple.

"I never said kids," she replied with a smirk, and biting her bottom lip, she revealed, "Actually, I'm a drug dealer."

"What!"

"I made five grand this month alone." She smiled excitedly with widened eyes and mouth.

"Five thousand dollars?" Leslie sputtered nervously, and wondered how he was going to extricate himself from this criminal. Before he could formulate a response, she started giggling.

"What's so funny?" Leslie asked, slightly agitated.

"I'm kidding," she laughed, and recomposing herself, she said, "You want the truth? Truth is, I'm a dominatrix."

"Wait a second, are you saying that you . . . you don't do it . . . ?" His voice trailed off.

"No, unlike Thomas Jefferson, I don't have sex with my slaves," she replied, slightly indignant that he would suggest such a thing.

"What exactly do you do?"

"I act out their fantasies. I whip them. Tie them up. Dress them like little girls, the usual."

"What advertisement did you answer to get that kind of job?"

"First, tell me how you dated a porn actress."

Leslie felt too embarrassed to confide his voyeuristic obsession and subsequent pursuit. He simply said that he saw Sky Pacifica in a film and later met her in a bar.

"Now, tell me about being a dominatrix."

"Come on, there's got to be more than that," she pushed.

"What can I say?"

"Look, if you want to have an honest relationship, this is where it begins," she said, looking at him sincerely.

Leslie really liked her and didn't want any lies to start. He rose to his filing cabinet and located the only porn magazine of Sky Pacifica that he hadn't tossed out. He handed it to Cecilia.

She looked at the picture of the sexy actress tonguing another girl and felt herself grow quivery. Although there was no actual resemblance, the lesbian imagery reminded Cecilia of her old college girlfriend. Softly, Cecilia muttered, "My god, she's beautiful."

"She's a complete nut."

"So how exactly did you meet her?"

"I became infatuated with her. I tracked her down on the West Coast, and through a weird twist of fate she ended up coming back here and living with me."

"You are kidding!"

"I wish I was. She lived with me about a month before I found out she was stripping and taking drugs behind my back. I got a call from a strip joint one day that she had overdosed right on the strip floor."

"Wow," Cecilia said, and staring at the magazine carefully, she asked, "Did you love her?"

"I loved what I thought her to be."

"Was she a spectacular lover?"

"Far from it."

"Do you still love her?" Cecilia asked, sitting up.

Leslie could see a hint of insecurity. Silently, he took the magazine from her, opened the window which overlooked a garbage-strewn courtyard, and threw it out. "That's what I think of her. Now, tell me how you got into S&M."

She explained that while studying in southern Italy during the mid-seventies, she had become involved with a wealthy older man, Lorenz. In his youth, just after World War Two, he had hobnobbed with the great artists and writers of his generation. She mentioned several artists whose names Leslie did not recognize.

"Anyway," she released in parts, "he . . . brought me . . . into it."

"How did it happen?"

"Very slowly. Lorenz actually lured a new persona out of me." She described how he was very warm and loving, but gradually grew aloof.

"When we first made love, he would not say a word or show any tenderness," she explained. All the while, though, he knew exactly what he was doing. Sternly, he teased and tormented her with equal parts pain and pleasure until the two became one.

"What did he do?" he asked.

"A lot of things."

"Like what?"

She wanted to tell him, to bring him into it, yet she was reluctant. Sex with him was still nice. It was edgy without being out of control. She decided to leave the insanity for later. Instead of giving a complete lesson, she skipped to an isolated detail of Lorenz's habits: "While we would make love, he'd choke me, not hard, but . . ."

"You like it?"

"Not at first, but now, whenever I get strangled, I kind of get turned on," she confessed.

"Maybe we should try it," he suggested.

"I don't know. It sort of got out of control. Lorenz became either too submissive or too controlling."

"How was it controlling?" he asked.

"You know, the usual ways. Didn't you ever read *The Story of O* or Marquis de Sade?"

He nodded no.

She sighed, not really wanting to go into it. "He would make me take off his shoes and socks when he came home. Since I was a student and usually broke, he would give me an allowance. Soon he decided when I ate, when I slept. He even picked out what I could wear."

"So you were his slave . . . How did you become a dominatrix?"

"That began accidentally. One afternoon in early fall. We were in Rome for the weekend. He took me to all the fashion boutiques. In one store there was this incredibly sexy miniskirt. We were going to all the ritzy discos at the time so I really wanted it. But it cost a lot; a designer's new line. So Lorenz made me this offer. He said he'd buy me the skirt if I wore it without panties for just half an hour."

"That doesn't sound too bad."

"You've never been to Rome. There, you don't walk around the streets too long in a skirt, let alone a miniskirt without panties. But I figured a half an hour with an escort, that I could do." She rose and went to the kitchen, where she checked the expiration date of the orange juice and spritzed it with seltzer. When she returned, she kissed Leslie on the lips. He kissed her back. She slid down his chest, kissing her way to his thickening cock.

"Finish the story." He pulled her back up.

"Oh, right." She sat up, took a sip of her glass, and resumed: "So I'm looking at my watch and we're walking around, not far from the Coliseum, and the half hour is ticking away. So far, so good. We pass a public square. He asks me if I would mind sitting down. He's getting tired. It's approaching dusk and I'm lucky because there are only old folks and women around. I could see that he was getting really pissed."

"Why?" Leslie asked.

"He had just spent a zillion lire and was hoping for

a humiliating experience. It would have been a real turn-on for him if I got gang-raped. Eventually we pass the thirty-minute mark. I begin to relax. Then, out of nowhere, a group of young guys in their twenties appear, and before I know it, the cocksucker reaches down and pulls up the front of my miniskirt!"

"So what'd you do?"

"I smacked him across the face, hailed a cab back to his place, and started packing my clothes."

"You left him?" Leslie asked, uncertain where it was all leading.

"I was about to leave him, but before I could, he came up to me apologizing, begging for mercy. I went crazy. I started hitting him, screaming, pulling his hair, kicking him. And the more I did it, the more subservient he became and the more I liked doing it. I told him to do as I say and made him keep begging for mercy. He had me tie him up and I started doing the same things to him that he had been doing to me. By the end of the summer, though, he became so whiny that I got sick of him and split."

"So how'd you get into the S&M game?"

"First, tell me more about your little porn actress," she countered.

"I pretended to be a photographer and she used me. It was a bad experience and it's all behind me now," he said, and asked again, "So how'd you get into S&M?"

"Actually, through paralegaling. At another firm, when I was temping. I worked for this older lawyer. No sex, he was almost fatherly. He invited me to dinner and I simply saw it in his eyes. The entire game. They start by treating you like shit. Bossing you around exactly like Lorenz did. That's how Tanen started."

"So Tanen's a slave . . ." Leslie said, and smiled at

the thought of the older man being bound up and humiliated. "He was always such a cocksucker."

"They're all just little SAMs," she replied.

"SAM?"

"A smart-ass masochist. They taunt and tease you until you have to straighten them out. That's all they really want."

"So explain about the first time you did it professionally," Leslie said.

"Well, this attorney asked me if we could get together. He offered me a lot of money, a thousand dollars for an evening, so I did it. No sex or nudity."

"How did he know you were into it?"

"I don't know. Maybe I was putting out a vibe. Or maybe he just came on to everyone."

"What was his thousand-dollar fantasy?" Leslie pressed.

"Let's see, it was really cliché." She smiled and looked away, slightly embarrassed. "It was his prom night and I was, like, lead cheerleader and prom queen, and he was the class nerd. I humiliated him as he jerked off. Stupid stuff."

"And now you've suddenly decided to rent a storefront?"

"They call them dungeons."

"So you simply rented a dungeon somewhere?"

"No. He introduced me to his old mistress, this lady who has a dungeon over on Twenty-first between Fifth and Sixth. I've been working there for a month, and now I have all the naughty boys I can handle."

"Where do these naughty boys come from?"

"Word of mouth, mainly, but Madame Leah runs an ad in all the sex papers."

"What's the name of this dungeon?"

"House of Fire," she blurted.

"And what does your boyfriend say about all this?" Leslie asked.

"Boyfriend?" She was caught off guard.

"I knew you were lying!" he shouted, as he jumped on her and jokingly wrestled with her. In another moment, he angled his hard-on into her and they were making love again.

◄◄

Throughout the Spring of 1980, they ate out almost every evening in all the finest restaurants in the city. Sometimes they'd catch a foreign film at a repertoire theater. Cecilia loved Italian filmmakers: Fellini, Bertolucci, Wertmuller. As the months grew warmer, going out became part of their foreplay. In public, leaning against parked cars, in doorways or movie theaters, she would usually initiate it as a kind of dare. With her bold sexual background, he always felt he had to raise the stakes and prove himself. They'd tease each other until they couldn't bear it any longer. She gave him handjobs on the benches around the Central Park Boat Lake and blowjobs in the Brambles or the trellis behind the Band Shell.

Once, Leslie play-raped her in the train tunnel under Riverside Park. Her skirt was hiked up and his zipper was down. He had one hand over her mouth, the other clamped around her neck, humping her from behind as she winced and mockingly fought back. When a homeless woman accidentally walked in and saw her struggling, she started screaming. A crowd raced over and an officer was notified.

After that they would only do foreplay outside, then

grab a cab home and fuck all night. Cecilia loved to play games. Sometimes he'd be a cop and she'd be his prisoner, or he'd be an immigration officer and she'd be a terrified illegal alien. Sometimes the fantasy would involve a third party, usually a woman who they both pretended was there.

By September, Leslie decided that it had been the best summer of his life. He also realized that he had never felt so much love for anyone ever before.

APRIL 3, 1980, SF

THE TENDERLOIN SECTION OF SAN FRANCISCO WAS the closest patch of bustling urban decay the hilly city had to Times Square. Dealers, hookers, and panhandlers aimlessly rotated from doorways and shelters. Although she had only stayed there with Leslie for four weeks, the Big Apple was the perfect habitat for all her bad habits and Sky missed it. The past few months in San Francisco had been dizzying. The recent murder of the mayor and the gay city councilor gave the place a strange crisis quality.

Today, instead of taking her usual bus, Sky decided to walk to the Naked Angels Strip Club. She hiked up the concrete hill toward North Beach, the unmythological land of tits and tourists. With each labored step she wondered, When is it going to break? How is it going to break?

Stripping was a quick fix, an instant injection of cash. One step above waitressing, but way below everything else. Her tarot cards said that something big was supposed to break for her. Fate was duty bound to offer not just anything, but something new and exciting, something she could rail her life onto.

"Hey jugs," she heard and ignored, not even bothering to quicken her pace.

She couldn't—wouldn't—do porn anymore. Stripping obviously wasn't merely moving around naked. You traded the job for some invisible and limited commodity inside of you. Once that part of you was gone, the bloom was off, you were toughened. Imperceptibly, men and all illusions of them were forever changed.

"Sky!" someone yelped from behind.

She kept walking. There were a lot more guys she didn't want to see than those she did.

"Sky! It's Denver!"

Sky turned to see Denver Wades, an undiscovered rock and roll star turned out-of-work porn actor. At twenty-five he looked fifteen years older. His thin-lipped smile, dark leathery complexion, and oily tassel of inky black hair made him look like a flamenco dancer who had drunk way too much tequila.

"Hi," she replied kindly. Only once did they screw for the camera. He had complications of the woody, but he was sweet, sensitive, and funny.

"I haven't seen you since when?" he said. "At least a year?"

"It's good to find a familiar face," she replied, as she hugged his bony body.

He wore hippy-dippy psychedelic clothes that looked like they had been reclaimed from Goodwill. His haircut seemed self-administered. At least he appeared momentarily clean of drugs.

"What are you doing, Denver?"

"Changing my name to Frisco," he kidded, and laughed at his little joke. "I've started a new band and I'm living with Riley. Remember Riley?"

"How can I forget?" Riley had been another member

of the fuck gallery. Sky once got into a fight with him during a sex scene. He had held her head down to get off, turned on by making her gag.

"You know who I'm still in contact with?" Denver asked. "Your old bud Laurel. She's still in LA."

"Oh! You've got to give me her number." Sky perked up. Denver started walking up the hill in her direction. "So, how you making money, darling?"

"You know, pushing, scratching, peddling." The merchandise didn't matter. "How 'bout you?"

"Dancing," she said softly, with obvious embarrassment. "What else is new?"

"Where you crashing?" he asked, and took a joint from behind his left ear.

"I got a place on Larkin," she answered.

"Did you hear that Sally Mar married money?" He lit up and took a deep toke.

"Sally Mar? Get out of here!" Sky replied, pausing for both a breather and to punctuate his news.

"She wore the white train. Didn't invite any of us. The guy was some real rich kid too. A nouveau riche socialite!" He handed her the lit joint.

She took a long hit. "Holy shit, doesn't he know?" Sky exclaimed. The big joke a few years ago was that Sally's promiscuity was forcing hookers into working at McDonald's.

They stopped walking and passed the joint back and forth. As he talked about life in San Francisco, Sky felt envious of Sally. Getting high, she struggled to understand Denver.

"What's in this joint?" she asked, suspecting angel dust.

"Just grass. Want to know my mystical secrets of living on three dollars a day?" She nodded yes as she took another toke. "Snag free lunches at the Hari Krishnas, but not at the Moonies—they don't let you leave; eat food right out of the wrappers at night at large supermarkets, only don't steal it; use found and old transfers to ride the buses, most drivers don't check; get clothes by dumpster-diving in donation bins after hours; sleep in Golden Gate Park, though it is warmer to sleep downtown; always wear a sweater because the west side is ten degrees colder than the east side of this fucking town."

When the roach was unpinchable, Denver flicked it down.

"Shit!" Sky muttered, spotting a clock in a store window. "If I'm late for work, the cocksucker fines me ten bucks."

To the cling and rattle of a passing cable car, the two resumed their climb up the sharp incline. Denver asked her questions but she didn't feel like talking. Shortly, he began lapsing into reminiscences about the good old days in LA, talking about events a few years back as if they had taken place a century earlier.

"I don't know about you," he concluded sadly, "but the summer of '77 I had more money, went to more parties, had more friends, got more pussy, had more everything than ever before. I was at my peak. One party after the next. Money. Friends. Drugs and booze all free and no hangovers or ODs I couldn't recover from, no weight stuck to my thighs or belly. It'll never get better than that. That will always be my Zenith TV year."

When they reached a street that wasn't slanted at a forty-five-degree angle, Sky gasped for air and exclaimed, "This city is too fucking steep!"

"This is where I turn off, kiddo," Denver replied, staring sadly at the distant bay.

Before she knew it, he planted a quick kiss on her cheek, then scribbled down and handed her a phone number where he could receive messages.

Walking west, down another hill, she remembered the time he had taken her home after a wild "bisexual bicentennial party" in the summer of '76. As usual, she had been high as a kite, passed out in someone's bathtub. He must have carried her about a mile on his back, because he didn't have a car. He put her on his couch and wrapped her in a sheet. The next morning, when she found that her money was still intact and she hadn't been fucked, she had decided that Denver was a genuine male anomaly.

She turned around and could see him walking away, the back of his colorful threadbare jacket fading into the distance. More than sadness, the sight sent a chill down her spine, because she was right behind him, one step away from living on the street.

Strip for a couple weeks, she thought, and then blow this place. *I've got to find my big break. Some way to get into . . . life.*

PART TWO: FAST FORWARD

APRIL 24, 2001, NYC

AFTER HITTING A HUNDRED AND TWENTY MILES AN HOUR and almost joining my dearly departed, I figure I better slow down as I enter Queens, the land of cemeteries. I don't even notice them at first. St. John's Cemetery, Lutheran Cemetery, Mount Olivet, Mt. Zion. Inevitably, though, the graves pop up. Little gray monoliths dotting the green lawns. When highway barriers bar their view, I can't stop thinking about how they go on and on, a miniature skyline of lifeless buildings.

They should have a chute where one can drop a body off without even exiting the highway. At Cecilia's cemetery, nearly twice the population of New York is buried. The graves of its youngest sons are backhoed in and crushed down onto the caskets of fathers, grandfathers, and great-grandfathers.

I de-ramp and cruise through a maze of small roadways that divide the manicured lawn of Calvary. Occasionally I have to slow down while passing a variety of poorly parked vehicles marking an internment in progress. I find the spot, pull over to a shoulder, and walk to her stone.

During the first days when I would visit, I'd note the growth of grass on her grave. Now, the green texture is as thick and consistent as the grass of those dead over a hundred years. I feel something like envy at the newly buried plots. I lie down on her grave, and staring up, I consider the overcast sky then drift off, joining her in velvety blackness.

I feel the hand, but in the stew of darkness can't see the face. A flashlight is shining in my eyes and then it goes out.

"Excuse me," says the bristling darkness, "it's wake-up time." A groundskeeper is gently touching me.

"Must have dozed off."

"No problem," the man replies philosophically.

"You know, Edgar Allan Poe used to sleep on his wife's grave," I say, scrambling to my feet. The groundskeeper smiles. I had informed him of this fact three weeks earlier, the last time he woke me here.

Pathological bereavement, Beckwith called it. "Do you ever fantasize yourself talking to her?" he asked.

"No, I don't fantasize that," I replied. I *do* talk to her everyday, but I didn't tell him that.

What's a healthy length and depth to grieve, particularly if you're the killer and she's the only person you've ever loved?

Stiffly, I jaunt to my Jaguar, glad that it is still early when I pass over the Triboro to Harlem River Drive and down the West Side Highway to my rented parking spot. Before going into my building, I stop at the local supermarket, where I pick up a half-pound cut of filet mignon and a head of broccoli.

"Hey, boss!" says Luis, the eager doorman who reeks of hair gel and cheap cologne. Probably the same cheap brands he's been using since he was a boy in Cuba. I go up to my apartment. Early man first lived in caves, then in trees; now we live in large caves higher up than trees. Hungrily, I plug my Camcorder into the TV to inspect my day of stalking Jeane in Long Island. On my forty-five-inch Sony Trinitron, the fruit of today's labors comes down to six minutes of poorly focused, wobbly-held, under- and over-exposed footage of the artist formerly known as Sky and her daughter. The film set, that ghastly mall, is distractingly tracked with the banter of me and the nitwit security guard. In short, it is a disappointing preview.

I put the filet on a baking sheet, cover it with minced garlic and fresh thyme, and slide it into the oven. I cut the broccoli, place it in a basket, and steam. Scanning the wonder windows through my telescope, I catch a clothing change. She is an ill-faced, beaut-bodied lass with a large pair of symmetrical breasts. The greatest moment of excitement isn't seeing her nude, but right before, as I am focusing my telescope. Seeing is having. Focusing is still craving.

My steak is burnt on the outside, bloody within. I eat the filet with a glass of Chateau Neuf du Pape. I leave the raw, inner rectangle of meat on the plate.

The red light is blinking on my answering machine. This used to make me anxious. When Cece was alive, the receiving tape filled up with calls quickly. Now, weeks can go by before I rewind it. The messages are a variety of wanters: seven soulless telemarketers, six automated stock offers, five angry messages from Holtov about the Sewter fiasco, and five golden rings from old friends.

I no longer feel guilty about not returning their calls. With soft hands and miles of blah emotional distance, they have rolled from promising young men backwards into big Howdy Doody dolls. Some are lean, a side effect of neurotic health-clubbing and dieting. Sacrificial-lamb vacations have become the greatest offerings of their moneyed lives: For months they'll plan a sailing trip on the high seas, or a mountain-climbing expedition with an entourage of luggage-carrying natives, or witness a natural phenomenon halfway around the world, volcanoes, eclipses, etc., but for them it's like some interactive cybermovie or a week in a futuristic theme park.

In the barbaric midst of a primitive third-world country, they are vertically dipped, hermetically protected, and surgically transplanted back into their twenty-first-century world without any real risk or aura of experience. Then, over the next fifty years, when that ravaged region of the world suffers plagues, civil wars, and famines, we, the friends, have to listen as they point their fat arms at the TV and say, "Yep, I was right there."

The worst part of seeing them, though, is that I am acutely aware of my own devastating failure. I've exchanged the rose of my youth for toys. A highly specialized legal expertise has earned me prestige among people I've come to loathe.

I turn my Camcorder and television back on and watch her again, my trophy of beauty, my atrophy of will, my entropy of spirit. While reviewing the "Jeane at the mall" segment, I push the magnification button on my TV to blow her image up like a balloon. I pause and slo-mo the entire tape. What escaped me the first time, I see clearly now: it's in her eyes. As little Kate is chirping with her friends, her mom's eyes are fixed on her the entire time. A shine of pride sparkles on her face. You can see the love and sacrifice and delicacy this mother put into making her daughter, the countless hours of patience and concern. A few years ago, Cecilia and I agreed never to have kids for a reason. They would grow stronger and more resentful as we would become frailer and weaker.

The marionette strings controlling Jeane are tied to the daughter. This revelation gives rise to a new plan: I could hustle the daughter into a rented van. I wouldn't hurt her or molest her in the slightest. I'm Humbert Humbert in reverse trying to get to mother through daughter. I'd have to hire an operative to hold her while I explained to Jeane that I would release her unharmed, provided she did as I say.

Suddenly I hear a flapping, the rustling of feathers. My rifle is leaning in the corner. I walk over to the balcony, calmly make sure there is a cartridge inside. The winged gargoyle is not there. It must be on the bathroom windowsill. If I try to kill the bird through the bathroom window, I will probably scare it away. Leaning out from my balcony, I bring the pigeon into my sites, a large bull-necked male.

I aim for the bird's fat garbage-fed heart and shoot. The miserable creature topples forward, spiraling, attempting to catch itself, but is unable. It tumbles all the way down to the outer deck of the building, right above ground level, where all my kills collect. I put the gun away and reward myself with seltzer and a square of Godiva chocolate that has been in my refrigerator since Christmas when my wife bought it. Then I take an Aderol, watch a little TV, and fall asleep.

▶▶

I awaken early the next afternoon. The Sunday *New York Times* is on my doormat, so it must be Sunday. Through the cover stories and various sections I dig to the comic strips for middle-aged men: the obituaries. A minor politician, sixty-three; an admiral, seventy-eight. An investment banker named Owens died at fifty-three of Amyotrophic Lateral Sclerosis. When I knew him twenty years ago, he was either with Shearson Lehman or Salomon. We once had a spat about the Fed and interest rates. After spending his life accumulating money, he never had a chance to really blow it. We might have that in common. Cecilia always said I was well-off with lower-middle-class spending habits. That was another reason I needed her, to teach me how to spend money.

Owen's obit mentions that ALS attacks the motor nervous

system. His diaphragm atrophied. All that money and power didn't rescue him from drowning in his own phlegm.

Although the earth lost no giants today, it's the little unmourned deaths that bleed us. One day we sit up, look around, and we're surrounded by strange young faces. The principals might still be there, but all the old character actors have slipped away. The second fiddlers were buried unnoticed. We're just another tearless, second-tier death waiting to happen. Owens is dead, long live Owens.

I check to make sure all the sections of the paper are there, then roll the overweight Gray Lady of journalism into a corner, where it'll sit until the middle of the week when I customarily chuck it out unread. I dress to go to my exclusive new gym franchise and bring a change of clothes. Yesterday's plan of kidnapping the daughter is obviously insane. I decide while knotting my sneakers that being a lawyer means breaking the spirit while preserving the body and letter of the law.

After the treadmill, the weights, I sit trembling on the Nautilus, hyperventilating, dripping with sweat. Endorphins racing. My biceps, triceps, and pecs are all engorged with blood and throbbing. Is pleasure the subtraction or the addition of pain? This is how personalities are divided. Cecilia was the only person I have known who could give as well as take it.

An aerobicized anorectic who had been waiting for my machine puts down her *Elle* magazine, and when I notice the Calvin Klein fashion ad on the back page, inspiration comes. I shower, change, and leave.

Stopping at a magazine store, quickly scanning through several glossies, I survey all the new clothing ads. A pair of teens on a beach sitting back to back, their legs join together in a single spread-eagle pose. A small purse tossed at the ankles of another model doubles as a pair of yanked-down

panties. Tiredly folded elbows cocked outward faintly simu-
late pert breasts. A woman's head thrown back languidly
with a man reclining at her feet doubles for the post-coital
ecstasy of oral gratification. All those years of looking at
pornography have taught me how to decode the hidden and
obscene glyphs of Madison Avenue; they have fully prepared me for this job. Photo advertisement is the trick of
turning the ordinary and insipid into the unbelievably profane. Women like it subliminal. One particular orgy of the
ordinary is a group of teens loosely and tiredly collapsed
into each other. Their position of heads and tails makes a
thoughtless daisy-chain of blue jeans—another Calvin Klein
ad catches my eye. The photo credit is one "Perry Cruz."

I walk over to Central Park to hammer out ideas. Passing
through the Brambles behind the Boat Lake, I deduce that I
have to scope out Kate's high school. That's where I'll set the
trap. Among cruising gays and scouting bird lovers, I see
that I am going to need some photo equipment as well as a
fake ID.

Back home—a quick call to the nefarious Ron Marauder,
who provides me with an operative, the surreptitious services of a graphic designer named Assif Sunjohnny. I call
Assif and explain that I need a fake photo-ID by tonight.

"Exactly what kind of ID are we talking?" the accented
voice sizzles on the phone.

"I want an ID for a photographer who works for Calvin
Klein," I explain without shame.

"Should I use any name or . . ."

"No, Perry Cruz." Names don't come cooler than that.

"You know," Sunjohnny replies, "it'll be easy to confirm
that you're not this Cruz man."

I explain that this isn't a problem.

"Do you want business cards as well?" No. The entire task
would cost but two hundred dollars. Fine. The graphic

designer explains that I have to sit for a passport photo which is not included in his price. Nice try. I already have some. Sunjohnny replies that a wallet-size ID will be ready for pickup at 8 p.m. He gives me his address—Forty-fourth and Eighth—and concludes by asking that I please bring cash.

I spend the rest of the day going over tomorrow's plans. I also consider a wardrobe, prop pieces, and equipment for the task. A couple hours under the sunlamp at the gym would make a nice glaze, but I don't have time for that. I know I'll have only one shot at this Long Island pigeon. Beyond that single chance, the surprise will be blown, the enemy will be on full alert, preparing for a counter-strike.

I go to the bathroom mirror and look me in the eye. Even though I look damn good for forty-six, I have to look younger. Since I haven't shaved in four days, I am able to carve a mustache and goatee out of the bristle.

Once outside, I purchase a corduroy shirt, a gold-plated necklace and bracelet, black hair dye, and three contemporary rock CDs: Limp Bizkit, Kid Rock, and Girls Against Boys. My final touch is in a tattoo parlor called Body Language. Kids trust tattoos: They think there is something exciting about befouling their silky flesh, making their thin arms and tight torsos look dirty and scrawled like a public toilet. Inside, the place is loaded with malingerers and nitwits chatting about nothing, using rock music to fill the gaps between their ears. I select a big stupid colorful icon called the Alien, based on the monster movie—a vengeful Gregor Samsa.

I pay for it up front, a hundred bucks. I am given a release to sign. No one wants responsibility anymore. A girl in laced-up leather pants leads me into a bathroom and gives me a razor. "Shave wherever you want the tattoo," she says, with a disaffected attitude that's regarded as cool.

I shave the fine hairs on my right shoulder. Then I'm shown to a wooden armchair where a skinhead takes a seat next to me. He puts the stencil on my arm and pulls out this futuristic tattoo gun with different needles and a color cartridge.

"I hope those are new needles," I warn.

"Yep," he replies. The gun sounds like a mechanical mosquito, with its million little pricks. Fifteen minutes, a half hour, an hour, I watch the disgusting figure coming to life on my arm. He keeps covering it in Vaseline. Soon it's done.

He tells me I'm supposed to take vitamins for the next week or so, and to keep the tattoo out of the sun and covered with Bacitracin. "It'll flake, but there's no need to worry."

Although approaching Jeane's daughter as a fashion photographer is a cliché, it worked with the mother twenty years ago. Besides, I have faith in the vanity of teenage girls. When I arrive at her school I'll talk to another girl first. I'll offer a fee, reveal my credentials. That'll show that I'm not singling out Kate.

As I prepare to leave, I nervously down a handful of assorted pills that make the world more colorful and friendly.

The receipt on my ATM withdrawal says 7:58 p.m. I check the mirror above the cash machine to be certain that the homeless man at the door hasn't seen me withdraw the max, five hundred bucks.

Outside, I grab a cab from Broadway and Seventy-seventh Street to the graphic artist's place in Hell's Kitchen. The driver is a small Asian man. His T&LC license reveals that his first name, Heu, is only a transposed vowel away from his last name, Hue.

I take the liberty of sliding open the unwashed plexiglass partition and use the man's presumed faith as an icebreaker: "You might have heard the old Buddhist axiom that each man has a limited amount of sperm. Only so many ejaculations, yes?"

"Dunno." He pronounces it as one word.

"Well, Heu, if I may call you Heu," I assume it's pronounced *who*, "truth of the matter is there is only so much of anything. You can take a life and chop it up into so many shits, pisses. So many bankruptcies and restructurings. So many cab rides . . ."

"Dunno."

"We don't have to be dead in order to die, do we? We burn out, but the body presses on. Our imagination allows us to reinvent and re-create ourselves." I lean up so that I am directly behind the cabby's little tulip ear. "But what happens when the imagination has reached its own burn-out, Heu, when the re-creation no longer re-creates? Buddha didn't mention that one, did he?" No response.

"In the days of old, Medieval farmers planted crops until they sucked the nutrients from the soil, then they let the land lay fallow to regenerate. Females of other species only have sex during a certain time in their cycle, only then are their genitals engorged. Very few species have recreational sex whenever they damn well want. Is that the secret? Does happiness lie in deprivation? Am I suffering the punishment of excess, Heu?"

"Dunno, dunno."

"Right! Why am I muddling the issue? Hell, I abused it."

Appropriately, Heu senses my nihilism and exhibits nothing.

"Does imagination live in innocence? And innocence, when we finally extinguish it—with all the shit and bitterness in life—do we kiss off all rejuvenative power?"

"Don't know." He separates the words, so I must be getting through.

"Where the fuck do you go when . . . when . . . ?" I can't talk anymore. Much to my chagrin, I start weeping. The cabby drives faster, passing through a red light.

Pulling myself together, I ask, "Why do we strive to destroy our own innocence? Where does that come from? Is innocence the price we pay for pleasure? I don't mind my physical vigor becoming dead weight and eventually rotting, but to still have energy and no innocence, that is unthinkable. Without innocence you can't recharge, can you?"

The cabby finally pulls up in front of the requested address. But I don't want to get out.

"Hey, what's your email? We could catch a ballgame or something."

"No," he replies bluntly. "You pay fare now."

Poor guy. He's probably got a cranky wife and as many children as grains of rice in a bowl. No available time for big American crybabies.

I give the man a well-earned twenty-dollar tip, get out, and wipe the tears off my face. The taxi zooms off with my woes in the backseat. The pills are kicking in.

Assif Sunjohnny, a stout, water buffalo–like man meets me at his downstairs door. He wears a silken embroidered bathrobe that outlines silos of fat; well-stocked for the next great famine. His stubby feet are squeezed into thin Oriental slippers. The long flight of wooden stairs sink and squeak like mice being squashed under his hooven step. With each landing, a different smell awaits: first floor, mothballs; second floor, mosquito repellant; third floor, incense. His floor smells like shit.

A dingy loft space filled with dust is Sunjohnny's Graphics Studio. The furniture looks like it was hauled in from the sidewalk. All lights are shaded and indirect. Sunjohnny points to a filthy sofa and excuses himself, vanishing behind a makeshift partition from which emanate strange gurgling noises.

An old black-and-white TV blares. He lowers the volume.

It is turned to MTV. A row of bikinied blondes shuffle in synchronized step. That MTV fertility dance might be the most important thing that those girls will ever do. That's how life is. I spot an old Helmut Newton calendar thumbtacked to the grease-streaked wall. Sunjohnny has a sexy-girl motif going.

"So, where's the photo?" the heavy-set operator asks, peaking from behind his tattered scrim. Some sauce is glistening from his lips — apparently, he is in the middle of dinner.

I offer a selection of three passport photos that I had taken a year ago. Sunjohnny chooses the most youthful one and vanishes into a small room. In a moment the man returns, proudly handing me a hot, unsealed wax-paper envelope. A large owl-eyed Persian curls around my ankles while I inspect the just-laminated ID. Sunjohnny kicks the cat away, not wanting to share any credit. Tastefully printed on beige rag paper, the ID has a Calvin Klein logo top-center. Under it is my face and my new name, "Perry Cruz, STAFF PHOTOGRAPHER." It looks utterly credible. I pay the man and promise him future business.

"Your wish is my command," Sunjohnny mutters, as if stating his business slogan.

A major fallacy of love is that such exclusive feelings are reserved for one particular person. But is there really such a person? A non-fungable, holy-grail person, a unique snowflake for your tongue alone?

"Let me ask you something," I put it to him. "Do you have a girlfriend?"

"A woman comes," the man replies flatly.

"Do you love her?" I perk up.

"If I don't, she won't come," the endomorph muses.

"But you're a realist. Here you are, counterfeiting IDs. What illusions can you have?"

"First of all, I make novelty items. Not for illicit purposes,"

Sunjohnny says, in case he is being taped by an undercover consumer reporter.

"I'm merely saying you seem to see things for what they are."

"I don't understand."

"Well, isn't love a little naïve when you think about it? Even a bit silly?"

"In what way?"

"The belief that one person can find another who is unreplaceable in a world of six billion: one person who is only for them, who's really worth . . . worth loving."

"Oh no, you shouldn't see it that way!" the Asian man urges.

"What way should I see it?"

"Women bring out an important side in us. We need them for this."

"What side?"

"You know, they make us . . ." — he searches for a word — ". . . considerate."

He misses the point. Women might be meat tenderizers for us gristly males, but does that merit love? I thank him and leave. Downstairs, I hail a cab back home. The driver, a flabby-necked, cliché-named American, is absent of any enigma or exotic aura. It would take a saw to cut his fat throat. During this trip I neither talk to the cabby nor cry. I consider what I said to Sunjohnny. The taxi slowly passes through Times Square at the exact hour of the releasing of the well-dressed hordes. These suited people sit in large multi-doored prisons for absurd, boring spectacles, and they are set loose around 10 o'clock. This strange middle-class ritual of wealth and status is concluded by a great cab competition. As they frantically wave for taxis I wave back at them from mine like the Queen of England.

With a sudden desire to get some hands-on experience for tomorrow's pickup, I instruct the loose-necked chauffeur to stop several blocks short of my home on Columbus Avenue. Paying the fare, I get out and walk into a corner bar called Sundry's. Its clientele appears to be mainly middle-aged gay men in penny loafers. The second bar, an old-age home for young people, is called Annie's Joint. The patronage seems as close knit as an ant farm.

Walking several blocks further, I stop in a new sports bar predictably called Hoops, where a TV is always watching you, always playing a sport. Everyone hoots in unison when someone on TV interacts with a ball. The venue appears to have an equal mix of guys and dolls. Squirming past the video–juke box, dodging the dart game, I make it to the bar, where I order a mug of lite beer. There I spot her. A bargain-basement Britney Spears. She's looking for me and doesn't even know it, sitting next to a liquor-scorched couple. They all look like off-duty cops. I pull up a stool next to her. It's not that she's pretty, or even attractive, but I can see in a million little ways that she is the type of girl who's attracted to the type of guy that I really am. Poor her.

She is solidly built. Pretty in a plain way, plain in a pretty way. Stocking-legged with laminated blond hair. Under a sheer button-up shirt and black Wonder bra, I can make her out, tight and pointy. Along with the couple to her right, she watches a basketball game on the overhead TV. After a much-challenged play, the Knicks score a basket. All yell thunderously. I yell too, a bit out of sync.

"Knicks rule!" shouts a young paunchy drunk with bushy eyebrows sitting next to me.

"They probably do," I say to blondy. She smiles and pops open a brass cigarette case.

I grab a match and offer her a light. She takes it, smiles. That's my cue: "I'm Perry, new in New York."

"Hi Perry, Sheila. What brings you to us?"

"Money. I just got a job here." Someone accidentally knocks over a bunch of bottles. All cheer.

"Where are you from?" She takes a long drag from her cigarette.

"California, LA. How 'bout you?" I stay in beat.

"I was conceived in Paris. Born and finished in Connecticut," she explains, downing the last of her beverage, "but I've been living here since '98."

"Did anyone ever tell you that you look like Britney Spears?" I ask.

"Yes, actually," she says modestly.

"So, what do you do?" I pray she is a cop.

"I'm an editorial assistant at a book packager. How 'bout you?"

"Photographer." I hide my disappointment.

She circulates cigarette smoke from mouth to nose like a gaseous snake swallowing its own tail.

"You look pretty young. Are you legal?"

"My, you're the charmer — twenty-four. You?"

"Thirty-three," I reply, and add, "the age Jesus was when he got nailed to the cross."

"So, *Jesus*," she pronounces the Lord's name in Spanish, "what's your IQ?"

"One-fifty, rock solid. Same as my weight," I reply, and gently slap my two-pack abs.

"And do you like women yellow, like your beer?" Stale pretzels and humor.

"Hey, Sheila, who's your cute friend?!" the male member of the rancid couple calls out.

"Perry, this is Lyle and Carol."

I shake hands with the pair who seem perfectly matched in weightiness and witlessness. The bartender, who knows he has a Pavlovian grip on the group, chimes in, "Anyone want a drink?" All order.

I, last in the group, say, "Gin and tonic, hold the gin and tonic." All laugh, failing the first of many little intelligence tests.

For the next two hours, I relish the game: the mindless banter, the silly jokes, the wary advances toward intimacy — only to blindly retreat when they are reciprocated. I keep score by Sheila's nervous teeter. Although she'll never be my mate, in no time at all it's checkmate. Her laughter says, Take me if you must: one night for a guilty sampling, two nights or more for the commitment package.

I listen to Sheila's discursive drivel with outward fascination and inward condescension. I can only live an evening like this once in my life and find it amusing. How do others do it for sustained periods? I buy her a three-drink consolation prize and two for myself.

By 11 o'clock, I've given as much as I've taken, so I issue the signal yawn. I look at my Rolex and proclaim that despite the boundless fun, it is time. I have an early shoot the next day, nothing like the magic hour of sunrise.

"Come on," Sheila encourages, "the night's in its infancy."

"Then I'll have to abort it. If you want to give me your number, I'll call you later in the week."

"No way." She is stalwart. "I've done that. Give my number out and wait forever. I'll give you my number only if you give me your number."

"Have you ever considered joining the police academy?" I ask, as I hand her a scribbled and fabricated phone number.

"Police academy?" she replies. "What for?"

"To be a cop."

"Me, a cop?" she says, baffled.

"Oh sure. Cuffs and uniform. You'd make a good cop."

"Why do you say that, Wesley?"

"Just a joke, Sheba." I sip the dregs from my tall tubular glass. But when I look back up, she is staring right at me. For the first time that entire evening, she is really seeing me, a smug bastard, out to make myself feel a little smarter by contrast.

"Look, I . . . I didn't want to be alone tonight," I mea culpa.

Sheila nods silently. Not particularly angry. Conveying her pain even more so.

"Goodnight," I say, just above a whisper.

"Look at you guys. Like a pair of love birds," calls out Lyle, whose blood-alcohol content now makes him talking while intoxicated.

"Remember, Lyle, AA and AAA don't mix," I reply casually, as if I've known him all my life. The couple seem to think that this is supremely funny and laugh. Sheila turns away.

All roads lead to self-contempt. When I get home, as an act of contrition, I play my answering machine, which bottles up the world's anger at me. This time there's an automated message from the phone company reminding me that I'm vertiginously close to being disconnected. Holtov is again asking for my input on the Sewter bankruptcy. Different associates from different departments on conference calls are cantilevering together complex questions which I no longer have the answers to.

Sky, I need to control your uncontrollability, that's my only haven. I locate my Nikon packed away on a high shelf and several boxes of film in the back of the fridge, which I thaw in my knapsack.

After taking a couple sedatives, I fall asleep in my chair.

Awaking to the dissonant echoes of the noon-time street, I lean forward and hoist up, clutching, clawing along the wall in desperate need of the toilet. I still linger in the afterwash of a Hieronymus Bosch dream-tableau: squatting knees out, hanged arches, heels jutting, naked on a window sill. Filthy and vestigial hands squeezed into fingerless balls nestled in my spiky armpit hairs. My little arms folded like quill-less wings and testicles dangling low. My subconscious is saying, It's bad to kill the pretty pigeons—BAD! Guilt's a healthy sign for a psycho.

By the time my feet hit the cold tiles of the bathroom, I am fully conscious.

Who's that middle-aged grunger with the goatee and mustache staring in the mirror? Me. And a huntin' we will go. I dress in the clothes I had selected the day before. Studying myself carefully in the mirror, I realize to my dismay that I am unintentionally creating that image that panicky male actors acquire just before resigning themselves to middle age, a clinging-to-youth quality. It is a sad and spurious look, but for a suburban post-adolescent girl it could work. Aided by a brush, scissors, hair mousse, tweezers, and a dab of male mascara, items that had actually belonged to Cecilia, I work the look. Upon satisfaction, I locate the falsified Calvin Klein ID, my bag of photographic tricks, and I leave for my hot wheels.

NOVEMBER 27, 1980, NYC

AS OUR FIRST THANKSGIVING TOGETHER APPROACHED, Cecilia wanted to introduce me to her folks in Connecticut. But the firm was in the throes of a big lawsuit. I had jockeyed myself to an enviable position for a second-year associate and couldn't get away. She headed out alone and it was the first time, the first evening, that we'd been apart for months. Like a door left open, there was a menacing chill of freedom in the air. The haunting chorus of a thousand pornographic sirens sang, "*Leslie come out and play with us.*"

That night I headed to a bar, but after a while, when it became clear that no chicky would yield either phone number or affections, I lost patience with the living and headed for the prosthetic. I browsed through magazines in porn arcades before checking out sex-trade papers—*Screw* and *Wife Swappers Gazette*—that routinely advertised porn actresses who were dancing the strip circuit. I was eternally curious about Sky's whereabouts. It had been eleven months since she vanished from my life.

That's when I spotted the quarter-page ad for Madame Leah's House of Fire. This was where Cece worked. I figured it would be a hoot pretending to be a new client. Take in the tabooed surroundings. It was only about 9 p.m. From a pay phone on the corner of Forty-second and Broadway, I called the place and inquired about their services.

"Well," said a murky female voice, "we have a wide variety of madames and a questionnaire. You can come in and pick your mistress and write out your likes and dislikes."

"Can I come right over?" I asked excitedly, knowing that I didn't have to worry about being caught since Cecilia was visiting her parents.

She supplied the address, and within five minutes I was walking into a drab, renovated warehouse under the triangular shadow of the Flatiron Building. An automated freight elevator hoisted me up to the fifth floor. The steel doors opened and I found myself in a Vincent Price movie set: faux stone walls, orange candle-shaped bulbs flickering in torch-light wall fixtures.

A sexy receptionist in a tight, electric-blue dress and gothic makeup offered me a seat and launched into her standard pitch: "The House of Fire features half a dozen select mistresses to suit all your slavish needs." She slid a photo album over. Each of the mistresses had several pages spotlighting them in different dramatic dress, along with props, sometimes with semimuscular slaves bound or kneeling before them in leather masks.

Skipping through the pages, I located Cece's persona, Madame Guinevere, a Medieval trade name. In the first photo, she was wearing a leather corset and fishnet stockings. Her hair was in a bun and her mascara was exquisitely applied. A slave was kneeling before her. He was athletically built, yet somehow his wrists had gotten fastened together with a tight leather thong. She was holding a shock of his enviable golden hair, yanking the poor lad's head back ruthlessly. His eyes were bent up mercifully, a minimum-wage Saint Sebastian.

On the next page, Cecilia was *Achtung* all over: appareled in an SS costume, with regulation stockings and garterbelt, inspecting the icy drip at the tip of a long hypodermic needle, probably used for horses. This time her hapless loverboy was manacled to a table. His ass was shoved upward, ready for the naughty night nurse. Actually, this slaveboy was an overweight slob who looked to be in his fifties and had a spooky resemblance to a Supreme Court judge I had once argued before. In the third photo, Cecilia was reclining in a burnished throne with several of her minions hooded and bowed before her. They were eagerly awaiting orders.

The hostess interrupted me with a form. In addition to asking if I had any medical disabilities, the form listed the various activities of this painful spa. Next to each of the destructive delights was an empty column, where I was supposed to gauge the intensity of my interest on a one-to-ten yikes scale. The options listed were whipping, spanking, paddling, caning, slapping, bondage, sensory deprivation, mummification, humiliation, foot worship, and even a vocational skill, maid training. Props offered were blindfolds, hoods, straight jackets, suspension gear, and gags. The categories for role-playing included puppy training, mean auntie/nephew games, prisoner interrogation, death simulation, nipple and anal torture, and—Cecilia's personal favorite—erotic strangulation.

Yummie! All that pain and terror tickles me up and down. 'Course, that's not what I thought way back when. Twenty-one years ago, sitting before that receptionist, reading that magna carta of ghastly horror, I felt something inside me coming to a screaming halt, not so much from the shock of what I was seeing, but because of the innocence. I was still loaded with what used to be called hang-ups. Even if I harmlessly incorporated a bit of slap-and-tickle into our love play, that didn't mean I approved of my most intimate alpha-bitch becoming a sexual tool for the pleasure of corpulent, corporate dogs.

In the concluding paragraph of the sexual inventory form, there was a short exculpating statement intended for my signature: *"I hereby certify that I am a sane, consenting adult. I understand that this is a psychodrama and role-play service only and there is absolutely no nudity on the part of the dominatrixes and/or acts of prostitution. I swear to behave in a courteous and gentlemanly fashion at all times while on the premises."* I could spot legal loopholes in the statement, but pro bono is a no no if you might wind up the plaintiff.

I remember asking the blue willow to elaborate on mummification. She bluntly stated that it meant being spooled up like a sandwich in cellophane. The rate was a hundred dollars per hour. I remember feeling smug about charging more for my legal services.

Before I could politely decline, the downstairs inter-com beeped and the receptionist buzzed back.

"Were you curious about anything else?" She hinted at impatience.

"What's this?" I asked, pointing at the line that read "anal torture."

"Your dominatrix might perform a variety of tasks."

"Like what?"

"You might be taken to the examination room and given an enema if you like, or perhaps your mistress might feel you need to be fisted." Did the AMA certify this proctological subspecialty?

"They fist you here?" I clarified.

"Not if you don't want them to, but if you do, it's all quite safe, I assure you. They use lubricants and wear surgical gloves."

Suddenly the elevator door opened and an aluminum walker appeared in the doorway with a pair of shriv-eled hands clutching it. A protracted step later, a scaly man, perhaps in his eighties, entered, more a skeleton than a body.

The receptionist picked up the phone and disclosed, "He's here." Then, before the guy's mandible could drop off, she announced, "She's waiting for you, Mr. Boyd."

"Huh?" he yelped, then gulped.

"She's waiting for you!" she yelled.

"Who?" He gulped again.

"Mistress Brunhilda! She's in the fist pit!" Apparently the geriatric was hearing-tortured.

"I hope this one's stronger," old man Boyd said, "and

I'll tell you why. The last girl couldn't do a thing with me. Not an ever-loving thing!"

"Madame Cleopatra's here. She's good with first-timers," the receptionist cooed. Wham, a stunning woman instantly appeared. She was younger than me. Not much older than twenty. Her burning red lipstick and pale white skin were curtained by a black bob with perfect bangs. She took the clipboard from my hand and led me to a back room.

"You didn't write anything," Cleopatra said, glimpsing at my paperwork.

"I never did this before."

"You're nervous, aren't you?"

"A little."

"You poor man. You do want to try this, don't you?"

"I suppose," I replied. After all, I was there.

Pulling up a seat across from me, she said, "Give me a name, whatever name you want."

"Bob," I said, appreciating her sensitivity.

"Okay, Bob, you know the rate. How do you want to pay?"

"Cash."

"You pay up front for a full hour, which is non-refundable. Understand?"

"Yes." I counted out the amount. I didn't want her to see my name on my credit card.

"You have to sign down here." I signed "Bob" and handed it back to her.

"Now, Robert, the safe word is 'mercy,' that means . . ."

"I know what it means."

"Let's go to the play room." She led me into a darkened chamber.

"Two things will heighten your experience. First,

take off your clothes and put on a terry cloth. Secondly, I'm going to handcuff you to the wall." The cuffs, which were each connected to a long, thin doggy chain, offered a wide range of motion, while introducing a sense of submission. I accepted her advice as she cuffed me to the wall.

"If at any point you want to touch yourself, don't feel ashamed or self-conscious. You're here to get off."

"Fine."

She smirked. "Let's talk about your fantasies."

"I don't really have S&M fantasies."

"Forget the S&M. There is no S&M. Just tell me a simple story."

"Let's see." I felt ashamed and self-conscious. "I haven't had any fantasies today. I know that sounds strange, but I've been involved with this girl."

"You must have some fantasy?"

"You mean, like I'm walking down a street and maybe I see a pretty girl and want to fuck her?"

She smiled and decided to help me along: "You stop by your girlfriend's house to drop something off. Just before you leave, her message machine beeps. Some guy is saying that her office line is busy. You think you recognize the voice. He's calling to confirm her appointment. He doesn't say anything unusual. He has a deep voice and an unusually familiar tone. He just says, 'See you at 4:30 on Tuesday.' Your girlfriend is a professional. It's not an unusual call, but that night after a dinner you take her home and have sex. Then your curiosity gets the better of you and you sneak into her purse which is sitting on the kitchen table. You grab her appointment book and slip into the bathroom. You look at Tuesday at 4:30. You see it's circled. No name or place. You put the book back and the next day you tell her the upcoming Tuesday you're going to be in her office building. Can she come out for a coffee? She says no, she has a big conference then. There's no way she can get out. She's obviously fucking with you."

The young temptress didn't miss a beat in her narrative, giving me the feeling that she had told this very story a thousand times before.

"You take off early in the afternoon and stake out her office. At 4:30, you see her leaving the building. She goes out front and he's waiting for her. He's around fifty, big belly, pushy, a classic daddy figure. He hugs her way too hard, not afraid to be sighted. He doesn't merely kiss her, he runs his fingers along her lips, across her face and hair, down into the crack of her ass. Then hails a cab and off they go. You grab a cab and try to follow them, but you lose them."

I could feel her eyes touch on my erection. Yeah, I could see it all, Cecilia getting fucked by some silver fox exec in his early fifties. The post-adolescent beauty gently put her hand on my own.

"It's later that evening and I'm your girlfriend." She lowers her volume and picks up her cadence. "And you know I've just been thoroughly fucked. I mean, I'm bow-legged sore." She moved a little closer. "This guy's done *ev-ry-thing* to me."

"Did he have a second girl waiting somewhere?" I asked, softly.

"'Course," she said, "I had to eat her while he did me."

"Let's fuck," I say, playing right into her trap.

"I don't think so," she utters, with an entirely new change of face and tone.

"Why not?" I asked.

"Want to know why, stupid? Because I'm having an affair. I thought I made that clear."

"With who?"

"Your boss, asshole."

At the time I was working under Tanen, which felt weird since Cecilia supposedly had a session with him. The fantasy was working.

"And he's the type of man you'll never be," she continued. "When we were alone in my office, he put his hand over my crotch and could feel my heat. He bent me over and took me right there."

"You didn't resist?"

"No self-respecting woman ever consents to getting fucked. Of course I resisted, asshole."

"So he raped you?"

"He sure did, like you never had the balls to." She reached around and gave the chain to my handcuffs a tug.

"What else did he do?"

"He does whatever he wants. I don't have a say in it. My pleasure is in servicing a real man."

"Service me," I commanded.

"Why would I service some pathetic little schoolboy?"

I didn't know quite how to respond, so I defensively smirked to show I wasn't volcanically erupting inside.

"You want to suck my pussy? It's still dripping with his cum. Would you like that, faggot?"

"Yes," I said, because I sensed that I was supposed to.

"If you want, I'll let you watch from the closet as my man fucks me. You can learn something."

"All right," I said, but I didn't like it. I didn't like it one fucking bit.

"What's it like being an office boy for someone like him? For the guy who fucks your girlfriend?" she asked with a grin.

"I'm not an office boy," I corrected her softly, unable to play her game anymore.

"You're a little faggot office boy who spends his days sucking cocks of older men."

I found myself getting irritated.

"Say it. Say, 'I'm a little faggot who wishes he had a dick.'"

I tried to ignore the comment.

"Say it, you little faggot."

"Fuck you!" I shot back.

Astoundingly, she spat in my face. Without thinking, I jerked my hand up to slap her and although I caught myself, the cuff, with its long chain, whipped across her cheek.

"Hey!" she hollered, grabbing her face.

I instantly felt something new.

"I'm sorry," I muttered. "I really didn't mean to do that."

"I know," she replied sternly.

"I don't think this is my cup of tea."

"I agree. Session over," she proclaimed, looking at me nervously. She undid my wrists and left the room. I dressed quickly and went into the receptionist's office. It was only fifteen minutes later, but I had to forfeit the rest of the hour. Still, I left with a hard-on that lasted twenty years.

I said goodbye to the slinky blue-dressed receptionist and slipped back into my own sludge. Over the next few days, images both grotesque and sensual cooked and stirred in my imagination: rats danced with babies, sheep spoke French, and pain was a sexual pleasure. I felt too guilty to mention the episode when Cecilia returned home.

"You know, we haven't done it in a while," she said, as she caressed my crotch that night. Before I could find a passable excuse, she had the zipper down and the ornament out. At first I thought there would be no chance that I would even get hard. That's when I discovered a big surprise. As she started sucking my cock, I placed my hand on her neck and squeezed it. She gagged a bit but sucked harder and deeper.

Then we began fucking; it had started tenderly enough, but suddenly I pinned her down and clenched my opponent's neck, and it wasn't role-play.

"Don't mark me, please," she rasped, barely able to breathe.

I had to lock my hips to prevent myself from shooting right then. When she started moaning, my hand clamped across her sweet mouth and we were on our merry way. Soon I felt her silent tears trickling across my fingers, ending in my climax. After she crawled out from under the wreckage, she should have stuck a knife in my back. I wouldn't have budged. Instead, she woke me with a tender massage, thanking me lovingly, kissing me softly. She swore that she had never experienced such an intense orgasm in all her life.

I was as confused by my actions as she was, but since she had more experience at this, she slipped contently into her docile little role. After that first fuck, we showered the sweat away, but the roles stayed. Ironically, she would come to teach me lessons from her workplace, bringing home toys of the trade—clamps, whips, gag balls.

Occasionally, when I really Sodom-and-Gomorrah'd her, she would start weeping in a tender schoolgirl way. She said that she did this out of shame, not pain.

All of us can form a divisive committee of at least three, consisting of what we were, what we are, and what we wish to be. At that time, one part of me was emerging, sloughing off the old me like an outgrown foreskin, and it scared the hell out of what I wanted to be.

If this wasn't enough, I discovered a post-coital pay-back. Following a good whack and spurt, I would feel my guilt rising in me like vomit. I would have to approach her gently. Hold her lovingly. Comfort her paternally. Hate myself for how I had treated her. I would tell her I loved her. I would love her (I think). The closest thing a salty cynic has to romance is cruel truths. The nearest and most identifiable feeling we have to love is guilt.

It would take all the cruelty in me to rip back my epiderm of shame and come into contact with the underlying tenderness. I would smother her in kisses. Buy repentant gifts. Baby her with hugs. Gently stroke her beautiful body. Gobble her pussy lovingly. Only to fiercely confront myself the next day: How could I treat her so well? Dominatrix bitch! Vile humil-iator of men! How could I indulge that vulgar slut so utterly? She would manipulate me as surely as she was manipulating any of her scrotum-twisted slaves. Then I'd get worked up into a frenzy, we'd make vio-lent love, and the wheel would spin again: cruelty, guilt, tenderness.

Each time we'd fuck—as the credibility of my ruth-lessness would slacken a touch, and she would become a tiny bit less sensitized to the lash, and I'd get harder—I'd have to whip and rage that much more. But all that came later.

At first I was scared about what I was becoming. And like anybody scared of something new, I took refuge in the old. I started going back to the dark arcades, watching primeval porn in unlit caves of secrecy, collecting and hiding pagan magazines of my screen-star goddess, Sky Pacifica, high priestess of the jerk-off.

NOVEMBER 28, 1980, SF

WHO? WHO THE FUCK . . . WHO? HE WAS FUCKING her, fucking her, fucking her, fucking her. Sky couldn't keep her eyes open, falling, falling asleep. She could hear a trolley car rolling by.

"Hey," was all she could say, wanting him to stop. But he only increased his pace more frantically. He obviously was trying to cum. The cool moist air felt good.

"Say you love me!" he blurted. His voice was weird, tinny. The banging was keeping her awake. He was still there fucking her.

"Stop!" she groaned.

"You want me to cum—say it. Say you love it!" She tried to twist to her side, but he held her up ironclad. "Say it!"

Wait a second, she wasn't home. There was dirt and grass around her ass and legs. She was in a park! She was still dressed. Wait a second! She didn't know this guy. She was outside. Wait a second!

"HELP!" she screamed. He grabbed her mouth, still fucking her.

"Say you love me!" He hit her, cracking her across the face.

"I luff ya!" she could barely get the words out.

Her lip stung. He slapped her again. Blood poured out of her nose. Dumb cunt, she thought, you deserve this for stumbling home high. Dumb fucking cunt! She saw herself like someone else on the far side of an upside-down telescope. Finally, when he came, she lay still and watched as he rose. A skinny, skanky little shit who had probably followed her from the bar. Zipping up his pants, he skedaddled away. It was not a foggy night. From where she lay she could see past the bay to the distant hills of Marin County. She tried to get up but felt stuck to the ground like gum. Couldn't even keep her eyelids open.

She pulled her dress up to cover herself, and realizing that she was too high to find her way home, she curled against the barky base of a tree and just let herself go.

APRIL 26, 2001, NYC

MY CAR IS AS SNUG AND STYLISH AS A SPORTY COFFIN, and at a hundred and fifty miles an hour, I'd love to wrap it like a yellow ribbon around an old oak tree. But with all the clunky cars in this city, it's impossible to get up that kind of speed. I turn to an AM news channel and, as I cruise downtown, I listen for traffic reports.

"Perry Cruz, pleased to meet you," I say to my windshield. "Sure, I photographed Kate Moss—you shoot one snot-nosed kid, you shot them all. Evangelista's okay, but Turlington is probably the prettiest for my money. Anyway, they're all grandmas now." I don't even know the names of hot contemporary models.

The radio announces that the bridge traffic is packed, so I head for the tunnel. I submerge into the earth on Thirty-sixth Street while reciting in a throaty voice, "Hey, you're as attractive as any of them. Don't kid yourself. It ain't the looks, it's the attitude."

The tunnel, with its shiny tiles and florescent yellow lights, makes me feel claustrophobic, so I play *La Figueroa* and sing along to manage my stress. But a swooping string aria in a D minor sets my prolapsed heart valve aflutter. Merging onto the Grand Central Parkway, I begin to catch myself in the rearview mirror. I feel more and more like a phony until I disintegrate into a sleaze. Spotting a young black guy at the side of the road leaning despondently against a dented Japanese compact, I pull over. He is wearing a black leather baseball cap and a matching leather jacket. He looks to be in his early twenties, and inspects me with my goatee, detail of mascara, and idiotic tattoo. Can he guess that I used to attend rallies against the Vietnam War?

"Need help?" I offer.

"I got my spare tire, but got no jack."

"Well, I'm not jack, I'm Leslie, blood type B negative," I say, sensing the man's apprehension, and head to the rear of my Jag.

"Kent's my name, like the cigarette," the fellow in the leather baseball cap replies.

"Well." I materialize from the rear of my car with my tire iron and hold it for just a moment as though I might wallop him with it, then I reach back in and get the jack. "This is your lucky day, Kent State."

I hand them to him. Kent fits the jack under the side of the car and cranks it up.

"You can see the difference between people by the love that went into them. Some are bolstered with love and given the leisure to find themselves. Others are drained; the love is sucked out of them by the love-debt left by their parents."

Because of the whirring of passing cars, Kent can't decipher any of my platitudes. He quickly unscrews the nuts.

"Most of us are just thrown together," I wax on, "like a last-minute omelette. Whatever's in the fridge. Our parents don't protect their investment very well, do they?"

"Guess not," the fellow absently replies, replacing the tire.

"You know, a number of years ago, I was attacked by two black youths in a subway," I tell him, as he twirls the lug bolts. "It wasn't the humiliation that bothered me, it was the fact that I was so frightened. They made me realize what a coward I was. But you can't hold one attack against an entire race. That's how people become bigots. Looking back over the years, what's bothered me a lot more are those moments of civilized cowardice, when I deal with white-collar cock-suckers, lawyers, clients, judges, who really think they're empowered by God, who bump into me, and before I know it, *I'm the one saying sorry.* Those are the bastards I'd love to execute."

Handing back the jack and tire iron, he's done. No hub-cap. Kent thanks me carefully.

"Don't mention it," I say. I needed to feel magnanimous.

Kent zooms off. I get back in my car and resume my drive. After a while, I detect a slight vibration which at first I assume is caused by the speeding engine, but then realize is coming from me; I'm running on a diminishing reserve. No longer ambitious, I'm burning up tragic energy.

While driving, I think of my relationship with my wife. We never swapped clichés like "I love you." There was always a fine tension to the sex because the emotional dis-tance made her a stranger. Yet I didn't feel she was with-holding love. She was beautiful, cultured. She could make love in three languages. But her affection was quiet, even hidden.

She must have loved me. That was the real S&M. The kinky shit was just a cover. Why else would she put up with all the abuse? She had accumulated many clients over the years, powerful men. Investment bankers, stock brokers, high-powered lawyers, private investigators. Even a bankruptcy judge. Men were addicted to her.

They claimed their genitals were gnarled and empty but for her. She'd be their erotic expedition leader. Testing their horizons, scaling their insurmountable traumas, turning them into ever-unfolding fantasies. Their hearts were mazes and only she could find the way in. Yet she chose me. That must have been love.

Despite the countless times each day that I recall her beautiful face and forgiving personality, I still can't cry for her. At my age, people commonly lose it. Forty-six is an age when the happy-go-lucky feel neither; when material, sexual, artistic, and spiritual distractions all fail; when minor compulsions and dirty habits surface and become major addictions. Still, forty-six isn't what it used to be. It's now a lot closer to thirty than fifty.

Although I haven't crashed yet, I'm in that interstice between the failure of the old and the salvation of the new. This is when things go topsy-turvy and everything is up for grabs. In extreme cases, it is when whores become nuns, bankers become beggars, and lawyers go lawless.

That's when suicide casanovas like me start popping out of their shells. For some, it happens a little late: Woody Allen dumped his wife, Mia, for her daughter, Soon Yi, who Woody emphatically points out was not *his* daughter, as if that makes a difference; O.J. slashed Nicole from ear to ear and got out of jail, but not free.

The denial of guilt is part of the tonic, but somewhere between hubris and scandal there is a solitary eroticism for the powerful and isolated. This syndrome isn't to be confused with youthful indiscretions like Hugh Grant and Rob Lowe stuff. Or public misfires by PeeWee or George Michael. A suicide casanova peaks in his profession and is given such awesome affirmation that he has to test his power.

These are people who can have any girl they want, but they pick that one person who will test the patience of their followers. Clinton might be a touch of a suicidal casanova, but who would've guessed that Monica wouldn't even launder a cum stain—now that's a souvenir for your grandkids. I'm merely an amateur next to these hall-of-famers.

I pop a disc of *Turandot* into my CD player. This opera seems appropriate to my situation: a princess asks a riddle to a string of would-be suitors; if they answer wrong, they are executed. I start singing along with the opera in Italian. Cece taught me the proper pronunciation. I remember seeing an overpriced production of it with her in Atlanta. The diva playing the princess sung well but was too physical for the role. The lighting was garish, the costumes boring, left over from some other opera.

By the time I reach Long Island, I am weeping to the music. Nothing like a good rainfall. Making the turnoff at exit 26, I wipe my eyes, check my watch, and slip on my Foster Grants.

I pull over onto a side street and unfold my map. I check the address of Borden High School. Suddenly there is a siren behind me. A pecker-head traffic cop is growing larger in my rearview, one hand casually on his pistol. "Just went through a red."

"No, I didn't." But the truth will not help.

"May I see your license and registration?" the cocksucker sucks.

"Fine," I say, fishing for my ID. "I don't blame you. You see that I have an expensive car and the former senator's brother needs his cut."

"Excuse me?" he replies challengingly.

"All of Long Island with its exorbitant taxes and shrinking

economy has been misrun for years by the local Republican party. Did they hire you?"

"No sir," the motherfucker fucks.

"Well, just the same, this place is a hotbed of patronage and corruption. 'We don't need no stinking badges,' right? I only hope all of this money isn't going to brown-bag politicos, I hope you little guys get a cut." He writes me a ticket and tosses it into my window.

Further down the main road that runs through Borden, I spot Kate's high school with a red-dirt ball field on one side and a gray concrete rec yard on the other. I drive up through a parking lot to the entrance. A placard on the grass reads, "Borden High School"; underneath is written, "Proud home of the Eagles." On the announcement marquee out in front of the shell-shaped auditorium, I read: "South Pacific, June 6-9." Some enchanted evening you will meet a stranger.

Unlike New York City schools, this place is new and loosely moored in a sea of grass. Kids wander around the front lawn like large birds. Kids have landed on and around cars. Kids are perched on stone steps. Small, frantic, and hairless, still filtering in all the nasty little habits of parents and culture that will one day bloom into full-grown neuroses, phobias, and ailments. Kids come out of nowhere and vanish into nowhere. A din of kid-chirps fills the air. Their lack of emotional ballast and experience, combined with their kamikaze gas tanks of fiery energy, make them a dangerous liability as a group. Lax gun control laws and hate-group websites notwithstanding, it's amazing that there aren't high school massacres every single day. But what can one do? Ritalin and other psychotropes make parents nervous. Kids eventually become rat consumers and our cat economy eats them.

I sit in the parking spot waiting, wondering what to do next. I can hear buzzers going off and megaphones calling out names across the large, fenced yard.

Go out there and be a fashion photographer, I coach myself. Look for fresh faces. Make friends. Act like you own the place. Thick dick and big balls. I gather my gear. Pop a mint Lifesaver and go out to the front of the building. Then I plunk down on the school steps.

I watch students come and go and notice a young man with a peroxide puff who has a snake hanging limply around his shoulders. The young guy leans against his polished muscle car and talks to girls. Snake-man has that breezy carefree look that I want. His vehicle relays his message: its windows are rolled down invitingly, its engine purrs. Rock songs blare from its speakers. That kind of mindlessness cannot be imitated.

The real secret to the man's success is the snake. The reptile isn't long or fat, but colorful, green and red; a handy icebreaker. Kids like snakes. Snakes and tattoos and cigarettes. I realize I too have a decent gimmick but I'm not making use of it. I pick up my camera and start shooting photos. I take pictures of the rec yard, the parking lot, and the baseball diamond, but I have to photograph students.

I'm shooting long shots. Going to the end of the school's cement walkway, I wait for groups of students to exit and then, aiming my Nikon, I execute them all at once with wide-frame photos. A group dashes to their cars. I nab them before they can unlock their doors. A couple of kids try to run back inside but I get them before they can make it.

It is 2:43 and I don't know how long I'll have to wait before Jeane's daughter exits. Time elapses. The shutter click, click, clicks. Rows of kids scream and yell. Mayhem. More kids. More shots. More screams. Some of the girls, the true beauties, catch my eye, scintillating like specks of Mica Schists from the dull granite of surrounding faces. Even though I stare, I know it's not their beauty I'm attracted to, it's the power of their beauty — more specifically, the power they have on men. A time-limited currency, beauty can move and motivate, and they won't appreciate its full value until they've lost it.

"Excuse me," approaches a freckle in a friendly blue, V-neck sweater. The skin around the freckle is albino with a receding hairline. "I'm a teacher, can I help you?"

"You're a teacher?" I ask this semi-adult. "What can you possibly teach?"

"Science. Why are you taking photos?" He's adorable!

"Ever watch Channel 13, *Nova*?" Here's my effort to be a personable moron: "There was an episode a few weeks ago on how a space probe was sent to orbit a planet in our solar system. I forget which . . . Venus, I think. For the life of them scientists, they couldn't figure out how the planet released thermal heat. All planets do, you know. They looked for volcanoes but they couldn't find any. They scanned the meteor patterns on the planet's surface. They figured that wherever meteor craters were missing, that might be where the planet had a recent volcanic explosion, because the lava fills in the gaps. Weird thing was they found a consistent meteoric pattern over the entire planet. Isn't that weird?"

"Yeah, but why are you taking photos?" he asks again.

"Generic student photos. Text-book margin fillers. For Scholarly Books. Anyway," I return to my subject, "one of the scientists theorized that on a cyclical basis, the entire planet surface melted down. The entire planet would become one big volcano! A big fiery orb, huh?"

"Yeah," he acknowledges nervously.

"It would hold all this tension and energy for millions of years and periodically the entire surface of the place would all melt and bubble out." I chuckle.

"Well, I teach biology," the teacher states.

Before I can ask if fish can fart, he's gone. My cosmological cry for help goes unheard.

The series of bells and buzzers release small pockets of students periodically. I keep pulling the trigger on my camera, taking rapid-fire photos. After one particularly long bell, all the remaining students erupt down the steps. I had better save some ammo, so I stop clicking and simply look through the viewfinder for Kate. Halfway through the student exodus, I spot her, a real head-turner. Immediately, I start clicking shot after shot, falling in love with that tight spring and that high-speed recoil reload.

Over her shoulder she sports a light green knapsack. In her right hand is a can of Diet Sprite from which emerges a straw that invites intermittent sucks. I snap several shots, getting as close as I can without being noticed. I watch her until she vanishes up Peninsula Boulevard with a friend, homeward. She is going to go through a lifetime of hell for the price of being so beautiful. She too will be stalked by strangers, falsely coveted. Treated too well initially and then abandoned soon after. Have doubts about a more real value. Mutilate herself with kids, drugs, food, booze, or in a million other little ways. Sacrificing her beauty before she can eventually discover her real self. But all that's some other guy's psychodrama.

I have saved the opera *Aida* like a fine wine for my celebration drive home. For me, there are few operas more majestic than this one. I remember once seeing a miraculous production of it with Cece at Lincoln Center. Zeffirelli had designed the sets, and during one scene, when the army returns victoriously to Egypt, a long line of sweaty, sinewy soldiers wound slowly downstage, accompanied by a string of actual camels and horses. I feel that kind of grand and total victory right now.

►►

That evening, I take my day's photographic kills to one of the ubiquitous one-hour photo labs near my house. An hour later, the photographic taxidermist gives me the developed shots. Reviewing the day's work, I have a half-dozen photos enlarged. Another hour, when I bring all the photos home, I locate the clearest shot of her. With a red wax pencil, I cross out several faces and crop the shot like a photo editor. I circle Kate, and, with a flourish, I draw a big arrow and sloppily scribble, "HER!"

I take myself out on a date to a nice new restaurant called Anthropomorphi's and enjoy a dinner of swordfish, ordering a two-hundred-dollar bottle of wine, which I leave half full. Cece used to say it was aristocratic to leave steak on the china, wine in your crystal. Her mentor Lorenz taught her well.

Arriving at home, I strip, take a pill, either a Xanax or Aderol or vitamin E, and go to bed. But I don't sleep. I watch as the sky grows dark with distress and I listen to the street noises that echo upward into infinity. Under car horns and screams, below rumbling trucks and dropping gates, I finally locate silence. The darkness palpitates and I can't stop watching the rhythmic shudder of emptiness. After two hours, I finally grasp that I am monitoring my own imperfect heart beat.

Next morning, I am awakened late by conspiratorial cooing. A small committee of large pigeons, like military leaders under their gray capes, are plotting my overthrow from the balcony. I never noticed the pigeons before Cecilia died. Perhaps her presence, all her little stirrings and shufflings, hid their ghastly plans. But now they are taunting me, mapping out my downfall. Still naked, I grab my gun and shoot the leader. The others scatter. Whenever they're around, my luck goes sour.

To my horror, the assassinated leader, who was lying still, suddenly hops to his feet like Rasputin and limps around in a circle, dragging one wing like an old overcoat behind him. When I put my pellet rifle to the bird's head, it makes no attempt to flap away or even show remorse. Usually, before the coup de grace, the bird makes some cowardly gesture at evasion. Inasmuch as this bird doesn't seem to fear, much less consider death, its murder loses its meaning. Not wanting to create a martyr, I put the gun down and scoop up the wounded animal. The pellet had hit the wing, but it doesn't look broken. The hole is small and bloodless. I put some iodine on the wound. Bandaging it seems ridiculous. Emptying out a cardboard box of legal files, I place the pigeon inside, along with a small champagne glass of water and a hunk of an old Portuguese roll.

I dress and get ready to leave. When I visit the box, the bird is sitting quietly, probably recalling the great skyscraper flights of its youth. I grab my bag in one hand and the bird fits nicely in my other. I carry it out and press for the elevator. When the mirror-paneled doors whisk open, I enter, holding the pigeon. Inside is a young woman who stares at the tiny winged descendant of the dinosaur. I survey her hair, all bobby-pinned and clasped up high like a black leaning pile of Pisa. She looks back at me through a large pair of black-framed glasses and inquires, "Your pet?"

"Actually, I'm his pet," I reply with a smile. Extending the bird toward her, I ask, "Would you like to pet him?"

"He's adorable, but no thanks." She smiles at me and I feel my heart pop open like a cuckoo clock. With very little effort, I feel as if I have known this lady all my life. I have a powerful sense of her. But instead of remembering her in the past, I see her in the future. In short, I truly love this woman. By my definition, that means, unfortunately, that I am entitled to certain things.

"I'm Leslie," I plunge forward in my unilateral marriage.

"Oh, I . . ." she flusters away.

"I know that there are strict rules for meeting and mating," I begin. The elevator slows, stops, and its doors slide open. A blurry couple who make middle-age seem like a contagious disease enter. The doors close. I lower my voice politely. "Consider how few people we can meet in a lifetime if we strictly adhere to that old protocol."

She doesn't reply, only looks at me. We could be like these two gluttonoids if we're not lucky, I don't say.

"How many men do you properly meet in a year? And from that group, how many do you circumstantially find yourself with one warm, lonely, intoxicated night?"

The elevator stops again and picks up another young attractive woman who, along with the middle-aged couple, eavesdrops on me. The pigeons must have summoned these people to fuck me up.

". . . I'm talking about a guy who you can be at ease with and maybe if things get amorous—who knows?"

All are silent, looking dead ahead, listening to me behind them. I smile and lower my voice a bit more. "From that narrowest group of men, how many call the next day and talk to . . ."

"I have no interest in you," my lady love angrily flirts with me. I am piquing her interest. Again the elevator stops, this time collecting a very old boy.

"These people are less important than this pigeon. Don't let them rule your life." This time she plays it coy, taking a step away from me.

"I'm simply saying that if you're going to let fate be your dating service, well, even sperm whales with entire oceans separating them have a better chance of mating."

"You're not nearly as clever as you think you are," she shoots back. That never occurred to me before.

"Then there's another reason I need you," I say. Some eavesdropper chuckles.

The elevator opens again and now four laughing and chatting people get in. When one of the two men in the traveling quartet invades my personal space, my siren goes off: "Watch it!"

Like a flamingo, the colorful, cologne-spritzed male hops away. In a moment the elevator has slowed, lowering the last remaining inches to reach the liberating lobby. But right before the doors slide open, I pitch my final ball. "All I'm saying is, don't make this a moment you'll always regret."

"You already did that for me," she retorts cleverly, which is yet another reason I love her.

A second later, when the doors glide open, the woman yells back, "Fuck you!" She is the first one out, racing through the lobby as if I might kill her. All the others exit calmly behind. I should have sidestepped the philosophical prose and told her my financial worth instead.

No, I don't kill the pigeon in retribution, I forgive it. After five minutes of walking, I arrive at the dark stone wall surrounding Central Park: my gates of hell. Bounding over it, I squat down and release the wounded plover. It immediately flies away to report what it has seen to the others.

I look up at the large digital building-clock high above Columbus Circle flashing 1:30. Although there is no rush, I have to catch Jeane's daughter as she is leaving school at 3 p.m.

DECEMBER 22, 1980, NYC

WHEN SHE CALLED ME AT WORK THAT DAY, SHE spoke in nebulas and tangents. Cecilia didn't mind the previous night's bloodied lip; she knew the bruises on her throat and other parts of her body were mere arabesques and pirouettes of the impassioned choreography before the ejaculatory crescendo. But after a month of being on the receiving end, Cece began to get curious, she wanted to know why our lovemaking had suddenly gone from vanilla fudge to bloody cherry. I think she suspected that I had a lover. She must have read about how infidelities sometime have a stimulating effect on primary relationships.

I didn't have the guts to tell her that a month earlier I had snuck into her dungeon, at which point caresses had been traded in for slaps and outpouring turned into withholding.

Fortunately, at that moment, Dorothy buzzed me on the intercom: "Someone is downstairs to meet you."

"Can we talk about this tomorrow over breakfast?" I asked Cece. We were both working late that night, but were available through morning the next day, so she was going to meet me at my place for a loving breakfast.

"Tomorrow, then," she agreed, and hung up.

I called the downstairs receptionist and learned that a counselor named Herman Katz was waiting to see me. Grabbing my jacket, I figured it was some other lawyer who I'd catch on my way out. In the waiting area, I was pointed to a deflated, gray-haired man in a conservative suit, buried deep behind a copy of the *Wall Street Journal*.

When the man peered up from his newspaper, I felt a jolt: the facial resemblance was remarkable. The only difference was that this man looked visibly older. When he rose and smiled, I realized that it wasn't merely a resemblance. I immediately shouted for the receptionist to notify security.

"Relax, I just want to talk." The shriveled porn purveyor put his hands out harmlessly.

I surveyed the room for a hit man, and seeing there was none, I fixed on the older man—Fillip from LA. This was the guy who had turned Sky into a porn queen.

His physique had changed dramatically. His body was thin. His posture, stooped. Deep ruts ran up and down his face as if he were sinking into himself.

"If I wanted you dead," Fillip whispered, "you'd be dead."

"Cancel security," I told the border-collie receptionist after a moment.

"How did you find me?" I wondered aloud.

"You left a trail a mile wide, kid." Fillip exhaled deeply,then sat back down and sighed. "I'm fresh out of surgery. I've been in the hospital for the past few months."

"What happened?" I feigned concern.

"Death," he answered. "Come on, let's walky talky."

He freely evaluated the tops and bottoms of secretaries and office personnel as we headed northward through midtown streets. For him, it wasn't lechery, it was work. Apparently he was always holding open auditions, constantly muttering business-minded critiques, like, "Boy, could I make a mint off her ass."

"I heard that you put out a contract on me," I began.

"Who told you that?" he marveled.

"Sky." It was one of the last things she had imparted before her timely departure.

"Is she living with you?" Fillip asked, accenting his words with a wrinkled brow.

"No, but I wouldn't tell you if she was."

"Look," he stated, "I have colon cancer and I've been told that I only have six months at the most with chemo and repeated surgery. They've cut a bucket of guts out of me. If I make it to 1982 it'll be a fucking miracle."

"I'm sorry, and I know you have money and muscle, but . . ."

"I'm sixty-two years of age, and I'm here less as the spurned lover than as the concerned father."

"A father? After what you did to her!"

"Come on, pal-sy, your slip is showing," he leered. "Let me show you my long division. You saw her at the flicks. Went mashugga. Showed up at my strip club and put on a charade so you could nail her. Yes or yes?"

"I admit it. So what?"

"What boys like and what girls like are two different things. I showed Sky what boys like. I'll tell you something else," Fillip said. "The reasons that a woman is attractive are not the same reasons we stay with them."

"Let me assure you—"

"Now, you take Sky," Fillip interrupted, "a knockout, sure. But she's sneaky, selfish, whiny, uneducated. She has no integrity, no ambition, no loyalty . . ."

"What the hell do you know?" I pushed back.

"The reason I know Sky so well is because I designed her . . ."

"That's the stupidest thing I've ever heard."

". . . and she's no compact. She's not fuel efficient. She's big and costly . . ."

"Give me a break."

"Go look at her muscles. Check out her stomach and arms: me. Look at where the hair is carefully waxed off her pubic wings: me."

"What crap!" Only by identifying with her that closely had he been able to thoroughly exploit her.

"Compare them to photos in her early days of porn.

I was the one that created her look. I dieted her, exercised her, gave her a taste for clothes. I shaped her. She was a little hippie chick when I got her."

"Give it a break!" I paused in the middle of the busy street. The lunchtime rush was in full swing.

"All right," Fillip said, stopping as well. Without lowering his voice, he added, "Look at the way she reaches around and strokes your balls when you're about to cum. Or how she massages your prostrate when she's sucking you. I taught her how to suck cocks!" The flow of lunchtime employees bumped into us as we stood there.

I accused him of being responsible for getting her so deeply into drugs and porn. I told him to fuck off. He accused me of making her into my own private concubine. Right there on Park Avenue we had a verbal tug-of-war as to who deserved her more, and I remember him eventually saying, "Me and Sky are two pees in a catheter."

I argued that she had fled LA to be rid of him, and that with me she was developing herself into someone valuable, someone strong with self-reliance. I remember a sudden smile curling out of Fillip's loose bulldog face; lowering his voice, he had muttered, "That only means you became the producer and director. And the fantasy has changed. Script's different, that's all. So why don't you tell me where she is?"

The old fart insisted that she was still with me, so even though she never did me any favors, I decided to do her one and set up a final smokescreen, while making him feel crappy in the process.

"You never did anything for her and she never cared for you."

"How the hell do you know?"

"Did she ever tell you that she loved you?"

"She *loves* you?" he replied, and made an expression that a child makes in front of an adult if he accidentally uses a profanity.

"That's right," I said emphatically. "Meaning, there's no place for you."

Slapping his palms together, he said confidently, "So, she did dump you."

"What are you talking about?" I asked.

"Sky never used the word 'love' in her whole shameless life," Fillip said, as if he were citing a code. I didn't reply, but I suppose my silence was articulate.

"You got to understand who you're dealing with," he went on.

"I know who I'm dealing with."

"No, you don't. You think you're dealing with me, but you're not," Fillip explained. "Sky's who you're dealing with, who we're both dealing with. And she is a genius at being underestimated."

"Give it a break."

"The Titanic could sink, that girl'd be on her own lifeboat. A plane could go down, she'd be the only one with a parachute. I'm telling you, she is the mistress of survival. She's not a giver. She's Madame Taker. She needed a ticket out, and you were a fast-moving vehicle."

"That might be, but if you didn't beat her up on that last night in LA," I said, playing the only card I had on him, "then she never would have ran to me."

"Beat her up?" he said in disbelief. "That night, before she went with you, she called me, crying on the phone, 'Wawa, Julian hit me. He tore up my clothes 'cause I didn't give him some bullshit modeling money.' That's when I told her I didn't much appreciate having you come to my club sniffing for her and then calling me up later and insulting me." He paused. "That's all I did, and she turned it into a hook to sink into you. Hit her? I didn't even see her. I was angry at you for calling me a kike."

I told him that I was sorry for the slur, but that he had ripped my heart out with his spiteful lie that Sky had been disfigured in a car accident.

"Yeah, 'cause I was pissed at her!" he exclaimed. "You know why I was pissed? 'Cause she showed up the day before coked out of her skull. She drove to work high as a kite. She could have killed herself! She's been eighty-sixed from every strip joint in LA 'cause of fucking drugs. The only reason I had her working at my club was so she could pay her rent, and the only reason I didn't set you up with her was 'cause I saw it would wind up as nose candy!"

I knew he was telling the truth—she had lost her New York stripping job for the very same reason.

"No one else cares that much about her but me," he resumed, "so cut me a little slack, kid." Then, without so much as a goodbye, the human bulldog turned heel and strolled away. Watching the man vanish into the crowd, I knew he was right. I had been used by Sky, screwed over bigtime.

The old fart had spotted it instantly when I had said Sky loved me. Love was nothing more than a con.

▶▶

After work that evening, I tried to control myself. I ate self-hatred, drank quiet suffering, and, by late that night, I became one dark cloud, despair on the move.

It was raining all evening. Although I was done with work, I couldn't go home. I was meeting Cece for breakfast and I couldn't face her yet, even if I wanted to. Sky, like a virus, had lodged herself in my feverish head. Eventually, I grabbed a cab to one of the Seventh Avenue porn arcades. Several gray and defeated-looking men were also evading their own psychological downpours, burying themselves in bargain back-issues, flipping through boxes of porn magazines like they were record albums.

I remember approaching the vendor, a chimp in a vest who sat behind an altar-high counter, trained in the art of turning paper into silver. I handed him a ten-dollar bill and he pushed an upright cylinder that dispensed four quarters at a time. He clicked it ten times and carefully spilled the coinage into my greasy palm so as not to touch contagious me. I slid the change into my pants pocket and checked my shirt pockets for Kleenex.

The rear of the arcade broke into a catacomb of booths. Each enclosed stall was a little bigger than a church confessional, about two feet squared. If they had knocked down the stress-bearing walls and tunneled under the streets connecting all these jerk-off shelters, they'd have a labyrinth beginning around Thirty-eighth Street and reaching as far north as Fiftieth, burrowing from Sixth Avenue westward to Ninth Avenue.

Browsing the still-photo releases framed on each door, I searched her out. The very possibility of seeing her made my heart pound in my ear drums and hula hoops spin in my head. Fillip's little revelation that Sky had used and dumped me made her all the more erotic. For a quarter, I could harvest a squalid revenge. But her reign had peaked and her short films were growing scarce. Inescapably, I located a booth that featured her. I slipped inside and slid the bolt shut, careful not to lean against the lower half of the wall that was still streaked wet.

As I inserted my first quarter, the bulb snapped out and the film started *in media res*. Despite a mercenary penis visibly hammering into her, Sky seemed oblivious. In most films, she was great with reaction shots, oooing and aaaahing where agony met ecstasy, right up to the money shot. But in that paradoxical loop, Sky's facial expression cast her in some remote Tibet of abstract thought, a lacuna of peace, while everything around her was in *loco* motion. She seemed too enigmatic to second guess. Too unfathomable to comprehend. She looked to be eternally bored by the quotidian circles and bourgeois cycles of life.

Moments later the quarter was sapped dry. The film blinked out and the dull-watt bulb snapped back on. I put another coin in, and then another.

When I was back where I started, in the middle of the film, I opened the door. Another guy was waiting, but I wasn't done. I headed to the arcade next door and then a place beyond that, until I found another Sky flick in a dive on Eighth Avenue. They had two loops there. Down on Thirty-ninth there was another film, an old one; over on Forty-third and Sixth Avenue, I saw yet another.

Bit by bit, the footage seemed to excise the memory of the lying, selfish bitch I had been briefly saddled with, and replace it with the fictitious Sky who once lived fully formed in the locked booth of my skull—charming, mysterious, brilliant. During my descent on that Walspurgian night, I purchased several sex magazines with Sky, and despite the fact that I didn't even own a projector, I bought an eight-millimeter flick of her. When I eventually got home, before going to sleep, I gulped down a few shots of bourbon.

The next morning, I didn't hear the door open. I didn't know how long Cecilia had been there. Squinting out from sleep, I watched her flipping through some glossy magazine. I was in the guilt-tenderness cycle of our relationship after having thrashed her lovingly two nights before. I saw her go to another magazine before I figured out that she wasn't looking at *Cosmo* or *Vogue*, she was flipping through the raunchy porn magazines with Sky that I had purchased the night before.

"What the hell are you doing?" I asked, bolting up, pulling the stroker out of her hands.

"It's . . . it's . . ." she struggled, as though thumbtacks were pressed into her larynx. "They're . . . her."

"What are you talking about?" I retorted in a slight panic.

"This is why you've been . . . why things haven't been . . . You're still . . . You haven't gotten over her!" Before I could even attempt to formulate a response, Cecilia was out the door.

DECEMBER 17, 1980, LA
"COME ON, BABE, THIS IS GOING TO BE A REALLY happening party," explained Sky's bubbly haired friend. It was 7 o'clock and Laurel was excited about that night's gala.

But Sky felt too listless to even watch the black-and-white TV which was blaring before her. Lying on the worn and stained corduroy sofa, Sky watched

Gilligan's Island, suffering all the way through it as a form of punishment.

She couldn't get it out of her head: She felt so shitty about getting raped. She found herself repeatedly pushing things out of her way, repeatedly defending herself against twitches and pillows and anyone who came too close. Repeatedly she burst into tears, feeling she had deserved it. Deserved that sleazy, infected psycho's dick sticking deep inside of her body. What was worse was the fact that he wasn't big or strong, just some junky kid who had seen his opportunity. If she had been sober, she could have kicked his skanky ass in a flash.

"Christ, Sky, lower the TV, I can't hear!" Laurel screamed from the kitchenette; the obnoxiously effervescent roomie was now on the phone, talking in her loud, perky voice.

All her life all she really amounted to was an opportunity for one skank after the next to make use of her; but this time, the guy was the skankiest of the skanks.

How many fuck-ups are you allowed before fate kills you off? She had known people who had died from far smaller mistakes. Life was getting worse and worse: fleeing LA with some poor sap who was infatuated with her; ODing on stage in New York; raped in San Francisco, only to wind up back here in Cocksuckerland, unable to even get a stripping gig because of her bad rep.

With forty-two bucks in her pocket and another ten in food stamps, Sky wondered how she was going to get cash. There had to be some place in LA that hadn't heard about her. She could use a false name. Barring that, she could always go back to porn. If that failed, she'd have to whore. Not streetwalking shit, but dating-service work. And worse comes to absolute worst, there was always scumbag Fillip.

A few years back, for maybe a day, it had been exciting. A little degrading, a bit scary. Then only drugs sustained it. But now she pictured it as if she were being pulled through a kind of human carwash, naked and coked, where guys and girls fingered her, ate her, fucked her, came on her, and she emerged out the other end, showered and with a bit of cash.

Unlike a lot of girls, she had never completely surrendered herself to it. She had loaned herself out to porn. The shame and filthiness were part of the problem, but even more disturbing was the general despair about the whole lifestyle. Even on the sunniest days it made life feel so pointless. Existence was a sort of ride. And you had to be going somewhere.

About a year or so ago, her whole hazy, drugged-out, party-down lifestyle had created the environment for it. But porn-fucking wasn't like regular fucking. It wasn't something she could simply hop back into. She was no longer adjusted. Yet all toilets seemed to drain back into it. After making hundreds a day for film-fucking, the idea of waitressing was unbearable. The notion of being a cashier or doing some suck-ass minimum-wage job was utterly unthinkable. Fuck-money was a million times easier, and yet . . .

"Sky! What do you think of this dress? Do you think it'll go with my new pumps?"

Sky nodded approvingly. It was sweet of Laurel to put her up, but there was always a price. Her frizzy-haired friend who she had found interesting a few years ago now talked incessantly about nothing. Different clothes and mascara. Different guys and girls who were equally meaningless. If this wasn't bad enough, Laurel demanded undivided attention. Why was it that morons couldn't make themselves smart, but could make themselves endlessly sensitive about whether you ignored them and regarded them as morons? Sky tried to be a co-moron. A moron who listened to a moron. But she knew that in a week's time Laurel would see through her little trick. Laurel would sense that Sky was only pretending to listen, pretending to care, and that would be the end of her welcome.

I'm not a fool, Sky assured herself, I'm just stupid all the time. There was a subtle difference. Where a fool could see no alternative to their hideous life and, in fact, was deluded into believing it was a good life, Sky knew she was deep in shit. She got up from the couch, turned off the TV, and headed to the closet where her unpacked suitcases were piled. She knew that if there was any chance of getting out of the shit, she had to go to this party tonight and try to hustle up some work.

APRIL 27, 2001, LI
I NESTLE MY CAR INTO THE BATHROOM COMMUNITY OF Borden. Going straight down the main road, past the turn-off that leads to Jeane's house, I stop at a convenience store and pick up a cup of black coffee. I am out here so frequently I can now find my way around the neighborhood without the map. It is 2:38 as I open my car door. I sling my camera around my neck and locate the envelope with yesterday's photographs of exiting high school students. My heart beats. My head floats. Panic ensues at the thought of returning to yesterday's crime scene.

People collect fantasies like flowers from the imaginative garden of their dull existence. We keep them in the greenhouse of our head and nurture them till they blossom. Everybody has fantasies. Someone at work, a neighbor, or the unlikeliest of strangers might be blown up as the inflatable doll of endless whack-whack sessions. We might treat this person with utter formality, or even contempt, but in our private twilight zone an entirely different relationship awaits. This is normal, or at least everyone does it. But for a stalker — I'll admit what I am — the ivy grows right out of the crack in that greenhouse.

I pop my hazy cocktail of tablets and capsules, the unfinished prescriptions of various stimulants and anti-depressants. It's Russian roulette as to which pills have had their active ingredients expired and which haven't. I have faith that together they combine the highs and lows of a single day. I wash it all down with the black coffee. Things slow down, flatten out, and become manageable again. I drive back to Kate's school.

Eagerly watching the pubescent faces spinning like Rolodex cards of tight jeans, bright shirts, hairstyles, and wildly oscillating voices, maybe it's the pills, but I start growing dizzy. Seeing the youth with the snake, I try to silently command the serpent to take a bite out of its handler's nondescript face, but, probably in league with the pigeons, it ignores my pleas.

I stare at the guy as he leans against his car. I can't believe that the little prick has the audacity to try and stare me down. I approach and ask, "You got a license for that monster?"

"I don't need no license," he remarks with a disparaging leer.

"Sure you do."

"Fuck off," he says with callowness.

I punch him in the chest.

"Hey! You cocksucker!" the youth shrieks.

"Get the fuck out of here." I shove him. He falls onto the car fender against his snake.

"Hey, you motherfucker!" he curses. I slap his snake.

The ninety pounds of reptile is pissed and starts constricting around Snakeman's chicken-bone neck.

"SHIT!" he hisses, turning red, trying to pull the serpent off. He then flies into his car and drives off, with the Loch Ness Monster still attached. It's not that I'm strong or powerful, I'm only insane, so if he had pulled out a knife or gun or merely beat the hell out of me, as he should have, it wouldn't have mattered that much. The result is that I now feel a syringe-full of self-confidence.

A flurry of fiery faces later, I see Kate walk down the steps with a hip-to-shoulder rack of girls. Each one a little high-speed metronome of frantic chatter. I check the rolled-up sleeves of my shirt to make sure that my Vaseline-slicked tattoo is still visible, and I pinch my silly goatee.

"Excuse me!" I commence. The entire string of chicks fall silent. I produce the group photo from thin air and stare straight at Kate. "Is this you?"

All the girls in the group stare at the photo I had snapped of them from a distance yesterday. I can see by Kate's slight smile that she identifies her own face sucking a straw from a can of Sprite. The thick red-wax pencil encircling her coronets her from the crowd of other Miss Teen contestants.

"Yeah, that's me. What's this about?"

"Who are you?" one of the pushier girls intervenes.

Vainly, I take out my counterfeit Calvin Klein ID. All the girls inspect it. One girl with a nose-ring claims that she recognizes my name—Perry Cruz.

"He did the *Kids* photo spread," she confides to all.

"And it got me into a heap of trouble, thank you," I reply smarmishly. "But that's how good I am." Pointing to Kate, I ask, "May I have a word with you?"

"We can talk over here," Kate says, pointing a bit out of earshot.

"We'll wait," the pack leader informs Kate, who follows me several steps away. Locked eyeball to eyeball with Kate, I feel something click deep in my transmission. This young woman was that little girl who I had almost adopted. I saw her popping out of her mother. I recall holding her in my arms, changing her diaper, feeding her, wiping off her excrement. Her baby cries kept me up, night after night, years ago. Those burning eyes, though, are still the same, and staring deep into them, I drop my mask and ask, "Do you remember me?"

"Remember you?"

"You don't remember me?" I smile slightly, and have to fight tears.

"What the fuck?" She begins to worry.

"I was here yesterday, that's when I snapped the photo," I shoot back.

"Oh," she replies, visibly relieved. "No, I didn't see you."

"I work as a fashion photographer for CK. You can call and confirm it if you wish. As your friend said, I did the *Kids* campaign a while back."

"So?" She shrugs.

"This year we are preparing to do a new summer campaign called Texas Tornados, which hopefully will be more wholesome. This time we don't want models. We're really looking for some new facial types."

"I'm a new facial type?" Kate replies indignantly. "You mean, because I'm bi-racial?" Sounds like someone who has sex on two continents.

"I only know that you have the look," I reply. "You're born with it. It can't be replicated in a studio."

"My mother was an actress and a model," Kate discloses, to my surprise.

"Well, you're beautiful as hell. Don't let anyone tell you

differently. And believe me, we have had photographers combing New York and Long Island. Anyway, I took a variety of photos yesterday and my editor held this one up." I hold the photo up. "And he said, 'She's it!'"

"Tell you right now, my mother will never go for it." Kate's not impressed.

"Okay, then let's not tell Mama," I suggest.

"What do you mean?" She takes a step back.

"I've been in this situation before. Parents are reluctant in the early stages, but once they're staring at a twenty-thousand-dollar contract with another possible forty thousand, and a heftier contract with residuals if we go to TV, they find it difficult to say no."

"So you're saying that we do the pictures and don't tell my mother until your editor gives me a contract."

"It's up to you, doll. To be honest, you'll be going up against literally hundreds of other beautiful faces for just a dozen or so slots. If you want to take a crack at it, I'll pay you for the preliminary sessions out of my own pocket."

"How much will that be?" she inquires.

"I'll give you fifty bucks an hour." I can see by the expression on her face that Kate is seriously wrestling with the idea. Soon she sighs, however, suggesting that she is going to decline.

I sense that if I were sexier or younger, or simply had more panache, she would accept the offer, and this depresses me.

"Look," she states, "I don't think you're dangerous or nothing, but I don't know you and I'm . . ."

"You're afraid to be alone with me?" I ask, astonished, having changed her diapers.

"Not alone like now. But indoors somewhere."

"That's okay. We can shoot outdoors. The only two problems will be that people will watch and that you'll have to find somewhere to change into certain apparel."

"I don't mind that," she replies hopefully.

"Then we got a deal," I conclude, and we shake hands to seal it. "When can we do the first shoot?"

"Whenever," she replies.

"How about tomorrow?" I ask eagerly.

"Okay."

"Fine, we'll meet here and go somewhere."

"Fine," she confirms.

"What are you, an eight?"

"Six," she says proudly, though I'm not sure why.

Driving home that afternoon, I put *Wozzeck* on and sing aloud, feeling pumped up. Before the tragic crescendo, when the kids dash off to find the victim's body, the orchestra yanks all that tonal desire hidden in the score right up to the surface. But it's far too lachrymose. I switch from CD to radio and turn to a news station. Hearing that the temperature is going to be in the eighties and clear, swimsuit weather, I decide that I had better move quick. All these meticulous plans could fall apart in the blink of a shutter.

After parking in my spot, I enter a magazine shop across from Lincoln Center. *Cosmopolitan* has a feature on swim gear, complete with the standard positions that most models employ. I purchase it and cab it to Bloomies, where I purchase six different bikinis in various cuts, colors, and sizes. I also buy a plastic tube of Coppertone suntan lotion, SPF 15. When I get home, I unfold my map of Long Island and find that Borden is thirty minutes away from Robert Moses beach.

That night, I visit my video store. I want to study the theatrical style of men in control. Despite all the billionaires I have met and deals I have been a part of, I find most moguls to be pretty blah. I rent *The Last Tycoon* and half-watch it while gleaning the salient parts of two of the latest books on corporate loan restructurings.

Smugness and muted power are what De Niro exudes in the film. I hit the rewind button and shut down for sleep. At 4 a.m. I sit up, wide awake, and notice a distant light on in an apartment across the way. It is a penthouse occupied by a woman I call Hildi. She is the mother of two children, without a husband in sight. Through the telescope I watch her crying in the nude.

The fact that she has had two children has taken its toll. The real reason I still watch her is to compare how she behaves in front of her kids to how she acts when alone. After seventeen years in the intrigues of corporate law, all social interaction is a performance to me. I used to wonder about fellow attorneys I knew over the years. Could they take off their war masks? Had the real them become sacrificed in the legal process?

In the bedroom at night, Cece used to remove the pins, unhinging my mask, revealing the squirming mess of maggots below. But now that she's gone, I'm trapped inside of me forever. I fumble through my pockets for pills. I find some old Prozac and nervously pop them, only to taste something odd. It's a wrinkled-up phone number that happens to be a palindrome. I dial and get a groggy female.

"Hello. My name is Leslie. Who is this?"

"This is Sheila. Who the hell are you?" says the small voice.

"Are you an attorney?" I ask, wondering if she's connected to the Sewter Case.

"No, I work in publishing," she awakens.

"Oh, you're the stiff blonde I met at the bar a few days ago. This is Perry."

"Oh, thanks," she finally divines. "You're the asshole with the bullshit phone number."

"And that's why I'm calling you now."

"Well, it's 4:30 in the fucking morning," she fires back.

"What can I tell you? I was in one of those moods. You know, when your head aches like it's a dam holding back a flood pounding behind it. And little sluice gates of foaming words allow for some of that pressure to trickle through, but that strain you feel is what most people perceive as insanity."

"Take two aspirin and call me in the morning," she dismisses.

I hang up and feel the pile of pills taking me away. We dread utter and complete obliteration until we absolutely can't live without it.

NOVEMBER 30, 1979, LA

WEST HOLLYWOOD WAS A CITY OF DROOPING PALMS, closed stores, and barren sidewalks that night. Several months before meeting Cecilia, I had made an effort to break free of my voyeuristic compulsion. It had started in New York while scanning the sex trades. I spotted an ad in *Screw Magazine*: "Fillip DeNuncia's sextacular palace of worship, My Fair Lady, is pleased to present Screen-Queen Sky Pacifica for one week only."

The club was located in Los Angeles somewhere. Urgently, I requested my vacation for the following week, booked a roundtrip ticket to LA, and bought a book on photographing the female form, *How to Shoot a Pretty Lady*. On the last day she was to strip, I took the transcontinental flight west and rented a 1978 Duster at LAX. I drove slowly, searching for the fateful strip joint. Pulling up to the only pedestrian I could find, I took out the My Fair Lady ad and asked the youth if he could direct me to the address.

"Keep going straight. You'll bang right into it," the kid replied. I thanked him and cruised on.

I could see "Fillip DeNuncia's My Fair Lady" pulsating colorfully in the distance. Parking the car in the lot out front, I entered. My eyes adjusted quickly to the darkness within. The place was busy. It had one central bar and was divided evenly by three small stages which looked like satellite dishes under hot lights. Rotations of strippers were either performing or working the house, getting guys to buy them drinks. Three tit-wigglers and butt-jigglers were dancing against a wall of music and spiraling colors. None of them were her.

I pushed right through the crowd to a boustier-bound bartendress and asked, "Where's Sky?"

"Fil-l-l-l-e-e-e-p!" she hollered into the loud darkness.

That was when I first met future cancer victim Herman Katz, a.k.a. Fillip. Unable to see his face at first, I remember an extra-large polo shirt and floral Bermuda shorts pushing through the distance like a charging tourist. His face was of the Mel Torme species. Charming in a thin-legged, beer-bellied, and thick-armed way, he shoved past me, asking the bartender, "What's up, princess?"

"Hi," I said, "you're Sky Pacifica's agent?"

"Depends," he smiled. "Are you with Immigration or Bunko?"

"No, I . . . I'm not a cop. I . . ." I was but a skinny lad fresh from law school.

"What's your accent?" Fillip cut me off and tugged my hand for a shake.

"New York." I smiled submissively.

"Oh! I'm from Nueva York, the Lower East Side," he said, as if the Big Apple were a small berry.

"Really? With a name like Fillip, you don't seem like . . ."

"Deena, give us both a beer." The bartender put two

mugs under the tap. "My given name is Herman. I know that I pass for a California golden boy, but I'm an old-fashioned, pickle-peddling New York Jew."

"I'm a photographer looking for models," I said earnestly.

"Aren't we all?" Fillip grinned and quickly asked, "Are you with anybody?"

"A new magazine coming out of Chicago called *Debutante*."

"Sounds like a winner," Fillip said in a congratulatory tone. "Always looking for an investment."

"Sky Pacifica—isn't she supposed to be dancing here tonight?" I gulped down my watery beer.

"Sky Pacifica?!" he remarked with some awe. "Firstly, she's a grandma."

"What do you mean?"

"She's not a new face," Fillip said, rubbing his stubby jaw which looked like it was sprinkled with poppy seeds.

"Oh, perhaps," I countered, "but she's not had much exposure in soft core."

"Well, I was trying to put it an easy way, 'cause the fact is, you're too late." Fillip took his beer in hand, swallowed it in one gulp, and slammed the empty on the counter to punctuate what he was about to say: "Last night she suffered a car collision. That's how life is. So, unless of course you plan on doing freelance work for *New England Journal of Medicine*, you better look elsewhere." Fillip tipped his head toward the girls on the three stages, his latest offerings.

"Killed? Last night?" I couldn't catch my breath.

"Fortunately, no," he said stiffly, then started loosening up. "From what I heard, she lost a kidney and an eyeball, but she will live. She was a gentle flower.

Snorting and driving is a no-no. But hey, there's a lot of four-limbed comeliness right here on these prosceniums."

"My god." I was mortified. Fillip slid his business card into my shirt pocket and vanished back into the noisy void.

A concave dashboard did its final duty in my appalled imagination by crushing down on Sky like a hydraulic press, disregarding flesh, muscle, snapping bones and gouging vital organs. If something pierced her eye, it probably ripped open her face. The sounds of her screams, blood gushing, the waning of consciousness: All the gruesome details presented themselves.

If I could still offer comfort, at the very least give condolences, then my trip out here would have a purpose, I thought. I looked for the slithery manager, but he was nowhere in sight. I spotted a new bartender, a young blonde in a slinky half-cut tank top, and waved her over.

"Perhaps you can assist me." I had to compete with the blaring disco beat. "I was talking to Fillip about Sky Pacifica and . . ."

"About last night, you mean?" she asked.

"Excuse me?"

"I never saw him blow up like that!"

I figured she was confusing me with someone else. "Like what?"

"Like last night . . ." the bartender said, and vanished to pour a drink; she returned a moment later.

"So Fillip no longer represents Sky?" I struggled to follow her.

"She's with that kid Julian now." The bartender seemed eager to show that she was in the know.

"Well, if you could give me her number, I was hoping to deal directly with Sky."

"Hey, I'm not some Zony, I don't give out no info," she replied, immediately suspicious, a little too late. "If you got a message, I'll see that she gets it. She hasn't picked up her envelope yet, but she's supposed to come by tonight."

"Fuck it." I feigned indignation, veiling relief. "I can't wait for her all night." And I stormed out.

As the evening turned into a wait, I thought to myself that there was no one else in the world who seemed more unattainable.

When a maraschino-cherry Corvette swung to a halt in front of the club some hours later—more precisely, when the door on the passenger side popped open— there she was—the Alpha and Omega, the embodiment of all solutions, the riddle to all problems—striding casually before me. That moment became indelibly etched in the now-dried concrete of my memory.

I can still close my eyes and see her strutting in ruby-red snakeskin boots, wearing iridescent green Spandex pants, with a bright scarf flapping behind her. The martini mix of fantasy and reality had never been more perfect. The sides of her firm milky orbs were generously revealed in a loose white tank top. Three long struts and two small shuffles, and she vanished into the loud strip joint.

Julian, her driver/lover/agent, looked like a beefy phantasmagoria who couldn't get enough of himself in his rearview; his face was a paradigm of geometry, color, and consistency, right down to the white cigarette transversing the side of his bluish lips. His slicked-back hair looked painted on in a hi-gloss black.

Moments later, Sky came out counting cash from the

envelope and waving it between her long beautiful fingers. In a well-rehearsed gesture, the cocksucker boyfriend flipped open her door and in she hopped. When their Sting Ray zoomed out of the parking lot, I was trailing in my clunky rental. Leslie Cauldwell, amateur stalker.

Venice Beach, next stop. They parked near the boardwalk. I cruised up the block. Sitting at the light, I watched the marvelous couple in my rearview mirror. The Sting Ray released them from its metallic jaws. Sky's money appeared to have a euphoric effect on them as they sprinted into their condo. I parked on the next block and backtracked. Her home was in a three-floor apartment complex that popped out like a pair of boobs around a large V-shaped pool.

I bounced up the steps, two at a time, and walked along the outdoor balcony. Frosted thirty-watt bulbs and nothing more. From several apartments I could hear televisions or stereos blaring. Through one door I thought I heard laughter or crying, but there was no trace of Sky or her princely driver. I nervously checked the names on the mailboxes downstairs. No Sky Pacifica.

I went back to the street. With its lean fenders and muscular hood, the stud's Corvette was ridiculously phallus-shaped. The seat covers and dashboard were lined in campy pink fur. The side window was rolled down. I opened the passenger door and touched her seat—still warm. Slowly I sat in it. In the ashtray among half-smoked cigarettes was a roach with traces of lipstick. I brought it to my lips. The car was relatively clean. There were no soiled Kleenexes, no used condoms, nor, for that matter, books of symbolic poetry or dusty philosophy. I jotted down the guy's license plate, and as I passed the right rear fender, I took out my car keys and deeply scratched into the polished gloss: my customized, souped-up way of saying, "Fuck you for fucking her." Little did I know that it was her car, albeit on the precipice of repossession.

A bright, all-night 7-Eleven was shining down the block. I went in, passed the teenage cashier behind the register, and grabbed a tall can of Budweiser and a Hershey's. As an afterthought, I located a freeze-dried ham and cheese sandwich that looked like it had been prepared on the surface of Mars. While it was being radiated in the microwave, I browsed through the magazines in the rack adjacent to the cash register until a low female voice hummed, "You mind?"

Sky Pacifica was in front of me, trying to angle a six-pack on the counter that I was leaning against. I jumped out of the way, falling into a miniature display of canned SpaghettiOs. She apparently was used to responses like that and did not so much as bat an eyelash. I stared at her, just a breath in front of me, as she fished money out of her tight, chartreuse purse.

Then the goddess spoketh: "Shit!"

Desperately she searched, then shook items from out of her purse—lipgloss, Tampax, Blistex, Binaca, Camel cigarettes, Juicy Fruit—onto the Formica countertop. The living vision was short of cash.

What is mine is hers. I'm hers! I'm her! The thoughts hopped up and down. I was about to pay her bill, but caught myself. If I were just another joe who happened to walk into the 7-Eleven at this late hour buying some stuff, would I give money to any pretty face?

"You can get three bottles," the ennui-generation cashier muttered. Carter was President.

"Shit!" she said again, clipping a broken cigarette

between her dazzling lips. "I swear I had a ten. All right, just three then." She added, "That means only Julian will be swigging tonight. Guess God is telling me something, huh?"

A skinny dishwater blonde who had friends waiting in an orange VW van out front, probably heading off to a Grateful Dead concert, came dashing in past Sky. When the woman opened the frosty glass door of the fridge in the rear, I moved toward her, smiling menacingly. "Hey!"

"What?"

"I got something for you," I said, sounding slightly insane.

"What?!" She was clearly nervous.

"You dropped this." I knifed something toward her threateningly.

"Back off! I didn't drop nothing!" The lady stepped away tensely.

"Anyone lose ten bucks?" I announced loudly.

"I did! I did!" Sky hollered enthusiastically, hearing the exchange and racing back. Not wanting Sky to take any notice of me, I shoved the bill into the hands of Dishwater, who dismally surrendered it to Sky. She thanked the other woman without acknowledging me, paid for her six-pack, and left.

I darted out a second later, leaving the magazine on the counter and the Martian sandwich sizzling in the microwave. The whole event had lasted fifteen seconds. Walking at a safe distance, I followed Sky to her condo. She was too happy with her serendipitous discovery to spot anything odd.

She trotted up the three flights, made a left turn, then vanished down a hallway. I heard a door shut before I peaked into the unrelenting stillness of the vacant corridor. Three possible apartments could have been her destination. Painstakingly, I listened at all three doors and then returned to one. I could hear the TV inside, then the elated voice of a young woman. Although I couldn't detect what she was saying, I knew it was Sky. The apartment number was 3C. I went back downstairs and looked at the name on the mailbox—Julian Meyers.

▶▶

That night I napped in my rented car and was awakened early by morning traffic. I drank a cup of coffee, went to a corner phone, and got the number of a Julian Meyers.

The message on his answering machine was a seedy, reedy male voice. Julian rambled some nonsense about leaving "a cool, loving message" while The Eagles crooned "The Best of My Love" in the background. When I heard the beep, I said, "I am a freelance scout for an adult magazine and I would like to take some photos of Miss Pacifica for a possible spread . . ."

The high-pitched screech of someone picking up the phone mid-message was interrupted by Julian, exacting, "What you got in mind? Junction shots?"

"No, just standard poses. Should only take an afternoon."

"How much money we talking about, man?"

I figured that haggling was the same in any business: Offer the lowest and let them dicker their way up. "Three hundred bucks," I initiated.

"Hey, this lady is a *dick-nician,* know what I'm saying? At least four," the novice agent replied. "And that's way below her base."

"It's okay, I'll find someone else." I negotiated for a living.

"Hold it," the guy said quickly. "Make it three-fifty and you'll get a show that'll make your lens zoom."

"Thanks anyways, I'll call Casting Couches," I said, referring to a well-known adult modeling agency.

"All right. Don't get your balls in a knot," Meyers replied. "Three, but she wants half up front."

"Fine."

"Call me back in ten minutes to work out the details."

"Sure," I said. Despite an elderly lady looking down at me from a window above, I performed a jig of exhilaration. But a whiplash of anger followed when I remembered the terror I had experienced the night before, imagining Sky being mangled in a car wreck. I recalled the fat tan man, Fillip. Why did this stranger tell such a vicious lie? I reached into my shirt pocket and located the business card that he had slipped me. I found another dime and dialed the number. After a couple of rings, a young female voice picked up.

"Yes," I commenced formally, "I'd like to speak to Fillip."

"Whom shall I say is calling?" she replied, probably kneeling before him.

"I'm a photographer from *Debutante* magazine in Chicago. I met Fillip in his club yesterday."

"One second." She handed the phone up to him, and probably returned to her flesh-flute recital.

In a moment Fillip was on the phone. "How may I help you?"

"I have a question," I began.

"Who is this, please?"

"I'm the photographer who was at your club last night. Remember, I asked for Sky Pacifica?"

"No, I'm sorry. I don't remember anyone reaching for the Sky." Pun.

"You told me she was badly injured in a car accident," I confronted him with his mendacity.

"Sasha Hips was maimed in an auto accident," Fillip corrected.

"Don't fuck with me," I shot. "You told me yesterday that Sky was in an accident. You said she lost an eyeball. You called her a gentle flower."

"I'm afraid you're quite turned around. Sasha Hips is a gentle flower. And the actor Peter Falk is blind in one eye," he mocked.

"Bullshit!" I fired back. "You know that I caught you in a lie and you're trying to back out of it."

"My friend," he tried to soothe, "there's no need for ire."

"I just want to know one thing: Why were you trying to keep her from me?"

"Buddy, I have no interest in keeping her from anyone. Now, if I mistakenly said Sky was in an accident, I am truly sorry, but . . ."

"Don't give me that shit! You're a fat, sleazy, old fuck."

"You little shit!" Fillip hollered back, losing his patronizing calm. "Who the fuck do you think you are?"

"I just spoke to Julian Meyers and hired Sky, so you can go fuck yourself . . ."

"Julian Meyers?!" he roared. Apparently I had touched a nerve.

"I only want you to know that your little stunt didn't work."

"That motherfucker, Julian!" Fillip screamed. "You apologize! You show regard!"

"Regard?" I was amazed at how infantile this man was. "I regard you as a sleazy scumbag! I regard you as a no-good kike bastard!" I slammed down the pay phone.

After catching my breath, I started my car and drove around the neighborhood. Ten minutes later, I parked at the Suffolk Lounge Motel. Above seedy, yet definitely substandard, the motel could serve as a photo studio, but I would never spend a night there. Once inside the room, I called Julian the agent and gave him the address and room number.

"She'll be there in twenty minutes," Julian informed.

"I'll be waiting," I said, lying on the bed. Hanging up the phone, I closed my eyes and quickly fell asleep.

A knock awakened me. Inhaling deeply, wiping my hands, I opened the door. There she was, the protean princess in her physical form. I took a deep breath and dissolved into her face. She stepped through me, into the room.

"Sky Pacifica," she introduced. I smiled stupidly, closing the door behind her. She wore a dark-blue miniskirt, a brightly striped red and white blouse, and sported a small shoulder bag.

I watched her eyes flutter about like a butterfly, from thing to thing. After so many hours of viewing her, after immortalizing her in fantasies, after making her a sexual Czarina of all my Russias, I was now fascinated by her brilliant simplicity; it pulled at me. I had to get deeper into her, past the tits and ass, beyond the perfect face, to where the messages were sent to her nerves, to the alchemical processes that took the raw sewage of impressions and interpreted them into gold as only she could.

"So what's your name, anyhow?" she interrupted.

"I'm Harry Izzigliano." An instant bullshit pseudonym to hide behind.

"So where's the hundred and fifty?" she requested unblinkingly.

I counted out half the amount for her.

"So, Harry, should I just strip?" she asked, pacing in a small circle around the motel floor. None of her clothes lay flat on her. Each swath of fabric seemed to have a tight part where there was a canyon of flesh or a voluptuous, seam-straining roll.

"Well . . ." I said, stuttering a bit, "whatever."

She opened her bag and laid out panties, garter belts, and other assorted lingerie.

"You want me to put something on or get naked?"

I shrugged, gaggingly.

"What?" she asked.

"The underwear . . ." I was barely able to produce a sentence. "Put the underwear on."

"Which ones?" she offered.

"You pick," I sputtered.

When she disappeared into the bathroom, I nervously located the how-to book and flipped through its pages. It was supposed to be an amateur photographer's guide to the female form. "Step One—Choosing a Focal Point." The bed seemed natural. "Step Two—Lighting." It went into different lights and how they could be positioned. It was then I discerned that the volume, which was loaded with photos of nude women, was actually soft-core pornography masquerading as a textbook. Since I had to look professional, I pulled open the legs of the tripod and screwed the camera on top.

The bathroom door flew open and she emerged, looking like someone else. Her hair was slicked back and darker. Her sharp mascara made her high contrast chic. She was wearing black fishnet stockings, a garter belt, and a shelf bra. I excused myself, went to the bathroom, and sucked water from the faucet. When I returned, she had a transistor radio turned on, quietly playing rock music, and she was searching for something in her purse.

"I shouldn't be doing this," she said, "but . . ."

Although she was half naked, she didn't seem to have the slightest sense of modesty as she lay out two tiny piles of cocaine and prepared them into fine lines on her compact mirror. I watched as she rolled a dollar bill and sniffed a line. Next, she handed me the coiled bill.

I inhaled it and had to resist sneezing. I didn't feel any different.

"So let's take some photographs," she said, and bounced back onto the mattress, squirming around a bit. I wanted to jump into bed with her. She looked up and I could anticipate her asking what to do.

"Just be yourself."

She started striking poses, squeezing her luscious tits together, rolling over, shoving her ass toward the tripoded camera. I kept staring as she curled and twisted, utterly dazzled.

Tiredly, she yelled, "Take the photo, asshole!"

I reached over and nervously snapped a photo.

"Is it focused? I didn't even see you focus it." That was when she bound up, pushed me aside, and looked through the lens.

"This shot is ridiculous!" she exclaimed. I replied that I was a little new at this.

"Where's your lighting equipment?"

"I . . . What happened, you see, was . . . they lost my lighting equipment on the plane. They sent it to Winnipeg."

"Your lighting is in Winnipeg?" She looked out the window. "Well, it's a nice sunny day out. I know a great place on Mulholland . . ."

"Look, these photos are really just to solicit an assignment, and frankly, I always feel that pornography should be indoors. Guys feel more comfortable seeing women indoors. In the outdoors a bear can attack, it's difficult to concentrate if you get my . . ."

"All right, well the least you can do is . . ." She got up and unscrewed the shade from the lamp and moved it to the floor in front of the bed. Then, looking into the viewfinder again, she lowered the tripod so that the camera wasn't looking down on her. Watching her take charge in her scanty underwear was even more erotic than her posing. She hopped back onto the bed, and when she was positioned, she yelled, "Okay, shoot!"

I took a couple of well-focused shots.

"Bracket," she said after a few minutes.

"What's that?"

She explained that it meant taking photos at different F-stops, changing the amount of light in the picture, so I bracketed.

"Maybe you should take a course or something," she suggested, and wordlessly placed a corner of her gauzy scarf over the lens. "That'll create more of a soft-focus effect. Your lighting's a mess, though." Getting back into view, she posed, and continued asking where her frame was. I would tell her and she'd position herself for the camera.

"If these photos are just to solicit an assignment,"

she thought aloud, "you really don't need a tripod. Unscrew the damn camera.."

I took a couple photos and kept staring at her, loving her. She must have picked up on it, because she finally smiled and waved me over to her.

Hesitantly I approached. She reached up, silently grabbed me by my collar, and pulled me down so I was directly in front of her. Up close, alive, after years of seeing her in film, she was a breathing vision—perfect skin, large, widely spaced eyes, a small dainty nose, prominent cheekbones, narrow cheeks, arched eyebrows, an open smile, and, to top it all off, soft, inviting coke-dilated pupils. Her thick red lips looked like a luscious fruit. I moved closer, barely caressing my lips to hers. My fingertips brushed the tips of her nips.

My hands slid down blindly. Lips on lips. Shoulder to shoulder, my body an arched canopy over her. I glided my fingers along the flat of her stomach, then abdomen, until I accidentally touched the electric coils of her pubic hair and jerked my hand away.

"It won't bite you," she whispered.

She wildly combed her thin fingers through my hair and ran the tip of her tongue along my lips. I felt her fingernails scratch along the serrated track of my bulged zipper.

"Christ, I love you," I muttered with utmost sincerity. The remark didn't seem to stick.

A song by the BeeGees came on the radio and she pushed me upright, tossed her hands up, and fell back on the bed. Ready for Mister Camera.

"All right, pretty boy, shoot away."

I slouched forward onto her, inhaling along her breasts, stomach, and pelvis. Running my fingertips across her perfectly bowed hips, gently trying to hold them.

"I love you," I prayed to her.

"'Course you do," she cooed, and added, "Now, back to business."

"But I love . . ."

"Come on, shoot the fucking camera!" she yelled, shattering my idyllic mood.

I grabbed the Nikon and shot a sequence of unsteady, ill-focused photos as she rocked and shuddered. When my erection became excruciating, I excused myself and staggered into the bathroom, slamming the door behind me.

"Hey, what the hell is this?" I heard her scream.

I stepped into the shower fully dressed and turned on the cold water.

"Give me a second," I said, and after a couple of minutes of cold water, I steadied myself.

"This is too weird!" she yelled.

I opened the bathroom door to find that she had packed her bag, dressed, and was on her way out.

"You can keep the remaining cash," she said, and closed the front door behind her.

"You left something!" I yelled out to her in the parking lot, and held up the pair of panties that had fallen beside the bed. When she approached, I didn't know what I was going to do until I clutched her wrist, yanked her back inside, and slammed the door.

"HELP! RAPE!" she started screaming. I pushed her against a wall, covering her mouth gently.

I could see terror in her radiant eyes.

"Just listen to me! That's all I ask! I beg you."

She nodded yes and I released my hand from her mouth.

"About two years ago when I was fresh out of college . . . I saw a lot of porn, but then I saw you and . . . I don't know why, but I had to meet you . . ." I released her.

"So you're not a photographer?" she confirmed.

"I'm a first-year associate in a corporate law firm in New York."

"I knew it!" she shrieked. "I knew this was bullshit. Fucking Julian! Said he knew you. Said he'd never send me into an unsafe situation. Didn't even have the decency to bring me. The only reason I came is 'cause he said he worked with you before. Fuck!" She stood there staring furiously at the bed.

"I collected everything of you . . ."

"You mean pornography?"

"Yeah, back issues, catalogues, everything. I mean, I wrote away to distributors. I have stills and loops, stuff you did in your early days under the name Sue De Grace and . . ."

She stared at me. In her face I could see curiosity, uncertainty, and disgust. Humiliation overwhelmed me. All I could do was screw my face into a paralysis of muscles. I sat at the edge of the bed and waited for her to leave.

"What do you want?" she asked plainly.

"I only wanted to meet you. Just get to know you."

"Why?" She sounded like an adversarial attorney looking for a quick settlement.

"Actually, I want an end."

"An end to what?"

"I thought that if I could see that you were as normal as anyone else, my interest in you would cease, or . . ." I smiled. She could see I was benign.

"Or what?" she asked with an odd smile.

"Or you'd fall in love with me." I tried to hide an adolescent embarrassment.

"Well, the joke's on you," she replied. "I'm less than anything you could have thought." She sat down next to me and added, "Hell, I'm . . . almost nothing."

"Don't say that."

"So you live in New York City?" She changed the subject, I thought, to save me added pain.

"Yes, but what I really wanted was to get you out of my head," I attempted to explain.

"You have a nice place? Good job?" she pressed further.

"And I want to return to it in peace."

Silently, Sky went to her purse and took out the stack of ten-dollar bills I had paid her and threw them on the bed. Apparently, this was her attempt to balance her books.

"You helped me," I told her. "You earned that money far more than if you had posed."

"Take your money. I don't want it." She then said in a murmur, "It was only going to go to rent."

I wanted to believe she was being magnanimous. Of course that was not it. Now that I was a self-confessed sucker, she spotted a larger con in the offing.

She broke into a histrionic hush. "So you're not . . . attracted to me anymore?" I couldn't figure out if this was what she feared or wanted.

"Well," I started slowly, only certain that I wasn't sure of anything, "I guess I invested all these things into you." I spoke awkwardly, wondering if any of the things I fantasized could have the slightest semblance of truth. "Did you ever attend college?"

"I once made a collage," she joked, and then confessed, "I never read a book in my life."

"Well," I said sincerely, "I was impressed by the way you handled this photo shoot."

She smiled modestly. "Did you really collect all that stuff?"

"Yes," I said quietly.

"Don't you think what I've done is horrible?" she asked, searching for some indication of guilt or innocence.

"If you did something wrong, then so did I," I replied, attempting to vindicate the both of us.

"I don't have any hang-ups about it," she declared. "I mean, don't misunderstand me, I'm not proud of it, but I ain't ashamed of it either."

"There must be something else you want to do with your life," I suggested. Even I knew that the career span of an average porn actress ranged from a few months to a couple years at best.

"I once wanted to be a veterinarian. Isn't that a joke?" She went through her bag and took out a cigarette. After a moment of silence she said, "I ought to get going."

I accompanied her to her shiny red Corvette parked out front.

"I'm really sorry about all this, Harry," she said with her head tilted to one side.

"My name's not Harry. It's Leslie, Leslie Cauldwell."

"You're a nice, good-looking guy," she said. "I'm sure you can find yourself a nice girl."

After all the facial phrases in all her films I'd watched, perhaps as a parting gift, she gave me a beautiful earnest expression like no other I'd ever seen. It linked delight and concern with embarrassed sorrow. I would have given anything to kiss her—not for me, but for her. She seemed so alone, but her car window was already rolled up and she was backing out. I watched as she drove away and figured I'd never see her again.

I stood there as long as I could, not wanting to let go of the moment. I had met the only movie star I had ever fallen in love with, a dream come true. With an open-ended ticket back to New York, I called the airline from a corner pay phone and got a reservation on an early-evening flight. I bought a Big Mac at a nearby McDonald's but I had no appetite. I considered doing some sightseeing but felt a fatigue. Actually, it was a profound disappointment.

Back in the motel, it was still early when I lay on the soft, springy bed watching TV. Unintentionally, I drifted off to sleep.

►►

Banging woke me. I rose, fearing that I had slept past checkout and missed my flight. I unlocked the door. Sky pushed in and closed the door behind her.

She couldn't catch her breath. When I flipped on the light, I saw her mascara smudged and a distinct red welt across her left cheek.

"I got beaten up!" she cried out. Tears streamed down her face.

"By whom?" I held and hugged her.

"A fat fuck! He somehow knows you," she replied, battling tears. In a shrill gasp, she blurted, "I think he's going to kill me!"

"I don't know any fat fucks," I replied.

"Fillip! He beat the living shit out of Julian and totaled my car." She started crying and mumbled, "I took a bus here."

It was all because of that telephone fray in which I had called him a kike. I had provoked the old fart. The fat fuck had attacked Sky to get back at me, or so it seemed.

"When did all this happen?" I asked, having lost track of time.

"Just now! He held me against my will," she replied. "He only let me out 'cause he thought I went to get cigarettes." She took out her pack and lit one up.

"So what exactly happened?" I was still unclear.

"Someone told him that Julian was agenting for me. The fat son of a bitch thinks he owns me. So when I got home, he was there waiting. He had already beaten the shit out of Julian." I felt immeasurably guilty, realizing I was the one who had squealed.

"Does he know where you are right now?" I asked, wondering if Fillip could track me down.

"He heard I did a shoot for some magazine, *Dilettante* or something . . ."

"*Debutante*," I corrected her.

"Yeah, anyway, he said he wanted the money. When I told him I didn't take a fee, he thought I was holding out!"

"I can give you the cash." I quickly dug into my pants pocket.

"It's way beyond that," she said tensely. Then, with a flash of horror on her face, she declared, "Oh shit! Julian knows you are staying here!"

"Let's get out, quick!" I realized that Fillip or his goons were probably on their way over. We were being pursued.

The sky was chalky white, slanting toward rain. It was only 4 o'clock. There was still time to catch my plane. I threw my belongings into the backseat of the rented car. Sky followed me out, holding my Samsonite suitcase.

Once we were both in the car, I asked, "Where can I take you?"

"Fillip knows everyone I know," Sky replied distressfully, and then muttered, "How the fuck did he figure all this out?"

"I should tell you something," I said, deciding to come clean. "I met Fillip at My Fair Lady."

"That's his club," Sky said suspiciously.

"I know. I saw an advertisement that you were dancing there." I had to tell all. "Anyway, I spoke to him there. He told me you had been in a car accident, so I called him up this morning and called him a liar . . . and we got into a fight. He kept telling me to show 'regard.'"

"Oh! So that's it!" Her tone became accusatory. "So you were the one! Now what the fuck am I supposed to do?"

"Give me a second," I said, and went to the motel manager's office to check out. A sign hanging on the door read, "Will return in five minutes." Having already paid for the room, I slid the tagged key in the mail slot and returned to the car.

Sky was sitting inside chewing her lip nervously. But she must have been disguising ecstasy. Her plan was working. To be young is dumb enough, but I was a dumb youth, double the idiocy. I silently started driving, and after a couple of minutes asked, "What kind of relationship did you have with Fillip?"

"He kind of discovered me," she admitted, and then softly added, "and we became lovers."

"That fat old man was your . . ."

"Yeah," she said. Sky's voice took on an uneasy

pitch. "See, everything has a place. And, well, his place has everything: a Jacuzzi, a sauna, pinball machines. If you were there . . ."

"So you had sex for . . . for what . . . toys?" I shot back, not hiding my disgust.

"No, necessities. Clothes. Great meals. Wonderful trips. Not to mention incredible coke. Top mesc. Pure heroin. Sometimes hundreds of bucks of it a day."

"So, I mean . . ." I endeavored not to be too judgmental.

"Look, you're right, okay!" she grew inflamed. "I'm sorry! I'm an addict. I'm a materialist. I like having things and not looking at price tags."

We rode in silence a while, watching the cityscape unfold before us, then seal up behind.

"What are you going to do?" I broke the silence.

"What's New York like?" Sky asked introspectively. I could see the New York inside of her: soaring skyscrapers, glamorous crowds, twin spotlights figure-eighting in the sky.

"Listen to me." I pulled over and whispered, "There must be someone here in LA you can stay with."

"There isn't," she said flatly.

"New York can be an awful place," I replied, just as flatly. The Big Apple of the late seventies was a far cry from the safe, slightly boring metropolis of today.

"See," she edged her little request forth, "I had always intended to go there. I have some money saved up. If I could stay somewhere a few weeks until I get my feet on the ground, I know people there."

Be careful what you wish for—that was the lesson. Here was my dream come true. I was still a skinny kid barely able to get a date. There was a reason I needed porn. But even then I could see that this three-dimensional parade-float of a woman was going to be a serious project. The prevailing feeling that tipped the scale, however, was that I had disobeyed the prime directive and fucked things up on her home planet.

"What will you do in New York?" I asked her, baffled.

"I could get my life back on track. Go back to school," she responded hesitantly.

She was very young and had already passed through a very strange world. Inasmuch as youth meant spinning the roulette wheel of possibilities, she was still in the game. To her, New York was merely a bigger casino.

"Maybe you could help me," she added, playing on the urge of a naïve thrill-seeker to realize his life-rescuing fantasy.

"Sure I can," I said with a dismal smile. "But if you have anything here, any life at all, I caution you to stay. If you don't, though, you're welcome to come with me."

The spontaneous honking of a car made us both tense, and aware that we were still prone to attack by our common enemy—Fillip.

It was an hour before my flight when I pulled over to a pay phone and booked a second reservation for Sky to accompany me to New York. On the flight I got a glimpse of what was to come when she grew anxious about trading the West for the East Coast and started popping down sleeping pills with mini-bottles until she passed out in the middle of the fly-over states.

MAY 12, 1981, LA

"HOLY SHIT, I MUST BE HALLUCINATING," THE OLD man labored to speak. "Look who it is." A smile crept over Fillip's face as Sky entered his hospital room.

"Laurel told me you were here, so . . ." Sky surveyed the room quickly, the IV drip, the strange old lady sleeping in the opposite bed of the semi-private room. She could see Fillip's watery eyes fix on the young black man behind her. "I'd like you to meet someone who's heard a lot about you."

"Please to meet you," said T-Bird, as he grabbed the limp hand of the man lying down before him. Fillip mustered a courteous smile.

"Nice to meet you, son."

T-Bird turned to Sky and said, "I'll be waiting outside."

"Who's the schwartza?" Fillip whispered, as soon as they were alone.

"Someone Laurel introduced me to. We're going to a party later."

"It's so good to see you," Fillip said hoarsely, yet earnestly. It was evident that he had just woken up from a long sleep.

"Laurel kept telling me you had surgery. I'm sorry it took me so long to come and visit."

"You know, I was in New York about six months ago," he murmured, "visiting my sis up in Utica. I tried to find you."

"I was only there for about a month," Sky replied curtly.

"I met with that boy lawyer."

"You saw the geek?" She smiled, amused by the thought of the two of them together.

"Did you part on bad terms?" Fillip asked.

"Why? What'd he say?"

"Nothing, actually, he covered for you."

"Yeah, well, you know me, Fil, I slipped off the stage one night while stripping and fucked everything up."

"You always got high while stripping." He smiled.

"That's 'cause I always hated it," she replied.

"You didn't hate it," he corrected, "you were bored by it. I used to watch you. You enjoyed yourself, but you didn't treat it like a job. It was a big joke. When you were up, you acted like you could get away with anything. That's always been your problem—all of you, you act like school children that don't need hall passes, like you are above the rules."

"Whatever," she responded.

"So you stripped in New York?"

"He didn't know I was stripping. I mean, what else was I supposed to do? I don't know anything else."

"So you got high, passed out, and he tossed you out on your ass."

"Yeah."

"Shame."

"Why is it a shame?"

"When I went looking for you, he said you were still with him. Any other guy would've said you weren't around, whatever, but this guy still cared for you. I kind of hoped you *were* still with him."

"I went out to Frisco," she said, no longer interested in talking about Leslie. "I bumped into Denver Wade . . ."

"Hey," Fillip said, still thinking about the boy lawyer, "why'd he think I was after him?"

"Oh, I played with him a little." She grinned.

Fillip laughed. "You always were a better head-fucker than body-fucker." She giggled and nodded yes. "You know, you're not always going to be young, hon."

"So they tell me." She had a sudden urge for a cigarette.

"The only angle to doing porn is if you're putting a nest egg away. Having something to retire with. 'Course, no one does that, especially with all those bad habits they pick up." Fillip started coughing. It was a wet rattling hack that sounded like he was barely hanging on. Sky began to pour him a glass of water, but he waved it away. After he calmed down, he said, "I missed you, dear."

"I missed you, too," she said politely.

His glassy eyes stared at her silently, as though he had finally found a course, a direction to head in. "You know what I'm thinking?" he asked softly. She nodded no. "I'm thinking that at the age of sixty-three, this is where I get off. Lived through a depression, a war, all that shit, and the show's over. I'm dying in 1981. And if you don't fuck it up, you've got at least another fifty years of the show. You're going to see deep into the next millennium. You're going to see how all this shit turns out. And I envy the hell out of that."

"Nonsense," she replied after a moment, "you'll be fine and outlive me by miles." It was an empty remark intended to make the dying man feel like she at least cared.

"You know, the state took My Fair Lady," he said.

"Taxes, I heard." She had gone there on her first day back to try to get some work.

"You know the one thing I like"—he produced a twitching grin—"the one good thing about this is I'm dying in debt. Which isn't so bad. I'll actually be fucked if I don't kick. 'Cause once I step out of this hospital, I'll die of starvation. I don't have a cent. 'Course, the sad part is I would'a liked to have left you something." He looked at her face as he sensed that money was the real motive for her visit.

"I'll be okay," she replied, poker-faced.

"You take the Mona Lisa or any oil painting by one of the great masters, a beautiful woman to me isn't just a boner. This is God's paint." He pinched his skin. "Woman is the greatest high—the only real intoxicant. Cocaine, booze, heroin—all bullshit. The moment I see a truly beautiful woman, I can feel myself get all tingly and start to . . . transcend. That's why I know there's something more to life, because I can actually feel my spirit rise when I see a beautiful woman. She fills the depth and breadth of my very being! Last thing I ever wanted to do was hurt any woman's feelings. I know that most people regard me as a greedy scumbag, but I could stare forever at a beautiful girl and that's how I know there is a higher being, 'cause only a god could create such a wonderful thing."

"I know, Fil," she replied, wondering how long she was expected to stay there.

"Jeane, you're one of the sharpest and coolest chicks I know. That's the truth. And you got a will of steel. Aside from a face that should be hanging in the Louvre, you are really as quick-witted as the greasiest ambulance chasers I've ever met, and, by the by, you've got yourself an ass that kicks out like a shelf and a pair of knockers that—"

"Thanks, Fil," she interrupted, with a smile and a glimmer in her eyes. His compliment was collapsing under the weight of its own sleaze.

T-Bird leaned into the room, smiled at Fillip, and tapped his wristwatch when the old man wasn't looking. They had to go.

"You know, that's going to be the death of you," Fillip shifted his tone. "Guys like that are going to plague you your whole life. Screw you over, throwing nickels and dimes at you till they throw *you* out. And the next guy who picks you up will be a little lower on the ladder."

Although she wanted to, Sky didn't tell Fillip that he *was* one of those guys—in fact, one of the first. She was trying to hide it, but Fillip knew that Sky had found a new pimp, and they had a john waiting somewhere.

"Give me my coat," he instructed, pointing to a coconut-creme sports jacket hanging in the closet.

Sky did as he asked. Fillip took his checkbook out of the inside pocket, scribbled into it, tore a check out, and handed it to her. "You can snort this up your nose. But I'd like to think it's escape money for when you wake up and discover this is a game you can't win."

"Thanks, hon," she said, folding it quickly so T-Bird wouldn't see.

"When you left Julian with that lawyer kid and vanished out to New York, I was really rooting for you," he confessed. "I was hoping you'd break free of all this—and me."

She put a kiss on his ashen cheek and was about to leave, when he warned, "Don't take too long in depositing that check."

Sky thanked him again and left.

PART THREE: PLAY

▶

APRIL 28, 2001, NYC

COUGHING, FALLING, STRUGGLING UPWARD, AWAKENING, unearthing myself from the bed sheets, from the suffocating void, sliding onto the floor, sleeping there a while, reawakening, rising, falling back down, refusing, fighting that steep descent of black sleep, busting through, trying to open my eyes, struggling to my feet, leaning against the wall, I finally drag myself into the bathroom and stick my head under the cold shower. My heart starts thumping, blasting through all those fucking pills I popped last night. They'll gracefully soar you to the dark domain, but their jaws won't release you so easily.

It's late—2:15 in the post-meridian. With at least an hour of driving needed to get to Long Island, I fear that I have missed my vital photo shoot with Kate. Size-six bikinis at the beach. I dress hastily. The remains of yesterday's coffee tastes like warm soy sauce. I grab my bag and dash out the door, racing all the way to my car and driving like a maniac to the bridge. Only then do I realize that I should have taken the tunnel; bumper-to-bumper traffic in the burning sun, coupled with jitteriness. Exiting, I gingerly rear-end a slow-moving van. Both of us do the whole pull-over thing, inspect this, chat about that, decide against insurance, then back into our vehicles. The only damage is to my Jaguar, which now has a visible indentation in the chromium front fender. Halfway through Queens, as airport-bound vehicles exit, the traffic starts loosening up. By the time I arrive a few blocks from Kate's school, I can see the last ripple of kids flowing out.

It is 3:39 and this institution of lowest learning is virtually drained. Driving down the lawn-lined lane toward her house, past kids-at-play signs and kids at play, I spot them. Two girls in the distance, walking and squawking. One is Kate.

"Hey there." I slow down. "Still up for a shoot?"

"Where were you?" She stops, hands-on-hips, incurably pouty. Tell me they don't know they're sexy.

"I'm sorry, I just got out of a meeting with my assign-ments editor. It ran late." I am suddenly aware that I have not combed my hair, and I make a gesture of matting it down.

"That's okay," the kitten purrs, "'cause I was going to say no anyway."

"That's ridiculous. You said you'd do it," I shoot back, and then grasping that I'm coming off violently, I smile abruptly. But nothing is stupider than a sudden smile, so I unsmile.

"I'm sorry, I can't." She's being coy.

"Look," I reply in a consoling tone, "we made a deal. Remember? We shook on it."

"I didn't sign anything," she returns, pulling legalities on me. I stop the car.

"Listen," I say calmly, allowing a speckle of sourness in my tone. Taking out my camera, I begin adjusting the lens. "There's something called a verbal contract, but let's not talk about that. Let's do it. Right here! Right now! A half an hour is all. Your friend can watch and you get a hundred bucks!"

"Thanks, but no thanks." She walks away blithely.

I feel a snapping sensation as the taut cords of hope connecting me to Sky begin to pop free.

"A hundred bucks! You made a deal!" I turn the smile back on.

"What are you, sick?" Kate turns nasty. "Fuck off!"

In twenty years of deal-making, no one has ever spoken to me that way. The process of degradation is complete. I'm Stroheim in *Blue Angel.* I hop out of the car, grab her by the wrist, and insist, "You apologize!"

"Get off me, you old freak!"

"You apologize!" I know that Jeane would never have let her daughter talk to me that way, so I give her a shake.

"I'm sorry!" she yells. Her girlfriend peels off. Kate tries to run, but I hold onto her.

"Look." I shove Kate back toward my car. "I'm only going to take a couple of photos, then you can go. Understand?"

"Yes! Okay!" Kate relents nervously. I snap close-ups of her. Through the viewfinder, I watch her, arms folded, face and mouth tight. Eyes widened. Cheeks trembling. Trying to control her breathing.

I hear the shriek of her friend at the screen door of an adjacent house, "HELP! QUICK! CALL THE POLICE! My friend's being raped!"

I hear an elderly male voice respond languidly in the distance: "Calm down, dear. What's all this about?"

"I know how it is," I tell Sky's little girl. "You're young and you really believe that your beauty and youth will last forever and be rewarded; that every cute boy, every nice car, every creative act, every perfect house and thing will be yours. We all believed that, but it never turns out that way."

"What do you want?!" her terrified voice barely whistles out. She is in a state of shock, with no idea who I am. And that's when I awaken to the fact that I'm the enemy. I return to my car and zoom away.

While driving back to the city, I feel myself coming up well-done. I try to hold it in and represent myself methodically to that singular jury of my peer—me: 1) I was nice to her; 2) I didn't try to do anything lewd or lascivious; 3) I regard her as the daughter I almost had; 4) I intend to leave her an abundance of money in my will. Summation: 1) she betrayed me; 2) I have never been so humiliated in all my life; 3) the whole project was a flop. The verdict: 1) no real harm was done; 2) fuck her; 3) squeeze her out of your head and wipe it clean.

I put on an opera, *Kingdom of the Black Swans*. Wagner's son wrote it. He was always trying to keep up with Dad. Always turning up inadequate, mediocre. Maybe it's simply my interpretation of the moment, but I can hear the full encyclopedic range of musical doubt and uncertainty. By the time I park my car, I feel shaky with anger. What's worse than bottled rage? And the vintage of my fury goes back centuries. I park, and as I walk home, I punch a parking meter, hurting but not injuring my knuckles. Where's Cece, who rewired my hate into love and vice versa?

Through the hard streets I stomp. Someone in front of me turns into the photo lab, so I follow him, frantically rewinding the roll of unfinished film. I pop it out of the camera, slip it into an envelope, and hand it to the Indian clerk, who tears off the receipt. It's not my fault she resisted.

As I am heading toward my apartment, a man jumps out of a car and grabs me. I twist his arm behind his back and knock him to the ground, only to find that it's David Polk, Holtov's number-one bootlick. His scrubbed collegiate face looks at me in horror. Luis, my doorman, sees our little scuffle and jumps out of the building to help me.

"It's okay," I assure the door specialist, who returns inside.

"Sorry, David." I help him up and pat the street off of him.

"Sorry for surprising you," he says, rubbing his bruised back. "Les, your phone isn't working."

"I turned off the ringer." I don't care to elaborate.

"Are you okay?"

I'm not sure if he's looking at my goatee and mustache, my clothes, or the complete picture.

"Why wouldn't I be?"

"You look . . . different." Then, noticing my shoulder, he asks in complete astonishment, "Is that . . . That's not a tattoo?"

"What wrong with it?" I can see tomorrow's headline: "Forty-Six-Year-Old Corporate Attorney Gets Crazy Tattoo."

"Leslie, Bill has an appointment with Sanders next week."

"Look, I'm out of it."

"Out of it? Les, you're supposed to be handling this." He is getting indignant, a real turnoff.

"I'm supposed to handle this? Hey, I'm not in the firm any longer, so fuck off!" I still feel freaked about what happened today. Polk is standing in shock as I enter my building. I see him dash off in my periphery. Luis asks me if I'm okay.

"Just beautiful, man," I reply with a polyester smile, and stopping myself, I amend, "Luis, listen, do me a favor. If anyone at any time asks, I'm not here—ever."

"You're never here to nobody?" he inquires, with the wonder of a small child.

"I owe big money, Luis." I put my arm over the brown-noser's shoulder. "This is a big secret, but these bastards are trying to shut me down. Well, they can go fuck themselves."

"That can be dangerous, Mr. Cauldwell."

"Trust me, Luis." Then, in a hushed tone, I add, "Don't tell them I'm here if you ever see them."

"Gotcha," he replies, eager to have a little romance in his dreary life.

I stand alone in the solitary confinement of the small, mirrored elevator. The leashless dog run of my fury is fenced in with fear, regret, guilt, and benign fetishes, watched over by a selfless specter named Cecilia. As the elevator rises, I painfully come to terms with the fact that I have lost all chances of ever sipping the lost wine of Sky. Due to the caprices of a teenage girl, my last love has vaporized. I am left alone with a desperate animal that is me.

The elevator slides open like a cage, but I see that I have to forever close the door that allows me out. I push the lobby button and slip back down to planet earth. When the door opens again, I rush out to the corner liquor store and pick up a pint of Absolut. At the Koreans, I grab a pint of English Toffee. Pre-stamped postcards are for sale behind the counter. Bill was always fair, and my secretary of many years, Dorothy, will want to know what's up: A suicide note is owed. Too bad Hallmark doesn't make them:

As the last of hope rushes out of my life,
My blood joins it, freed by a knife;
Was just thinking about the few I rue,
Was thinking about my contempt toward you.

Guilt—the final parting shot of the bitter and hateful.

Standing on the corner, I address the card to dear Dot. I scribble it out with a pencil, then erasing several parts, I revise and read it:

Dear Dorothy,

Thank you for always providing the illusion that I was worth working for. Please notify the authorities that I have filed my final Chapter 7 in my apartment. Now that my estate has been assessed, let me just say that you were always a pleasure to work with. Live happily. Cry not, I had a damn lucky life.

Cowardly Lion, Scarecrow & Tin Man, all in one,
L.C.

Just the right balance of humor, humility, and homily. I drop the card in the corner box and head home quickly, fearful that she might receive it before the deed is done. It's a strange, lighthearted, bounce-to-my-step kind of feeling. The very idea that I'm going home to kill myself actually thrills me. The great accumulation of life—every achievement, good or bad, every object, every mask and thought—is like a weight that I've had to balance on my back. I can't describe the joy I feel in being able to get out from under it.

Virtually skipping across the pavement, the last time I had looked forward to something so much must have been during my childhood. If death is a journey to some vast, invisible world projected up behind this one, that's fine. At best, I'd love to have the opportunity to make amends to Cece. But even if it's a slip of blank nothingness, no matter, so long as it's an end to this increasingly painful twitch of meaninglessness.

"Hello, Mr. Cauldwell. How are you? He's not still out there, I hope," the doorman with the Chihuahua face greets me.

"No, Luis, everything's *simpatico.*"

Despite the fact that I had seen him only five minutes ago, he's all hopped up because of the big secret I confided. He continues saying flattering things about me—I look good, I smell great, I'm well dressed. Christ, he's giving me a hemorrhoid with his incessant ass-licking, but he does that to everybody.

"You know," I point out, "if you're indiscriminately nice to everyone, even the sons of bitches, your kindness has no real point."

"Oh, I don't discriminate," the idiot hooks onto the biggest word and replies pleasantly.

"No, I notice how you always make it a point of saying hello to all the people in the building. See, I've spent a lot of time with rich people. Hell, I'm rich. Money protects us. Those people you brown-nose all day, they're fucking phonies."

"But you got to be nice to people, Mr. Cauldwell. You got to try to love everyone."

"Why?"

"It's written in the big book, Mr. Cauldwell."

"But they're phonies!" I explain.

"I know they're phonies, but that's their loss. What else can you do, Mr. Cauldwell? How else you supposed to act?"

"Actually," I revise myself again in accord with something I heard on TV, "the answer has something to do with conducting yourself with dignity — that's the secret."

"Dignity. Got you, Mr. Cauldwell."

The most pragmatic philosophy a poor person can hammer together among the rich is being an ass-licker, isn't it? Before I can impart this wisdom, I watch him opening the door for a flabby middle-aged lady, flattering her hairy little armpit dogs. I quickly grab the elevator so that I don't have to ride up with her.

In a moment, I am back in the anarchy of my apartment. In another moment, I am sitting naked in the womb of my bathtub as it fills up with embryonic fluid. My latest toys are gathered around me — vodka, ice cream, and sleeping pills. Leisurely, splendidly, unrushedly, I suck gulps of booze, spoon globs of gooey, semi-melted English Toffee ice cream, and pepper it with the occasional pill. *Gulp, gobble, pop — gulp, gobble, pop — gulp, gobble, gulp, gobble — gulp, gulp.* The gulps and gobbles are a lot more fun than popping the sleeping pills. *Pop, pop, drift, drift, oh what a relief it is . . .*

JULY 11, 1981, NYC

NERVOUSLY, I PACKED MY ACCUMULATION OF pornography—from genteel mainstream, *Playboy* and *Penthouse*, through *High Society, Cheri, Hustler*, right down to the Swedish Eroticas and other hardcore—into a large garbage bag and waited until late that night. Then I hauled the black plastic bag to a wide metal dumpster several blocks from my house and heaved it over as if I were disposing of a body. It had been a while since Cecilia left me, and to nurse my loss, I had purchased a stockpile of photographic companionship. Unfortunately, we don't know how much we acquire until we have to toss it all out.

Afterwards, I headed to a nearby bar, ordered a vodka martini extra, extra dry, and went over to an Aspen-looking blonde who was sitting at the bar. She resembled the porn actress Marla Lillian. I noticed a ski pass on the large stainless-steel zipper of her parka.

"Downhill or cross-country?" I asked. She turned away.

I stood next to her a moment and breathed her in, weighing whether I should try to force her to like me. Then I finished my drink and ordered another. Within half an hour I had downed two more martinis and been rejected by two other minty-fresh girls. One curious-faced woman smiled at me, so I went over. Her visage was an intriguing amalgamation of child and woman, and when I said hi, she returned it.

"You know," I said drunkenly, "I'd love to talk with you, but you don't look anything like Cecilia."

"I see," she replied.

"In fact, you alone look like two completely different people." She left the bar.

After another string of vodka martinis, I was furiously drunk.

All seemed very amusing, and then I thought, it's all Cecilia's fault. Why did she have to be a dominatrix? But that was the rumor that had attracted me to her in the first place. She was into "weird shit."

Everything then began to get very maudlin. I went outside. Hailed a cab. Got in the backseat. Before the driver could ask where I was going, I vomited. The cabby was about to punch me, so I gave him a twenty and hailed a second cab. This one took me to Cecilia's house.

I walked up to her doorway and rang her bell repeatedly until she said, "Who the fuck is it?"

"Your beloved."

"It's late," she replied over the intercom, but I kept my finger on the button until she rang me in. Once upstairs, I told her that I loved her.

"You're a drunken asshole!" she barked. "Go home!"

"But I loves you," I joked.

"If Gina were here . . ."

She put me to bed.

"I love you, love you, love you," I said over and over. Sleep.

I awoke with a jump and a hangover. It was noon and I wasn't sure whose couch I was sleeping on.

A girl was sleeping in the adjacent bed. She looked beautiful. Only when I spotted Van Gogh's Starry Night spinning on the wall did I know I was at Cecilia's. I took the phone into the bathroom and whispered to my secretary that regrettably I would not be in for work that day. Dorothy said she understood.

I quietly dressed and was about to leave, but as I looked at Cece, I found I couldn't stop staring at her.

Love usually began with sexual attraction, followed by guilt, resignation, and boredom. Did I still love her? Or was it just guilt I felt? Was constantly thinking about someone love, or was it obsession? Can you love two people at once? Can you want someone and yet not love them?

I took off my shoes and coat, and gently lay in bed alongside her. Slowly, carefully, I worked my arm up around her, hugging and holding her.

"I went to your dungeon," I whispered to her. "I saw those pictures of you in your mistress garb, then I had this weird session. It made me see a whole new you . . . and I guess that's why I, why the way we made love . . ."

Although she snored faintly, I felt easier making my confession. Soon, I fell into a deep and tranquil sleep.

"Let go!" she abruptly shrieked, and leapt up in her undies. "You touch me again and I'll fucking kill you, I swear it!!"

"I'm really sorry," I said, not for touching her, but for causing the pain responsible for such wrath. She covered herself with a blanket and threw open the front door. I picked up my shoes, grabbed my coat, and staggered out.

JULY 20, 1981, LA
"SHIT'S RIGHT FROM HEAVEN," T-BIRD PROCLAIMED, as he opened the small packet and delicately peppered a paltry white pile on the glass tabletop. He then cut several lines with the gold-plated razor blade hanging from his necklace.

Sky smiled, knowing exactly what he wanted. She was supposed to crawl over to it and snort it bent over.

Doggy-style. That was the routine. First, to save any fuss, she went into the bathroom and quickly removed her pantyhose and underwear. The last time this happened he had ripped her undergarments right off. The nylon tearing against her skin had given her a visible burn.

She returned and bent over on the shag rug. She could hear his huge belt buckle clicking as he undid it. When she picked up the half-size plastic straw, he kneeled behind her and started kissing her neck and shoulder blades. Chivalrously, he didn't touch her while she siphoned up the candy. No one wanted to risk a spill. But once she threw her head back to snort it deeply, he reached around front and snapped open the buttons of her shirt. His large hand moved down, over her stomach. Reaching around, he slipped his fingers into her, steering slowly, firmly working his way in.

"Oh, fuck me, baby." She said her lines convincingly.

His muscular black body was firmly pressed behind her, supporting her like a living scaffold. She limply nestled into him, a kind of fleshy bar to perch upon.

Sky didn't particularly want to screw. She never would have guessed that last night's horny little john with the cocoa tan and white suit would have so much fuel in him. He paid for the whole night and fucked her three times in as many hours. The second girl was a jail-bait bleach job who the john seemed to own. She played fingers and tongue on the side. When he was finally done and dressed, he gave Sky five crisp one-hundred-dollar bills.

Then the tan man took his little girldo and left Sky in the hotel room. She showered, gargled, and, before she could dress, heard a knock on the door. T-Bird, who had been in the lobby, had spotted the cocoa john leaving. When Sky opened the door, he simply held out his hand. Sky gave him the bills and they left.

Now, she felt T-Bird's tongue swabbing her ear. She opened her lips and the tongue slugged in, occupying her mouth. His cock rocked inside her in short, hard jerks.

"Fuck me, baby, fuck me deep," she urged, and thought, I've put at least sixty grand in his pocket over the last three months and gotten less than six back.

"You want me, hon?"

"You know I love you," she replied, and knew he believed it. That's the best weapon she had right now. But he already had a new girl lined up. T-Bird was diversifying, moving out of dealing and more into prostitution. She knew that over the next few weeks his percentage would get bigger, his treatment of her would get worse, and the johns would get sleazier. She had seen it all before with other older girls once they became washed up. Now it was her turn.

"Oh, babe, that feels so fine!" she moaned, as T-Bird's hands massaged her breasts. She knew that in the next two weeks he was going to make a big score. At least twenty grand. She had to act quickly. Make plane reservations. Grab the cash—not all of it, only enough so he wouldn't come after her—then a cab to LAX. It wasn't really the money she was after but her life. She hadn't had a period in over a month. The doctors said she couldn't get pregnant, but with morning sickness and swelling, what else could it be? T-Bird had fucked her almost every day since they first met. She knew if he found out she was carrying—if she was in fact pregnant—he'd rip it out himself.

He started fucking her faster, slamming her, approaching orgasm. As she feigned her own climax, she figured either Miami with cokehead Norma or back with the geek in New York.

APRIL 29, 2001, NYC

TEN HOURS LATER I AWAKE WITH A SPLASHY JOLT. I'VE been regurgitated: Instead of joined with Cecilia in something- or nothingness, I'm shivering in a freezing tub of icy water. I jump up, kicking over the bottle of vodka, stepping in a slick of melted English Toffee ice cream. I lumber into bed, covered in shriveled, languorous flesh. Why aren't I dead? Just as I thought: I'm already in hell.

Four p.m.: I awake woozy, dehydrated, and with the mother of all headaches. Remembering that my life is but a growing weight and this was supposed to be my last day on the earthly shell, I close my eyes and decide to rest my liquified skull and inflamed brain for another ten minutes. When I finally get myself out of bed, it is 9 p.m. I make a pot of coffee and recollect that I had sent my secretary Dot a postcard regarding my much-exaggerated demise. Although it shouldn't have arrived today, the card might arrive tomorrow.

Since the ice cream and booze are a pool on my bathroom floor, I need new ingredients to painlessly chill myself. Outside, I purchase vodka and ice cream again. If you can't competently kill yourself, you should be dead. I've read how women will attempt suicide repeatedly, deliberately botching it, searching out that rescue fantasy, and when they eventually do kill themselves, it's usually an accident. Men, on the other hand, tend to off themselves the first time, no fucking around. Stepping off buildings, jumping in front of trains. This makes me wish I was more masculine. On my way home, I spot the Indian clerk preparing to close his little photo lab.

I pay for the Kate pictures, open the envelope, and start

laughing. The clerk smiles, wanting to share in my joy.

"Look." I proudly show them. With an eager smile on his face, he flips through the snapshots. They cannot be staged. Kate attempts to hold back great fear. The blur of tears in her eyes, the token resistance of the spirit, the shallow retention of dignity — all captured in her face and stance. The clerk hands them back, looking worried.

"Time to snuff the molester," I confide to him.

Before returning to my oblivion upstairs, I remember that I haven't fetched my letters in a while. I struggle to open my mailbox. It's jammed by the density of my fan mail: catalogues, final notices, utility bills, letters from work, and a yellow notice slip that a certified letter is waiting for my signature at the post office. Half of them are for Cece. One can live a second lifetime after dying on recycled mailing lists. The closest thing to a personal letter is a note from the D.A.'s office:

Dear Mr. Cauldwell:

Please be alerted that we have received a letter from Dr. Beckwith, your designated psychiatrist, claiming that you have refused to see him. Keep in mind this is a violation of our agreement . . .

We believe that our terms were generous. If you would prefer another psychiatrist, we can provide you with a list for the New York area. We urge you to comply with this agreement. If we have not heard from you and compliance is not met in fourteen (14) days, please be aware that the State still has the right to pursue charges . . .

Go ahead and pursue. All I'm stalking now is a hot and unsuspecting bath. Still, I'm fortunate. No jail-time or trial. The D.A.'s office would have had a difficult time pressing charges against me as an accomplice, considering that at the time of the accident I was handcuffed. My face, hooded. The perfect crime. Poor little Lana was not so fortunate. Negligent homicide with a previous conviction of purchasing narcotics carries a sentence of two-to-four in a medium-security facility. She'll get out while still young.

Her real sentence will be the fact that word got out. Hell, the accident even made it onto the Net. No slave's going to trust you with cuffs if you have a reputation for strangling a client. Maybe that's the real reason Sanders is pissed at me.

Reading the zillionth letter from Holtov about my handling of the Sanders ruling, I figure now is the time. The extorted judge isn't going to call me, so I Rolodex Sanders's home phone number. What does it matter if he's taping the call? I'm dead anyway. I hear the phone ringing and then an elderly female voice. "Hello?"

"Hello, Mrs. Sanders?" I say with complete professionality.

"Yes," she replies.

"Is the judge home?" It's important to be polite, because I might be faxing his wife the stills.

"One second," she says, putting the phone down.

"May I help you?" the sexually bankrupt juror speaks. In that one phrase, I can detect the great tradition of brocade settlements and cherry-paneled bribes.

"Your honor, this is Leslie Cauldwell."

"Yes," he replies.

I've got you by the balls, I silently think, *don't you want to rip my heart out, you cowardly bastard?* But he doesn't utter a sound. "I sent you some photos. I assume you got them?" I ask suavely.

"I suspected it was you trying to extort me." His soft voice remains calm.

"That was over a month ago. I was waiting to hear from you. My wife tried to civilly break free of you, and you threatened to report her to the police, despite the fact that she never broke a law in her life."

"That was our affair!" says the guardian of justice.

"Fine, I just wanted to give Honey a final chance before I send the videotape to your wife." *Let's hear you beg, fucker.*

"Would you like to speak to her?" he offers. "My wife knows all about my little proclivities. I've never lied to her, nor have I ever broken the law."

No wonder he's so calm. I consider calling his bluff and asking to speak to her, but instead I up the ante: "How about if I pass the tape around the courthouse?"

"Do whatever you want. I'm retiring later this year. Nothing is going to remove me any quicker." It's the first time I have ever *heard* a smile.

"So," I chuckle, and reply, "you're going to force the Sewter Corporation into a Chapter 7 as retaliation against me."

"If you think I'm doing an unfair job, feel free to take it up in appeal," he says, and hangs up the phone.

He's enjoying this immensely. With his damn dom dead, he's able to have one final mini-session with me. Holtov isn't going to be pleased with this one. Ten years ago I would've been wiggling on a hook over it, but now I really don't give a shit. There's a chance we could win if we keep pursuing it, though appellate isn't inclined to reverse.

It's difficult not to admire him. The old man who dresses as Honey, the disobedient little girl who repeatedly needs to be corrected, drives a hard fucking bargain. Even if I had taped it and played the conversation to the D.A., I would only implicate myself. He didn't say one word out of joint.

Soon I'm back filling the tub. Again, I position the lubricants of death. Again, and for the last time, I perform my ritual of demise. If man was able to drain all repetition from his life so that each moment was a unique creation, if each place, each event, each thought were new and filled with the risk of uncertainty, chased by a small demitasse of anxiety, with the awesomeness of novelty and surprise, that would justify a real life, not like these mass-marketed, manufactured little existences we live today, where each scene in our concocted existence is set in a home or job, with the same recurrent cast of minor characters. We are trapped in our own cheesy sitcoms, replete with the inflated laugh-track and fraudulent sentiments.

Before touching the Absolut or ice cream, I pick up the container of pills. Putting my lips around the top of the burnt-orange plastic, I toss my head back and gulp them all down at once. Then I lean back in the hot water and slowly wait for my self-consciousness to uncoil.

Jeane: It isn't simply her that I love. It is what she did. She once described her porn career as having a relationship with thirty or so people who have sex with each other over and over for just a couple of months, like a big, bisexual Mormon marriage that ends after a summer. Getting fucked is not exactly a herculean task, but the willingness to turn yourself inside out in front of a camera for the benefit of a sexually frustrated and crippled world, that is the trick. (A lawyer is exactly the opposite: We'll fuck you over and put massive effort into concealing it.) If that isn't enough, Jeane then pulled a major one-hundred-and-eighty-degrees. One day she's a drug-dependent porn actress, and the next—breaking out of a fucked-up, foredoomed life and tunneling under a mountain of shame—she's a mother and career woman. Now that's resilience.

What one thing do you think you'll miss most when that final moment comes and you are lying immobile in your lonely body slipping away? Will it be that you'll never see another sunny day? Or dash into the breaking ocean waves on a glorious summer morn? Or maybe that you'll never taste another wonderful meal? One last time to see Sky's face—that would be my last meal, my last sunny day, my last splash in the ocean.

JULY 25, 1981, NYC

LESLIE WAS AWAKENED BY FRANTIC RAPS ON HIS front door. It was 5:34 in the morning. He stumbled out of bed and yelled, "Who?"

"Me," he tiredly heard Cecilia's response. It was just two weeks after he had arrived at her house drunk, only to be tossed out in the morning.

The messengered bouquets of roses and Hallmark cards must have softened her, he thought. She was intruding upon him the same way he had pushed himself upon her—drunkenly, in the middle of the night.

When he opened the door, though, he took a couple steps back in shock. A new incarnation of Sky Pacifica entered. She had cut off all her hair. It was now spiky and dyed jet-black, which made her skin look pasty and her eyes a turquoise blue. Under a large overcoat, she donned a punk outfit: black pants with zippers that ran along her calves and a grimy black T-shirt that shouted, "Never Mind the Bullocks, Here Come the Sex Pistols." Overall, she appeared haggard. She looked much older, even though it had only been a year and a half since he had last seen her. When she entered his overly lit living room, he saw that the fur lining of her coat was matted and sticky as though she had been sleeping in it.

"Well, aren't you going to say something?" she asked, but he didn't respond. She wondered if he was going to throw her out.

Despite the stinging recollection of how she had left him after he discovered that she was stripping and mainlining during their brief stint together, he felt sorry for her. When she hugged and kissed him, he didn't reciprocate. But he didn't push her away either.

"I've been through hell and back," she finally confessed. "Leslie, I'm sorry for wheeling in like this without warning, but I just got here."

"I'm flattered, but . . ."

She sighed, and looking around the room she noticed that the place was a mess. "Tell you what. If you let me crash here a while, I'll clean up."

"I don't need a maid," he replied tiredly, covering himself with a bathrobe.

"I'll get a part-time job and pay half the rent."

"Sounds familiar, but I'm loaded. Thanks anyway."

"Then I guess I'll just have to let you fuck me," she joked with exasperation, and smiled. Sitting herself down on his couch, she knew she should have made herself look sexier.

When she glanced out the window, Leslie saw the despair in her eyes. He couldn't believe the punishment she had put herself through.

"I have a girlfriend," Leslie uttered, attempting to curtail her visit.

"Okay, so you're not getting laid," she kidded. "Now you need a mistress."

Leslie didn't respond, refusing to lighten up.

"What's her name?" Sky tested him.

"Cecilia," he replied. Sky lay back on the sofa and wondered if his girlfriend was in the bathroom.

"You look awful." He decided to let her have it.

She blurted out a laugh. "I'm not exaggerating when I say that this has been the worst fucking year of my life. I cannot tell you what I have been through." She started chewing on her fingernail, trying not to smoke. How long, she wondered, was she going to have to make small talk before he let her spend the fucking night?

"What are you doing back here?" he asked formally.

"It's all changed. San Fran, LA. I don't know the West Coast anymore."

"But you don't know New York either. You were here for less than a month," he reminded her.

"Yeah, well, my star was waning long before then. Anyway, I couldn't get any real work." Sky dreaded having to recount her time away. She didn't want to have to humiliate herself by listing the times she got drunk or high and raped or robbed or slapped or pissed on. She only wanted to spend the night—one fucking night! She was owed that much. She kept smiling and looking at him with interest, despite the fact that she could barely keep her eyes open and he wasn't talking.

"I don't know what to tell you, Sky," he finally said, and took a seat across from her.

"I saw a psychic and she said my future is bright in New York. She might be bullshit, but I know for certain that there's nothing out in LA for me." The psychic had actually said that her future was bright in the Far East.

"Well, I wish you the best of luck," he said neatly.

She kept the smile going, but silently wished that he would just say "Fuck you, whore" and toss her out.

"You know, I got my GED degree out in California because of you," she replied, deciding that she wasn't leaving until he did throw her out.

"Good," Leslie said, "but I don't have the energy anymore."

"Look, I know I was wrong." She fumbled through her purse for a nicotine fix. She needed more octane if he was going to put her through this shit. She snapped a cigarette in half, slipped it into her chapped lips, and lit it. "I'm sorry if I hurt you. I really am. But I need a little help."

"I'm sorry," he replied.

Without thinking, she let loose her bomb: "I'm three months pregnant, and I've decided to keep the baby."

"Shit!" Leslie coughed out, fully awake now. After a measured pause he said, "Your old pal Fillip came here looking for you. He was worried."

Nice try, she thought, find someone else to pawn me off on. "Yeah, I saw him. He died in June, deep in debt."

"So who's your baby's daddy?" Leslie rose and paced about the room.

"A very handsome man," she said in a firm tone.

"What's his occupation?"

"You wouldn't understand," she responded, but immediately realized that she should have said that T-Bird was a truck driver or a cop.

"What wouldn't I understand?" He paused parentally.

"He's a coke dealer. But in Los Angeles, that's a legitimate profession, like being a business manager or a personal trainer." He snickered. She knew there was no point in trying to explain it to him. "Look, Leslie, I have six thousand dollars on me. I only need a healthy environment and a good routine."

Leslie nodded in disbelief and speculated about what awful things she must have done to earn that money.

"I broke my drug habit," she said proudly. "I haven't touched a thing in two months." She doubled her one month of sobriety. "I'm not even jonesing anymore."

"Two months, huh? That's damned near forever." He didn't know what *jonesing* meant.

"I'm not out to prove anything," Sky said, and took an anxious drag from her half cigarette. "I got a belly full of reasons to stay clean now." She pet her abdomen and exhaled a plume of smoke. Leslie wondered how he could have ever gotten involved in such a mess.

"I'm going back to bed," he said, deciding to end this nightmare.

"Fine, I'll sleep here." She took another drag from her cigarette.

"No way," he replied. And there it was.

"For Christ sake, Leslie, let's not get melodramatic. At least, not tonight."

"You're not staying here!"

"You want me out, call the police!" she replied, but warily recalled the last time she had said that to a guy, a restauranteur who had then shoved her backwards down a short flight of stairs.

"You dumped me," he reminded her. "I don't owe you a fucking thing, Sky."

"My name is Jeane," she said, her voice crackling. Then she rose, grabbed her bags, and stormed out of the apartment, slamming the door behind her.

Leslie sat for a moment. He still smelled her scent in the air. It was a mix of tobacco, a generic perfume, and something earthy, like soil after a rain. Leslie wanted to help her. He knew that she had experienced more than her share of adversity, but he feared the possible entanglements that could follow a single moment of wreckless kindness. Leaning forward so that he could glance out the window, he watched Sky cross the avenue.

She headed north up Amsterdam. The faint glow of orange was just peaking on the horizon high above the streets, reflecting downward from tall buildings.

Her throat still felt tight as if she were choking. As

she walked, her large purse slid off her elbow and dropped to the pavement. She was too tired to even think about dumping the larger bag strapped around her shoulder.

For a couple of minutes, Leslie managed to think that she would be okay: Like Fillip said, she's a survivor. She'll find someone else. After ten minutes of trying not to think about her, Leslie rose, dressed, and hurried down the stairs. It was warm and humid outside. The morning streets were nearly empty, and the orange street lights revealed her absence. On Seventy-fourth, he saw her large purse lying on the sidewalk. He picked it up and continued walking. He spotted her on Seventy-sixth hauling her big bag like a dead companion along the ground. He followed her a while, hoping she would hail a cab and head to a hotel. Instead, she just continued plodding, not so much to a place as into time, away from the advance of morning, back toward the vacancy of last night from which she came. Leslie watched her cross Central Park West. When a police car zoomed around a corner and almost struck her, his heart froze.

There would have been no difficulty in getting out of the cops' way except for a great weight. She didn't even know what was dragging her down. Becoming aware that she was still holding the pointless bag, she released it in the middle of the street and pressed on another block up. She plopped down at the first available bench in front of Central Park as though she had walked a thousand miles, and closed her eyes.

What the hell did she drop her bag for? Leslie wondered. He picked it up so that he was now holding both bags, and approaching carefully, he said, "What a wonderful life you have, where someone always picks up for you."

"I don't want them," she grumbled, without looking up.

"What do you mean?"

She wasn't going to gratify him with a response. Reaching up, she yanked the bags from him and shaped them into cushions. Stretching out on the wooden slats of the bench, she pulled her coat tightly around her and seemed to instantly fall asleep. She decided that she wasn't going to off herself until he was gone. But Leslie merely stood there and sighed.

During the short time that they had been together, she had used him all she could. But now he just remembered the lonely, desperate hours sitting at his desk above Times Square, emotionally frozen, and only by envisioning himself with Sky, sometimes even as her, only then was he able to laugh or cry or care.

If he had to pay royalties on the countless fantasies involving her, he figured, he'd be broke by now.

Leslie sat on the far side of her bench. Another police car zoomed by with sirens blaring. Leslie watched Sky sleep. Eventually he nudged her.

"What?" she asked blandly, not looking up.

"Look," Leslie said lucidly. "If you get an abortion, I'll put you up for a while, I'll help you get a job, a new start . . ."

"Fuck you!" she cursed behind closed eyes.

"Think about it. A good salary, a nice place to live, a TV . . ."

"A TV? Do I look like a moron?" Her eyes popped open.

"All right! My conscience is at peace." Leslie rose dramatically. "I tried. I'm leaving now."

"Fine! Fuck you!" She turned her head away, took out the other half of her broken cigarette, and lit it.

"What am I saying that's so fucking unreasonable?"

he asked, as she continued puffing. "Fillip said you were a user, and he was right. He told me how all this was a scam. And now you're pulling this again. Well, find some other sucker, you already used me."

"You're right! I did use you. I am a fucking user, but you want to know something? I used myself up. I can't use anyone anymore. Why do you think I'm here? I've hit bottom! I'm completely fucked!"

"I don't know what to tell you," he said flatly.

"At least have the strength to say fuck off and leave me alone!" she barked.

Leslie walked away. He made it half a block before he accepted the fact that he was not going to be able to go back to sleep knowing she was out here. He turned around, marched over to her, and said, "Look, I'm willing to be used one last time, if you get an abortion."

"Leslie, I can't. Believe me."

"Fine. Goodbye." He turned to leave again, satisfied that he had tried.

"The fact that I'm pregnant is a goddamned miracle," she announced before he was out of earshot. "This baby is my only chance! And with it, I'll live or die."

"Sky, I wish I could believe that it makes a difference."

"I'm not asking for any special favors," she replied. "I'll take care of him."

"Hon, there is only one seat on this lifeboat. Do you understand?"

"Yeah, and you can't force me to have an abortion."

"You're right. It's your abused body, but it's my home you're asking to share."

"I was only looking for a place to stay a little while." She instantly expanded her proposed stay beyond the night because he seemed to be expecting it.

"We both know you're not stupid. Even you have seen this kind of shit before, these teenage mothers who think having a kid is going to redeem them. Look at you. Honestly, Sky, you're homeless. You're smoking while you're pregnant! What do you have to offer this kid?"

Sky stared into the distance and puffed furiously.

"Fine," he replied, "don't answer me. I'm going back home, but these questions need answers. These are the questions that your kid is going to prosecute you with some day."

Sky snuffed out her cigarette and decided that much as she hated going into it, the geek was decent enough to come out here, so she owed him an explanation. "*If* I don't have *this* baby . . . If I don't have this baby . . . I am dead."

"Why?" he asked, infuriated.

"Because!" She chewed her bottom lip viciously for a minute until tears came, and then explained, "Let's face it. My life is already ruined."

"It's not ruined."

"It's fucked up and I can't change that. I tried straightening out. That didn't work. I tried going the other way, getting back into the dance circuits and the porn. No one wants me there either. I can't even get laid anymore, do you understand? I'm always depressed. I genuinely have no reason to live. I mean, I'm only twenty-three! So when I have the opportunity, I just do coke and try to kill myself. Do you understand?"

"Yes, but this is so cliché," Leslie said unsympathetically, more disappointed in her than anything else. "This notion that bearing a child will save you—please!"

She didn't respond, so Leslie considered the dilemma and came up with his own theory. "You want to know what you're doing? You're having a victim fantasy, that's all. You see yourself as this lone mother against the world. Well, it's time to give up the dream."

"That's not it," she replied calmly. Gazing along the tops of buildings, she explained, "When I was living with you, I would do things I shouldn't. Not 'cause I was being childish—that was your own asshole way of seeing things. I just figured, it's only me I'm hurting. Somehow in your past you got a strong sense of motivation to live right and succeed. That's how you see and do things. For me this kid is high-octane motivation."

"But how do you know this kid will motivate you? If you can't do something for yourself, how do you know you'll do it for this infant?"

"See," she took a drag from her cigarette, "I'm attractive and sexy, so men give me all this attention, but I don't deserve it. Why do I deserve it? I got nothing to give back, I'm not even young anymore. You want me to tell you about the tricks you get to turn when you hit bottom? All the wormy dicks you get to suck? It's nightmare time."

Leslie looked up at her and was surprised by how effortlessly she could display her vulgarities. How could she degrade herself so freely?

"I think I could love a child, my child," Sky resumed. "I would love it, and it's been so long since I haven't hated and despised everything!"

"Have you ever taken care of another person?" Leslie asked sternly. "Do you know what you're getting yourself into? It's hard, particularly an infant! They soil! They wet! They get sick and cry all fucking night! You have to feed them every ten minutes. I mean, men have war. Women have babies, that's their hell! And kids never give anything back. They just keep taking! They're the worst investments."

"I used to take care of my grandma," Sky said tiredly. "She was an invalid; crapped in her pants, wandered around senile, the whole magilla. My mother and her boyfriend were always stoned or away. I'd cook, clean, look after her. Hell, I took care of everyone."

"When was this?" Leslie questioned. He thought he knew everything about her.

"Over ten years ago. I was twelve, thirteen. Right before we went to this ranch. You know, I look back on that time, before puberty, taking care of an old lady, making dinner for everyone, and I'd feel so proud of myself. It was the one thing I did well." She paused, wiped her eyes, and smiled. Looking down at her lower extremities, she joked, "If I didn't have this killer body and startling beauty, I'd'a been someone."

"How modest."

"I know you think I'm a selfish moron, but suppose you lived in a world where guys bought you things and you didn't mind fucking, and they offered a lot of money to do it, not with any fat-ass john, but with Romeos and Don Juans . . ."

"I'm sorry if . . ."

"All I'm saying is that those years didn't prepare me. They unprepared me."

"Look," Leslie appealed, "can't this awakening occur without the child? A kid will only exacerbate things."

"If I have an abortion, I'll keep being me until I OD. I know how pathetic this sounds, but the very last thing I might be is someone who can teach my baby how not to fuck up, how not to be me." She turned away and stared into open space, trying to hold back a flood welling up inside of her.

Leslie sat there as five minutes turned into ten, and then a half hour had passed. Finally, he conceded that he simply didn't have the guts to walk away, abandon her.

"All right," he said, and feeling that he needed to hold up some minor victory for himself, he added, "This is the stupidest gamble I've ever taken, but I want to see a steady line of progress."

"Obviously," she replied, not caring to be patronized.

"You must find some kind of job."

"I have always intended to." She restrained ending the phrase with the word *asshole*.

"Okay," he said, feeling he had no choice. Leslie grabbed her larger bag and together they headed back to his apartment.

While walking, Sky asked him what he was going to tell his girlfriend about her staying at his place.

"There is no girlfriend," he said dismally, not adding that she had dumped him over six months ago when she discovered pornography of Sky in his possession.

She leaned over and gave him a peck on the cheek. "Thank you, Leslie," she said tiredly, and added, "Would you hate me if I said I love you?"

"Please don't. 'Cause I don't love you. In fact, I want you to find a good boyfriend. Someone who'll be a good provider," he said, as they crossed Columbus Avenue. "And I'm going to tell you something else. Any bullshit and you are out. No drugs. No johns." She looked dead ahead, waiting for his power trip to pass. "I want you to get on your feet and find an apartment of your own—*a life of your own.*"

"I want to be free of all this shit," she responded,

hating herself for being in this situation, "free of everything!"

As Leslie opened the door to his building, Sky thought, Move over, Denver, I've bottomed out. At least with T-Bone I was earning my keep. Now I'm a fucking charity case. She went to bed immediately.

Leslie showered and dressed. Riding the crowded subway to work, he felt panicky and wondered what he had gotten himself into. She could bring in strangers, drug addicts, and criminals. I have a fucking porn actress in my apartment, he thought, as the train sped to Times Square.

APRIL 29, 2001, NYC
WHAT WOULD I HAVE TO LOSE?

What would it hurt if I approached Jeane and spent a day, only one day, with her?

Nothing. I'll be with her, be near her for one last day. Suppose she resisted. Hell, I can force her to be with me for one day. I'm entitled to that much. I took her in when she was knocked up and no one else would. I recently saved Wilbur the homeless man from dying! Money, charm, good looks, I have them all, but if worse comes to worst, I have a persuasive set of steak knives.

Sitting up in my Roman bath, I decide to postpone my imminent departure for yet one more day. Besides, I've drained all the self-pity and tears from this suicide fantasy. Getting up, dripping wet, kneeling before the toilet, I touch the back of my throat with my index finger and press the vomit button. As my regurgitating body contracts in agony, I focus on a nine-word mantra that comes to me from nowhere: *The vacancy of justification sustains the fluidity of desire, the vacancy of justification sustains the fluidity of desire . . .*

I keep vomiting until I can see all the shiny tiny bald heads, still loose in their wet gelatinous capsules, floating in the toilet. I continue regurgitating until my pyloric rubber-band twangs out no more. I take a stiff gulp of vodka and stumble face-forward into bed.

▶

The next day I awake at noon. Strike two: I'm still alive. It has been two days since my fatal photo pas with the bi-racial daughter/model. I make myself a cup of coffee. Absently looking at apartment buildings across the way, I spot a beautiful girl changing her beautiful clothes. I've never seen her before—but it doesn't matter. Instead of training my telescope on her, I go out to my balcony and yell through cupped hands, "PULL DOWN YOUR SHADES!"

She doesn't want to hear.

In the bathroom, I shave off the silly goatee and mustache, though I'm permanently stuck with the alien on my arm. Putting on a brand new Donna Karan shirt and a pressed Armani suit, I'm back in my old aesthetic. I spend some time making myself look like myself again. Dab some fern-scented Pen Halagan under my neck. Floss, brush, and gargle. Then I go to the kitchen and select a small sturdy steak knife which I will use against Jeane when she refuses to spend my final day with me. The sky is spotty. A tidal wave of a cloud bank is rising high on the western sky, ready to explode and drown all Manhattan Island.

I feel the fog of questions and ambiguities lifting as I drive—and I pen my own little opera crescendo:

Farewell fine moments that lit the lively road to death;
To all the alto tenors and great baritones

echoing in the gilded cavern of Lincoln Center.
Goodbye to all the meticulously prepared dinners
at the ritziest dives in town.
Thank you law partners by day
who brought me into my former firm,
And sex partners by night
who brought me into your firmer forms.
Thank you Cecilia for making a libidinous diet of all my per-
verse curiosities and hateful love.

Speeding through Long Island, I just missed her exit. Was it an accident? No, I must be heading to Jeane's workplace. Why? Because I have to grab her as she is going to her car. If I learned anything from the Cecilia accident, it's that my unconscious is a lot smarter than I am. It's just a matter of understanding it. I coast into a space in the hospital parking lot, turn the key, pull up the emergency brake, and wonder if I really have the guts to go through with this.

I am going to walk up behind her, put the knife to her throat, and say, *"Do as I ask and no harm will come to you. I have no intention of raping you. Just walk to my expensive car."*

As I try psyching myself up for the most insane thing I'll ever do, a tap, tap, tapping lifts my eyes. Through my car window, Jeane "Sky" Lindemeyer is looking right at me. Standing there with an expression of sheer delight.

"I can't believe it!" she says as I get out. While holding myself in, she tosses her arms around me.

"Jeane!" I reply, fighting bewilderment and fright.

"God, it's good to see you!" She hugs me so hard I hear my spine popping. I hug back sincerely and contritely until I almost cry.

"Hell, fate owes me a favor!" she exclaims. "The other day some cocksucker tried to rape my daughter!"

"What?" For a moment I don't even know what she's talking about.

"A few days ago some guy claiming to be a fashion photographer approached her. She fought him off."

"You're kidding me!" I'm shocked. She didn't fight.

"It's true. She slapped him and ran! But let's not talk about that." She stares at me, taking inventory of the present against her memory of me from years ago. "What are you doing here?"

"Visiting a friend. I just had a hernia operation and . . ." I flub my lines, but she doesn't notice.

"You know, I knew I'd bump into you one day," she says. "I prayed it would have been sooner."

"You prayed to see me?" Incomprehensible.

"Sure, I tried calling you a few years back." A feeling is growing.

"Oh, I moved about twelve years ago," I reply.

"And you're not listed!" Jeane chides. The feeling is rising and spreading.

"What the heck are you doing here?" I ask.

"I work here. I'm a social worker."

"A social worker!" I lift my eyebrows and smile like a schmuck.

"I got my M.S.W. about twelve years ago. Christ, I . . . I can't believe this. I haven't seen you since when?" Her eyes are still perfectly blue.

"1983, '84. Around there."

"Amazing!" Jeane says, and hugs me again. And me, her, lingering in each other's arms. I can feel her breasts pressed against my chest. My hands slowly move down, feeling her strong shapely thighs. Jeane tucks her face in my neck and kisses me on the throat. I still have a steak knife pointing up in my interior jacket pocket, and fearing that it might stick her, I gently break the embrace.

"So did you marry that girl?" she asks.

"No." I act embarrassed. "Close call, but still unattached."

"Typical Leslie. I got some girlfriends who'd love to meet you."

"What are you up to?" I try to act lawyerly.

"I have an appointment in ten minutes. But once that's done, I'm all yours," she replies. I smile and feel the heat radiate from my face—I'm blushing.

Unable to contain herself, Jeane grabs me yet again and gives me a kiss, smack on my lips. Without having to speculate, I see, almost to my dismay, that I have her—that simple. No stalking, no springing, no hostage-holding, no knife threats or painful compromises. Nothing.

"Come on," I say, walking her to the hospital. Inside the lobby, she leads me to the elevator.

"What floor are you going to?" Jeane says.

"I've got to ask the information desk what room my friend's in."

Jeane smiles and watches as I walk to information, out of earshot. She pushes for the elevator while I dialogue with the elderly volunteer. Jeane's unable to hear that all I'm requesting is different routes back to the city. The elevator doors slide open and she boards.

My entire fantasy was predicated on the belief, the hidden hope, that she was unattainable, that she would never want to have anything to do with me—the creepiest of the creeps, the lowest of the low.

When Jeane vanishes from my peripheral vision, I end my pleasant discussion mid-sentence and go out to my car. Checking the passenger seat, I fold up all maps of Long Island as well the dossier that Ron Marauder had prepared for me, and I lock them in my trunk along with the vest-pocket cutlery. Carefully, I search for any evidence that might reveal my recent surreptitious activities.

Back in the lobby, I take a seat next to an emaciated man and read my *New York Law Journal*.

"You look like a million bucks!" Jeane says, as she collapses next to me.

"I'm worth several times that," I say, showcasing my smile. Fuck modesty.

"Everything's a goddamn mess, Les," she replies, and stares off, not caring to elaborate. I feel my humility turn into humidity as I sweat with concern for her.

"Come on," says I. "Let me show you a good time." We head out to the parking lot where I show off my Jag again.

For that absolute instant that she sees it, I feel myself turn to granite. A Jaguar, after all, is not a common animal in these parts. Her daughter must have described the vehicle to her.

"Look at this car!" Jeane replies excitedly, fixed on my motorized steed.

"I'm starving," I blurt.

"Me too." She bites the bait.

"I know the perfect place," I say, without knowledge of any eateries within a twenty-mile radius. I start the car and zoom down the main street, looking for a decent restaurant.

"This is not something the Leslie I knew would drive," Jeane says under a smirk. "I drive an old Honda that keeps breaking down."

"If you need money, Jeane, I'll lend it to you," I state, knowing that she would never accept it.

"No, my luck was in the front end of my life. This part of life is all work. When I think of the easy cash I made through my loins and snorted up my nose, it makes me sick. Especially now, when I can barely afford to buy my boy a new pair of sneakers." Jeane leans forward, resting the top of her head on my glove compartment.

"A son!" I exclaim on cue. "You went and cooked up a son!"

"Oh yeah, Ed and I went to a fertility clinic where I got this procedure, and now I have a seven-year-old boy." I listen carefully, keeping my eyes on the road.

"And what do you do?" I ask, not sure if she has mentioned that she is a social worker or if I had only read it in the dossier.

"I already told you, I got my M.S.W., then my C.S.W., and I've been working here in Preventive Services. Eddie got a job driving a milk truck . . ."

"So you're still with Eddie?" I interrupt.

"Of course," she says. "We bought a nice house and had Joey, and we were happy."

"Were happy?" Is a divorce brewing?

"Well, Eddie decided to open a fucking video store on one of these strip malls."

"A video store!"

"Yeah, and it has become a money pit." We come to a red. I stop and look at her earnestly.

"It's great that you're still with Ed," I say, to throw off my hidden motive.

"Eddie's wonderful, but fifteen years of marriage and two kids pretty well knocks out the romance." Decoded — no sex.

"Well, I suppose it's a cliché, but you still look sexy as ever."

"Clichés like that I can never get enough of."

I smile at her, not wanting to make it sound like a come-on, but not wanting to sound insincere either. We drive and take in the scenery — trees, lawns, small businesses. South-central Long Island is nicer than eastern New Jersey, but that hardly seems worth saying.

"Actually," she says calmly, "life has been good. I feel like I'm doing important work and the pay is decent. I love the kids, even though Kate can be a little bitch and I think she's smoking."

"Kate! Christ, last time I saw her . . ."

"Oh," she acts tickled, "you've got to come home and meet everyone."

"Love to," I have to say, even though I obviously can't.

"It hasn't been entirely easy, Les. Eddie is sixty-seven and I don't know where he gets the juice."

"I turned forty several years ago and I wonder where I get it," I reply, reminding her of my relative youthfulness.

"So, two days ago Kate is at school and some guy comes up to her. Says he's a photographer. Perry Cruz. Offers her money. I mean, she's no dummy. I told both my kids about what I used to do. I learned that secrets all come out so it's best to bring them out the gentlest way and then have everyone adjust. Anyway, this sleaze-bag claims to be with Calvin Klein."

"How do you know he wasn't with Calvin Klein?" I inquire.

"We called them up. Perry Cruz is a photographer, but he's working in Milan, Italy. This guy was some pedophile imposter. We called the police. But I . . . I was terrified."

"Why?"

"He singled her out!" Jeane says. "He knew that she was *my* daughter. I've had nuts approach me over the years. This cocksucker was trying to get at *me!*"

"Not to be unsympathetic, Jeane, but how do you know?"

"He said it!"

"Said what?"

"He said, 'I know your mother was a porn actress!'" Jeane exclaims. I smile. Although I can't correct her, I see that her bitch daughter is pulling a supreme guilt trip. I took pains to not disrobe Jeane's former occupation. It's just like children to deliberately lie in order to put their parents through hell.

"So you called the police, I hope!"

"Of course, but teenagers, Christ. They can't remember

anything unless it's on TV. The guy was driving a nice car. Did they get the make? Either a BMW or a Ferrari. Did they see a license plate? No. One girl says the guy looked like Nicholas Cage with a mustache, the other girl says he looked like Kevin Spacey with a goatee. What the hell kind of description is that?" Jeane slumps into silence and exhales. I keep driving. "I know this guy wants me. He's not done yet."

"Is there anything I can do?" Jeane shakes her head no. I can see tears swelling in her eyes.

"I mean, if this cocksucker jumped out and raped me, I could deal with that. But stay the fuck away from my kids! They didn't do anything! Leslie, slow down!"

"Sorry." I tend to speed up when I'm described as a child stalker. "So exactly what did this guy do to her?"

"He terrorized her! She thought she was going to be raped!"

"Did he threaten her with rape?" I ask calmly.

"I don't believe you. Typical lawyer. If someone grabbed your daughter . . ."

"Did he grab her?" I ask, speeding through a yellow.

"Yes. Of course!"

Unfortunately, I did grab her. To hide my embarrassment, I do my Matlock impersonation: "See, that would be pertinent in court."

"Well, the police have been notified, but this guy's clever. He had someone at Calvin Klein print up an employee ID for him."

"Amazing," I mutter, as I spot a restaurant called Charlie's Steak & Grille that would never make *Zagats*.

The place has a smart-looking blonde for a maitre d'. With dark brown menus resembling a leather corset strapped around her, all she needs is the feather-tipped Broomhilda helmet. She leads us to the rear. It's not the large tinted bay windows or the candles and polished silverware that make this a classy Long Island establishment, but the absence of vinyl on table clothes, seats, or menus. This is the type of place where mid-level execs bring their Amy Fisher mistresses. Jeane and I follow the tightly vested warrior waitress to our secluded, overly upholstered booth.

"Would you like to order a refresh—"

"A gin and tonic," I blurt.

"Bloody Mary," Jeane joins.

She talks. First, on motherhood: joining the PTA; attending Boy Scout and Girl Scout meetings; vigil-sitting kids through illnesses; Kate getting left back twice; clothes shopping for children; church-going for a couple of years before everyone got bored; dental care; sleeping and eating habits.

Somehow we jump to her career: She has worked her way up over the years from C.S.W. to supervisor to Director of Preventive Services. She describes her work at Mercy Hospital. She's been burnt out for some time but still functions. Welcome to the club, hon. She deals with children of all ages. Doctors and nurses refer cases of mothers who don't seem to bond with their infants. Not providing prenatal care is a form of neglect. Postpartum depression is always a factor. The worst part of her job is detecting child abuse.

"Does this include sexual abuse?" I inquire tactlessly.

"Yes."

"How do you detect it?" I take a sip of my drink.

"A variety of ways. I've seen little girls rubbing themselves on their chairs in places that indicate they were sexually activated before their time." Play therapy is her predominant method.

"What is play therapy?"

She explains that children's games are customarily very repetitive, but within them traumas are acted out symbolically.

"That's how unusual sexual habits are shaped, isn't it?" I put it in the form of a question.

"What kind of unusual habits?" she asks.

"Deviant behavior, fetishes."

"I don't know."

"It is," I assure her. For years I've tried to wrestle with the question of what trauma made me the way I am. But I don't remember anyone touching me. Nor do I remember being particularly neglected. I wasn't held underwater. I don't recall being buried up to my neck in dirt. No relatives sucked me off or fucked me. No daycare workers, priests, building custodians, nor polite middle-aged boarders forced me to eat, or listen to, or smell, or do anything.

"Is it possible," I ask her, "to be fucked up without any reason?"

"How do I know?" she deflects, and takes a big gulp of her drink to push cruel reality a little further away.

"So we act out our traumas through games?" I murmur, envisioning children playing innocently on jungle gyms and feeling sorry for them.

"We probably act out our traumas in everything," she retorts. "I became a social worker as a way of dealing with my own past."

"Have you ever confronted a parent, a father, over abusing his daughter or son?"

"Yes," and she wants to change the subject. I've gone too far. I remember that she was abused as a child, so we're now back to her family's history: She talks about when she moved to Queens in the early eighties and then out to Long Island in 1987. They got a great deal on a house repossessed by H.P.D. several years later. Won a blind bid for the place. Eddie has been renovating it ever since.

Full glasses of liquor are discreetly placed on the table and empty glasses are quickly bussed off. I make a point of sipping my tonics at half the rate of Jeane's gulps. Also, twice when she orders drinks, I only order a glass of water. By the fifth round for her, an hour into her biographical musings, she starts slurring her words.

Eventually, looking at her Mickey Mouse Timex, Jeane says that she has to get going. Dinner has to be made. Laundry has to be washed, folded. While she has left her car at the hospital parking lot, she is in no condition to drive. I offer to drive her home and she accepts. I pay the check and Jeane takes my arm, leaning against me as we walk to the car.

"I can't believe no one snatched you up," Jeane says, as I open the car door for her. I don't tell her about my marriage and Cecilia's accidental death, and the fact that I am now a guilt-crazed widower. I certainly see no reason to explain that this is my last day on earth. Why ruin the mood?

When I get into my side of the car, I inadvertently rub up against Jeane. She takes my hand and holds it for a spiritual moment. I lean over and give her a quick peck. Instantly she kisses me back.

A life of obvious burdens makes her ripe for the picking. For the veneer of a moment, I attempt to control my lechery. But that's where I discover I am nothing. Right below these pants of skin lurks Perry Cruz, matinee villain and sinister predator of Jeane's little darlings. As I realize who, what I am, an erection periscopes. While she tenderly starts kissing my lips, I take the initiative of rubbing my hand up along the soft material of her loose-fitting shirt. Up, my hand whispers, fingering along her button line, spreading out, sculpting those wonderful breasts out of the billowy fabric.

"God," she swoons, "that feels so good."

"I shouldn't be doing this," I say, because it will take the pressure off of her if I'm the one providing the moral constraints.

"No one else has done it for years now," she purrs.

I start unbuttoning her shirt. Three buttons and I'm in. I unsnap the front of her bra. Her packed bosoms sigh as they drop, still veiled under her dark cottony shirt. I can feel the moist heat between her breasts and along her rib cage as I cup her right breast gently in my hand.

"I can't believe we're doing this," Jeane says, slightly mischievous.

"Shut up and kiss me," I instruct, and thumb her singed-brown, perfectly cylindrical nipple.

"Oh, please, I, I can't," says Jeane. I kiss her hard on the lips. Her mouth goes flush. Tasting the vodka on her darting tongue, I open my eyes a bit to see that hers are closed. She begins experiencing the slight respiratory irregularity that comes with passion. But the car is too cramped. Without another word, I start the engine, flip on the a.c., and speed the half-mile to an old, weathered dive called the Park Boulevard Inn.

JULY 25, 1981, NYC

BY THE TIME LESLIE GOT TO HIS OFFICE, HE FELT SO anxious that he closed his door, something he never remembered having done before, and telephoned Cecilia.

"What?" he heard her say groggily.

"I'm sorry for calling you," he began, "but she's back."

"Who? Who the hell is this?"

"It's me, Les."

"You! Quit sending me flowers and shit!" Cecilia shot back.

"Okay, but Sky is back," Leslie said, as if that changed something. "She came to my house at six this morning and she's . . ." Leslie couldn't bring himself to tell her that Sky was pregnant. "I don't know what to do."

"Who's back?!" Cecilia asked, obviously still asleep.

"Sky Pacifica! Remember—the porn actress?" Leslie bit his inner lip, aware that he was talking too loudly.

"The one I saw in the magazines?"

"Yeah," Leslie replied in a low, reluctant tone. He wanted to explain that she didn't look nearly that pretty in real life, certainly not anymore.

"What the fuck do you want me to do about it? Why are you calling me?"

A shrill female voice broke through the background: "Hang up the fucking phone!"

"Relax," he heard Cecilia console the other woman.

"Just hang up!" Her companion was definitely a she.

"Leslie, I'll call you later." Click. Looking through the glass partition, he saw Donna, a large-haired secretary from Sheepshead Bay, munching down potato chips, annoying him.

To keep his anxieties in check, Leslie kept busy all day. It was his first big restructuring case—the Sewter Company. He had to spend the day working with a partner and the head of the shareholder's committee. By that afternoon, Leslie was fully informed of the details of the restructuring proposal that had to be drawn up. Upon returning from a brief meeting with a debtor's committee, he received a message that his ex, Cecilia, had called back.

Returning the call, he received a stern warning: "Never call me in the morning. I can't get Gina out until noon."

"Gina?" he snapped. "So are we a lesbian now?"

"Fuck you!"

"I was just asking," he responded, disowning his former indignation.

"Well don't." She sounded irreversibly pissed.

"I have a porn actress in my house," Leslie flatly relayed his crisis.

"Call the police. Show them your lease and have her physically removed. Next problem?"

"I don't have the strength to put her out on the street." Leslie paused. "Look, I don't know if I ever properly apologized about the entire porn fiasco . . ."

"It wasn't the porn," she replied. "Although I admit it was disconcerting to see every angle of the same naked woman, it was you. You changed the way you made love, and that's okay, but for the first time I knew why."

"Before I disagree with you, let me understand this," Leslie clarified. "You're saying I was making love for the wrong reason?"

"Absolutely," she confirmed. "If you're having sex with me—not to mention all the other stuff—while thinking about her, there's an infidelity going on, isn't there?"

"First of all, guys and probably girls do that all the time." Cecilia issued a retorting snort, which Leslie ignored. "And secondly, I wasn't doing that. I have no interest whatsoever in this woman."

"Then why is she living with you?"

"Honestly, it's 'cause I feel guilty," he declared. "I feel responsible in some way."

"For Christ's sake, she was just someone you jerked off to in a magazine, and then you fucked a couple times." Cece was making him feel guilty about feeling guilty.

"It was much more than that," he argued.

"What more?"

"I don't want to go into it," he lowered his voice.

"I want to know," she maintained, now irritated that he was holding back.

"It's very embarrassing." He hoped she'd break off.

"Listen, Leslie, I have to tell you that it always troubled me that you went all the way out to LA and located this . . . this person. I've been utterly perplexed by what could have motivated you to do such an extremely uncharacteristic thing. I mean, I deal with men every day. What compels these, these . . . things?"

"You know, you're such a crock," he accused, no longer concealing his anger.

"What?"

"You're using your slaves to please yourself."

"Look, all I am is someone *they* use to purge themselves of their own fantasies."

"So why can't I have my fantasies?" he appealed.

"Oh, please . . . How many sexual fantasies are there?"

"They're not even sexual."

"Not sexual? Then what are they?"

"Please, let's not . . ."

"I want to know what they are."

"Okay." He decided to try candor: "But if you are going to make me feel embarrassed about this . . ."

"I'll only listen."

"Well, it's not so much role-playing." Leslie muted his tone as he looked out the window. He glimpsed down at the Times Square zipper and a billboard of a giant underwear model across the way. "It's more like role-creation. I worked up an identity for her. I gave her mannerisms. Nuances, subtleties. I would spend hours thinking of details to fit her with, qualities that

I would take from people I met, from women I saw. I filled her with characteristics that no one could ever live up to."

"Like what?" Cecilia's tone was slightly impatient.

"I made her ambitious, strong, clever. Someone I could idolize and worship. I put a lot of creativity into it," he said. For the first time, he realized the full extent of his work.

"So these fantasies—tell me more about them. I mean, you made her into a superwoman? She'd rescue cats from trees, or what?"

Leslie paused a moment and realized that Cecilia was actually jealous. Although he didn't want to go any further, he loved hearing her so captivated by him.

"Usually . . ." He cleared his throat and spoke even more quietly. "Usually they were little things."

"Like she'd laugh at your jokes or clean the house?" she persisted.

"Not at all. In fact, she'd usually be unattached to anyone. And she'd betray no emotions."

"What the hell would she be doing?"

He cleared his throat a second time. "I don't know. She might be able to play a musical instrument, or do some athletic feat, or write a great novel . . . Even then, it would be very slight, modest aspects of greatness, like I'd imagine seeing her night after night across a courtyard, sitting until the early morning, hearing the keys of her manual typewriter tapping away while others slept. Concentrating on her work, blocking the entire world out, and I'd dream that maybe I could be the one to wipe the sweat from her brow . . . something little like that."

Cecilia wished that he, or anyone, had ever felt that way about her, idolizing her quietly and simply. With a slight tremble in her voice, she asked, "How does something like this happen?"

"I really don't know," he said absently.

"How did you choose her? Why do you feel this way?"

"I don't know. I guess it grew out of the visual. If I knew, I would have prevented it. It's one of the most embarrassing, ridiculous, insane things that ever happened to me, and now I have to see it through."

"I don't understand why you can't simply dump her."

"It's like falling head over heels with some TV character, but here I got this drunken, has-been actress, the real person, and because she created the role, I feel I owe her."

"It sounds like such a load of shit, and it's such a fucking shame too, 'cause you're the only guy I think I might have ever . . ." Cecilia's voice faded, and then resumed, formal and anew, "I really don't think I can speak to you ever again."

He heard the phone click and thought that in his desire to grow close to her he had screwed things up for good.

"FUCK!" He slammed his fist on the top of his desk and turned away from the outer office, aware that someone must have heard him.

▶

When Leslie arrived home that evening, he immediately felt restricted by Sky's presence. She was his cellmate, and the length of the sentence was unknown. Sky consciously made every effort that first night to be quiet, but it only made him more aware of her.

Lying in bed, Leslie determined that although the pregnancy was going to be difficult, child-rearing was going to be unbearably nerve-wracking. He silently considered moving into a larger apartment, one that could comfortably house him, Sky, and the kid. Ever since his last raise, he had been intending to find a nicer place, somewhere he could bring dates without feeling embarrassed. The next day, though, when he opened the *Daily News* and considered some of the available apartments on the Upper West Side, he was shocked at the dramatic price hikes of rentals. In a few short years—between 1976 and 1981—the cost had jumped substantially.

That Sunday, Leslie tossed out years of accumulation: rotting books, stored legal files, old clothing. Sky helped him carry out several bulky pieces of furniture, which they abandoned on the corner.

At the local grocery store later that week, Leslie saw a flier taped to the wall advertising an independent contractor. "Free estimates" was bannered along the top. Leslie called the number and made an appointment. A lanky fellow with unruly hair came by the following evening.

"I want a wall going through the room and a door here." The carpenter took measurements, drew up a thumbnail sketch, made some calculations, and in a matter of minutes, produced a bid.

"When will it be done?" Leslie asked.

The guy said he could start the next day and would be finished in three days. Leslie gave him half of the amount and a copy of the door keys.

After a week and a half of sporadic construction, littering the apartment with wood shavings, drywall screws, and sawdust, the wall was up. Sky and Leslie went out and purchased a new bed and a small desk for her little room.

Subsequently, she had to walk through his room when she entered the apartment, and he passed through her room to use the bathroom and kitchen.

Soon, Sky took a waitressing job in a restaurant called Fire Sticks. A cute Argentine waiter named Marcos developed an instant crush on her. With his beautiful Aztec cheekbones and a thick wave of shiny black hair braided in the back, Sky thought he was irresistible. In no time at all, she found herself making out with him in the stock room, getting felt up in the walk-in fridge. When he asked for her phone number, she gave it to him. But since she couldn't afford another phone line, she explained that she lived with her older brother Leslie, who was very Catholic. Marcos assured her that he'd be respectful when he called.

Within a week, Sky was wondering if she should tell Marcos about her shady past. But she knew without any doubt that he would never be able to handle it. What the hell, she thought, everyone has a few skeletons in the closet. It would only be a matter of time before her pregnant belly would betray her. They started seeing each other almost every evening after work. Leslie was happy to get calls for Jeane, and he hoped against hope that if all went well maybe this guy would snatch her away before she dropped the kid.

At the end of the second week, after a romantic evening out together, Marcos tried to get Jeane drunk. Conscious of her pregnancy, she said that she was allergic to alcohol. Marcos kissed her, but as much as he tried to move things further, she refused to take off her clothes, afraid sex could jeopardize her pregnancy. She explained that she was an old-fashioned girl.

"Why are you so shy, my lark?" he asked, staring deep into her eyes.

"I was raised by nuns," she replied, delighted with this fantasy.

"Are you a . . . virgin?" he said, with such tenderness she felt dreamy. Almost imperceptibly, she nodded yes. He kissed her and told her that he loved her all the more. That someone so beautiful and sensuous could still be virtuous was a miracle to him. She instantly wished that she hadn't lied, because now it was going to hurt that much more when it was time to part. She was careful not to mention any of this to Leslie, fearful that it might confirm his suspicion that she was deceitful.

For a while, she felt as though she had captured something she had always missed out on, the gallantry and sensitivity of a courting gentleman. Over the next few weeks, he wooed her, babied her, brought her aromatic flowers and little gifts. She loved being perceived as innocent, and dressed simply for the new role. To assuage his urges over the ensuing weeks, she would put up a false protest and finally capitulate, giving him a handjob and later a blowjob. Soon he was winning these little battles about once a week. She was careful to hide the fact that she enjoyed handling him. His uncircumcised penis had an unusual corkscrew form that she thought of as an exotic piece of fruit from his native land. When he ejaculated, he would throw his head back, contorting his face like a demon on fire, and release a symphony of muffled screams and muted cries.

About a month into the courtship, a young college kid who was friends with one of the other waiters visited the restaurant. "Holy shit," he muttered. "That's Sky Pacifica!"

"You know her?" the waiter asked.

He explained who she was.

"No way," the waiter replied, and repeated what Marcos had said, "she's a virgin."

"Ha! Go to a porn place. Check it out."

When the waiter confirmed this, he told another waiter and soon the rumor spread until everyone except Marcos knew about her past. One of the waiters purchased a sex magazine with Sky, and the entire staff saw endless photos of her doing the unimaginable.

One afternoon, when some of the guys were snickering at Marcos behind his back, a cook took his friend aside after work and broke the news to him as gingerly as possible.

"Your girlfriend is a sexual . . . performer."

"What are you saying?" Marcos grew livid and insisted that this was a sadistic lie. The cook quietly handed him the magazine. Marcos looked through the pictures with mouth agape, throat constricted, tears in his eyes.

Sky was in the middle of her waitressing shift when Marcos raced up to her and yanked her by the arm, causing her to drop a tray.

"You are a fucking *puta!*" he screamed, waving the magazine at her. "A dirty whore!" Marcos displayed the pictures to all, waiters and patrons alike.

"I'm sorry," she said, as the manager tried to calm him down. He continued screaming, and Sky retreated into the office downstairs.

After Marcos left, Sky wrote a brief note:

Marcos,
I'm sorry for hurting you. Yes, I did some crazy things when I was younger and didn't know better.

I'm really sorry these things hurt you. I know I should have told you about it immediately but I was kind of ashamed and didn't think you'd like me no more. There's nothing else to say except I really enjoyed hanging out with you and I'm real sorry I hurt you. I was hoping to tell you someday in my own way. Anyways, try to forgive me if you can.

Thanks and sorry,
Jeane

P.S. You made me feel like a real lady.

Sky handed the note to the manager, a grouchy older man who had observed the entire incident.

"Could you give that to Marcos?" Sky said tiredly. "It was all my fault."

The manager told her not to worry. Uncharacteristically, he said that Jeane was a fine waitress and gave her the balance of her earnings with a bonus.

"If you ever need a recommendation, call me," he concluded.

Initially, she felt guilty about the incident. Within three weeks, though, when she started putting on serious weight, she figured her relationship with Marcos would have come to an end anyway. In September, Leslie helped her locate an Ob/Gyn. The doctor performed a sonogram in October and told her she was carrying a little girl.

APRIL 30, 2001, LI
THE OUTLYING WINGS OF THE DILAPIDATED MOTEL ARE

bordered by a splintery balcony. I park toward the far right end of the wooden structure and flip off my car lights. This flophouse is an insurance company's nightmare. A small spark and the entire place is in embers.

Still combating the five Bloody Marys she had downed at Charlie's Steak & Grille, Jeane starts, "I don't have time . . ."

"No one does," I battle.

"It costs too much."

"I make enough," I mollify.

"Les," she leans forward, "I'm married!"

"Just stay in the car." I go into the central shack. Ma and Pa Kettle are camped in front of a TV set that has no off button. She looks like an ashtray; he resembles a liquor bottle. With minimal words—one day, no luggage—lest they offend their antennaed god, we do the keys-for-cash exchange. I sign the registry: Jethro Bodine. Maybe they'll read it during an infomercial. One struggles to remember what mankind did before TV. Back to the Jag.

"Come on," I say, opening the car door. I hold Jeane in my arm and escort her to the room. She doesn't have a clue. Her head flops against my shoulder. I unlock the door and flip on a light. There is a telephone on the end table and an old TV against a wall. With the necessary furniture, clean walls, and no unbearably bad odors, the room is serviceable. Jeane turns on a lamp, I turn off the overhead. I sit on the old queen-sized bed with her, gauging its springiness. After kicking off our shoes, we're back to square one.

Slowly, while we kiss, I curl up in the director's chair of my fantasy: In the prior scene, Perry Cruz had extorted this virtuous wife and good mother with nude photos of her daughter. Perry needs to believe that she is doing this not because she wants to, but because she has to. It is not so much that I want to believe I am forcing her, but to attain turgidity, I need to believe that my will is inexorable—I have to be a fiend with single-mindedness of purpose, and she has to be one of the unsuspecting innocent. Otherwise, my erection engines will stall and I'll start to lose altitude.

Action: As I grind my crotch into hers, I remember her character: She is married, a mother of two, a career woman. Her motivation: She is offering me her body in place of her daughter's innocence. I kiss and rub her, and slowly stroke her thighs down to her midsection and stomach. Inevitably my fingers prowl along the outer area of her moistened panties.

Soon I push aside the thin fabric and I am fingering her tenderly, stroking along her pubic mound. She is moaning and opening her legs wider. Looking at her closed eyes and panting little mouth, I can see she's having her own fantasy. Probably *Bridges of Madison County* crap. With most women, sensations are emotions; a touch means they like you, a fuck—total vulnerability—is love.

Without taking off my pants, I unzip and rub my hooded bob against her blossomed rose, spreading open her mois-ture, flicking myself along her bulged clitoris. It's as though a dam has broken. She's wet all over. With my pants still on, I enter her gradually. She lets out a back-of-the-throatism that resembles a soul fluttering.

"Should we really do . . . this?" I ask remorsefully. She doesn't respond; I ask again.

"Yes! I need it, but . . . but I feel so guilty."

I pull out punitively.

"No! Fuck me! Please!" It's better than any of her old films. Working it back in, I lap up her bouquet of facial expressions, perfect silent tulip lips surrounded by dainty baby's breath of exquisite winces, articulate floral gasps. On to the next fabulous sphincter of hell: "Have you cheated on Eddie before?"

"I'd rather not talk," she mouths more than mutters.

"I need to know," I demand, as I stridently drive my thickness into her. She reaches around, grabbing the cheeks of my pants-sheathed ass, and moans, "Yes!"

"Yes what?" the interrogation commences.

"Yes, I cheated!" Her closed eyelids are like the mouths of tight little fish, and again I have to catch my breath.

"More than once?" I begin again.

Yes, her mouth forms, but only a bubble appears.

"How many times?" I toy.

"A couple, for goodness sakes," she replies. Now she is trying to turn her head, trying to hide her abominable shame in the contours of an old pillow.

"Were they good?"

"Yes, yes," Jeane pants. I give absolution by worming my forked tongue into her creamy, silky mouth, but she won't have it. As I'm slamming myself against her cervix like a wrecking ball, she squeezes her legs, pushing me back, retaining a modicum of control. I flip her over on her stomach, yank her knees out from under her, and plug the tip of my cork back into her. Her right hand slips slowly downward. Her surreptitious index finger strums her string as I continue to bang away. When she is close to eruption, I pull her plucking fingers from her nub and say, "Now, did I say you could do that?"

"Please!" She desperately tries to touch her fuse box.

"Who fucked you?" I push.

"Nobody!" she shoots back.

"Where'd you meet him? At work?" It's confession time.

She shoves me backward and spins around, angrily looking at me. "What the fuck's the matter with you?"

For an instant I am powerless. "I'm sorry, I guess I lost myself a little."

"I guess you did," she replies. Then she lays down again.

After a pause, I reenter and resume gradually, building up to our former pace.

"Fuck me!" She orgasms as she screams insanely through walls not much thicker than cardboard. "Fuck me! Goddamn it!"

Perry Cruz loves the yearning pitch of her voice. Since he can't mind-fuck anymore, he hopes someone hears.

I pull out and squeeze several solid streaks of Elmer's glue on those perfect ten-gallon orbs of her butt cheeks. Jeane slips forward hyperventilating, super-extended. Within moments, she is snoring, fast asleep.

With the tip of my index finger, I rub the stripes of semen along the purple-brown crack of her glistening butthole and the soft maroon tissue below her vagina, into her jet-black pubic hair—that's for you, Eddie boy.

And I did the entire scene without ever having to remove my trousers. I take a couple steps toward the tiny bathroom, but stop a moment. I stare at the chimerical scene; I would give ten grand to have my Camcorder with me. Biting my lip, I try to magnetize the image into the videotape of my memory. Looking around the room for a pencil, I consider sketching the vignette, this skyscraper of euphoria, this Mount Everest of erotica, which I plan revisiting time and again. There is a fresh pack of motel matches in an ashtray. I slip the matchbook into my jacket pocket and enter the bathroom.

Time to clean up the crime scene and dispose of the body. I wash myself, then dip one of the rough motel towels into hot water, squeeze it dry, and go back to the bed where Jeane is still lying on her belly, exhausted and intoxicated. I gently clean the semen and other DNA evidence off of the victim's beautiful back, only to realize that she's softly whimpering, delicately crying.

"Are you okay, hon?" I whisper. She curls into a ball and falls asleep in my lap.

PART FOUR: STOP

OCTOBER 7, 1981, NYC

SKY FELT LIKE HER BODY WAS BEING INHABITED and no longer belonged to her. Everything about her seemed to be changing. She was losing her hair. Her fingernails felt weird. Of course, the biggest problem was her expanding belly. She wondered if she'd ever look normal or attractive again.

Just after her first trimester, early one morning, Sky had slipped on the ice outside of Leslie's apartment. She didn't fall, but she panicked, and resolved to sit out the remainder of her pregnancy. Through the half-inch plasterboard wall, Leslie would hear Sky stirring in her bed. She'd usually be watching the small black-and-white TV she had bought or reading a romance novel, careful not to be overly physical, terrified of accidentally miscarrying her one chance at motherhood. Leslie would routinely call her from work in the late afternoon and ask if he could pick up anything for her at the store. When he came home at night, she would be waiting for him. Initially, she tried to keep tabs on the money he spent on her. He'd explain that this wasn't necessary, and eventually she stopped.

Over the weeks and months, she was amazed by his discipline. Despite how late he'd come in or how poorly he'd sleep, by 8:30 each morning he'd be up—scrubbed, dressed, and out the door. His conduct, which she had once found overbearing and condescending, took on a new value. Now, Leslie was magically responsible, incredibly poised, and wonderfully cautious. He was marvelously in control—imperative qualities for raising a child and building a career. Although Leslie began to regard his own professional life as form at the expense of any real content, a dull ache that had to be suffered stoically, she regarded him as a model for how to conduct her new life.

She felt herself drawing strength from him. Never panicky or sad or dependent on any dangerous vices. Always clean, calm, and reassuring; he was simply perfect. In a million little ways, she mimicked his behavior and set her clock to him. She'd eventually pull herself out of bed when she heard him close the front door. Soon, for the first time, she was flossing her teeth, and without even thinking about it, she'd made a habit of never leaving an uncleaned dish or utensil in the sink. In difficult situations she'd find herself wondering what Leslie would do.

She started becoming aware of it at night in her little room. While lying in bed she'd touch the adjoining wall, thinking that maybe she'd feel his body heat from the other side. For the first time in her life, not ever intending it, Sky felt she was actually beginning to fall in love. Although she was sincere in her promise to become autonomous and move out, she caught herself staring at him while he was reading or doing legal work. Secretly, she fantasized that Leslie might love her back, that he might marry her, adopt her child, perhaps even have other children with her.

Leslie sensed her increased affections in the endless household chores and little tasks she performed, which initially included attempts at making him difficult dinners from old cookbooks. In the evening, she was willing to rub his back. He always made a point of politely rejecting her offers.

APRIL 30, 2001, LI

HOW DID HUMILIATION EVER BECOME EROTIC? THE WHOLE scene, so charged and frothy, miraculously drains of passion and refills with self-loathing. When I was younger, all my fantasies were tender and loving. When I hear Jeane softly snoring, I whisper, "I was the one who terrorized your daughter. I didn't mean to hurt her or scare her or even involve her in any of this. Things got out of hand and . . . for some reason, pain, giving or getting it, is the only way I can . . . feel. Forgive me."

I check my watch. Ten o'clock is fast approaching. Not wanting her to get in trouble with hubby, I awaken her with caresses.

"Sweetheart," I whisper, "it's time to get up."

Jeane silently rises and lumbers into the bathroom. I listen to the water running for about ten minutes. When Jeane comes out, she silently starts dressing.

"Everything okay?"

"Well, you know," she says, as she puts her face on, "I don't like cheating."

"If your husband isn't satisfying your needs . . ."

"I don't need excuses," she replies, not angrily.

"Can we get together again?" I ask.

"I have to think about it," she says, buttoning her blouse. In a moment she is ready to go. A five-dollar tip for the immigrant maid, and I leave the room key in the door.

Together we sprint through the pattering rain. In the car, we speed out to the highway, toward her home, unaware that I am about to make a fatal mistake of showing that I know where she lives. Fortunately, she mutters, "Take me back to my car."

Jeane lowers her window and the slight spritzing of rain awakens her. I look over and watch her. She's silent-eyed, peering off. She seems to be assessing the damage our motel infidelity has had on her marriage contract.

"Jeane." I pause. "Years ago when we were young, I found the idea of a porn actress too much."

"God," she mutters, "I never thought it would be such a big thing."

I chuckle at the remark. "What do you mean?"

"I don't know." She struggles to explain: "When I was a girl, my mother was usually nowhere around. I used to take care of my grandma."

"I remember."

"The only guy who would visit was Todd, this really sweet, funny guy who would stop by and ask if we needed anything at the store. Stuff like that. He was so nice. He'd buy me candy and clothes and . . ."

"Was he the first guy you ever had sex with?"

"I suppose so. It happened so slowly and he was being so sweet and tender, it didn't even occur to me that he wanted sex. He kept saying, 'If you don't want to do this, you don't have to.' I couldn't figure out why he was saying it 'cause it all felt so good. Rubbing my back and stuff. I was lonely as hell. It didn't occur to me that everything led to something else."

"Like where?"

"Well, that tenderness led to sex. And then one day after we had been doing it for a while, he asked if he could take some photos, and he pulled out an eight-millimeter camera."

"How old was he?"

"Not old, nineteen or so."

"And how about you?"

"It was right after puberty, I couldn't have been older than fourteen at the time. Hell, the whole thing was a big joke. I only remember how good it felt. I didn't orgasm or anything, but I remember feeling this incredible power in making him cum. And I liked him. He was really sweet and generous. After several years, we ended up going out to LA. He said he knew someone who knew someone, and that, of course, turned out to be Fillip.

"We did a bunch of shorts and I remember when Fillip took me aside one afternoon and told me that Todd was exploiting me and making all this money off of me."

"So he turned you against him?"

"Yeah, but Fillip wasn't lying. The guy really was taking a ninety-percent cut, so I dumped him and worked directly for Fillip, but I could never handle money, I'd blow through it in a few days. There I was, having sex and making great money, and soon I was doing it all the time. What I didn't know was that these films would take on a life of their own and become this *thing.* I mean, Eddie got ahold of this film of me a couple years back and I'll tell you right now, it reminded me of the fact that most of the time I was so tired or hopped up, I didn't feel anything."

"What was the worst part of it?"

"Aside from the occasional creeps, probably the bright lights." She smiles. "In the summer, I felt like a fucking chicken roasting on a rotisserie under those beams."

"So you're saying you really didn't enjoy it?"

"Well, I mean, what kid wouldn't enjoy it? I was addicted to it. The whole lifestyle. I was a teenage sexpot partying, fucking, coking my head off. God, I was a kid in a candy shop." Then, flashing her eyes, she seems to catch herself, embarrassed, and caps off the subject. "Ever see that movie *Lost Horizon?* Remember when the gorgeous young girl leaves the enchanted land and suddenly ages into this old hag? It was kind of like that—the prostitution, the drugs, all the trauma I had to get over." She takes a deep breath to move on and says, "I really enjoyed being with you tonight."

"You don't have to say that."

"I'm not just saying that. I don't know if you know how much you meant to me." She smiles and adds, "You were the one that helped me through all that."

We sit in silence, taking in the Long Island darkness, and I can't help thinking how I used to get off on the idea that she was getting off.

When I reach the hospital the rain subsides. I drive perpendicular to her parked car, one of the few vehicles left in the lot.

"Here's my home number." She looks at it pensively. "I want to be with you, so it's going to be up to you."

Jeane takes the card, and without kissing me or even saying goodbye, she steps out of my $80,000 sports luxury and into her $200 jalopy. I wait for her to start off before I begin the long, lonely drive back to the city.

NOVEMBER 21, 1981, NYC

AS SKY'S FETUS GREW, SO DID LESLIE'S OWN HOPES of being free and happy. Over recent months, his definition of happiness moved from simply having his place to himself to meeting and having sex with a large carousel of beautiful, playful college girls. He decided that the only reason this and other wonderful things weren't happening was because a pregnant porn actress was encamped in his living room.

Eventually, his fantasies weren't merely about college girls, but also about an exit strategy for Jeane. If she pulled herself together, evened out the edges of her life, and found some sweet, not-too-bright construction worker–type from Bensonhurst—someone who enjoyed partying and wasn't too sleazy, therefore wasn't aware of Jeane's shady past, someone who didn't mind a stray child from a previous marriage—that man would be Leslie's ticket to freedom.

He envisioned this bachelor for Jeane clearly: He was living in the basement apartment of his parents' brick-face house, under the gaze of the Verrazano Bridge, getting up late on a Saturday, shaving in his tank top, smacking himself with Old Spice, before dashing out for a quick game of handball or pool with the boys and returning home for Mama's lunchtime bowl of pasta.

Leslie would look out his window searchingly and know that Mr. Right, the man of his dreams, was out there somewhere.

JULY 27, 1981, NYC
"HAVE YOU EVER HEARD OF DRINKING IN MODERA-tion?" Cecilia yelled above the jukebox, while sitting at the Duchess, Gina's favorite dyke bar.

"Have you ever heard of telling your faggot ex-boyfriend not to call in the middle of my fucking sleep?"

"I told him not to do it again," Cecilia countered, watching as Gina popped back her third Bushmills and chased it down with a Bud.

After routinely seeing Gina get thoroughly wasted, she knew this was not going to last. Cecilia tried to rea-son herself out of the relationship, but when Gina was sober, she was so sweet, so attentive, so giving, and so beautiful. The orgasms with Gina gave her out-of-body ecstacy like no others.

"Don't you have a session tomorrow?" Cecilia asked, checking her watch before Gina could order another whiskey.

"I'll cancel," she replied, and in a tickled, intoxicated tone added, "That's what's wonderful about slaves— the crappier you treat them, the more they love you."

Cecilia was about to dispute her, but didn't want to get into two fights in a single night. Instead, she thought, What the hell am I doing dating another dominatrix?

FEBRUARY, 14, 1982, NYC

EARLY IN THE AFTERNOON, WHILE LESLIE WAS IN conference at work, Jeane called to tell him that she had felt her first contractions. She left a message that she was grabbing a cab to the hospital.

By the time he arrived at Doctor's Hospital, he was informed that Jeane was already in delivery.

"Can I go in?" he asked.

"Are you her husband?" the nurse inquired.

"Breathing coach," he lied.

"Well, you're a little late. She's already in there with the doctor." He was given a smock and a mask, which he quickly changed into, then raced to the birthing room in time to see the most astounding event he had ever witnessed: the baby's head pushing out of Jeane. To a background of screams, the nimble shoulders, body, legs, all came shooting out along with endless fluids. Leslie looked on in awe as the shapeless bright piece of life wailed at the top of its little lungs. It was like watching a pink octopus being blasted out of a cannon. The infant was sponged and her umbilical cord was snipped. Then she was bathed, wrapped, and handed to her mother. Leslie stood numb until a nurse led him over to Jeane.

"How do you feel, hon?" he mumbled, exhausted, slowly returning to the moment.

"Now that it's over, fine," she responded, trying to catch her breath, covered in sweat. There were tears in her eyes as she stared at her baby.

"You have a gorgeous girl," he said, staring at the infant.

"We both do," she replied. A nurse congratulated them, mistaking him for the father.

She began to weep. Soon, he too was crying. He pulled himself together and gave her a big, proud smile. Noticing the olive complexion of her baby's tiny fingers, Leslie asked, "Is the father Italian?"

"No," Jeane replied calmly, "T-Bird's black."

"T-Bird?" Leslie lowered his head so that only Jeane could hear him. "I thought you said he was a cocaine dealer."

"Coke is white. The dealers can be any color," Jeane said earnestly, too tired to be sarcastic. She then began yawning. The nurse explained that Jeane needed to rest. Leslie kissed her on the cheek and left.

Although he never regarded himself as a racist, he knew a brown baby would complicate his plans to be free of her: Would Jeane's future husband, the gentle, ethnic construction worker with the calloused hands, understand and accept this? I guess he won't be from Bensonhurst, Leslie thought.

He hired a maid before bringing Jeane and the baby home. Within two weeks, however, she had fully regained her strength and dismissed the young woman, ready for the full brunt of motherhood. Leslie didn't try to change her mind. In the beginning, he was ready to comfort her should she discover to her misfortune that being a mother was too difficult. That way, at least he might be able to convince her to put the baby up for adoption—for the little girl's sake. He anticipated how he would console her lovingly, but it would be best for everyone involved. Then he could focus on her rehabilitation and his independence.

After the first month, though, he had to admit that he had never seen her take command of something so naturally, so fully. Purpose filled her when she was with Kate. She seemed to be continuously touching the little girl, stroking and kissing her, refusing to be apart from her for even a moment.

Leslie adjusted to all the alterations in his house. He quickly came to tolerate the endless flow of heated bottles that monopolized the kitchen and the mounds of disposable diapers that on unseasonably warm days gave the place a poignant fragrance. He learned to slip back into sleep when the little screamer awoke him again and again throughout the night. Inescapably, he was conforming to his unwanted family.

Late one lazy weekend afternoon, about three months after the birth, Leslie was dozing when he became aware that Jeane was rubbing his back, delicately grazing her fingertips over his skin.

"Les," she asked barely above a whisper, "I know this is unusual, but . . . can we do it?"

"Do it?" he replied, knowing full well what she meant.

"Me so horny," she said in a mock Chinese accent.

"Me so tired," he responded.

"Come on, you owe me a mercy fuck," she half-kidded.

"Jeane, please."

"Believe me, it's nothing personal. From time to time a woman needs this."

"It's biological?" Leslie asked, unsure if he was being bamboozled.

"Right up there with birds flying south and squirrels collecting nuts."

"Maybe if the squirrels didn't collect the nuts, the birds wouldn't have to fly south," he retorted.

She pulled open the sheet and got in, and without much fondling or kissing, they quickly linked and bumped. She exhibited some old tricks of the trade, and sensing when he was about to cum, she slowed him down. When he started going limp, she gently fondled and sucked him back to fullness. Her large, firm, lactating breasts were a special treat. A couple of times, while Jeane repeatedly climaxed, he closed his eyes and thought of Cecilia. When he ejaculated, she kissed him so hard on the lips that he thought she had bent his front teeth. Jeane hugged and held him and no one else. She never wanted to hold another man again. They drifted off to sleep clinging to each other. Within half an hour, though, Katie started crying. Jeane slipped back into her own room.

■

On weekend mornings, during warm days when he didn't have to go in to work, Leslie would occasionally grab coffee and accompany his roommates to the playground in Central Park, right off West Eighty-first Street.

One time when they entered the park, a hot dog vendor said hello to Jeane. She smiled and returned the greeting.

Jeane, Leslie, and Katie sat on one of the long green benches and Leslie inspected the food handler. He was a rugged man with broad shoulders and short hair. His face was an energetic brown, the color of his frankfurters, with fatherly good looks. Leslie watched him while he forked a steaming frank into a napkin-encircled bun, then lined it with a yellow stripe of mustard.

"You really think you should be encouraging guys like that?" Leslie said prudishly.

"Encouraging?" She smiled.

"Saying hi to strange men is encouraging, yeah."

"Who's strange? Eddie?" Jeane replied.

"You know his name?" Leslie yodeled in disbelief. "That guy's probably whacked off to you in filthy porn theaters."

"What does that make you?" Jeane said, silencing Leslie immediately.

After a few minutes of cleaning off Kate and then taking her out of her stroller, Jeane explained, "About two weeks ago, I was taking Kate to the park and this guy started following me . . ."

"This guy?" Leslie said, pointing to the vendor as if he were about to thrash the man.

"No, some stranger."

"You didn't tell me about this!"

"Actually, I did." She lifted her eyebrows. "You weren't listening."

"What happened?"

"This guy started following behind me when I was walking Kate. He said, 'I know you, you're Sky Pacifica.' Then he started going through the list of every actress and actor he had seen me make it with."

"What the fuck were you doing when all this happened?" Leslie asked her angrily.

"What do you think? I was with Kate, trying to get away from him, yelling at him to fuck off! There are never any cops in this city unless you're double-parked! I tried to get away from him, but he wouldn't leave me alone."

Leslie could see that Jeane was distressed just remembering the incident.

"Anyway, the asshole followed me in here. In front of all these mothers who I've gotten to know over the last few months," Jeane's voice dropped to a brittle whisper and began cracking, "he starts saying how I'm a porn star and for a few bucks I would take it up the ass. Shit like that . . ."

"I'm so sorry, Jeane," Leslie said solemnly.

"I cursed right back at the fucker. Then I tried to get someone to help me. Everyone walked away. Kate was crying. I asked the guy to leave me alone." Leslie could see tears in her eyes as she muttered, "He told me that if I said something, he would leave."

"What?" Leslie asked, feeling his insides fill with anger.

"If I said it aloud so that everyone would hear—"

"If you said *what?!*" he shouted.

"If I said that . . . that Don Jerome fucked my ass while Sally Springfield ate my pussy. If I said that, he would leave." Jeane sighed.

Leslie felt tears come to his own eyes. While he regained his composure, he could see Jeane fighting to regain hers. Trying to show that it was the only reasonable course to take, he uttered, "So you did that?"

"Yeah," she replied, "but he still wouldn't leave. Then, out of nowhere, Eddie grabbed the guy, twisted his arm behind his back, and threw him out of the playground."

"He did?"

"And the entire time, the guy was telling him, 'She's a porn actress. She has no right having a baby. She fucks guys professionally. You don't believe me? She's in this film and that film! Someone should take that child away from her.'"

"Why do you still come here?" Leslie asked.

"'Cause he said," she pointed to the vendor, "that if I didn't come back here, that son of a bitch would have won. And he's right. I'm not going to let that guy or any other cocksucker change my life a fucking bit."

Leslie's first reaction was to track the bastard down and kill him, but he caught himself, realizing that he was bonding with his captor. Jeane is not my girlfriend, she is an ex–porn actress who left me for a drug dealer and got pregnant, he reminded himself. He nodded calmly, ending the conversation.

Later in the week, when she told him that she still felt a little uncomfortable about going outside, Leslie muttered something about her having brought it onto herself.

"What did you say?" She froze.

"I don't want to get into a fight with you, but the fact is, that guy only described what he saw. It wasn't like he was making it up."

"That doesn't give him the right to talk to me like that!" she yelled.

"I agree, but I do see his point. In my own way, I've done what he did." He refused to make eye contact with her as he spoke.

"What are you saying?" She couldn't believe he would even think such a thing.

"I'm saying that your porn persona is a part of their

fantasy world." Cold and clinically, he offered a simile: "As if Bugs Bunny came to life for a kid."

She was too furious to speak with him about it anymore, and she knew if she let herself get worked up, she would start screaming and maybe even hit Leslie, and, in doing so, might get thrown out of his house. She couldn't do that to her little girl, so she just stormed into her room.

She regretted ever telling Leslie about the man who had harassed her. His blaming her for her pornographic past reminded her of her status. She was a charity case and he wanted his freedom. That night, she wept into her pillow until she fell asleep.

MAY 1, 2001, NYC

THE DAY AFTER SCREWING JEANE IN THE PARK BOULEVARD Inn, I take a medication holiday. I declare a moratorium on pigeon killing. In fact, I only peak through my telescope once. For the first time, I feel like I'm back in life. Like I've had a stay of execution. But I know last night's delight will be tomorrow's distress for Jeane. She won't be calling today.

The following day she does not call either.

Nor does she call the next day.

Nor the day after!

NOR THE NEXT!

Nor by the end of the week.

I get a million calls from Bill Holtov and associates screaming for help. Judge "Spank Me" Sanders is rejecting all restructuring offers. To those calls, I have no reply. I've fallen in love again, so all suicide plans are temporarily off. On Monday morning, while screening calls, I hear my secretary Dorothy on my machine and pick up. She nervously asks if I am okay.

"Sleepy, but fine," I reply groggily. "Nice of you to ask."

"You know, everyone's trying to get ahold of you."

"I know. Please don't tell them you got through."

"I won't."

"What's up, Dorothy?"

"Well, this is a little embarrassing, Les, but I got a postcard that looks like it's in your handwriting."

"You did?" I reply jovially, without a clue what she's talking about.

"It says you killed yourself!"

"Oh god," I say, instantly turning inside out with shame.

"I was about to call the police but thought I should call you first."

"Oh shit!" There is no point in issuing a denial. "See, what happened was, I was out with some guys, see. And I got drunk. And the next thing I know, we're playing truth or dare. I didn't know one of the sons of bitches would actually mail the card."

"Well they did, and it scared the hell out of me and a bunch of others here."

"A thousand apologies," I apologize.

"This is difficult for me to say," she says, "because I usually don't talk about it and it always sounds so corny, but you know, there's a world larger than this one."

Can she be referring to Disneyland? Canada?

"I mean Jesus, the son of God, who died for our sins. His saving grace could make life on earth heaven."

"When did you get into this?" I ask. In all the years I've worked with her I've never heard her mention God or any of his illegitimate children.

"I've always believed. I don't proselytize," she proselytizes, "but it sounds like you could use some help. So if you like, I can send you some literature."

"Sure." Knock yourself out.

"You know, truth is, you can go as far in life as your faith and love take you," she concludes. I thank her. My truth is, you can go as far as insanity and the police let you.

Certain that the suicide postcard must be thumbtacked to the community bulletin board, I feel wrung out and entitled to the much-awaited call from Jeane the Protractor. As the hours pass, I make excuses for Jeane: She has needy cases at work, dinners to make, a family to attend to, a lot of squeaky wheels competing for her valuable grease.

I refuse to leave my apartment all day. By 7:30 p.m. I end up shooting a bull pigeon with green phlegm-like blotches around its thick neck. By 9:00 I am spying on promenaders in Central Park with my telescope, wishing it was attached to a high-powered rifle. By midnight I pop a Prozac, but I know it's only a placebo because I'm not taking them regularly, as prescribed. I fall asleep rubbing the matchbook from the sacred Park Boulevard Inn.

Jeane doesn't call the next day. Or the day after that. By Thursday I realize that I had walked into a lucky dalliance. Lightning doesn't strike twice. She's never going to call again.

Where's the vertical hold? That night, my apartment officially becomes an unpadded cell. Staring out over the unheated black pool of Central Park, I restrain myself from diving into it.

Although it was over a week ago, I begin abusing myself to those brief, brutal motel memories, recalling how vulnerable she had been: I was in charge.

Midway through my fantasy, as I dissect the events, I detect a salient detail of her motivation—fear. It was not merely being at the right place at the right time. I had inadvertently created a crack in Jeane's safe little biosphere. That fissure was fear. Sex was the sealant.

It wasn't any stringent and intimidating terror I ignited, but a slow-burning menace named Perry Cruz. He had attacked her at her weakest point. In laboratory tests, mother mice are willing to sacrifice everything for the safety of their offspring. Compounding this fact, the offspring is a beautiful bi-racial daughter and the mother is a survivor of sexual abuse and a recanted porn actress. After fourteen years in this cozy community, Jeane's sleep cycle is suddenly invaded by this Freddy Krueger arising from her deep, dark past, her own rated X-Files. Because of the terror Jeane was experiencing, she needed a protector as well as a sexual vent for her anxiety—she was keeping the attack on Katie confidential from poor Eddie—so I filled both roles.

That's when it occurs to me that the only way I am going to get back into the sack with Mean Jeane the Porn Queen is through a phone call of my own, or rather a call from the monster.

Checking my watch, I see how late it is. They'll all be at home right now, the husband and kiddies, but that's okay. That will only gas up her own fear, which ultimately is everything. I pick up the phone, but realize that Jeane can star-69 me, so I dress and head out.

"Mr. Cauldwell, you still not here for nobody?" Luis the ever-kind doorman asks. "'Cause, you know, I've seen them."

"Seen who?"

"Those guys, they've been waiting for you around the clock."

"Yeah, you haven't seen me," I say.

"You better leave through the service entrance in the back then. They're probably watching the front door." I thank him and give him a twenty. He leads me downstairs to an outdoor courtyard, and from there to a gated exit where the garbage is dumped.

I walk around the neighborhood a bit, revving myself up. Finally I enter Hoops, the closest bar with a pay phone.

Heading toward the booth in the rear, I see the nickle-plated, Hong Kong knock-off Britney Spears—Sheila. She still sits at her stool, sexed up, smoking a cigarette, chatting with some pathetic geriatric in a generic suit.

"Are you really so lonely and depressed that you have to spend your evenings trawling like this?" I utter in passing.

"What the . . ." She flicks the ashes of her cigarette.

"Is this really preferable to loneliness?" I ask in all sincerity.

She looks flabbergasted. Her self-indulgent companion completely misses everything I say because he's boring away at some tired, predictable anecdote. I continue to the rear of the joint. The phone booth is empty. Amid a track of laughter, TV, and chatter, I dial Jeane's number.

After a short ring—*bingo*—Jeane answers.

"Jeane Lindemeyer?" say I, disguising my voice with a low rasp.

"Who is it?"

"It's Perry Cruz, to let you know your past has caught up with you."

"What?" There it is, right on the surface—the horror.

"Don't fuck with me. I saw you outside the hospital the other day. I watched you."

"What are you talking about? Who is this?" I can hear her tone drop as she tries to cloak the call from her innocent family.

"The other day, bitch. I saw you. I saw you with your husband and your attitude."

"My husband?"

"The peckerhead in the parking lot. The one with the sporty car. I followed you. In fact, I saw you go to that bar and then to the whore motel for the quickie."

"You *what?*" She's perplexed, poor dear.

"I looked in through the window. I watched you. I watched him nailing you."

"You *what?*"

"Now it's my turn. Either I'm going to slam-fuck you or I'm going to slam-fuck that offspring of yours. You pick." I surprise myself by slamming down the phone.

At the bar, I order a double single-malt, which I gulp down.

"Rat bastard."

"I know I am, but what are you?" I reverse the childhood deflection. Sheila is sitting alone.

"I know exactly who I am," she retorts.

"You disappointed me."

"I disappointed you?"

"That's right. 'Cause underneath a crappy upbringing I can see that you are really quite smart and attractive."

"A crappy upbringing?" She's deeply insulted, yet she remains seated, so she's deeply attracted to me.

"Tell me honestly, how many conversations do you endure here? How many stupid, boring, egotistical fat-asses do you and that hairdo have to put up with each night?"

"Like you, you mean?"

"Worse than me," I up the stakes. "At least I keep you awake."

"I don't know anyone in this crummy city! Is something wrong with trying to find friends?"

"There's no companionship for the soul, no light in the darkness, or warmth from the cold."

Suddenly, some sports team in TV-land scores and the bar-bulls bellow as one, nearly giving me a coronary.

"I can't stay here." I rise. "If you want to keep talking, walk with me."

"Walk with you?" She's outraged and can't believe her ears.

"Believe me, no more toupee-topped, wife-cheating, Viagra-popping fat-asses are falling in here tonight." I turn up my collar. "Shake a leg if you're coming."

Slightly drunk, tired, and frustrated, she accompanies me as I leave and retreat back to my apartment.

MAY 24, 1982, NYC

A WEEK AND A HALF LATER, WHEN LESLIE ARRIVED home from work, Sky was happily feeding Kate, humming a rock tune. There was an obvious change in her mood.

"Why so upbeat?" he inquired.

"I've got a fan." She lifted her eyebrows.

"A fan?" he repeated, a little nervous.

"Yeah, he wants to take me out."

By fan, he wondered, did she mean someone who liked her or someone who liked her films. Then Leslie figured, or rather, felt it. Even though she was smiling, her eyes were slyly focused on his; she wanted to see if he was jealous. He made a point of showing he was happy for her.

"So when are you going out with this guy?" Leslie asked calmly.

"When I can afford a sitter for Kate," she replied just as calmly.

"When do you need one?" he asked, instantly rising to the challenge.

"Friday night," she responded, knowing that he had to work late that night.

"I'll do it." He smiled.

"Fine," she said tensely, and repressed her anger for the remainder of the evening.

On Friday night, Leslie arrived home in time for her to make her date. Upon opening the door and seeing her, he felt a jolt. She wasn't just beautiful, with hairdo, cosmetics, and a new dress; this was her cinematic image come back to life. As she told him details about caring for the little girl, Leslie remembered that divine spark when he had first seen her on film, when he first fell in love with her. He considered asking her to stay, cancel the date, but he held it in, allowing the longing to pass through his system. He took a seat and grabbed ahold of the chair's arms.

"Good luck," he said. Jeane quietly thanked him.

"Jeane," he broke down, as she was about to close the door behind her. "You know, you don't have to do this if you don't really want to."

"I haven't gone on a date in ages. 'Course I want to," she replied curtly, and left the apartment.

For the first few hours, everything went well. Leslie had to change his first diaper, which he decided was the most grotesque experience of his life. While wiping Katie's backside, he tried to think of the baby as a delicate reptile. By the second change, it simply seemed alien and not quite so disgusting. When Katie started crying, he tried to give her a bottle. But she refused it and kept crying. He took her out of her playpen and discovered that she stopped whining when he held her. She stared up at him. He stared back into her dark, beautiful baby eyes and smiled. Leslie sensed that somewhere in the depths of her memory she was retaining everything.

"You understand me, don't you?" he whispered to her. She tilted her head slightly. "I love you, Katie," he said in a baby voice, and gently placed a kiss on her soft cheek.

Afterwards he spoon-fed her some beef-stew baby food. Together they watched *Wall Street Week*. Occasionally she made baby sounds. He would reply in kind and bounce her on his knee. Later, he placed her back into the cradle where she slept soundly. He fell asleep next to her in Jeane's bed.

He was still asleep several hours later when Jeane entered. She walked right into the bathroom and locked the door behind her. Hoping to drown out any sounds, she turned on the shower. The date had been nice. Eddie was a gentleman, though he was neither young nor sexy. He was the best catch she could get since Marcos, but as they had walked up Columbus Avenue among other, younger couples, she felt both pathetic and cruel. Poor sweet, kind Eddie, who sweated over his hot dog stand all day, had bent over backwards to make her happy, and she had simply dated him to make Leslie jealous. Tears blackened with mascara streamed down her cheeks.

When she opened the bathroom door fifteen minutes later, Leslie was standing there like a zombie. Swiftly, he asked, "Did you . . . I mean, you didn't . . ."

"What?" she shouted back. "Spit it out!"

"Well, you went right into the shower," he said, trying to ascertain whether or not she had had sex.

"Fuck you!" she yelled, unintentionally waking Kate.

Leslie retreated back to his room and she, to hers. He lay in bed, hearing the sounds of both mother and daughter crying. Soon he was asleep. Eventually he awoke to the sensation of a kiss, but he pretended to still be sleeping, hoping that she would go away. Jeane rubbed his chest. When her fingers grazed his nipples, he jumped up.

"Jeane, what are you doing?"

"Please," she trembled, "I just need this moment." She reached down and stroked him hard. A moment later she was sucking him. Quickly, they were having sex, and five frantic minutes later, they were both coming.

After a pause of silence, she softly said, "God, it would be so perfect if we could do this from time to time." Leslie didn't utter a word, didn't even breathe. "I could fuck you every night," she vowed in a desperate whisper. "You and no one else. I could make you so happy." She saw his tense silence as a positive sign. "We could reenact all the fantasies you ever saw me do in films. Would you like that, baby?"

He got out of bed and walked over to the window.

"I'd blow you every morning before you go to work and every evening before you go to sleep." She knew he liked blowjobs.

"Jeane!"

"I could come to your office and you could fuck me in the ass during lunch breaks." Fillip told her men loved this because they were all repressed faggots.

"Jeane, enough!"

"I love you. I never said that before . . ." she paused and added, "to anyone."

He groaned in response. "This isn't fair. You wanted to have a baby and I want what I had—my independence."

She exhaled, looked away, threw open the sheet, and muttered, "I'm sorry." Rising naked, she silently withdrew to her half of the apartment.

■

The next day as Leslie was eating cereal, Sky came into the kitchen with an embarrassed smile. She apologized for her behavior the night before, explaining that she had suffered a panic attack about being a single mother. He said he understood, and changing the tone, he asked her who the fan was that had taken her on last night's date.

"The hot dog man," she replied softly. "That's how low I've sunk." She sneered.

"He seemed like a nice guy."

Leslie had brewed a pot of coffee and was drinking his customary two cups. Jeane poured a mug for herself. "A really nice guy," she responded. "Smart, and he has real heart."

"How old is he?" Leslie finished his cereal and put his bowl in the sink.

"Thirty-eight," she answered, as she poured milk into her coffee cup.

"He's not too old," Leslie countered, buttoning up his dress shirt.

"He's lived through a lot." She took a sip of the coffee, set it down, and added a half a teaspoon of brown sugar.

"Lived through what?" Leslie asked, as he selected a somber gray tie.

"He got a scholarship to MIT and dropped out. He went to Vietnam. He was in the police academy. He writes poetry. A lot of stuff."

"You're sure he's not lying?" he asked, knotting the tie.

"I don't know. We saw a stupid film. Afterwards, he took me up to the projection booth in the movie theater." Jeane had another sip of coffee and put another teaspoon of sugar in the cup. "The projectionist was his ex-girlfriend."

"No kidding," he said, adjusting his collar in the mirror.

"He was very polite. I sensed that he was hot for me, but he was very respectful." She took a large gulp of her coffee. Now it was too sweet.

"Are you going to date him again?" Leslie asked, fumbling through his top drawer for a tiepin.

"Well," she went to the sink and emptied the cup, "I'm not really attracted to him, but I don't have anyone else in line." She washed out the cups and his cereal bowl, then put them in the dish rack. Leslie told her to have a good day and left for work.

■

He was asked to assist with a bankruptcy appeal in Delaware, so that night Leslie packed an overnight bag and boarded an Amtrak train to Dover. The next two days he worked busily on the case. He called home on the third day to learn that Jeane had decided to become a projectionist. Eddie, who had a background in math and science, was going to help her prepare for the licensing exam.

"A projectionist?" Leslie said. He could hear Jeane giving Katie her bottle in the background.

"They make a good wage," she assured him, and then took a suck from the bottle's rubber nipple; it didn't seem to be drawing.

"A projectionist," he repeated. "How proletarian."

Jeane explained that Myrna, Eddie's projectionist friend, was going to help her get into the union.

When Leslie arrived back home with his suitcase, Eddie was sitting at the kitchen table trying to teach Jeane the basics of algebra—all necessary in order to pass the projectionist exam. It was difficult to concentrate because little Katie wanted so much attention. Leslie agreed to baby-sit, so Jeane and Eddie went to study at a nearby diner.

Over the course of the next two weeks, the hot dog vendor taught her Ohm's Law and other rules of electricity. At Eddie's suggestion, Jeane wrote everything down on flashcards. After studying at the diner, Eddie would walk her home. One night after their session as she was about to say goodnight, Eddie paused in front of her. Oh god, he's going to kiss me, she thought, and decided, okay, I'll kiss him, but only once. No tongues. I owe him that much.

Instead, he looked away suddenly, then handed her a slip of paper and said, "Call this number and get a registration form. Also, find out how much they want. You'll have to enclose a money order for the exam in September."

"Will do," she said hastily, and dashed into Leslie's apartment.

When Jeane closed the door, Leslie commented, "He really seems like a nice guy, but he's gotta be older than thirty-eight."

JUNE 7, 1982, NYC

"SHEET METAL?" THE LITTLE BOY ASKED.

"No," Cecilia replied with a chuckle, "Sheep's Meadow."

Gina was with her older sister Rosie getting large Cokes at the red-brick concession stand in Central Park. Cecilia sat on the grass under the weekend sun talking with Gina's young nephew Albert.

Lying on her back, she glanced up along the fenced walkway bordering the north end of the pasture and spotted them. He was wearing red shorts and a white T-shirt. She was blocked by him, but Cecilia could see that she was shapely, in a cheap way. Leslie was pushing a stroller. Cece instantly felt a pain.

"My god, they went and had a kid!" She didn't think it had even been nine months.

"Why is it called Sheep's Meadow?" Albert asked.

Cecilia couldn't reply. She was doing everything she could to keep from crying. She couldn't take her eyes off the voluptuous mother.

"Aunt Cece!"

She knew at that moment that she loved Leslie. To her, he suddenly looked like the only real direction in her life. But she wasn't certain about what he really wanted. Despite all the flowers and cards he had delivered to her house and all the phone messages he had left on her machine, she wasn't sure if he felt guilty or merely enjoyed the kinky sex. Few girls would put up with it. She couldn't afford another crappy relationship, let alone returning to an uncertain old one.

Suck it down, she thought, Gina's going to be back in a moment. She'll sense that something's wrong and she'll needle it out of you, then all hell will break loose.

"Aunt Cece, where's the sheep if this is the sheep's meadow?" Albert's pesty little voice buzzed.

"They don't graze here anymore," Cecilia replied.

JULY 25, 1982, NYC

WITHIN TWO MONTHS ALL OF THE PROJECTIONIST-exam facts were neatly copied onto flashcards and the job was just memorization, so Jeane began reducing her time with Eddie. As the meetings became increasingly infrequent, Jeane commented to Leslie that she had started smelling alcohol on her tutor's breath.

"Let me ask you something," Leslie said pointedly. "Why are you doing all this?"

Jeane was in the kitchen and Katie in her pen, playing with a rainbow-streaked ball that sounded musical notes when it rolled.

"Doing what?" she asked, as she flipped through the stack of flashcards.

"You know." He took a deep breath. "This whole study bit." He reached into the pen and rolled the ball to Katie, who picked it up.

"To become a projectionist. The exam is only six weeks away." She flipped to another card.

"I know, but do you really know what you're doing?" Leslie watched Katie trying to chew on the ball's rubbery exterior.

"What are you saying? You think I'm an idiot?"

"No, I'm sure you could be a projectionist, I only mean, do you really want to do this?"

Jeane asked if Leslie was insinuating that this line of work was too common or lowly for her.

"Of course not." Anything was an improvement over doing porn, he didn't say. He took the ball out of Katie's mouth and gave her a doll.

"What do you want me to do, Les?"

Leslie interpreted this question as suggesting that if he chose to marry her, she would not have to subject herself to further torments.

"I want you to be happy," he said cheerfully. "I want us both to be happy."

She read another card, while Leslie watched Katie pull the doll's blouse open and yank its little dress off.

"Do you want to spend your life supporting me and Kate?" Jeane asked, checking another card. He reached into the playpen and redressed the naked doll.

Leslie unraveled his thoughts delicately: "See, I figured that you and Eddie liked each other and this little projectionist thing was a way of you two getting together . . . See what I mean?" He gave the doll back to Katie.

"The fact is," she paused and looked at another flashcard, "I like him a lot. But I'm not attracted to him."

"When you first met me you weren't attracted to me either," Leslie reminded.

Jeane looked at Leslie and wondered where his questions were coming from and where they were heading. She checked the answer to the next card, and said, "Look, Eddie's trying to cajole me into a relationship, and I don't care for it. But today he said something that, like it or not, was fairly true. He said, as people we need other people. It's the way we're built. Life is a two-seated vehicle, and even if you don't love someone, it's easier to live just being with that second person." She gave Leslie a self-satisfied smile.

"Well, I'm a unicyclist," Leslie replied bluntly, and taking away the mistreated doll, he gave the little girl her musical ball back.

"I'm really trying to get on my feet and move out," she countered just as blandly, then selected another card.

"Look, I put poor Cecilia through enough."

"Cecilia?!" She remembered that this was the ex-girlfriend-turned-lesbian. Jeane slammed down the stack of cards. "What the fuck does she have to do with anything?"

"I ended that relationship before it was even over."

"You told me she left you."

"She found pictures of you and thought I wanted you over her. She wanted me to prove my love for her alone." Without thinking, Leslie added, "And I've been punishing myself ever since." He watched Katie, who was enamored by the twangy tunes coming out of the ball, and smiled.

"Nap time!" Jeane roared. She then rose, grabbed her cards with one hand, and snatched Katie out of her pen with her free arm. She vanished into her half of the apartment in a huff.

MAY 10, 2001, NYC

"SO, TELL ME ABOUT YOURSELF?" SHEILA THE BLOND BARFLY buzzes around me as we walk through the late-night, early-morning Upper West Side streets.

"Only if you promise not to tell me about you," I say, because that's what she really wants to do.

Sure enough, she dives straight into the sewer of her childhood, which leads us down the pipeline of her post-adolescence, and drains out into the polluted spillway of her unrealistic ambitions. I know by how pat and rehearsed this is that I'm listening to touching-monologue numbers 24, 25, and 26, designed to paralyze eligible bachelors with her pain, bravery, and endurance. I'm still lingering on the devastating impact I have had on Jeane's little life with my Perry Cruz call.

"Tell me about you now," Sheila says.

We pass a huge Lhasa Apso pulling a microscopic lady. I reach down and pet it.

"Look at this, the creep likes dogs," she mutters. The dog and owner blow away.

"I had this neighbor years ago," I start, "in the building where I used to live, an old lady who kept two dogs."

"What kind?"

"I don't know, a brother and sister, large ones. One day the old lady croaks. Another lady in the building loved the two mutts, but she had a small studio. She could only take one of them. It was sad as hell but what could she do? She kept the male, and after failing to find a home for the female, she was forced to take it to the pound."

"What happened to it?" Sheila asks.

"The dog was about six so it was probably destroyed. Anyway, she told me how the final day she had the two dogs, she tried to explain to them that this would be their last time together. But how do you explain separation to dogs? How do you prepare them for loss or tell them you're sorry? Anyway, after that, she would take the male for a walk and it would pull her to the dog run, searching for his sister, smelling other dogs, looking everywhere for her. He had always been with his sister. It wasn't simply a matter of finding her, it was more like finding a part of himself. His sister was his protector. She was the more aggressive dog, he was the passive one."

"What ended up happening?" Sheila seems intrigued.

"Nothing. Do you think dogs are capable of mourning?"

"I don't know. Do you usually pick up girls with that anecdote?" she asks, and presses, "Why don't you tell me about yourself?"

"Myself? Okay, I was a crazy sadist. I killed my wife during rough sex and got away with it scot-free. But then I saw a court-appointed shrink and got cured. Now I'm half-crazed with guilt." I sigh and look uptown. "And I'm stalking an old lover, but I'm not sure why."

"Are you really nuts?" She smiles daintily.

A block away from my building, I scope out Bill Holtov and check to see if he's hired any summer intern thugs for surveillance work. Spotting a suspicious suit, I push Sheila into a doorway.

"What's going on?" she asks, fearing an assault on her maidenhood.

"Someone's trying to kill me." But checking again, I see the suit walk away. "False alarm."

"What were you like when you were younger?" she asks out of the blue.

"The short form — an asshole. The long version — someone who was unwittingly soliciting to be hurt. And that's the nature of youth. People have to suffer; you can't live their lives for them. I'm sure someone must have told you how all men are creeps. But you keep going back for more, looking for guys like me."

"Why are you so fucking angry?" she asks, obviously distressed.

"Probably because of the dead wife." I smile. Coast looks clear, no signs of Bill and associates.

"The one you killed?" she replies nonchalantly. I nod, and she asks, "You didn't really kill your wife, did you?"

"'Course not."

I pause outside my building. It is my intention to hail a cab and let her slip away, but then she says, "Why is it so hard to find a decent boyfriend?"

"If you just want a great provider, take some fat ugly bore who worships you, but who you find repugnant." And that's the truth.

"I want a good lover," says the victim to the serial murderer.

"Anyone can fuck. If you want your flesh to tighten three sizes too small and your heart to beat outside your chest," I hold out the noose, "take a slightly older sadist."

I dash inside my building, getting helloed all over by Luis. Sheila makes the mistake of following me, and asks, "You wouldn't happen to know any older sadists around here?"

Once in the elevator, I push the button for the top floor. She is still blathering away, confusing superficialities and romantic projections with a character assessment. Somewhere between the eighth and tenth floors, I place my sweaty palm on her right breast and start rubbing in ever-tightening concentric circles. Then I stop and pinch her pointy nipple through the garment. She shuts up, closes her eyes, and starts sucking air slowly, steadily, like someone who has just been taken off life support. She is shaped like a hurricane with an outer wall of self-confidence always rising and an inner wall of self-esteem always collapsing, yet lacking that peaceful inner eye.

I like watching her as she moans and groans and thinks I am feeling the same, but I pull the plug. She opens her eyes and sees me scrutinizing, smirking at her. Before she can say anything, the elevator doors open. I exit and walk up the steps to the roof. She follows me out the heavy door and onto the gravel toward the ledge. She is talking at me. God, they love to talk. I act listeningly and keep walking to the chest-high wall. The greasy city is smeared out before us. Yak, yak, yak, behind me. I grab Sheila, push her against the edge, and start kissing her. She finally falls silent.

Her little Britney doll eyes flip shut. I work my hands along her lower stomach and thighs. I can see the muscle tone developed from all those hours on the non-impact machine, running four times a week, imagining she's heading down a three-mile church aisle to the wedding altar. I lift the secret curtain of her dress and carefully dip my fingers into her foam, toying with her tumblers. Now this Jeane stand-in is groaning big-time, throwing off smoke and sparks. My hobgoblin is hard and hungry. Turning her around so that she faces the world of streaked and stained buildings, I bend her over, put a little spit on it, and work it in. She has a surprisingly nice body, lean and proportionate: good legs, a tight Midwestern cunt, smells fertile, a strong muscular ass. Twenty years down the road, when she has a shapeless husband and pointless children, this will be a recurrent touchstone, a shower fantasy. I fuck her steadily, and reaching around, I play with her clit as she moans faster.

I stop right before she cums, letting her measure my fullness in her.

"Please, please," she says. I fuck her until she is loose and wet. It's time to spear Britney. I spread her cheeks and quickly slip my cork inside her envious, pouting asshole.

"How's that, Jeane?"

"Wait a second," she sputters.

"I'm pretty sure I don't have AIDS," I try putting her at ease.

"No!"

I feel her go weak, and torpidly work it all the way in. Then I sway myself out. I can't shoot anymore, but for her sake, I make sounds like I am. Quickly, we wipe, zip, and without kissing her, I leave. She follows.

Waiting for the elevator, we begin a game of Simon Says: she hugs, I hug back, she kisses, I kiss back. When the elevator arrives, we both get in. I push the button for the lobby, but she doesn't see it. We kiss as we slip downward. Breaking off, she asks, "So, loverboy, who's Jeane?"

"No one."

"Are you seeing anyone now?" she asks sternly.

"Only you, but I need to suffer alone a while. Here, more important than a wedding ring." I take out my ring of keys, and removing the one to my apartment, I fearlessly hand it to her as though it were a dagger. "Come see me when you want."

"Are you kidding?" She smiles, unsure how to interpret.

The elevator opens.

"Hey, we're in the lobby," she comprehends.

"Yeah, well, I gave you my key and told you what a dog I am, didn't I?"

I step out, she follows. I give her a hard kiss and take one giant step backward into the elevator as it is closing.

"What?" she exclaims.

I watch her mortified expression as the doors slam shut. Simon says goodbye. Simon didn't invite you up. In the stairwell on my floor, curled in the light-brown canvas folds of the flaccid fire hose, is my spare door key. In my apartment, I strip, shower, and wait to see if she bounces back up. She doesn't, so with some of the pressure relieved, I go to sleep.

■

The next afternoon, a week and a half after the fucking of Mean Jeane, but just a day after my menacing Perry Cruz call, I finally capture it. It has flown into my little net. The more I replay it, the more I liken it to a rare and beautiful bird, small and neurotic, but a work of art, living, breathing, its little heart beating in the cage of my machine—Jeane's frantic bulletin, half in a whisper, half in tears, begging for me to call her at work. I virtually ejaculate without a touch.

I take the cassette out of the machine and snap off the black plastic tab in the back so that no other message can be inadvertently taped over it. It is easily one of the most erotic tapes I have ever heard. *"He saw us at the motel! He knows we did it, Leslie. He thinks you're my husband! You've got to call me!"* Jeane concludes, leaving her work number. For the first time in more than a week, I smile genuinely. It is too perfect. Her persecutor is her confidante. If being a psychotic means functioning in the straitjacket of a self-created reality, then I am no longer psychotic. My gestalt is gestalting, my animus is animated, my archetype is archetyping. I pick up the phone like a wand and relish the power. I savor the fact that Sky is actually waiting for me. She hungers to speak to me! Cecilia would have appreciated the irony of this construct.

I put the phone down, mix myself an orange juice and seltzer, and toast Cece's memory. Then I close the window, but open the patio door. I maneuver a chair, a lamp, and a couple other items in the room to create a visual balance to my lopsided apartment. When everything is *feng shui,* I sit down to make the call.

"Social Services, Mercy Hospital," I hear her apprehensive little voice part the silence.

"Jeane, what's going on?" I personify sanity, civility, and authority.

"Oh my god!" she replies. Then in a low tone, "It's him— Perry Cruz. He's stalking me! I knew it and I was right!"

"That's insane. Relax now." Daddy's home.

"It's not insane! He called me at home! He spotted me with you! He followed us to the motel! He thinks you're my husband! I couldn't even tell Eddie about it!"

"He thinks I'm your husband?" I react in horror.

"I'm so sorry for bringing you into this, Leslie," she says guiltily for putting me in harm's way of this crazed stalker.

"Don't worry about it," I reply, and add, "Better this way. If he comes after me, I'll handle it."

"Oh, Leslie, I feel so . . . I'm exhausted . . ." I hear a soft whimper.

"Jeane, I can't talk right now," I mutter out of the side of my mouth, as if others have entered the room.

"But I . . ." she clings on.

"Look, I'm going back out to Mercy Hospital to visit my friend. Why don't I stop in and we'll figure this out together?" It doesn't occur to either of us that hernia patients—I claimed my friend was one—would usually be discharged by now.

"All right," she says with a sigh, resigning herself to see-ing me.

"I'll be out there tomorrow, around 5 o'clock."

"You can't meet me any earlier, can you?" she asks timidly.

"I have a court appearance in the afternoon," I lie, wanting to hammerlock the appointment into a time when she'll be getting off of work. As I place the phone on its cradle, I'm sporting a granite erection.

■

The next day I dress as I would for court, even bringing my briefcase. I go down to my Jag but suddenly remember that my car might have been recognized and reported by one of the endless students that flowed by me during my trips to Kate's school. All future visits to Jeane will have to be done by rail.

Heading toward Penn Station, I stop in a photo shop to buy the vital tool missing from our last intimate encounter. I select a disposable camera with a flash. But when the clerk holds it out for me, I realize that if I take the explicit photos I want, they will be too embarrassing to develop in a lab. Privacy is everything. I end up purchasing a Polaroid that folds neatly into my pocket.

Near the subway about a block from my house, I pass an attractive young couple on the street. I vaguely recognize the woman, probably from work. The name Heather pops into my head.

"Heather?" I say timidly.

"No," she retorts with a smile.

"How do I know you?" I ask, and vaguely remember her in an amorous scenario.

"I'm sorry, I don't know you," the woman who is not Heather replies.

"But I do know you," I say with a smile that might suggest our one-time intimacy. I've seen her breast, loose and large outside a bra. Her red raspberry nipples float above creamy bosoms. Was she one of the love partners when Cece and I were still riding high?

"She says she doesn't know you," her male companion purports. As the two resume their walk, it dawns on me that she's one of the women I've seen nude on many occasions through my telescope.

While riding the train, I know that it is time to come up with a broader program. I can do anything I want. Anything I can dream up: If Jeane left her husband and children, if she abandoned them for me, that would be a start. She still looks great. The thing that would delight me most would be her startling re-entry into pornography. If she resumed her career of being filmed as she fucked strangers, men half her age, even though she hasn't made a film in over two decades, that would be delicious; to proudly show the world the poised middle-aged woman that Sky Pacifica has blossomed into — a kind of female clown, forty years plus, busting out of a miniskirt and tank top.

"Change at Jamaica for the train to Huntington," the P.A. hollers as the doors slide open. I grab the train on the opposite track.

I spend the remainder of the ride thinking about how I am going to get Jeane liquored up and back into the sack. Perry needs his fuck and photos. At Borden I check my watch. It is almost 5, so I jog through the streets to Mercy Hospital, then into the lobby. When I find I don't know her office number, I ask the front-desk receptionist where the social-service department is located.

"Who are you looking for?" the elderly woman asks.

"Only the office," I say, not wanting the nice lady to call upstairs and alert my little pigeon. I tap my jacket pocket and say, "I have to drop something off."

"Room 412. Take the elevator to four and make a right." I quickly find myself entering a drafty, large-ceilinged office with yawning windows and a sloppy paint job.

SEPTEMBER 12, 1982, NYC

IT RAINED THE ENTIRE NIGHT BEFORE THE projectionist exam and Sky couldn't get to sleep.

Leslie rose early the next morning to hear the baby girl crying against the whistle of wind and rainfall. He tried to go back to sleep, but soon found that Jeane was not attending to her. Something was wrong. The bathroom was locked. Leslie put his ear to the door and could hear water running and Jeane sobbing softly. Then the water was turned off and the door flung open. She emerged with reddened eyes, her face not even made up.

"It's 8:30, you have to be there at 9!" he informed her.

"I'm not going!" she screamed. "Are you happy? You fucked my life up!"

"What's the matter?" he asked groggily.

"What's the matter!" She stood before him, stark naked. "I never passed a test in my entire life! Where did I get it into my head that I could pass this?"

"Get dressed. You're going," Leslie shot back.

"What are you going to do, asshole, throw me out?" Jeane employed the tough street persona that he had not seen since that day she first showed up at his house.

"Yeah." To her surprise, Leslie lurched toward her and seized her around the waist, yanking her toward the front door. "You're leaving this instant."

Kate watched and screamed.

"You fucking bastard!" she hollered, pulling his hair and slapping him.

"You're out the door!" Leslie yelled. She had seen this in other men, but never in him, and it shook her.

"Okay! Stop it. Stop it! I'm naked!" she cried out. "Let me fucking dress!"

She ran into her room. He stood by her door for a few minutes in his underwear before he tried the knob. It was locked—she had barricaded herself inside.

"OPEN THIS FUCKING DOOR!" he yelled, and started banging. She opened the door, hastily dressed. Kate was still screaming.

"You are a shitty little geek and the only reason I'm doing this is to be rid of you!" Jeane grabbed her purse containing her test registration card and the stack of now crinkled and stained flashcards, then stormed out the door.

As she hurried down the stairs, Leslie yelled after her, "HERE!" She looked back, and he tossed her an umbrella. Then, turning, still pissed, she stomped down the rest of the stairs.

"USE ALL THE TIME! DOUBLE CHECK YOUR ANSWERS!" he yelled. Seeing her hand still clenched on the last stretch of banister, he added, "I LOVE YOU!"

When she heard this, she paused on the step, staring furiously into the empty space. She exhaled deeply, then bolted outside and grabbed a cab.

Tiredly, Leslie went to the crib. Kate was crying. He picked her up in his arms to find that she had peed. In the bathroom, he held his breath and quickly cleaned, powdered, and changed her. He then set the little girl down in Sky's bed and lay next to her.

He awoke when he heard the front door opening. Leslie looked at the clock and saw it was three hours later. Both were still in bed as she entered.

"How'd you do?" Leslie asked immediately.

"Failed." She issued her verdict and smiled demurely.

"Sorry for freaking out this morning. Thanks for making me take the exam."

"How do you know you failed?" Leslie couldn't believe that she could concede so abruptly. He had never failed a test in his whole life.

"I just know it, and I'd rather not talk about it." Kate's bottom felt wet so Jeane took her to the bathroom and found that Leslie had put her diaper on backwards. She changed her. Returning to the bedroom, she found Leslie asleep in her bed. Jeane was about to heat up a bottle for Kate, only to see that she too had drifted off to sleep. Jeane quietly slipped into bed with both of them, gently nestled herself into Leslie's arms, and joined them in a deep slumber. When she awoke sometime later, he was gone.

Jeane washed her face, checked Kate, and called Eddie to tell him that she had failed the exam.

"What? Did they grade it right there for you?" he asked facetiously.

"No, but . . ."

He interrogated her on some basic questions that he knew were on the test. She answered them all correctly.

"You didn't fail the exam," he said, almost bored.

"Yes I did," she assured him.

"Look, I know what you know and I know enough to pass that exam cold."

"It's all so simple, isn't it?" she barked, furious that he could be so smug about her success.

"Jeane, you're nervous, you're terrified. I understand, but . . ."

"No, you don't understand! You don't get it at all!" Jeane blasted, and then catching her breath, she calmed down and declared, "I am tired of being handled and helped along. I am sick of feeling like some mercy-case moron. Now, I really do appreciate your help. You're a nice guy, but I am not attracted to you. So I'm basically calling to tell you that I won't be able to see you again." She paused to let him digest what she had said and regurgitate any understandable anger.

"Jeane, I'm sorry," she heard him mutter, and knew she had taken out an unfair amount of frustration on him.

"Eddie, you'll find someone. There are a lot of pretty single girls out there and most of them are sharper than me and don't have a daughter, so . . ."

"Please don't do that," Eddie replied. "If you want to dump me, I'll survive, but don't pull the 'you can get better than me' crap. It's patronizing."

She agreed and apologized. They bade each other farewell and she hung up.

SEPTEMBER 12, 1982, NYC

"WHAT THE HELL IS THIS MESS?" CECILIA INQUIRED, trying to act angry. She was in no mood for Judge Asshole today. She still felt bad about last night's fight with Gina. In his little girl dress, the slave responded accordingly.

The thin-limbed, elderly man with the well-trimmed mustache had been keeping up appointments with her—Mistress Guinevere—every second Tuesday at 3 o'clock for months now. He had hinted that a legal acquaintance had recommended her, and at first he seemed like a typical slave. The first inkling she had of his true character surfaced late in their initial conversation when he asked her if she ever did bottom.

"Never," she replied.

"You wouldn't consider trying it once for a lot of money?"

"Not even once," she said uncompromisingly. "If that's what you're looking for, I know submissives who will do it under closed circuit supervision—"

"No, no," he interrupted, almost happily, "you're the one I want."

For the first few months the encounters were run-of-the-mill, stern-Mommy, mischievous-child role-playing, verbal humiliation, light beatings. He tipped nicely. He never once took out his pecker. He insisted on the same basic routine and Cecilia liked the structure. She knew what was expected and exactly how the encounter would end. Easy money. She was able to improvise and occasionally rephrase statements. But gradually something happened. Over the last two months, he was steadily becoming more demanding. Strict about her sticking to the originally agreed upon script. Time and again he would employ the safe word, correct her error, and they'd have to start again.

During every session, he was a little girl named Honey. Cecilia would do Mommy Dearest. She was supposed to come in and catch Honey playing with her cosmetics. Mommy had to be angry and spank him with the bristle side of a large wooden brush.

As she tiredly recited her lines that afternoon, she wondered if Gina had gone to AA. Whenever they got into a fight because of Gina's drinking, she would promise to go to meetings. But Cecilia never knew for certain.

"Hey! Mercy!" the slave called out. "I don't mean to be rude, but how many times do I have to say it?"

"What's the problem?" Cecilia asked absently.

"You hit me with the wrong side of the brush. Would

you mind if we start again from where you first put me over your knee and say, 'You need a little discipline, Honey'?"

OCTOBER 9, 1982, NYC

LESLIE ATTENDED A THREE-DAY CONFERENCE ON bankruptcy law that included a schedule of keynote speakers and several symposiums on discovery. During the after-dinner social, Leslie met a young associate from a corporate law firm in Chicago. Her name was Natalie, and although she was a bit awkward, she had a charming personality. She wore black-framed glasses, a crooked smile, and had a Gee Willikers Midwestern twang that Leslie found itchingly arousing. While they were alone, he began kissing and rubbing up against her. All the while, to his delight, she talked about the law.

On the last evening of the conference, after a couple of drinks at the bar, they retired to his room and smooched. Soon he was heavy petting. She began reciprocating his affections, touching him. Half an hour later they had their undergarments pulled off and were having sex. After they both came, they watched TV. Following a sitcom, they screwed again. Although the sex was vanilla simple—"I don't do that"—they kept it up until 5 a.m. They slept through the morning and into the afternoon, missing a variety of talks and new protocols. Natalie, who had just graduated from law school the previous year, promised to stay in touch.

When Leslie returned home the next day, he felt invigorated and actually looked forward to seeing Jeane and Kate. As he entered the apartment that afternoon, carrying his suitcase into the foyer, he was surprised to find Eddie sitting in the kitchen, holding a bag of garbage that Jeane had given him to carry out. She was strapping Kate into her stroller and the three were about to leave for a walk.

"Hi, Leslie," Eddie said, rising to his feet.

"Good to see you," Leslie replied cheerfully. When they shook, Leslie noticed that the older man's hand fully encompassed his own.

Jeane asked Eddie if he would be a dear and take Kate outside. She would join him in a minute.

"Actually," he countered, "why don't I take Katie to the playground? You two can talk as long as you like."

Jeane said fine and Eddie balanced the bag of garbage on the handle of the stroller and took the little girl out.

"Wow! You made him into a nurse maid," Leslie said, once the older man was safely out the door. "I guess you two made up."

"A lot happened." She paused, inhaled, and said in a declarative tone, "Les, I'm moving out."

"In what sense?"

"I passed the projectionist exam and I'm leaving. I'm moving out."

"What? When did this happen?" he asked, taking a seat.

She explained that the first morning after he left on his trip, she had received an official yellow postcard in the mail proclaiming that she had passed the exam.

"Congratulations!" Leslie replied, grabbing her exuberantly. She told him that she had been so excited that she had to call someone. She ended up calling Eddie, but his phone rang and rang.

"I know he stays home on his days off," she

explained, "so I dressed Kate up and we went over to his house. His downstairs door was unlocked. I went up to his apartment and knocked. After about five minutes he answered. He had these incredibly blood-shot eyes."

"Is he an alcoholic?" Leslie asked, with a slightly patronizing tone.

"Well," she said, looking down at the Formica table, "he told me he suffers from depression."

"Yeah," Leslie said disparagingly, "'cause he drinks."

"He told me he had been off the bottle until he met me," she revealed further.

"Oh, my favorite kind of trip," he smacked his hands together, "a guilt trip."

"Anyway, we were sitting in his place, two people, needing someone . . ."

"What did his place look like?" Leslie interrupted, always fascinated by New York apartments.

"Actually, it's huge. Sparsely furnished, yellowing wall paper, dust and crud over everything—you'd like it. Stacks and piles of everything. Paperbacks and hardcover books. Newspapers and strokers reaching up to the ceiling. I asked him if he was okay. He ran into the bathroom, I could hear him wrenching his guts out."

"He wasn't pissed that you dumped him?" Leslie asked.

"Well, kind of. He said that it was painful to see me. And it would be best if I didn't come by again. Funny thing is, I've been with him day and night ever since."

"What do you mean?" Leslie replied, feeling queasy.

"He said more than he intended to say. He acciden-tally let out that he had served in Korea, not 'Nam."

"If he was in Korea . . ." Leslie started doing the math.

"Yeah," she cut him off, "he's forty-eight."

"Forty-eight!" Leslie looked into her blue eyes and felt a sudden, frantic thumping, like he had to try to stop something that was already over. "So what happened? Is he helping you find a place?"

"No, Leslie." Jeane paused, looked off uncomfortably, and battled tears. "I need a father for my baby, and I need someone to love me. So I'm marrying him. We agreed on it. I'm moving in and we're going to renovate his place, which by the way is three times the size of this crappy dive." Jeane smiled at Leslie.

"Jeane! He's forty-eight! That's twice your age."

"I spent the night thinking about that, and I figured that it really could work."

"What could work?" he asked, baffled.

"At forty-eight, there aren't many more acts left in life, are there?"

"What the hell does that mean? What are you saying?"

She pursed her lips, unable to look at Leslie any longer. All the months of depression and floating anxiety that had pressed behind her optimistic face suddenly burst through. She collapsed forward into her hands and started weeping, shaking uncontrollably in her seat.

Leslie put his arm around her and thought, this is it. It's over. It's all over. After several minutes, she regained control. "I saw all those empty liquor bottles in his apartment," she sobbed, "and I realized that *I* was his drinking problem."

"Jeane, please listen. This man helped you study for an examination over a period of weeks. That might mean you owe him something, but you sure don't owe him your life!"

"It's not guilt I feel. I mean, all those empty bottles, I didn't think I could still do that to a man. I didn't think anyone desired me that much."

"How do you know he doesn't always drink?"

"Because he told me."

"Jeane . . ."

"You know what it's like to go to bed at night with a baby next to you and feel totally unwanted? If I don't have love, I can't give it. He made me feel pretty again." She smiled and opened her compact and dried her eyes with a balled-up Kleenex.

"It was never a question of anyone not wanting you," Leslie explained. "I would have married you when I first met you. I would have jumped off a building for you. I was obsessed with you . . ." He lacked the guts to tell her that something vital in him was missing. Although he knew he needed to love somebody, no one seemed to deserve it.

"Well," she said, hastily applying eyeliner, "but here I am now, and right now I can't even give me away."

"This is a rash decision."

"It's not going to change."

"He's a fucking hot dog vendor!" Leslie blurted out angrily.

"And what am I?"

"Don't do it. For god's sake, Jeane, don't do it! You should wait."

"For what?" She stared at him. "Are you going to marry me?"

"I . . ."

"Say it! Do you want to marry me?"

He stared at her sadly.

"Then shut the fuck up!" Jeane rose and grabbed her coat.

"Forgive me," he said, before she could storm out the door. "This is a bit sudden for me."

She slid back into a chair next to him. "I could have done a lot better. Hell, at night I lie in bed and think about the guys I could've had. I could've had you. But now I am this. And who else can handle me and my background and my baby? That waiter Marcos called me a *puta*. That's how most guys feel about someone like me. I mean, Eddie's not going to start calling me a slut or whore when the going gets tough."

"Sounds like a debtor's compromise," he stated, employing a bankruptcy term.

"I told him that if I had slept around less and if he were a few years younger we'd both probably get a better quality of partner, and he laughed."

Silently standing before her, holding her, Leslie could feel a small but poignant part of his life dying, waiting to disintegrate into his past. He looked around at his apartment which had been divided and occupied for over a year by Jeane and her baby. It had become cramped and smelly, but he had grown comfortable in it.

■

Over the next few days everything was in turmoil as her things were packed into boxes and moved out. When Leslie came home from work on Friday evening, Jeane and Kate and every shred of them were gone. His place and his life belonged to him again.

JANUARY 8, 1983, NYC

"I'M REALLY SORRY, I DIDN'T ANTICIPATE THIS," Cecilia said over the phone to her employer, Mistress Leah.

"Just get well. Fluids and vitamins," she heard her boss advise. Cecilia thanked her and hung up.

Cecilia was glad that she had never missed a session, because she knew she could lose her job for spontaneously canceling half a dozen appointments. She didn't really have a fever. That would have been preferable to a broken nose.

Why the fuck did I wait this long before breaking up? Although they weren't cracked, Cecilia's ribs felt sore as she lay down.

Gina had gotten shit-faced the previous night and had spun out of control. If that wasn't bad enough, Cecilia knew that she was out there now somewhere, getting drunker than ever before, wallowing in guilt about hitting her.

At least I get a vacation, if only to convalesce, she thought. But that still meant a week with two shiny black eyes and a bandage over her nose.

JANUARY 26, 1983, NYC

THREE HUMID SIXTY-DEGREE DAYS IN THE MIDDLE of winter compelled Leslie to take advantage of the warm spell with a walk. The oil-slicked streets northwest of Forty-second that night were slippery underneath Leslie's feet. Now and again he would hold his breath, trying not to inhale the waves of sulfuric smells, barbecued smokes, and cheap incense. Lights screamed out of the darkness against his watery pupils. Car honks, brake screeches, screams, and the blaring of distant radios blended into a hodgepodge of untranslatable wants.

When it started raining, he pressed close against the buildings, passing under dirty, torn awnings, careful not to rub against the rippled-metal drop-gates filthy with soot and graffiti. Doorways were filled with chanting or leaning figures. Posters plastered over posters plastered over posters thicker than the walls they were glued onto. At the convergence of Seventh and Broadway the avenues parted like a pair of concrete lips into a permanent traffic bubble of cars and pedestrians.

He crossed the intersection and took a couple steps toward the subway, but that night the thought of going home alone and zombying out on TV was acutely unbearable. He stopped at Nathan's Hotdogs on the southeast corner of Forty-third and Broadway and bought a burger and oily fries. He grabbed a handful of yellow napkins, and after eating, when the misty rain had subsided, he entered the first porn arcade on Forty-second between Seventh and Eighth Avenues. After flipping through magazines, gaining a bit of momentum with a series of semi-erections, he went into the next place down the strip. The rear of the store subdivided into a honeycomb of little booths that seemed to reach deep into the interior of the block. It was a grand bazaar of wonderfully exploited young flesh. Girls of all varieties had been cleaned, cast, filmed, edited, and cubicle-distributed.

Leslie went into several booths. First, he saw a stunningly beautiful blonde being devoured and dildoed by another stunningly beautiful blonde; next, a saucy brunette got rear-ended by a black man with a humongous schlong; the last film was a huge orgy, a Horn &

Hardart's of sexual delights. Then he spotted a publicity photo on the door. It was an old Sky Pacifica flick, and though he wanted to watch it, the booth was occupied. He waited a while before he thought, there's a reason this booth is inaccessible. Leave the memory alone. With a sudden force of will, he exited.

In the third adult entertainment establishment he entered, a gang of five women in colorful string bikinis— two young Latin girls, one black woman, and two whites—were leaning against a banister on the upper balcony, giggling and catcalling to the businessmen perusing porn magazines below. The thought of going into a private booth with a live female made Leslie shiver. After seeing the Sky photo, he felt too nervous to even venture into the booths in the back half of the arcade. He confined himself to the tables filled with magazines.

"Hey, you in the brown shit! What's that, a cucumber in your pocket?" one of the bikini girls called down to him.

"Hey babe! Up here!" another accented voice stirred in.

"Everyone married, look up," a different girl's voice called out. All the ladies giggled.

Leslie wanted to leave but surrendering would give them victory. So he slowly started looking at magazines near the door. Finally, when the girls got bored with the teasing, he dashed out.

He stopped briefly at four more porn palaces and bought three magazines. Since Sky had left him, the type of pornography that he found most effective were tight close-ups that completely obliterated any surrounding female features. The images were a succession of gigantic genitalia, hairy or shaved, which looked more like abstract art than anything else.

He slipped the magazines inside his trench coat and stepped off the sidewalk into the street for a cab. But the theaters were letting out and the frenzy had begun: Cabs were being snatched up as fast as they appeared. Couples in suits, families from the Midwest, tourists from the world over were vying with each other for the sacred golden vehicles. Leslie felt a drop on his head, and then another. It was starting to rain again, large splashy drops spitting from the dark surrounding buildings. He hurried down the corner subway entrance. An uptown express and a local train were simultaneously pulling out of the station. Leslie headed toward the rear of the platform, yawned, and picked up a *Wall Street Journal* that was ledged on a garbage receptacle.

As he read through the different waves of screeching trains, Leslie discerned a single, wiry voice twanging out. It was actually more of an intense whisper. Despite its hyperactive pace, its tinny tone was very articulate: "They want it posy rosy! They want it dean clean! They want sunlight! They want the normal. Even if it's the other way, they want the norm. Make it normal! Sure! I'll make it normal. Salt me down, well done on both sides!"

Looking up, he saw an old homeless guy with white hair sprouting out all over him. It even appeared to arise from the tattered, gray business suit he was wearing, along with the dirt-caked shirt and oily black tie. The man seemed to have mentally snapped right in the middle of his business day.

Leslie wondered if Sky had gotten married yet. He envisioned her dressed in white, walking down the aisle lined with Sabrett Hot Dog carts, a twenty-one-frank salute. She could have invited him to the wedding.

"They want it rosy red! They want it licked clean! They want it surgical tight. Well, fuck 'em. They can't have it. It's a big fucking joke to them! They don't got the balls! What do they know? Shards of glass to 'em."

An article in the *Journal* profiled a recent phenomenon in Japan. A growing number of older businessmen who had become successful in the booming economy were leaving their high-salaried jobs to become Buddhist monks. The article focused on one particular executive who was the head of a growing electronics firm. After the career man reached his mid-fifties and found his life empty, he disowned his former existence and took a sacred vow and became a monk. Now he lived with other pilgrims in a seven-hundred-year-old Buddhist temple. He spent his days in austerity and contemplation, in a world where not even a single grain of rice was wasted.

"They want the normal! Even if it's abnormal, they want the normal, so show them the norms, George!" the psychotic man yelled in the background.

Leslie read on. Occasionally the businessman-turned-monk would go out with other monks to neighboring villages where they would offer prayers in exchange for donations or whatever sustenance they could get. His great pursuit now, according to the article, was to trade in his former material gain for higher spiritual wealth.

Leslie wondered exactly what the word *spirit* meant. Wasn't it supposed to be the state which existence takes after the body dies? Somehow the word acquired moral connotations. There seemed to be an assumption that if a person made money, they were doing it at their spiritual expense. Leslie folded back the paper, stared at the subway track's third rail, and thought, shit, *I'm spiritual too.*

A shriek from the corridor above was followed by a scurrying of heavy feet hustling down the dirty concrete steps. Leslie gracefully ducked behind a pillar and noticed two black youths. A woman shouting obscenities down at them was presumably reacting to their hijinks.

"You a crazy bastid, Ville, you so fly!" Leslie listened to the shorter youth babble at the taller, older one.

"Make it normal! Sure! Make it normal!" The hairy homeless man was flaring up in the distance.

"Oh shit, look at this deep-fried mothafucka!" The youth called Ville was pointing at the homeless man.

Leslie watched as the two teenagers strutted over and inspected the slow-moving lunatic.

"Hey!" the younger one began. The homeless man ignored him, still railing on about normalcy.

"Yo!" the first one said this time, shoving the homeless guy. "Quit that crazy-ass shit!"

"Fuck them all's what I say! Fucking bitches is what they are!" The homeless guy was speaking more maniacally, starting to grow hoarse.

"You cured!" Ville yelled, as he kicked the man hard in his thigh. Both kids laughed.

"They're fucking bitches!" The psychotic scrambled a few steps away. "All rich fucking bitches!" Leslie could see the man limping now.

"Shut up," Ville responded, and shoved the homeless man hard, causing him to whack the back of his head against a steel column. The man scurried.

"Hey!" Leslie yelled authoritatively. "Leave him alone!"

The two teens slunk away guiltily. For an instant, Leslie felt victorious, but a moment later he heard one of them say, "Who the fuck are you?"

Ville was looking directly at Leslie, heading toward him. The second teen, still a boy, was in tow.

"This ain't none of your fucking business," he said, directly in Leslie's face.

"All I'm saying is you don't need to pick on him. He's a human being too," Leslie reasoned, trying to hide his fear.

The taller teen started looking up and down the platform as the shorter one stepped up close to Leslie. Without warning, he smacked him harshly across the face.

"Hey!" Leslie yelped, and jerked his arms up defensively.

"Looky here, mothafucka's gonna whip my ass," the short youth said to Ville, laughing.

"Oh, watch it, Moogy, he a bad-ass mothafucka," Ville replied, and the two started laughing.

"Ville say you bad, huh?" the smaller one taunted, approaching Leslie. He started edging away.

"Where the fuck you going?" Ville reached out, grabbed Leslie by his coat, and shoved him against a tiled wall behind the stairway. "Yo ass ain't goin' nowheres till we done with it."

"What do you want?" Leslie asked, trying not to tremble.

"We want you to shut yo mouf'!" the younger one shouted, as droplets of his spit shot into Leslie's face.

Leslie was sure he could hold his own against the little one, but with the older, stronger youth present, he didn't dare try. Without warning, the younger teen jabbed Leslie hard across his head, causing him to fall forward and drop the porn magazines he had bought. Leslie saw a woman on the opposite track staring at him and trying to make sense of the magazines.

"Oh shit," Ville said, reaching down and collecting the stash. "Looks like we hit jackpot." The two vanished up the stairs chuckling.

Leslie stood there a moment, paralyzed. A train soon swept into the station and opened its doors, sucking Leslie in. Nervously, he took a seat and tried to resume reading, but his tears dripped onto the *Wall Street Journal*. He wished he owned a handgun. Feeling like an utter coward, he slapped himself across the face, only to become aware that a dozen people had seen him do this and now thought they were locked in a car with an insane man.

Despite the fact that he was an Ivy League graduate and a promising associate in a powerful corporate law firm, Leslie felt stripped down to a schoolboy, fearful of bullies.

When he arrived home, he put a cold compress on his swollen face. He could still smell the lingering residue of Sky and Kate even though they had left over two months ago.

■

The following workweek passed slowly. Repeatedly he'd stop and think, was I put on this earth to file corporate bankruptcies? It grew increasingly difficult to focus. The next week passed even more sluggishly. *I'm bored by my job* turned into *I hate my job,* and that evolved into *I don't have a life.* Despite a pile of briefs and endless paperwork, he kept getting distracted and would find himself staring down at the traffic bubble around Forty-second Street.

Time seemed to be drawing to a torpid halt. Each

workday ended with Leslie moseying over to a porn arcade and flipping through the skin magazines. Sometimes he bought one, sometimes he didn't. He always perused the photos on the doors of the loops, but rarely went into the little stalls. One day he found a sex photo of Sky on a booth door. The little cubicle was vacant. He checked his pockets for quarters and went in, locking the door behind him. In the darkness, he couldn't bring his finger to release the quarter and start the flick. Sky's sudden departure had left him sad and angry. If she had ever loved me, she wouldn't have left. At least she could've given me notice instead of scheming while I was away on a trip. If she had told me that she was thinking of going to Eddie, he decided, I wouldn't have let her go.

When someone knocked on the booth door, he still hadn't dropped the quarter. He left without viewing her loop. Leslie went home and fell asleep watching TV.

The next day, as soon as he arrived at work, he called Sky at Eddie's house. She answered on the first ring.

"How are you doing?" he had difficulty saying.

"Fine. I wanted to call you . . ." she said, but didn't finish the sentence. Leslie knew she believed that by not calling him she was showing her gratitude.

"It's good to hear your voice," he said stiffly. His jaw felt rusty from disuse.

"You too."

"You know, I wish I got to know Eddie better," he replied, trying to relax.

"Me too," she said. Leslie could hear her chuckle politely.

"So, you guys get married yet?"

"Not yet. He wants to. But what's the rush, right?"

"You don't?" he asked. A good deal, he thought, should be closed quickly.

"Well, I'm not really in love with the man." Her voice dropped an octave and assumed a comical white-trash accent. "I feel like a child-bride in some Oklahoma mail-order marriage catalogue."

"If you feel that way . . ." Leslie responded, not intending to complete the statement.

They slid through a brief slick of silence before she said, "You know, I finished my hundred hours of interning and I got a two-week projecting stint."

"No kidding. Where?"

"I'm back in porno."

"What?"

"It's a porn theater," she relayed. "The El Dorado over on Forty-third and Eighth Avenue. I started last week."

"You're kidding!" Leslie gasped and cringed because he had been there just a few days earlier and hoped that she hadn't spotted him.

"Last week," she continued, "I showed a collection of shorts and there was one episode with me doing a girl-girl. It was fucking embarrassing . . ."

"No fooling!" He laughed with her.

"No one said anything. I don't think anyone noticed."

"What do you do for a baby-sitter?" Leslie asked, hearing Katie in the background.

"Well, since I usually work the closing shift, Eddie watches her. I actually brought her to work once."

"It sounds like it's all coming together for you," Leslie said sincerely.

"Almost all," she replied. They chatted a bit longer before Kate started crying and Jeane had to run.

MARCH 21, 1983, NYC

SITTING AT A BAR IN THE VILLAGE WHERE SHE AND
Leslie used to drink, Cecilia wondered how she could
have liked it. The cigarette smoke and loud music were
intolerable. The only thing at all enticing was the guy
in a black T-shirt sitting in the nearby booth stealing
glances at her. He looked young and pretty like a tough
Italian chick, a little like Gina.

The black T-shirt finally stopped being discreet and
looked directly at her. If I could screw him and shake
him, I would, she thought. Cecilia knew he was going to
make his move, but she couldn't handle it. Most
boyfriends, and for that matter, most girlfriends, were
lessons that didn't require repeating. Gina was a classic
example. Although she was passionate and loving, she
was an addictive personality. One type that Cece would
never deal with again. Leslie was the lover who troubled
her most. He was neurotic and dorky. Gina was actually
more macho than he. Somehow, though, it made him
very attractive. He was also great, though unpre-
dictable, in bed. But perhaps the most magnetic quality
was that she felt incredibly secure with him. After she
had dated an alcoholic, Leslie's problems seemed trifling
by comparison. Except for the occasion when she had
discovered the magazines, his strange obsessions were
always his own—private, hidden, shameful. But that
was all moot now. Leslie and that porn star had a kid.

The guy in the black shirt was smiling at her now,
and all Cecilia could think was, what is the weak link
in this guy's tacky gold chain? What quality would
make him painfully human and render him sexless
and destructive? She didn't want to think about it;
instead, she finished the dregs of her beer.

"Can I get you a refill?" the black shirt jumped, not even waiting for her to put down the empty mug.

"Thanks anyway," she replied. "I was on my way out."

MARCH 21, 1983, NYC

"LESSS-LEEE!"

Above the shuffle and din of city noise, he heard somebody bellowing his name down the busy street. Stopping, looking through the intermittent movement of the bustling masses, he caught glimpses of Sky hastily approaching, pushing Kate's stroller before her. Shortly after the little girl was born, Sky had lost most of the weight she had gained during her pregnancy. Now she appeared thinner than ever before.

"You look great!" Leslie greeted with a big smile.

"Actually, I was sick," she rebuffed.

"Sick?" Some guy handing out sales fliers gave one to Leslie, who crumpled it into a ball without breaking his conversation.

"A respiratory infection," she replied. An Indian man pushing a red hand-truck with a large cardboard box on it brushed by Katie, forcing Sky to move the stroller.

"Did you see a doctor?" Leslie asked, returning to her illness.

"Yeah, he kept asking me who I screwed."

"What do you mean?" A fire engine turned a corner, its sirens blaring. Both of them silently smiled a moment until they could resume speaking.

"He asked if I did all this sexual stuff," Sky elaborated.

"What stuff?"

"Used drugs. Made it with bisexuals. Oh! He asked me if I ever screwed a Haitian," she chuckled.

"What did you say?" he asked, concerned.

"You kidding? I told him to stand in line and see the film like everyone else. *Sky Screws the World*. I ain't giving the plot away!"

Both of them laughed until a flare-up of tourists started pushing them apart. Leslie moved Kate's stroller against a building, behind an open door, where they took refuge against the flow of people.

"How's it feel being an eligible bachelor again?" Sky asked.

"I've been filling the time with work," he replied, visibly bushed.

"Excuse me, folks." A tall, hollowed man approached. "Would either of you kind, wonderful people be able to spare a single quarter so that a decorated Vietnam Vet might be able to buy a subway token to go home?"

"Sorry," said Sky. Leslie shook his head no.

"Even a shiny penny would help," the beggar persisted. Both shrugged, but the man just stood there. Sky checked her watch and said, "Oh gosh! I have to take Katie to the pediatrician."

"I'd love to see you project a film sometime," he said, making a point of taking an interest in her career.

"I think the city of New York pays those guys to break up conversations on the street," Sky said, as the beggar went to harass another couple. She promised Leslie she would invite him up to a theater as soon as she felt it was cool with the management.

Sky leaned forward to give Leslie a kiss goodbye. While they had been living together, he was cautious of her affections, but now that she was with Eddie, Leslie hugged her, kissed her, and breathed her in. When he let her go, he watched as she and Katie vanished into the crowd. Leslie thought it odd how life seemed a succession of meeting strangers, growing very close, and eventually drifting apart again. Each friend and lover who had vanished into oblivion took away a little part of him.

■

Sky called Leslie at work a few days later, commenting on how good it had been to bump into him on the street. While they conversed, he could hear Katie crying in the background.

"How's your cold?" he asked.

"Oh, it cleared up."

They only spoke for a few minutes, but the conversation initiated a new and casual relationship. Over the next week, Leslie and Sky chatted a little each day. The light conversations usually touched on their respective routines and sometimes the news of the day.

MAY 12, 2001, LI

JEANE IS SITTING AT A FIFTY-YEAR-OLD DESK IN HER hospital office, listening to a twenty-five-year-old rotary dial telephone, scribbling something in a yellowing file. The overhead bars of dusty florescent lights are off and a single incandescent bulb shines a dull marble glow on her desk. When she spots me peeking in, she waves once, but makes no expression. I take the only available seat, an oak armchair facing her.

Where the hand meets the armrest all the shellac has been

scratched off — like an electric chair. While staring at the old window latch, buried under layers and layers of lead and non-lead paint, and listening to her on the phone, I remember Sky. Even though my life is a formula for regret, I don't feel regretful. The sexual part of her I was initially attracted to is now buried under age, propriety, and duty. What I am witnessing is a hardened outer shell. The old her is completely obliterated and the cast of decorum is all that remains.

After several monosyllabic words, she says, "Fine," drops the phone on the horns, and starts writing frantically.

"So, despite the present situation," I say, "how're you doing?"

Before she replies, the phone rings. She picks it up. I hate when people prioritize telephone calls above humans in their midst. After listening to another tedious work-related call, I feel myself tensing up and my impatience rising.

She finishes with this second call, and I quickly suggest, "Why don't we grab some dinner?"

"Actually, tonight's family night," she says, a clear, unambiguous message.

"Isn't every night family night?"

"Well, since everyone is usually running on their own schedule, we agreed to make Wednesday night family night. That's when we all have a sit-down together."

"How about a drink then?" I compromise.

"I really don't have the time. We are all meeting at 6:30. If you're thirsty, though, there's a Coke machine down the hall."

"No, I'm okay." I squeeze my heartbreak into a smile. "So the creep called you last night," I remind her. "Tell me, did you consider getting a trace on the phone?"

"When I star-69ed I got a recording saying it was a blocked number that didn't accept incoming calls."

"Slippery son of a bitch. What'd he say?"

"He said he was going to either have sex with me or rape Kate."

No, he said he was going to "slam-fuck" you, I correct silently in my head.

"I hope you notified the police," I counsel.

"We've been assigned a Detective Witowski who's handling our case. But all we can do is report incidents like this. God, I'd love to get my hands on this guy. I'd kill him. I really would."

"Jeane, I don't want to trivialize this, but all it comes down to is harassment."

"No! Don't you see?" Jeane leans forward. "This guy is very dangerous!"

"But an obscene phone call . . ."

"He's followed me—followed us! You've never been stalked. You feel them out there. You're connected to them. And they're connected to some sick, blind vision. Even *they* don't know what they're going to do next. He's out there and he's either watching me now or planning to watch me. I feel it!"

"You sound paranoid," I warn her.

"He saw us the other day when we were together!"

"What makes you think—"

"I told you!" That's right, she did. He saw us at the motel. It's difficult to keep track of what I'm not supposed to know. "He thought you were my husband!"

"Man," I reply, sorry for her. I sincerely wish that this would stop. A million wankers and strokers must have seen Sky getting fucked in the seventies. They jerked off, cleaned off, went off. Perfectly normal. Why do I have to pursue this? I don't know. Sex is the hardest addiction because with only a fantasy, we secrete our own glassine packet of heroin. And like all addictions, as I've grown more inured to the drug, I've grown more desperate. My fantasy grows imperceptibly stranger, rougher, and more dire, scraping further and harder into the bottom of my imagination, until it's come to this. I'm hunting down old sirens in the suburbs.

"I'm afraid to go home," she details. "At night, I have the hospital security guard walk me to my car."

Could I ever hurt her? Am I capable of going that far? I reach out and place a supportive hand on her shoulder.

"In a strange way," she confides, "I'm kind of relieved."

"Relieved?!"

"For years I was expecting this. I'd occasionally get a hang-up call. Glances from strangers that last a bit too long. I'm sure one of them was him."

Through the subtlest of clues, Jeane unveils her ancient fear that has had roots growing for over two decades. Her guilt, seeded in years of recklessness, has been springing up in the nooks of her nightmares and now emerges fully bloomed in her daily dread. From a place of titillation, shielded by a veneer of loving concern, I ask, "How do your kids feel about your past?"

"About my acting in porn?" she says, tearing the envelope wide open.

"The porn, yes."

"Initially, they seemed okay with it. But, you know, these things are time bombs. As Kate gets older and matures and comes to appreciate what it all means, well, her judgment is coming slowly. We got into a fight a few weeks ago, and she said something under her breath. I don't know what, but I know it had something to do with the porn." Jeane looks down for a retrospective moment. When her eyes come up they are wet. She adds, "With time, whatever it was she whispered is going to be shouted. Kids don't forgive their parents for anything."

"It might get worse," I clarify, "but as she turns into an

adult, when she understands how difficult and meaningless everything is, it'll get easier." The exchange carries a resonance for me. As I look dead ahead, I can feel the message echo down the cold, dark chambers of my own Perry-tortured soul. For the first time, too, without my immediately noting it, Jeane is looking at me.

"First they blame you," Jeane says, trying to lighten the mood, "then they feel sorry for you."

"Crap coming and going," I reply with a smile.

A golden crowbar of sunlight suddenly pries through the cast-iron clouds. I can't hold back from saying, "I'm sorry, Jeane. I really am." She thinks I'm sorry about this one thing, but I am sorry about everything to come.

Looking at her wristwatch, Jeane sighs and explains that she has to head home. Fine. I feel drained and politely ask if I might walk her to her car.

"'Course," she replies. Collecting her purse and jacket, she mentions the details of her workday, clients she saw, cases she handled. I respond supportively, letting her proudly exhibit her dollhouse in which she plays a benevolent god. As we leave, she locks the murky-glassed door behind her.

Waiting at the elevator, I stand with my back to the hallway window so that the rays from the late-day sun behind me shine in Jeane's eyes. I'm able to take a deep gulp of her perfect face close up. She's beautiful, but I see crows feet emerging at the corners of those never-aging eyes. Her skin is a bit runny as if she has been caught in a rainstorm. Motherhood is there; middle-age is alongside it. As she speaks about her family, I remember the her I once knew — terminally young, reckless, arrogant, with a brittle armor of confidence over every insecure move and gesture. Like a heartless Don Juan, her youth has abandoned her for ever younger women. But in 1979 nothing had come between her and her girlishness. Youth, ultimately, was the great love of her life. Her honey-toned skin, as I remember it, was so soft and luminous it looked edible. If the seventies ever had a reason for not proceeding into the eighties, it was to keep Sky young.

The clunky elevator opens and we enter. When the doors slide shut I feel comfortable next to her. We stand side by side and the last fifteen years vanish. We are comfortable together as if time had never devoured us and shat us out through completely different holes.

"About the other day," she finally refers to our motel interlude, "I'm embarrassed about, well, you know, I kind of lost it."

"Me too." Kind of.

"You have to understand that I was sublimating a lot of pent-up frustration."

Her psychobabble makes our passionate encounter sound like some freakish aberration. Although this annoys me, I balance a professional smile.

"You're not just anyone," she says, perhaps sensing my disdain. "I mean, you're more than a person. You're the clos-est thing I have to a hero." Jeane leans forward and hugs me. "I owe so much to you."

"You don't owe me anything," I say sincerely.

"Remember that day I showed up at your door preg-nant?" She lets out a chuckle. "God, when I add up all my clients that have pulled stunts like that, I mean, it's the only reason I can do this job, 'cause I was once them." She pauses and nods to remember it. "That day, I had nowhere to go but your door . . ."

"It was nothing," I dismiss.

"You initially threw me out, remember?"

"I threw you out?" I have no recollection.

"I showed up early that morning and tried to spend the night, and you said no and ended up pushing me out.

Remember? You followed me to Central Park as the sun was coming up?"

"Oh yeah." Amazing to think it.

"I only wanted to spend the night. I had about four grand which I stole from T-Bird and the bags I was holding. I was hoping to start a new life."

"And you did."

"I was young, dumb, and pregnant, and you came outside and got me, and instead of only letting me stay the night, you gave me a place and money."

"You probably could have stayed at the Y or something," I reply.

"Maybe, but you gave me a lot more. From you I really learned discipline, you had these . . ." she looks for the word, "principles! You let me get my feet on the ground."

"Well," I return the praise, "you were a good investment."

"That night, I had a bottle of sleeping pills and was as close to the edge as I had ever come. I was ready to end it."

I look away, feeling embarrassed. The man I was, for all his frustration and anguish, shames the creep I am now. She reaches over and hugs and kisses me. For the first time in so long, I feel warmth and connection.

Taking the biggest and stupidest chance, I pull back, look her in the eyes, and say, "I know this sounds ridiculous, but I'm forty-six years old and . . . you wouldn't ever consider leaving Eddie?"

"Leaving him where?" She grins, thinking I'm joking.

"Leaving him and . . . marrying me?"

"Leslie!" She smiles sadly. "You got to wait twenty years before your dreams are answered, and by then . . . Les, you were always the only love of my life. You know that, don't you?" Her eyes grow wet and I hold her.

"I love you and I need you," I plead.

"All these years, Eddie's been there." She tries to convey

her sympathy and adds, "I wish it were you, Les, I really do, but this is life."

"I was terrified! But I'm ready now." Kindly ignore the fact that I married another woman and strangled her.

"Don't do this!" She lifts her arms up and turns away.

"Look, I can wait. I mean, Eddie's not young and—"

"Please don't do this," she appeals, and is quickly losing patience. Of course, she's absolutely right. Melodrama is worse than pathetic, it's boring.

The elevator doors slice open a new reality. A small gathering of insects are buzzing outside, waiting for us to exit.

As I walk Jeane through the lobby, she talks fondly about old times: the Upper West Side of the late seventies and early eighties. For a short time, when she was on top of the world, it seemed she could go in any number of directions. It's odd that she chose motherhood in Long Island as her oblivion. But then, we never really make any choices. One day it's later and we are there.

Jeane and I are about to leave the building when a young, hip doctor approaches. Handsome in a twerpy way, with a springy pad of Brillo hair, he exudes a sexual self-confidence that shakes every jealous bone in my body. The doctor blocks Jeane's path with a cocky stare and a ballsy smile.

"Jeane, I tried calling you earlier this afternoon." He talks low in his larynx, vying for a throaty authority beyond his years.

"I was dropping off the Castillo kid at Protective Services," she replies. I detect subtle interest on Jeane's part. The fire in the old diva loins is not completely burnt out.

"I wanted to ask you about the Mol case," he explains.

"Oh shit! That's right. He's in court tomorrow, isn't he?" Turning to me, Jeane says, "I have to go back upstairs."

"Do you want me to bring it up?" the young doctor asks. Now it's crystal clear what's happening.

"You have the file?" she replies. They must think I'm a goddamned idiot!

"It's in my office. I finished his physical yesterday." This is the guy she mentioned during our brief encounter—Mr. Infidelity, her Rudy fuck.

"The lawyers will be coming to pick it up. Bring it to my office, I'll open up." I'm sure she will.

The young doctor leaves to fetch this suddenly needed file.

"I can wait," I say to Jeane, as she heads back toward the elevators.

"No, this is going to take a while. You go ahead." She thinks she can chuck me out like an old diaphragm.

"I really don't mind," I say with a gum-exposing smile.

"Really, I need to be alone to work on this." Translation: I'm done with your tired, middle-aged tool, now it's time for some young, nonstop cock.

"I'll wait down here." I calmly sit in one of the empty Naugahyde lobby chairs, demonstrating supreme leisure.

"Leslie, I'll feel pressured if I know that you're down here."

For a moment there is a fine tension, and I can see Jeane wondering why I am so desperate to be with her. I stand up and see that there is little choice.

"You're sweet, but I'm fine, really." She permits me a graceful exit. "You don't have to worry. Dr. Stein will walk me to my car."

"I'm a bit apprehensive," I whisper as a last-ditch effort, and leaning toward her, I ask, "How do you know this guy isn't your secret admirer?"

"Why do you think that?" she asks, wrinkling her brow.

"Isn't it suspicious the way he suddenly appeared, like he was waiting for you."

"Leslie, I appreciate your concern, but it's not him."

"Okay," I say with a big-sister smile. "Call me sometime. We'll talk more about this later." Now she's going to fuck the doctor and I have to go home like a good little boy.

"I promise I'll call," Jeane says, and gives me a quick embrace. I leave with a reassuring smile pinned to my otherwise despondent face.

Heading for the train station, I keep the smile on high speed, straining my facial muscles until they hurt. Touching my heart, I feel a cold and empty weight. The unused Polaroid is folded in my breast pocket. While walking up the steps to the elevated platform, I see the New York train pulling out. In the glass-enclosed waiting area, I envision Sky with the boy medic. Time for a quick exploratory. He's leaning her against the two-drawer filing cabinet, taking her from the rear, pinning her arms behind her, dipping into her bra. Or maybe she's lying on her back, legs open on the old desk with her heels still on. The next train won't be coming for another hour. I'm trying to hold him in, but in this solitary confinement, Perry's going *muy loco*. He breaks out, and I dash the six blocks back to the hospital, considering what I should do. I saved her life all those years ago, I should be the one nailing her now.

PART FIVE: EJECT

▼

APRIL 12, 1983, NYC

"WHERE TO?" THE DRIVER ASKED. THE QUESTION forced Leslie to consider *what* rather than *where* he wanted.

"Fiftieth and Seventh," Leslie blurted. As the cab sped across town, he wanted to correct himself and give his home address, but couldn't. The benign impulse had metastasized into a malignant desire.

Stepping into the arcade, he half-hoped that they had replaced the old loop. Porn no longer meant just sex. It was initially the excitement of a promise that could never be kept. Now, though, it was a measure of his own innocence that had been ground down to a nub. It was getting increasingly difficult, requiring ever more quarters to cum. But this wasn't even about jerking off. When he found her film, he briefly wondered why this unmopped booth had been overlooked; specifically, why this short reel of Sky, a relic, at least five years old, hadn't been rotated out like all the others. Few women were more beautiful than Sky, but novelty was always more erotic than beauty.

There were two loops inside for the customer's

choosing. One publicity still showed a photo of two Asian girls entangled in each others' bodies like a pair of wrestling Siamese cats. The other still was of Sky smiling between two men. He locked himself inside and instantly dropped a quarter in the "A" slot.

Sky sprang to life in the middle of an orgy. Two men, one black, the other white, were on either side of her. A pumpernickel and rye sandwich. He knew the loop; he knew her entire oeuvre. Yet every time he saw a Sky Pacifica film, he always learned something new. It was the only film in which she was ever DP'd— double-penetrated. But he didn't come to see that. Leslie put his hand over the junction of skewered genitals and watched the alternating shots of her face, which pulled half a dozen of the most amazing reactions out of her magician's hat. He absorbed her facial expressions as though he were deciphering some forgotten language. Even though the film had been made several years earlier, it seemed like another lifetime. Without so much as an erection, he held onto her face with the same intrigue he had in listening to a great opera.

When the camera pulled back so that the sexual act filled the screen, Leslie was overwhelmed and stepped back, bumping into the rear of the small booth.

"*Sky,*" he muttered. He tried covering everything up with his hands, but couldn't, and though he didn't want to see it, he couldn't abandon the cubicle.

The two men had pulled out and were standing over her, jerking and shooting onto that soft post-adolescent face. The woman he had lived with all these months— who had said she loved him and wanted to marry him—was now lying back with her mouth wide open, her teeth pearly and tongue wiggly. He wanted to feel sorry for her, but dicey clots of cum that looked like maggots covered her mouth. She gargled it into a frothy melange and spat it softly out so it oozed down her lips, bubbly, creamy, along her tongue and nose, dripping down her throat. She looked right at him as though she knew some day he'd be locked in that rotting booth on Fiftieth and Seventh Avenue, and she smiled. For the first time ever, he whipped open the door while the film was still running and ran out.

In a ridiculously overpopulated world, sex means nothing, he vacantly thought, as he stepped outside and hailed a taxi.

"Where to?" the driver asked, turning the flag up before Leslie even closed the door. Despite the fact that he had no answer, the cab hurtled north.

"Where to?" the cabby asked again.

Leslie sat frozen between embittered thoughts and the loosening grip of the image he had just witnessed. The cabby pulled the vehicle to a corner, craned his head, and, staring at Leslie, he asked, "Want to tell me where we're headed?"

The failure of his ability to love or forgive Sky had sealed one passage but inadvertently opened another. Leslie instructed the driver to take him to the nearest ATM machine. The cabby drove fifty feet and screeched in front of a bank. Leslie paid him and went inside. He withdrew three hundred dollars. Then he grabbed another cab and instructed the driver to take him to the Flatiron Building.

As his cab outpaced other taxis, racing and slipping down Broadway to Twenty-third, Leslie decided to turn his thoughts off. He didn't want to think about what he had to do. He simply looked at the blurry rat-tat-tat of bumpy faces while the cab zoomed down Broadway.

I've lived in this city my whole life and I don't know a single person out there.

▼

He went to the building that he remembered walking into roughly two years earlier and pushed the door-bell/intercom button.

"Can I help you?" said a square little voice.

"Yeah, I don't have an appointment, but I'm wondering if I can see Miss Guinevere." The buzzer sounded and Leslie entered.

The receptionist, a new girl, all limbs feathered in a billowy canary-yellow business suit, explained, "La Madame is not here."

"When will she be in?" he asked, poorly hiding his despair.

"I can make an emergency call," she said, picking up a golden telephone.

"She's not in today?" Leslie thought aloud, uncertain about calling her.

"No, but she's gotten emergency calls before. She's the most in-demand disciplinarian we have. She won't get here for at least twenty minutes—if she's at all available. It'll cost you double and you'll have to pay for the first hour in advance."

Leslie crossed his arms and contemplated what he wanted and how he could get it.

"Do you want the Madame or not?" the receptionist asked after several minutes.

"Here's what I want: Can another mistress bind me, hood me, and gag me so that when Mad Gwen gets here we can get right into it?"

"It'll cost you extra, and I strongly advise that she never hear you refer to her in that derogatory diminutive."

Leslie assured her that money was no problem.

"We take cash or credit cards," she explained. As Leslie paid in cash, she continued, "In the event that you want to end the session at any time, the safe word *du jour* is 'zebra.' Do you understand?"

He understood but wished she hadn't told him. He didn't want an emergency exit. He wanted to suffer to the end.

He was handed a pen and clipboard with a questionnaire on it. He scribbled down an alias and glanced at the menu of abominations: whipping, spanking, paddling, caning, mummification, humiliation, degradation. He looked over the role-playing categories: equestrian, puppy training, nipple torture . . . Anxiety prevented him from reading further, so he simply checked off all the boxes at level five—the highest degree of intensity in each category.

Under the paragraph that said "Other Interests," Leslie detailed that he had to be hooded and gagged. In capital letters he wrote, "MY SILENCE MUST BE RESPECTED THROUGHOUT THE ENTIRE SESSION."

The receptionist thanked him and took his payment for a one-hour session. She showed Leslie into a ghastly room that looked to be a medieval torture chamber, and she explained, "You can pick a costume from the closet."

When he touched the walls, he confirmed that the stone and mortar were plastic casting with intricate tones of paint that mimicked dungeon decay. A small modern closet holding a series of absurd costumes was situated in the rear. He undressed and carefully hung up his suit so as not to crease it. All the costumes were fitted with elastic form-fitting waist bands. Among various dresses and gowns, he selected a complete French-maid outfit that included a corset, nylons, glossy-black high heels, and a lavender-handled feather duster. No sooner had he squeezed on an absurd strawberry-blond wig than his dominatrix entered.

She was an athletically built, intensely eyelashed woman with Italian features, who introduced herself as Mistress Lucretia. When Leslie said hello, she called him a faggot and told him to keep his beghole shut. She promptly handcuffed him. An oversized leather hood was pulled loose over his head. He could smell the bad breath of the prior slave along the mouth zipper. Mistress Lucretia asked whether she had cuffed his wrists too tightly. He gratefully muttered, "Thank you, no."

"Not tight enough, bitch!" she cursed, and yanked his elbows up painfully. "How's that?"

"Yes!" he responded quickly.

"Yes, what?"

"Yes, ma'am!" he winced.

"Yes, Mistress Lucretia," she replied, and yanked his arms up again, still higher.

"Yes, Mistress Lucretia," he echoed obediently.

"Though I'm just dying to make your tight ass bleed, I'm gonna go easy on you. Know why?"

"No," he replied.

Reaching into his panties, she grabbed his testicles firmly in hand and corrected him, "No, Mistress Lucretia, I don't."

"No, Mistress Lucretia, I don't!" he repeated attentively. Although she didn't squeeze them, she held his testicles as if weighing them.

"Reason I'm riding you easy is because Mistress Guinevere makes me look like a kitten. She's an unforgiving cunt and you're calling her on her only evening off and I'll tell you right now, nothing pisses her off half so much as this. So I'm gonna save your white meat for her. What have you got to say about that?!" She was still holding his testicles like a handball.

"Thank you so much, Mistress Lucretia."

The dominatrix squeezed his testes only enough to make him flinch, then let them drop.

"Mistress Lucretia?" he appealed.

"What is it, slave?"

"I requested on my questionnaire that I be gagged and hooded for Mistress Guinevere."

Seizing the clipboard, she read it and mumbled, "So you did, slave." She pulled out a small clean piece of cloth from a bin. Removing his hood, Mistress Lucretia tied the strip of cloth loose around his mouth so that he could spit it out if he needed to.

"Let's see if you suffer from vertigo," Mistress Lucretia said, and hoisting him up onto a narrow swivel barstool, she started spinning him around. Turning the lights off, she left him rotating in darkness.

Shit, he thought, revolving in tight circles, trying not to fall, what the hell have I done?

Soon the swiveling slowed and stopped. After what seemed like a lifetime, the light was flipped back on. He was facing the faux stone wall, and although he could hear the footsteps, he couldn't see who was entering behind him.

"What little bitch needs a beating on my night off?" he heard Cecilia articulate, followed by a sharp whacking sound.

Instantly he felt himself again being spun about.

Standing before him, dressed in the full regalia, Cecilia could be seen through the eye-holes in the hood. She was harshly snapping a riding crop against her right thigh.

"You called me out of my manicure, so I don't know if my nails are done. You tell me, slavegirl!" She ran her fingernails deeply across his naked scapula just short of tearing the flesh. When she stepped back, Leslie registered her details: solid jutting shoulders; one hand on a hip; a smoldering cigarette; stepping hard on the heel; exhaling smoke in disgust; never lowering her nose and chin; her lips, constantly pursed; her tone, uncompromising, precise, disgusted. It was a vignette of pain soon to be inflicted.

She noticed that his unflinching eyes were fixed and fawning over her. Lifting her leg, she placed the hard leather sole of her boot against the crown of his stool, right over his flaccid penis, which protruded out of the black lace panties like a desiccated snake. She leaned forward into the barstool, tilting him slowly backwards. He closed his eyes, balancing fear with the faith that she wouldn't hurt him. But as the stool continued rising at a greater angle, lifting him higher and higher, he clung to the thought that the lawsuit would be prohibitive. He felt the stool reach the tipping point, and suddenly it tumbled beyond. He screamed through the gag as she let him fall backwards. He landed on a large and spongy piece of foam rubber discreetly placed on the ground behind him. She chuckled a bit at this practical joke, and muttered, "Did I scare my little baby?"

When he struggled to his feet, she pushed him back onto his belly and said, "Let's see if my little girl crapped her jammies." Yanking down the large black lace panties, Cecilia started giving him hard, open hand whacks on his ass. Leslie bit against his gag.

"Our little girl can stand to lose a couple pounds, can't she?" Cecilia said. "Does this little girl need a high colonic?"

Leslie decided that if she tried to give him an enema, he was going to end the session.

Instead, she removed the cuffs and had him crawl on all fours around the room with his panties down while she whipped his butt with her riding crop. Each snap left a sharp red welt. She stuck the lavender feather duster up the crack of his ass. Plodding around like an animal, he was grateful that she didn't remove his hood or force him to talk. Unlike Lucretia, she had read her chart.

After twenty minutes or so, she shackled him to the faux stone wall, and turning and scrambling through a box in the closet, she took out two tiny alligator clamps which looked like miniature jumper cables. Carefully, she fastened them to Leslie's nipples. The metal teeth pinched into his brown flesh. But this wasn't nearly as painful as when she started tugging on them. He cringed under his mask, and asked himself, why did I have to mark top intensity for nipple torture?

"Oh, baby doesn't like the clampys, does she?" Cecilia asked with a sexy smirk.

He bent forward, pulling on his shackles, trying to push her away with his head. She giggled and started tugging all the more, testing the elasticity of his nipples. He coached himself, let go of the pain, think about some other part of your fucking body. She'll stop focusing on them if she sees they don't bother you. As she pulled and twisted, he thought the word "zebra" over and over. Holding his breath, he yanked himself back sharply as she held the pinched clamps. Through a surge of pain they popped off. He was free of them. She moved away toward the closet. For a moment he believed it was all over, that she was going to turn her attention to a new direction of torment. But as soon as she moved away from the closet, he saw what looked like a tiny vice used to attach earrings to unpierced lobes. Cecilia was carefully fastening it to his right nipple.

"This'll teach naughty little girls!" she threatened, as she began pulling again. Unlike the clamp, this one was tearing into his tender flesh.

"FUCK! STOP! CECILIA, STOP!" he squealed through his gag, behind the leather hood.

Unscrewing the tiny vice, yanking off his hood, Cecilia stood agape, staring at Leslie, shackled and shuddering before her.

MAY 12, 2001, LI

BY THE TIME I RACE BACK TO THE OUTER LIMITS OF THE hospital parking lot, I see that her car is gone. I'm too late. Cocky Dr. Stein moteled her somewhere and is screwing her brains out. I hike back to the train station, wishing I had brought my happy pills with me. Stopping in a convenience store, I purchase a Diet Coke and a newspaper, which I drink and read while I wait for the next train.

Then, uncontrollably, I throw the paper and soda to the floor of the platform, dash back downstairs, and flag down a dented-up, hammered-out, white Ford station wagon that serves as one of the local getaway cars. I have the immigrant chauffeur drop me off around the corner from Jeane's house. Just to be sure the driver won't be suspicious, after I pay him, I stroll up the pathway that divides two manicured lawns toward some strange and empty house. When the car veers around a corner, I jog the two blocks and crouch behind a new pickup truck under a weeping willow. There I pose as if I am tying my shoe laces. Watching, waiting, I can see that Jeane's car is already parked in the driveway. Dr. Stein is a premature ejaculant.

During my ten minutes of stooping, an elderly male walks by with his ratty Jack Russell. I untie and retie my shoe. The husband finally parks in front of the house. Old Eddie-boy looks drawn. The video business, which he thought would be a good profession to retire with, turned out to be his Sisyphean chore.

Jeane's husband hoists their young child onto his broad shoulders. The boy in the blue overalls is a miracle of modern fertility. He reaches up and grabs at the leaves of a sycamore shading their lawn. As Eddie carries him into the house, I jot down the older man's clothes: teal-colored, peg-legged pants and a short-sleeve corduroy shirt. That would be enough for my purpose, but it isn't the prize.

Teenage daughter Kate is the type to hang out with her homegirls for as long as possible. Yet the pleasant numbness in my lower legs turns into a stabbing pain. I won't have to wait much longer. Jeane says the family dinner is at 6:30. It is now 6:23. I search through my jacket and locate my cellphone, but the only number that drones in my head is Sheila's palindrome.

"Hello," I hear her blond voice, tender and unaware it is me.

"Sorry about the other night," I begin, "I just wasn't myself."

"You motherfucker! Don't ever call me again." She hangs up.

I push the redial button and she picks up. "But I gave you my apartment key!"

"I threw it away!" the Britney replies, and hangs up again.

I push redial: "Oops, I did it again."

"Why are you calling me?" she snipes.

"You hung up on me, which any self-respecting woman would do," I reply, as if I'm giving her an award.

"I'm going to get you back somehow," she vows vengefully.

"And I'll give you the opportunity. A love like ours deserves retribution. In fact, that's why I called." She stays silently on the line. "I called to tell you that I can't get you out of my head. And I think, well, I don't really know what the term means, but I think I love you."

"You motherfucker!" She hangs up again.

I dial her back again: "Honestly, though, wasn't it incredibly hot, having sex with a stranger?"

"I was drunk and you took total advantage of me . . ."

"All I'm saying is, if I was sweet and kind and did all that crap, do you really think it would have been that erotic? Sometimes people need it that way."

"You mean being treated like a whore?" she says.

"Yes! And sometimes people need warmth and reassurance, and do you know how to distinguish between the kind of guy who might be doing a little role-playing and the kind of scumbag who you really should watch out for?"

She is silent.

"The guy who calls back the next day to apologize, he's the one you want."

"You need help."

"That has nothing to do with it. Remember, I told you about me." I elaborate, "How I'm a sadist, and I killed my wife, and now I'm stalking my ex-lover."

"Yeah," she says, with all the interest of a gum-snapping shop clerk.

"Well, it's true. I'm across the street from her house right now, waiting for her daughter to come home."

"You're sick!" But not sick enough for her to hang up again.

"I know I am, but what I'm trying to say is, I've reached a point where I have to end this. I have to end it or it will kill me, and I don't know if you like me—I think you do. But more specifically, the reason I keep calling is I have these feelings for you." Perfectly framed in the window across the street, I see Jeane washing her hands in the kitchen sink and, for a genuine and painful instant, I'm feeling and saying all the things to Sheila that I really want to say to Sky: "I'm sick of the game-playing. Sick of all the bullshit."

"Are you really stalking someone?" she asks, slightly intrigued. After all, I'm still cute and eligible, though nuts.

"Just you, Sheila."

"You're mentally disturbed," she tags me.

"I'd love to spend a long, romantic weekend with you at some country house on a lake, in front of a roaring fire, with a fine wine. I'd love to just kiss your sweet face, hold you in the curls of my chest, stare into those sweet, sweet eyes of yours." Tears start collecting in my own eyes as I talk. "I'd love to strip away the bullshit and get to the real you—the you that snapped me up, but no one else ever got to see . . ."

"Oh please . . ."

"I know that everything I say comes out sounding like bullshit, but when I'm not with you I'm fantasizing about you. I'm completely lost without you." My breath becomes baited. "I guess . . . if I've acted weird or conflicted . . . it's 'cause I really . . . honestly don't want to love you. There, I admit it. I hate feeling this vulnerable," I say earnestly, staring at Sky across the street. It's like Cyrano de Bergerac gone bonkers, talking through one Roxanne to another.

"You just fucked me and threw me aside, it was all you wanted."

"Loneliness is incurable," I explain. "Each person is a solitary cell, but sex! You hold and hug someone, and link up with them if only for an instant. But it's all we really have."

"Give me a break."

"You want to know why guys like me need sex?"

"'Cause you're fucking vampires!"

"You're half-right. We are, we're injured and self-despising. We're too selfish to have children or give love, and the only real morphine is sex. We're able to feel and connect with someone much more compassionate than we can ever be. It's a way of convincing ourselves that we're not creeps, but then we hate you for loving someone as despicable as us." Short, tear-gulping pause. "Please, this one last time, give me a final chance to redeem myself."

A long, vomit-digestive beat later, she says, "When do you want to get together?"

A car screeches to a halt in front of Jeane's house and I flip off the phone. Enough purple dogshit. It is 6:35, fifteen minutes or so later than I had intended to wait. A fire-engine-red VW bug driven by a copper-haired girl with a silver nose-ring is idling in front of Jeane's house. Kate hops out. She is wearing a hot-pink tank top that reveals her muscular midriff. As she bids farewell, I can make out the word "Princess" studded with brass spangles on the front of her T-shirt. Oversized jeans hang loose on her hips, the notorious "gangsta" style, mimicking the most enviable strata of our society—convicts.

From my crouched and silent dickblind, I motionlessly jump for joy. When Kate vanishes safely into the abode, I rise painfully. But I have a bounce in my step on the long walk back to the train station.

▼

A half an hour later, I arrive at the LIRR station. I have only a short wait for the 7:15 train. I use the twenty minutes that it takes to get to the Jamaica station to rehearse my script: Perry Cruz is going to call Jeane regarding her daughter's naughty apparel. The clothes I observed will be cruel proof of my sinister shadowing.

But how should I put it? I consider explaining that I had to resist tugging down those gangsta-bitch threads and showing her an authentic shower-room buttfucking.

Perry, after all, is an ex-con. I just realize this. My Walter Mitty alter ego is expanding before my hungry eyes. He's what's enhancing my fantasy nowadays, not Jeane. Once I hear the fear in Jeane's voice, he'll order her to discreetly excuse herself from "family night" and retire to the telephone extension in the upstairs bedroom. There I'll give the orders. Remove your clothes. Unclasp your bra. My nerves will extend through the phone wires. I'll feel her warm, sticky glow. Hell, Perry will be right on the bed with her. His steroid-inflated muscles bulging from his T-shirt, my sweaty, prison-tattooed arms wrap around Jeane's own. My large calloused hands and powerful hammer-edged fingers manipulating her small nimble ones. Her body encased within my own. She'll want me as I instruct her to touch herself, bringing her to a quivering frenzy.

My heart is fibrillating in the confining chamber of the train and I have to catch my breath.

I will tell her that she has to get ahold of a Polaroid. Every household owns one. Tonight, when all others have gone to bed, she will have to quietly rise, tiptoe to the bathroom, disrobe, spread herself to her most exposed, legs V-ed back in the air, and in the mirror snap several flash photos of herself. Having her submit to this private photo session is enough, but, if I can somehow get the photos — the physical evidence — those I could retire with. It then occurs to me, I could instruct her to give the ransom photos to her "husband," which Perry believes is none other than *moi*, Leslie.

Sending Judge Sanders his Honey photos was a picnic compared to this, but look where that got me—I've sent the Sewter case down the sewer.

Just settle for the phone sex and have her consent to take the photos, I counter-offer myself. To have her agree to it on the phone even though she won't do it, that's thrilling enough.

No, I need those photos, I hold out. After all, I never expected to follow the daughter at her school. I did that. I never expected to meet Jeane again. I did that. I certainly never expected to fuck her, and I fucked her sore. The photos will actually be a minor achievement after all that. When my train screeches to a halt at Jamaica, I get off and wait for my connecting train.

An announcement comes across the P.A. that the New York train will be delayed for five minutes. The Perry in me impatiently demands, *Call her now!* From right here in Jamaica. Better this way. Less traceable than her constantly star-69ing Manhattan. I race downstairs to the bank of phones and grab the one farthest from the stream of people. Quickly, I poke in Jeane's number.

After two short rings, the wrong voice answers. It is the little kitty. I am about to ask for the big feline, but no, wait! This is much better. This is the one she protects.

"Hi, hon, how are you?" I say with patronizing concern.

"Fine," she meows, unsuspecting, "how are you?"

"Okay, my pretty pink-tittied princess." I give special nipple-tweaking emphasis to the consonants.

"Excuse me?" She doesn't understand.

"How's my princess?" I ask the little girl who I once babysat.

"Who is this?" I can hear the sudden ruffle of uncertainty giving way to fear.

"Who was driving the cute VW? She looked tasty too," I say.

"Who is this?" Horrors!

I employ an exaggerated Spanish accent: "Dis is yo boy-toy, Perry de la Cruz."

"Fuck you!" she shoots back.

"You want I should come over right now," I bark, "pull down dose loose pants and spank your tight ass? I will!" I pause and yell, crazily, "You think I'm fucking kidding?!"

"NO!" she hollers back.

"You apologize to your elder!" I treat with thunder.

"I apologize!"

"You know, Princess, I took photos of *Mamacita* when she was your age, had her open those delicious long legs and fucked her silly when I was done. Maybe it's time we bring you into the family business."

"Mom!" she shrieks. "It's him!"

"Who the fuck is this?" I hear Jeane's voice screaming from an extension. I slam the phone down.

I hurry to the train platform upstairs. Maybe now Jeane'll have time for an after-work drink with me. Following a minute of gluttonous delight, the New York–bound train rushes into the Jamaica station.

While the train rocks toward Manhattan, I try to imagine the havoc unfolding in Jeane's little household. I consider the awful accusations that Kate must be hurtling at her mommy. *Why the fuck did you have to open your legs for strangers? For money! How can you ever be a mother, let alone a social worker?* By the time the train reaches Penn Station it is 8:15 and my pleasure is diminishing. The first twinges of guilt are returning.

I pass by the subway, deciding instead to unwind with a walk home. Glimpsing south on Seventh Avenue, I see the sky vivisected by buildings. But a clean slice of mackerel clouds roll south. Their copper-hammered indentations are dramatized with different distressed colors — bruised-yellow, burnt-orange, and blood-red sunlight — a quick peep-show of nature's forgotten beauty.

I head up Seventh Avenue and pass through the desolate trench between Herald and Times Squares. When I cross Forty-second, the streets narrow and accelerate. First there was sex, but because that felt so fucking good, it begat guilt. The guilt begat sleaze, and so sex was zoned to the land of Nod in Midtown. There the sex begat cheap trinkets and tawdry mementos alluding to its trick sensation. And those pornographic ancillaries becameth guilt-strewn and dirty. And then the dirtiness blighted the marketplace whereuponeth it was peddled — Times Square was shameful and pornographic. And the city of the plains needed to be destroyed yet again. All the strip bars and most of the theaters are closed and gone. The theater marquee where Sky and I stood during our last meeting when we were still obscenely young, that too has been razed. The stainless-steel future stole the spermy, squirmy past, leaving us to doubt the fading stains of our memories.

Built upon unfruitful seediness, the new Times Square has got religion. It's shimmering in baptismal splendor. These large new corporate cathedrals, filled with overpriced icons and worshipping mothers pushing strollers, were recently occupied by godless porn palaces where thousands of men gathered and ejaculated.

Clean, young, disposable titans now look down from billboards — morons in Calvin Klein undies. Various zippers flashing irrelevant numbers and words, cryptic messages from high. The Dumbotron and Megacrap, the duel of company names and logos, the dominos of billboards advertising TV shows, the rivalry of blurbs for big Broadway fiascos, soda and liquor brands cluttered like overcrowded cereal boxes along the upper shelf of a giant's kitchen cabinet, all about to avalanche down.

Shoved by Ameri-trash families, tugged by Euro-tourists, passing my old law firm, through the whitewater of Sham Canyon, I can't help but miss good old porn-central as I inspect this Madison Avenue concept of an American house-wife's fantasy.

The heads of Easter Islands, the Pyramids, Stonehenge, and now the Times Square Redevelopment Program, a monumental project to supplant the false god of sexual gratification with another golden calf. Soon the streets slow down and I'm moving up the conveyor belt of Midtown, about to get price-tagged and shelved in the sparkling quality of America's superstore—*It's up to you, New York, Neeew Yooorrrrk* (©First Performance 1979, Frank Sinatra).

APRIL 12, 1983, NYC

"WHAT THE FUCK ARE YOU DOING HERE?!" CECILIA demanded, baffled at seeing Leslie bound in her dungeon wearing a maid outfit.

"Unlock my hands!" he beseeched, pulling at the shackles.

"Leslie!" She took out the little key and unlocked him. She let him catch his breath before asking, "What the fuck?"

"I had to come here," he said. "You saw my porn, I had to do it. I had to have you do it to me."

"I hope I didn't hurt you," she snickered, rubbing his chest.

"You're a real bitch." He was still catching his breath.

"You were a pretty good slave yourself," she replied, amused and confused. "You need a goal when you're doing this, so I was intent on trying to get you to scream."

"You were getting off on it," he observed. "You can say you weren't, but you were."

"So what if I was?" She smiled and glanced at a brass candelabra.

"You spent all this energy explaining how you are professional and telling me how clean and sanitary this job is, how your fantasies are cliché, but you're no different than I am."

Cecilia started chuckling.

"What's so funny?"

"Sorry, but that maid outfit doesn't become you."

"Well, you look too comfortable in your outfit," he retorted.

"Give me one second," Cecilia said.

Leslie took off the maid outfit when she left the room and carefully put it back on the rack. He rubbed the stinging pain from his nipples. By the time Cecilia came back in the room wearing a bathrobe, with her dramatic mascara wiped away, he had his suit back on. Seeing her with her makeup gone, he still felt a residual nervousness toward her. That feeling, he decided, was as intense and close as he was ever going to get to a lasting love.

"Why did you spend a hundred and seventy-five bucks?" Cecilia asked tersely. "I'll give you back my cut, but the house gets a hundred and seventy-five."

"Fuck the money," Leslie said, and stepping closer, he explained, "I want another chance."

"Leslie . . ."

"I love you," he said without faltering.

"Aren't you married? Don't you have a kid?"

"Hell no, where'd you hear that?"

Cecilia grinned and nodded her head in disbelief. Leslie didn't relieve the silence with any apologies or displays of embarrassment.

"You're timing is wonderful," she finally said.

"Why? Did you get married?" he asked nervously.

"No," she disclosed. "I broke up a month ago."

"Sorry to hear it," he replied, smiling. Cecilia looked at him and wondered if love was just a matter of timing and availability.

"You don't have to be sorry, only grateful."

"Why's that?"

"Because I just broke up with Gina. You would know her as Madame Lucretia, the first mistress you were with, and if she had known you were my ex-boyfriend, you would've suffered more than you ever thought humanly possible."

"Lucky me."

"Leslie, before we broke up, you . . . you suddenly . . ."

"You're talking about the . . . strange sex."

"Yeah. Where'd that come from?" Cecilia could see Leslie sigh, and realized he was blushing.

If only to show that it had nothing to do with Sky, Leslie decided to come clean: "I came here behind your back one day."

"You came here?"

"Yeah, and I don't know why, but it released something in me that I suppose was there all along. If it bothers you, or if you think that this is the only reason I'm here . . ."

"No . . . you have to understand something about me," Cecilia explained. "I'm not a very forthcoming person. The role-playing, the mock humiliation, all that stuff, it's incredibly cathartic. Everything convulses out. And even though I can be a top with strangers, I can only be a bottom with someone who I absolutely love and trust and have faith in. After our little sessions, I needed equal amounts of love and reassurance.

Otherwise I felt like some whore. And I can't be left feeling that way. You understand?"

"I think so."

"Coming here, doing this kind of work, I don't simply get off on it. It repairs me. It complements that other side."

"You can whip men to hell and back, long as it never turns up on a film," he concluded.

When she leaned up toward Leslie, her bathrobe parted and he could see her leather corset. He hugged and kissed her.

"I can't deny that I have strong feelings for you, but I also occasionally like girls," she said.

"Look, I love you."

"I'm not entirely sure I'm ready for all this." Cecilia caught herself and added, "We'll have to take it a step at a time."

They agreed to have dinner and proceed slowly.

Leslie asked if she could leave with him. Cecilia said it would be best if he left first. She could meet him on the corner.

"If Gina knew she had you under her whip and let you get away, I'd never hear the end of it."

▼

That night the two went for dinner at a new French restaurant Cecilia had heard about, La Chambre Idéale. They talked about their time apart. Leslie recounted his baby-rearing ordeal with Sky. Cecilia talked about her tumultuous relationship with an alcoholic lover who broke her nose. He ordered an expensive Chardonnay and Cecilia got a variety of appetizers. By dessert, they were both tipsy, kissing and touching each other beneath the table. When they arrived later at her apartment, they made repeated and desperate love. Leslie slept through the morning.

At noon, he arrived at work to find a message from Sky waiting for him. It was at that moment that Leslie decided he couldn't see her anymore. Merely thinking of her made him anxious. She both attracted and repelled him.

Sky had called him from work, saying she had a big surprise for him. Leslie called her back to learn that she had secured a one-day gig at a theater right down the block.

"Great," he said glumly.

"It's the Metropolitan. It's not porn. It's an old carbon-arc projector and the manager said I can have visitors, so if you want to come down, today is your big chance."

He had to say farewell in person. "Can I come by right now?" he asked softly.

"Sure, great!" Sky said, full of energy. "When you get to the box office, tell them I'm expecting you."

Leslie ran downstairs, across Broadway, past Seventh Avenue. As he walked briskly along the north side of Forty-second Street, he considered what he was going to say: *The good news is I'm back with Cecilia. The bad news is she's unbelievably jealous.* When he neared her theater his heart raced.

The Metropolitan, a large old theater which was constructed during the gaslight vaudeville days, was now a run-down third-rate movie house, showing low-budget double features. *High Kick*, a karate film, and *Bad Black Blood*, a blaxploitation film, were featured on the marquee in broken red-plastic letters. Two Latino kids in front of Leslie paid the two-dollar admission and pushed through the old wooden-paddle turnstile. Leslie told the elderly woman behind the plate-glass box-office window that he was a guest of the projectionist. Leslie watched the woman pick up the intercom to confirm. Pressing a button, she instructed him how to get up to the projectionist booth.

He walked through the once-beautiful lobby, past the corroded cameos and torn felt curtains that bordered the walls, into the cavernous showroom. Leslie ascended the long staircase that ran up the center of the huge auditorium as an elite team of Kung-Fu masters made excruciating sounds while delivering chops and kicks to a never-ending rampage of villains. In the semi-darkness, the daylight scene on the screen illuminated the faces of teenagers sitting in rows, munching pop-corn and shouting up at the large screen.

At the uppermost step to the booth, Leslie located the black door and knocked softly. Jeane opened it and he stepped inside. She gave him a big hug and kiss, but he didn't reciprocate. He stared at the two large projectors side by side behind her. One machine was spinning its reels, humming its engines, generating a bright light from its center. The other projector was off. They looked like a pair of old battlefield guns.

"So this is it," he said, inspecting the instruments.

"This is where fantasy becomes reality," she replied tiredly. "And you're just in time for a lesson, in case you ever get disbarred."

Leslie watched as she hoisted a full reel of film onto the metal pin on the upper arm of the waiting projec-tor. Then taking the end of the ribbon, she started slip-ping it into the machine. "You open the gate, thread it through the intermittent sprocket, through the sound head, past the exciter bulb, and loop it into the receiving reel down here."

"Amazing," he muttered, strangely fascinated by her little lecture. "When do you switch it on?"

"During the change-over. We still have a couple of minutes."

Looking at the bolt of light punching from the running projector through the small glass onto the large and distant screen, Leslie felt like some behind-the-scenes gargoyle. This is where minute mistakes project themselves on a massive scale, he thought.

"I kind of wish I never saw this place," Leslie proclaimed. "Pay no attention to the man behind the curtain."

"Hey, this is only a projection booth. Be grateful you were never part of an actual film shoot. It gets a lot more disillusioning."

"Thank you for making it all too real," Leslie said, and looking at her eye to eye, he remembered what he was there to do. His eyelids beat and his focus fluttered around, finally alighting on a capped gas pipe protruding from the wall. He felt his heart sinking as he tried to find words. He deliberately recalled that pornographic scene of the two men ejaculating on Sky's smiling face.

"What's the matter?" she asked, making final adjustments on the projector.

"Well," he began, "I'm back with Cecilia."

"And she doesn't want you to see me anymore," Sky replied, pulling the thought right out of his head.

"Yeah," he said stiffly.

"Did you tell her that I loved you and you didn't want me?"

"I told her everything."

"Shit, oh well." Sky's stare joined his on the filthy gray wall, conveying no emotion. "Other women, rivals, know what men can never guess at."

"What's that?"

"I suppose I was still hoping to somehow land you," she conceded.

"I'm sorry."

"I only hope you're not in love with some idea of this girl like you did . . ." She didn't finish the sentence.

Leslie didn't respond.

"I'm happy for you," she said softly. A moment later, to shake off the melancholia, she added, "Hey, I still got a surprise to show you."

She grabbed Leslie by the hand and led him through a small, dimly lit bathroom and up a dark flight of stairs that ended at an old door. Sealing its aura of antiquity was a battered crossbar that held it shut. Jeane used the heel of her palm to hammer the wooden beam up and off. Swinging her powerful hips, she shoved the door open. Pigeon wings flapped and sunlight obliterated the darkness. She stepped out onto the filthy tar-bubbled top of the old marquee. Leslie followed her and looked down Forty-second Street. It was bright and lined with other marquees that reminded Leslie of the hulls of ships, moored side by side on a long, land-locked pier. Crowds of people swarmed below them.

"You know, Les," Jeane said, "in all relationships the sex eventually stops, the conversation gets boring, and that's when you really get to test that love."

"So they tell me," he replied with a smile.

"I kind of feel like we were married," she said, and tenderly put her arm around him.

"We sure went through a lot together," he mulled.

"Call me if you ever need to," Sky said tenderly.

He promised he'd keep in touch. Then they gave each other a gentle kiss. Soon Leslie was downstairs, heading back to his office.

MAY 12, 2001, NYC

THE LAST GRILL MARKS OF THE CRIMSON SKY CARBONIZE into blackness as I cross Columbus Circle, mindlessly missing cars that buzz and spin around me like huge mechanical bugs.

Marching up toward Sixty-fourth Street, I pass under a construction site filled with makeshift nooks and crannies inhabited by the sundry homeless. Among them, I spot Wilbur, the middle-aged orphan that I had saved not so long ago. He is snoring, curled behind a Siamese water pipe. I am careful not to step in the stream of urine stemming from him like an umbilical cord that connects him to the gutter. I remember rushing through the street with this limp man in my outstretched arms.

His thick patches of torn and scarred skin are swathed over a funny concave face that in turn is collapsed under a mighty brachycephalic forehead. These disruptive features combined with his small primordial body and abnormally large hands doomed Wilb from the start. He is ugly. This means he is born with an inability to draw love from others; a visual stiletto in the heart of all who see him, forever exiled into the ghetto of people's awareness. Attracting love, inasmuch as it eventually draws support and self-confidence, plays a large role in success.

Sky is his flip-side: sexy, charming, tall; her most trivial remarks are given prime real estate in any conversation. Between intelligence and good looks, the latter is invariably preferred. All Sky had to do to survive was want to.

The longer I stare at him, though, the more I begin to envy him. My whole life I have worked toward making more out of myself, building a skyscraper of money and power. Now the only pleasure I have from my little sandcastle is in kicking it over. How much of myself can I destroy and how far can I fall? Eventually, if I'm lucky, I'll be in a situation like yours, Wilbur.

I take three folded twenties from my wallet and invest them into the empty pocket of Wilbur's filthy sailor jacket.

"What the fuck you doing?" he awakens, grabbing my wrist—a reflex for frequently rolled drunks.

"Charity for all." I hold up the bills. "Robbery in reverse."

"Why?" He snatches them.

"I was the one who saved your life a few weeks ago. You don't remember that, do you?"

"You're the motherfucker that saved my life?" He staggers to his oafish feet as if preparing to hit me.

"Yeah," I say immodestly.

"Well, fuck you!" he coughs out, and then shouts, "If it wasn't for you, I'd'a been dead!"

"I thought I was doing you a favor," I murmur.

"You did it for your fucking self, you goddamned self-righteous yuppie!"

As I walk away, he keeps yelling obscenities at me, but of course never throws the twenties away.

Amid garbage cans brimming with debris, I pass gregarious weekend people, inflatable Macy's-parade girls and their protective, anchoring boyfriends. Their normalcy rancors me. Their joyous idiocy ruffles me. And I feel it growing once more, a new hydra-headed erection. It's Perry-time again.

When I reach my corner, Luis spies me through the glass front doors. But out of the sky, a massive hand reaches down and spins me around.

"Leslie," says Big Bill Holtov. The angular Anglican is

wearing his gray forty-foot overcoat which resembles an office building. His ten-foot-tall fedora looks like a water tower. "Polk says you beat him up."

"How old is that guy, thirteen? He's not even born yet. How can I beat him?"

"Well, I just spent four hours in my car waiting for you."

"Gee," I smile cheerfully, "I wish you had shown me that kind of loyalty when you cocksuckers hung me out to dry."

"I did." He immediately leads me down the street, away from home. "Leslie, we have clients, remember? When they see headlines like 'Rough Sex Lawyer—Not Indicted,' it hurts business. You're still 'Of Counsel' with us. Tell me any other corporate law firm in this city that would cut you that much slack."

"I tried to get the reorg accepted. I really did," I cut to the chase.

"Les, the Sewter Corporation is still worth a billion worldwide. Now, initially Sanders was tough, but he was willing to play ball. Something happened and now he's vetoing every fucking plan and returning every disclosure we send him. He's not just debtor happy, this fucker is intent on liquidating us."

"So that's good, it shows he's being unreasonable—appeal."

"This is the second reorganization plan, and we have a heap of angry creditors. Right now I'm trying to figure out why a tough but fair judge suddenly turns into the world's biggest asshole." He pauses very cleverly so that the street light is shining down in my eyes. "I've known Sanders for the past twenty years. I've met his wife, I've even played golf with him a couple times. I'm supposed to have lunch with him and Ratner in a few days." Ratner is the attorney for the other side. "Leslie, I need to know what the fuck happened."

I want to look away, but this is Bill, and we all have a Bill. There is a seven-year grace period called "up or out" in any corporate law firm. At the end of this time, young lawyers are either going to be partners or dumped. During those combat years, Bill and I were each other's best buds, flying each other's wings, and recently, when my scandal broke and the executive committee convened about my ouster, he was the one who stuck up for me, the truest partner I've had in that fucking firm. Like it or not, it's confession time.

"You know what Cece did for a living?" I ask him slowly. "It was all over the newspaper."

"To be honest with you, I was shocked," he replies absently. "Cecilia always struck me as such a society girl."

"The Honorable Peter Sanders was one of her clients. He does this freaky Pollyanna act. Needs to be disciplined. But he's full of mind games. Cecilia couldn't stand the son of a bitch, but he threatened to shut her down if she barred him." I pause and spin around so the light is now in his eyes. "I had a private investigator take compromising photos. I tried extorting him."

"Oh shit!" he unravels. In slow stop-action moments, I can see dread splash up, on, and over his face. It's worse than anything he ever expected.

"I know it was a major miscalculation," I attempt to vindicate, "but I wasn't sure he was going to go for it."

"What do you mean?"

"I didn't think Sanders would buy our plan. This, I thought, was our guarantee."

"We had a good plan!" Holtov appeals.

"I agree. Generous. Realistic. But you said it. It was our second big one and he has a history of going hard on multiple reorganizers. The son of a bitch won't forgive a cent. Plus, we had a bunch of screaming creditors."

"But extortion, Les? I mean . . . what the hell kind of person are you?" Incrimination becomes recrimination.

"We needed a guarantee for our billion-dollar baby." I

don't mention that I had also wanted to avenge Cece. "I got dirt on a dirty judge. Two wire ends waiting to be twined."

"So why didn't you connect them?" he asks with a chill.

"I tried," I smile. "I threatened to send the videotape to his wife. Guess what? She knows she's married to Shirley Temple. That's a working marriage for you. I threatened to pin stills around the court. He's retiring this year—'Go ahead,' he says. I offered to quit the case, I offered to resign from the firm, he doesn't care." If you can't shame a Republican, what's left?

"What an unbelievable fucking mess," he mutters under his breath. His eyes start ricochetting off of dark windows and distant buildings. "The reason I went into law was because it was supposed to be boring."

"If it's of any consolation, I'll tender my resignation."

Bill is beyond hearing. He has that rattled look on his face like someone who just stumbled out of his car after a bad accident.

"Let's see," he starts mumbling, "I'll tell him we unloaded you. You're nuts. You can get a good plea bargain. No jail time. Maybe we can get you committed. In and out. You already have that psychiatric release with the D.A. Tell him the whole thing was a major fuck-up."

Poor Bill meanders away babbling strategy, but we both know the Sewter Company hasn't got a chance. He's one of those people who saw a higher meaning to restructuring. Aside from losing a sweet advance, all their little holdings— mills, factories, warehouses—will close and the countless individuals worldwide will be out of work. Thousands of tiny lives, like rows of suburban tract houses will fall over like dominos in this acute economic catastrophe. All of those people will be laid off at the end of America's longest period of uninterrupted financial growth.

▼

Once in my castle, I take a useless Prozac and drink a detoxed bottle of wine. Then I take another useless Prozac and drink some more liquor — gin, vodka, bourbon, working my way down to the creme de menthe, cassis, and triple sec.

Picking up the phone because this was once something that made me happy, I listen to the dial tone. Finally, I push in the palindrome number because this is what the phone wants.

"Hello?" the phone says.

"Hi," I greet it.

"Leslie, is this you?" The phone seems to know me.

"Wait," I recognize, "you're the teenage superstar."

"That's right, I'm Britney Spears." It's my rooftop rube. "Why did you hang up on me earlier?"

"Oh, yeah. My cell died. Listen, I was wondering if you weren't doing anything, maybe you can come over. I'll pay for the cab."

"What will we do?"

"I'll recite some of my poetry," I proffer timidly.

"You can read that on the phone," she dismisses.

"Come over. We'll play a new board game called *The Mistress and the Slave*." Always offer the controls.

"All right," she says.

Another useless pill and glass of hair tonic and I drowse to sleep and am awakened.

"I used your key." She tosses it on my lap. She is standing before me in all her MTV glory. "So, recite some of your crappy verse."

"Beshrew that heart that makes mine to groan . . ."

She makes a buzzing sound.

"When in the chronicles of wasted time . . ."

"Next!"

"My love is as a fever, longing still for that which longer nurseth the disease . . ."

"Yuck! Next!" I'm on the freaking *Gong Show.*

"Those lips that love's own hand did make breath'd forth the sound that said 'I hate.'"

"Bzzz!"

"Thine eyes I love, and they, as pitying me . . ."

"I don't think so."

"That you were once unkind befriends me now . . ."

"All pretty shitty," she interrupts. It doesn't matter, I'm too drunk to recite anything entirely. Cecilia used to love Shakespeare.

We move to the poetry of the senses: touch . . . and kiss . . . and rub and strokes and . . . she unbuuuckles me and pulls my pants down . . . and . . .

"Sky, I love you, Sky . . ."

"Who is Sky?"

"I mean Jeane."

"Who is Jeane?" She roots around in my drawers. "Come on, tell me, who is Jeane? Look at these women's clothes. And these pictures. You were married, weren't you?"

"Yes."

"You killed your wife, didn't you?" Killed her when she was alive, but I kill her more now that she's dead.

Reading a form from my filing cabinet, she asks, "Who the hell is Cecilia?"

"You are."

"Who's the lover you're stalking?"

"You be her too."

"She's the dead bitch and you're the brother dog, aren't you?" she interprets. "Well, Cecilia wants a little something in return." She hands me the phone. "Call Jeane."

"I'm sorry," I reply.

"Fuck your apology. If you're sorry, call Jeane!"

"But it's no longer 1981."

"Call her . . ."

Sheila puts her lips tenderly around me—liquid grace. "Oh, Cece, don't . . ."

"No, asshole, keep talking," she says, swallowing me deep.

"Oh, Cece." I focus on dialing as my balls get a marvelous sponge bath. "Jeane, this is . . . this is . . . Perry." I can barely catch my breath.

"What do you want?"

"Show and tell time. Get that fucking Polaroid. Do it before I make your daughter do it!" and on and on.

Cecilia slaps me and I fall down, dropping the phone.

"Jeane, I love you . . ." I say to her.

"My name's Sheila, asshole!" She stands up and spits in my face. I struggle to get up, but she knocks me down again and stomps on my ribs and stomach. "You ever fucking call me again, I'll kill you!" She kicks me right in the balls for good measure and storms out.

APRIL 13, 1983, NYC

AFTER HIS FINAL FAREWELL TO SKY, LESLIE STARTED dating Cecilia. The relationship moved cautiously for the first few days, but by the week's end they were back into the swing and whip of things. During one particularly heated evening of love and loss—and what would become a costly visit to the microsurgeon— Leslie accidentally left several delicate white scars along Cecilia's right cheek and neck. He also crushed part of her larynx, causing her to talk in a low rasp for roughly two months.

As a way of apologizing, he showered Cecilia with more affection and romance than ever, and before he knew what he was saying, he had proposed marriage.

Six months later, he testified his eternal love to her before a priest. Standing in a new tux, having paid over thirty grand for the festivities that indulged nearly a hundred friends, relatives, and business associates, all he could think was, this is a hell of a price for one night of excess.

Soon after, Cecilia started her own dungeon, Excalibur, and Leslie made partner in his law firm. They were both pulling in good money, so they gave up their leases and together moved into the newly completed Deacon Arms Apartments.

APRIL 13, 1993, NYC

OVER THE NEXT SEVERAL YEARS, THEIR RAMBUNCtious sex life began to taper off. From time to time Leslie would visit the porn arcades, and though he'd survey the films, he no longer went into the booths. The idea of getting caught by a coworker inside the arcade became almost a greater thrill.

One afternoon he arrived home unexpectedly and heard Cecilia in the bedroom having sex with another woman. He had suspected something for a while and although he didn't really care about the cheating, he was annoyed that she wasn't at least honest about it.

After they showered and dressed, Cecilia introduced Leslie to Betina, a Latin beauty with a territorial glare.

The next day at the breakfast table, Leslie decided to tweak his wife with a lie: "I've been seeing someone at work."

Cecilia sat perfectly still for a moment before asking if he was jealous of her occasional dalliances.

"Well, it's nice of you to ask," he said.

"I thought we understood each other," she replied. "Remember, I told you about this."

"I don't mind it, but I feel like an idiot coming in on the middle of things."

"Look, I don't do this often, but if you'd like, I'll tell you when I'm using the . . ." Leslie looked down and nodded. "What?"

"Nothing," Leslie said with a detached air.

"Well, we're not having sex with each other anymore," she stated.

"Fine."

"But I do love you and I think a relationship should be more than mere sex," she returned, and asked, "How about if we try some arrangement?"

"A threesome?" Leslie responded with a secret smile. "Not with . . . your Latina firecracker?"

"She'd never go for it. I know others though."

"Let's try it, see where it rolls."

Cecilia made some calls and found a clean young girl who charged five hundred dollars for the evening—condoms a must, no anal.

Two nights later, Cecilia and Leslie met a small blonde named Yvette at a cozy restaurant on the Upper West Side. She was a student at FIT, studying to be a fashion designer. She reeked of patchouli oil and dressed like a hippy.

After a light dinner, Yvette joined Cecilia and Leslie back at their place where she playfully started kissing Cecilia in the elevator. Once inside the apartment, Cecilia lit candles, put on music, and took out some grass. They smoked, then the two women stripped each other, touching and kissing. They seemed so comfortable that Leslie began wondering if Yvette wasn't one of Cecilia's former lovers. Eventually he joined them and was soon having sex with Yvette. Then he did it with Cecilia. By 4 in the morning, they were all asleep.

Leslie woke Yvette early the next day for sex again. Cecilia brushed her teeth and joined in. While Leslie fucked Cecilia, she serviced Yvette. By noon they had all showered and dressed. Yvette was paid and tipped handsomely, and she said that anytime they wanted to do it again, just give her a call.

▼

During the next two months, Cecilia and Leslie had sex with each other about once a week until the frequency tapered down again. One evening, nearly three months later, Leslie suggested a tryst with a new girl.

Deborah was a tall, quiet undergraduate with beautiful brown hair, getting her B.A. in communications at NYU. Although she was reluctant to do anything other than straight sex with Leslie, she would occasionally have sex with Cecilia. Her orgasms were tumultuously loud and tearful.

Vivian was from Thailand. She was slightly overweight, but very sweet and affectionate. After making love with her several times, they learned that she was supporting a husband and two kids.

Charlotte, a dyed red-head who painted the mascara on and had no fashion sense whatsoever, was the sluttiest of the group. She was willing to get down and dirty and try anything twice.

Anique was the prettiest, but her constant compulsion to talk about the sexual abuses she suffered as a child, accompanied by wild mood swings, compelled Cecilia to cancel further engagements with her.

Melissa took turns making love to one of them while the other would watch, refusing to sleep with both at the same time.

Ursula, from St. Petersburg, Russia, was gorgeous and incredibly curved, but there was something about her that reminded Leslie of Sky and it turned him right off.

Mistress Theodora, a.k.a. Lana, was an imperfect lover. But even before meeting, Leslie secretly knew he wanted a piece of her. At night in bed, he would listen to his wife's commentary on the different young dominatrixes who had come and gone over the years. Lana's name kept popping up again and again.

Although she looked it, she wasn't simply some stripper with a whip. She had come to the city from the West Coast, where, Cecilia insisted, the bond & dom scene was far wilder. A blitz of rich, middle-aged slaves always crowded to please the buxom blonde. Cecilia said she had not seen anything like it. Masochists were tumbling out of the rackwork for her. Cecilia utterly feared that the young girl would run off, start her own dungeon, and steal her clientele. Leslie knew that Cecilia really didn't care about losing her patrons, only her edge. She was jealous of the young mistress and he found that instantly erotic.

One night Cecilia brought home a photograph of the young ingenue in full garb. With a Teutonic wave of blond hair, lips twisted into a smirk, eyes glowing with contempt for any prospective slave, Lana was completely irresistible.

"You wouldn't be interested in having Lana join us, would you?" Leslie asked late one night, after they both had a couple of nightcaps.

"Lana?" Cecilia replied, bewildered. "But . . . but she's not a call girl."

"So what?" Leslie shot back. "You'd like it, wouldn't you?"

"She only does one thing, and you don't like it. Remember?"

"I'd like to give it another shot," Leslie confessed. "It might be time for a change."

"A change?"

"Well, the three-ways are getting a little monotonous," he replied. "I'm beginning to feel like I'm molesting foreign exchange students . . ."

"It's not that I mind. It's only, well, she might refuse," Cecilia said diffidently. "And if she does—"

"You're not worried that she's going to spread rumors about you, are you?" he baited. "After all the freaky stuff you've done all these years?"

Cecilia couldn't believe that he was making such a request. "I don't even know if she's bi."

"This isn't really sex," Leslie corrected.

"I've never done anything with anyone I've worked with." She was angry with herself for not having seen this coming.

"You were the one who said that we could share our fantasies," he softly muttered. "And once we stopped doing that, the marriage would be over."

Cecilia eventually nodded her head; if Lana was willing, it would be done. Leslie sighed. Without even attempting to hide how excited he was by the little contest, he made love ravenously with Cecilia that night.

FEBRUARY 10, 2001, NYC

LANA MOVED WITH A SHAMELESS SAUNTER, STRUTTING about the changing room, wearing nothing but lace panties, a sheer black bra, and polished black cowboy boots. Kid

Rock was faintly playing on the stereo and she was buzzing. She stopped for a moment before the wall mirror and inspected her beautiful self. Perfect, except for one detail. She took out a lipstick. She was still young enough to hold firm, but mature enough to be voluptuous.

Cecilia stepped in quietly, waited for another girl to leave, then asked if she could have a moment of Lana's time.

"I'm late for a 3 o'clock mummification," Lana said, pursing her obscenely full lips, giving them a thick, ruby redness.

"Okay, when you're done with that, stop in my office," Cecilia said prissily, and attended to awaiting business.

Cecilia had observed that two characteristics make a dom exceptional. Either they had perfect self-control, which was where she excelled, or they had to be a touch psychotic, able to really *be* the role—this was Lana.

At 4:15, sweaty, wrapped in a terry-cloth towel, Lana entered Cecilia's office. She closed the door behind her and plunked down into an upholstered chair.

"What's up, darlin'?" she asked in her typically carefree tone.

Cecilia took off her reading glasses. Looking to the blotter on her desk, in a tense whisper, she said, "I've got an extremely sensitive and confidential case."

"Who?" Lana asked, always eager to get the dirt on any celebrities.

"Actually," Cecilia's volume bottomed out, "it would be for Les and myself."

"But you're not . . ."

"It's not really for me," Cecilia amended, "it's for him."

Lana silently bit her tongue. Cecilia always seemed so professional and low key. Lana never envisioned straightening the older woman out. With her constant power trip, Cecilia would be a wonderfully sexy slave. Lana smiled and thought, hell, I'd do this just for kicks.

"When are you free?" Cecilia pushed ahead.

"Unfortunately, not for about the next two weeks," she replied, then pausing, the young girl said, "I ain't got anything happening tonight."

Cecilia knew she and Leslie were both available and thought, the sooner I get this over with, the less anxious I'll be. "Fine, tonight then."

▼

When Lana came to their apartment early that evening, she was thrilled to meet Madame Guinevere's husband. Aside from a lean body and good looks, she could see that he had a serious rocket in his pocket. The three discussed time and money.

By speech and mannerisms, Leslie assessed her white-trash upbringing. He poured drinks as Lana and Cecilia chatted about different girls at work.

"Fuck, I'm tense," Lana remarked, massaging the back of her neck. "Been a long day."

"Have another drink." Leslie offered the bottle of Glenlivet.

"I wish you didn't get me started on this," she said with a smile.

"You don't have a drinking problem, do you?" Cecilia asked politely.

"I got arrested for carrying pot once, but I'm not addicted to nothing." She gulped down half of her drink. "This moonshine is too good to only drink a glass."

"Have the whole bottle," Leslie replied jokingly.

"It would take that much just to get me going. I don't get drunk easily," Lana said, dropping ice cubes into her glass and pouring herself another. "So, what's your pleasure?"

Cecilia fell silent as Leslie edged forward with a smile and said, "Our pleasure is your pleasure. We're here to serve you, Mistress Lana." Leslie heard Cecilia sigh.

"It's Mistress Theodora," Lana corrected, then asked, "Are there any do's or don'ts you want to . . ."

"We're here to please you, Mistress," Leslie repeated, steadfast.

"Naturally," said Lana, already getting into role. When she went to the bathroom, though, Cecilia caught her and discreetly re-specified the rules.

"He's not into anything too extreme," Cecilia whispered. "He doesn't like penetration or nipple torture. Mild verbal and physical humiliation should do him fine."

"I was going to tie you guys up, spank you, insult you, maybe whack him off."

"Do whatever you want, but don't touch his dick," Cecilia said, not looking at her, "and try to be careful."

"How about you?" Lana asked politely.

"No welts, no pain. You can play with my breasts as much as you like. Mild strangulation. There's some stuff in that box on the sofa. No large dildos or fingers. This evening is really for Leslie," she said. "Make sure he gets to see whatever you do to me. And make sure it's all wrapped up in an hour tops."

"Fine," Lana replied with a wink. Cecilia turned heel and headed back into the living room.

Lana didn't like Cecilia's smug tone. She thinks I'm some Mexican maid looking to steal the ashtrays, Lana dissected. Don't worry, bitch, he'll get his and you'll get yours.

Clothes came off and other apparel was slipped on. Bit by bit, roles were assumed. Lana continuously lubricated all her movements with tiny sips of Glenlivet. The session started out as a polite series of rises onto plateaus of token pain and exaggerated humiliation. But as Lana's attitude crystallized, the humiliation Leslie and Cecilia incurred grew more real.

Steadily, other accessories were fitted and clasped and ultimately strapped on. Within half an hour, Lana had them rolling over and sitting up on chairs, begging.

Every time a question was asked by the dominatrix, it would be quietly countered by the husband and wife with the synchronized reply: "Yes, Mistress Theodora."

Lana cuffed their hands behind their backs. Tired of his smirking expression, she yanked a hood over Leslie's face.

"I've got to get a picture of this," the young madame said, slurring her words drunkenly and spotting a Polaroid on a book shelf. She snapped a photograph of Cecilia with clamps on her nipples and a perforated gag ball strapped in her mouth. Leslie knew that Lana was showing Cecilia extra attention because of who she was, and he was thoroughly titillated by it. The dominatrix wiped the drool off of her employer's chin, then tugged a leather hood down over her face.

After forty minutes or so of insertions, squirmings, occasional swats, and other mild degradations, Lana started getting nasty.

"You're such the little queen bitch, aren't you? Well, tonight you're my little suck slave." Lana reached down and twisted Cecilia's nipple red and raw. The employer didn't so much as wince.

Lana slipped her hand down into Cecilia's panties and combed her fingers through her pubic hairs. Staring into the eyeholes of older woman's leather hood, Lana detected her nonplussed attitude. She abruptly slipped her middle finger up into Cecilia's wet twat. The shackled dom didn't bat an eyelash. After a moment, realizing she had disobeyed the instructions, Lana pulled her finger out. She didn't use the safe word, Lana noted, and realized that her boss had something big to prove.

She took off Cecilia's mask. This is something between the two of them, Lana decided, don't get in the middle of it.

Besides, there were only twenty minutes to go. For the crescendo of her session, she wanted to let them torture each other. Lana cuffed their hands behind their backs and flipped them both on their bellies. Through a mirror reflection, Leslie derived a silent pleasure from watching the line of spit run down Cece's chin, until Lana pulled the large hood back over him.

"What a pathetic pair of shits you are," Lana said drunkenly. "Let's see which of you is the more devoted slave."

Cecilia was impressed by Lana's strength as the young woman lifted her in the air and spun her around, heads and tails, on top of Leslie. She could feel her husband's naked extremities below her. Lana shoved a sofa cushion under her breasts. By the far wall clock, Cece saw that the encounter was only fifteen minutes from ending as Lana fastened the dog collar tightly on her neck. She knew that Lana was using seesaw collars, something she had perfected during a twin-slave session: a chain connects the necks of the two victims, allowing them to pull at each other. She's supposed to use the broadnecked posture collar, Cecilia thought, not these narrow ones. She considered ending it, but instead closed her eyes, feeling the stinging of her nipples and the tight pressure around her neck. She clenched the plastic ball in her mouth and counted off the last few minutes, thinking, fuck you, Leslie, fuck you . . .

Thrusting a bunch of pillows between Leslie's chest and the floor, Lana then tightened the doggy chain linking the back of his neck to the back of Cecilia's neck. She pulled his leather hood halfway up, just over the bridge of his nose, then strapped on a small black dildo and commanded, "Suck me off, faggot!"

As he pushed his head down, Leslie could hear his wife struggling at the far end of their connective leash.

Still blinded, Leslie pulled down on the chain and was

able to push the plastic penis aside. Lana could feel Leslie's tongue shove under the acrylic toy, past the loose-fitting harness, through the fabric of her panties, over her moist crotch.

"What a randy slave boy you are," she said, amused. Removing the dildo, she pulled aside the crotch of her panties, allowing Leslie to slip his tongue through her golden bristles and dart into her. He eagerly licked her clitoris as the young woman threw her head back and moaned. The shiny, taut dog chain that connected him to his wife conducted her gasps and wiggles.

Wishing Lana would do more girl-girl stuff with her boss, Leslie rubbed his cock against the thickly carpeted floor below him. As he jerked himself up and down he could feel Cece struggling in ecstasy. He balled his tongue into a tight little roll and worked it all the way into Lana's snug young vagina. Pulling hard on the chain, he lifted Cecilia in the air by her neck.

He never found a limit to his wife's patronizing patience, a point where she'd say "Enough!" After about ten minutes of tonguing Lana and rubbing himself, still handcuffed, Leslie spurted onto the carpeted floor. He lay still for a moment, catching his breath, when he realized that dead weight was hanging from behind his neck.

"Lana! Cecilia's choking!"

The young girl immediately unlatched the chain and pulled out the ball.

"Cecilia!" Lana shook her. She quickly flipped her over and started applying mouth-to-mouth and CPR.

MAY 13, 2001, NYC
THE REPEATED NERVE-FRAZZLING BUZZES OF THE DOOR-man send an electrical current down my Frankensteined body. They draw me up. I'm still intoxicated and multiply

bruised. From the blasting volume of the intercom, I hear Luis say, "Mr. Cauldwell, there's a pretty lady here to see you."

"What's up?" I groan groggily.

"Okay, I'll send her up," Luis misunderstands me, as usual.

By the time she arrives at the door, I am back in sleep. Only furious and persistent pounding drags me to my wobbly feet. It must be Sheila, who after a good night's sleep and having learned the pleasure of being a top, has decided to come back and kick me a bit more while I'm on bottom. My pants and underpants are on the ground. I tiredly tug on my boxers.

When I swing the door open, I see Jeane standing there, dripping wet, and my heart pitterpats. I notice the sky out a window. Thick clotting clouds are breaking up. The balcony, the entire city, is drenched in a sticky rain.

"He called me twice last night!" she says, entering with a crazy glint in her eye.

"You want a towel?" I mutter automatically, barely able to open my gum-sealed eyes.

"Perry called last night!"

"Perry? Who the hell . . ."

She doesn't respond, only glares at me.

"He did, huh?"

I remember and stumble back into my living room, into my soft recliner, with Jeane following, explaining how the monster threatened her beloved daughter. "So then I grabbed the phone and I spoke to him."

"You spoke to him, huh?"

"Yeah, but he hung up."

"Oh," I reply, and curl my legs into my chair and make myself into a ball. The alcohol and pills still dominate.

"But he called back later." She has a stiffness to her.

"Later last night?" I repeat through mush and fuzz. Could I have?

Jeane glares down at me. Her eyeliner and mascara are streaked from the humidity. Some of the rain from her clothes is dripping onto my hair and semi-clad body. Lowering her volume, she articulates, "He told me to go to a separate room, away from Eddie."

"He did?" I reply, battling floppiness. Staring up at her, I ask, "Does Eddie know you're here?"

"He told me to pull down my panties," she continues heatedly. "You know what he told me to say? He said he'd leave Kate alone if I said Don Jerome fucked my ass while Sally Springfield ate my pussy."

I sit solemnly.

"I wonder who the bitch in the background is," she says.

"What bitch?"

"I heard a girl laughing in the background. He's got a girl." She's baring her teeth in a kind of diabolical smile.

"He does?" I reply.

"He told me to get my Polaroid. He said every family has one. You know what he wanted? He wanted me to take photos of myself. Can you imagine that? 'Take photos of yourself in the bathroom mirror!'"

"I . . . I'm . . ."

"Were you married, Leslie?" she asks. "Said he was going to fuck me to death like he did his wife."

"I'm sorry he said that," I whisper hoarsely.

"Say it!" she finally snaps. "You're Perry Cruz!"

Instead of trying to explain that Perry was a role I was stuck in the same way I had been locked in the Leslie-the-geek role when she lived with me, I simply nod my head.

"I trusted you with everything!" she exclaims. "I don't have sex anymore. I let you fuck me! I let you have me!"

"I don't know what you mean." The last reflex of lawyerly self-preservation wrings out.

"I star-69ed and it was your answering machine. But I

knew it while you were speaking to me. I recognized your voice. I even heard the girl saying your name in the background. You didn't even bother to disguise your voice!"

Mimicking me, Jeane makes a wide-eyed innocent expression that was one of her trademarks during her early porn days. She begins walking around the apartment, searching. I can hear her pulling out drawers, yanking books off their shelves. From Cecilia's room, I hear the dusty tools of her trade falling to the floor—whips, clasps, masks—and hear Jeane calling out, "Holy shit, it's loaded!" Then, stepping into the living room, she asks, "Who the fuck is this?!" waving a photo of an older man dressed up in a little girl's dress with a Goldilocks wig and a big swirling lollipop shielding a distinguished mustache.

"A judge," I disclose. She flings the picture to the floor and resumes her scrambling search.

"What's this? A file on me?!" she raves from the other room. She has located the dossier Ron gathered for me. I don't respond. I only listen as my little world is torn asunder in her desperate investigation.

Then I hear silence and a single, sharp, almost elegant cry. Now her boots are marching toward me. Displaying the photographs of Kate at school and the one of her held in terror, she shoves them in my face. She tries to say something, but gags with disgust.

I watch Sky go blank, and in the space of seconds, without even twitching a single solitary muscle, that amazing face rolls through a vast spectrum of emotions: starting with humorous disbelief, pausing for an attempt at compassion, a check for nostalgic understanding before blowing open betrayal, and the last stop of violent, intractable fury.

When I see Ron Marauder's handgun that she found in Cece's box, I bound for it. She pumps a slug into my well-deserved chest, punching me back onto Cecilia's nineteenth-century chestnut coffee table, which splinters to the floor. I wish I could have done that for her. That's the final division of human beings: those who sacrifice themselves for others and those who sacrifice others for themselves. The door slams shut. She is once again a part of the permanent past.

A delicate circle of smoke spirals up, rising dead center from my Armani shirt. I pick up the phone, put it down. The blood isn't hosing out, only oozing. Now that I've played out perversity, I'm ready for professionality. I have a new wild card to play. Flipping through my Rolodex, I locate Judge Peter Sanders's numbers.

Since it is Sunday morning, I call him at home. The phone rings, he answers. "May I help you?"

"On Monday," I speak carefully, "William Holtov has an appointment with you."

"Don't call here again!" He hangs up. I push the trusty redial.

"I want you to know he has nothing to do with any of this."

"I've known Bill for years," he replies, "and I know he'd never pull a stunt like this. In the thirty years I've been on the bench, no one has ever dared to fuck with me and no one ever will." He slams the phone down and again I push redial.

"The administration and shareholders of the Sewter Corporation didn't have anything to do with this either."

"What the hell do you want?!" he says, with a tone of zero tolerance.

"I want you to know that the administration and shareholders of the Sewter Corporation had nothing to do with this."

"I agree. I believe you and you alone are the culprit. Are we done?"

Now that I've isolated myself as the problem, I pitch the compromise: "Suppose, Judge, I were to file a Chapter Seven."

"Let the Sewter Corporation be the headstone for your career."

"No, I don't mean Sewter. I mean, suppose I were to liquidate." The euphemism finally sinks in. He doesn't respond. He's waiting to hear the full offer before answering. "Would that change anything regarding the Sewter case?"

"What are you saying?" He lowers his voice, comprehending that my offer is part of an overall proposal.

"If I were to file a Seven, which you would read about in tomorrow's obituary, would you let Bill file his plan of reorganization for Sewter?"

"If I understand exactly what you're saying, I would strongly reconsider Mr. Holtov's plan with great partiality," he responds, and I know for him that's a yes.

I thank him, and when I hang up the phone, despite the fact that I've bled all over myself, I feel good.

One down, now I have to consider my last client. I have to fabricate a reasonable doubt. What possible alibi and motive could I devise for a bullet hole in the victim's chest? I am still too drunk and tired to resolve a strategy for this one. I decide to rest a moment, but my mind and mood drift to new, innovative fantasies in a more evolved calculus of pornography.

Love, that curve ball out of nowhere, bops me on the head: Sheila the bar vixen, who I used like a rag doll, suddenly comes to life and now I'm left with a bloody heart; Sheila, who connived drunken me into calling Jeane. It doesn't feel like a bullet has entered my chest, it feels as though a heart-shaped metal plug has been yanked out and, yes, I am deflating.

Looking out the window to the stretch of sky before me, I can see that the clouds have completely dissipated. The magician of the heavens reveals a beautiful blue sky. The glass windows of the adjacent buildings are staring at me now. She shot me, and it is my final duty to cover for her—a dying testimonial will hold endless water in a court of law.

I pick up the phone and ask directory assistance for the number of a building in Manhattan called the Deacon Arms. Information's automated operator gives the number and says that for a cost of thirty-five cents they will dial it if I press 1. What the hell, I press it. I hear the ever-obsequious Luis answering the lobby phone.

"Luis, did you see my friend?"

"You mean that lady that just left? She was *muy bonita* . . ."

"Is she safe?" I ask frantically. "Has anybody hurt her?"

"Why? What happened?" The blood is a spring trickling down my chest into a pool in my lap, hot and dark along my legs. I feel myself expanding, diversifying. My stock is going public.

In the dark jaws, where all things tumble, where societies crumble and old men stumble, love is the air we breathe, the earth we walk on, the economy we function in. It's not a passion or a fixation or a desire or a guilt. Love should have been a conduct, a process of life, an axiom, a grandeur we evolve . . . Its connective nature, its transferal powers, make utter sense.

"Listen, Luis," I ask, "can you get up here?"

"I can't leave my post, sir."

"I'll give you a thousand bucks. It's vital. I'm in trouble!" With every quiver, a little more life shakes out of me.

"What's the matter?" His voice takes on an urgency. "Those guys up there, Mr. Leslie?" I won't be alive long enough for him to get here anyway.

"What guys?" I ask.

"The mobsters who've been following you?"

"Oh! Yeah! Luis, listen! They shot me."

"They shot you?" He's astonished.

"Yeah, listen, I made big bets, worked up huge debts."

The crescendo of so many operas, so many porn flicks, so many memories I've had and'll never have. I feel my body squeezing out diamonds, pearls, and sapphires. It's a wonderful feeling as if my whole body is orgasming, shooting out from itself. I wish I could buy a thousand bodies to kill in order to experience this wonderful swooning, swirling departure a thousand million times over. Death takes all the sustained mediocrity and monotony of existence and presses it into a sparkling, garlicky drip of a perfect scintillating moment.

"Mr. Cauldwell! You there?"

"Sky, Shecilia, I'm sorry, forgive me."

"Hold on!" she says.

That's why I pulled on the leash—she always loved a good throttling. With every ejaculation love seemed to grow more distant. You can either have desire or fulfillment—not both.

But love is both. As I splatter in my blood, I feel as it fills me, all the innocence, all the naïveté, all the strength and ideals, all the crispness is returning, flushing out all the jaded and crippled and ugly and old—it's love, not moralizing love but a tidal flood, connecting and forgiving everyone.

"Mr. Caldwell, I'm coming up!"

The city of life is getting smaller, but before it vanishes, the Times Square of my 1970s, with all its gritty shameful authenticity that makes us woefully human replaces the Disney of manufactured innocence. I try to impart this: "Mercy!"

"Yes!" Luis cries out.

The doorman already knows—

▼

Thanks:

Henny Ohr

Johnny Temple

Johanna Ingalls

Lynne Tenpenny

Bernie Mooney

Special Thanks:

Everyone at Center at Cain

Jan Cain

Mike Vadino

Jason Marder

In Memorium:

The Real Times Square

Leo Samiof

Also available from Akashic Books:

MANHATTAN LOVERBOY
by Arthur Nersesian

203 pages, a trade paperback original, $13.95, ISBN: 1-888451-09-2

"*Manhattan Loverboy* is paranoid fantasy and fantastic comedy in the service of social realism, using the methods of L. Frank Baum's *Wizard of Oz* or Kafka's *The Trial* to update the picaresque urban chronicles of Augie March, with a far darker edge . . ."
—*Downtown Magazine*

THE FUCK-UP
by Arthur Nersesian

274 pages, a trade paperback original, $20.00, ISBN: 1-888451-03-3
Original Akashic edition, available only through direct mail order

"I was utterly charmed (disarmed and seduced is actually closer to the truth) by Arthur Nersesian's masterly evocation of the early eighties Lower East Side. *The Fuck-Up* is an unerringly accurate rendering of a place, time, and experience lived by many, but its true power lies in Nersesian's narrative voice. This really is one of the few books you want to take to bed with you, cuddle close, and wrap your arms around its characters."
—Darius James, author of *Negrophobia*

BROOKLYN NOIR edited by Tim McLoughlin

350 pages, a trade paperback original, $15.95, ISBN: 1-888451-58-0

Twenty brand new crime stories from New York's punchiest borough. Contributors include: Pete Hamill, Arthur Nersesian, Maggie Estep, Nelson George, Neal Pollack, Sidney Offit, Ken Bruen, and others.

"*Brooklyn Noir* is such a stunningly perfect combination that you can't believe you haven't read an anthology like this before. But trust me—you haven't. Story after story is a revelation, filled with the requisite sense of place, but also the perfect twists that crime stories demand. The writing is flat-out superb, filled with lines that will sing in your head for a long time to come."
—Laura Lippman, winner of the Edgar and Shamus awards

WITH OR WITHOUT YOU
by Lauren Sanders

280 pages, a trade paperback original, $14.95, ISBN: 1-888451-69-6

"I hate the term poetic, but Lauren Sanders's writing has such a slick mean surface and her subject is such a truly bad girl, a murderer. I mean, so that poetic suits *With or Without You* just fine. It's a hot poetic book I wouldn't kick out of bed."
> —Eileen Myles, author of *Cool for You* and *Chelsea Girls*

HEADLESS stories by Benjamin Weissman

157 pages, a trade paperback original, $12.95, ISBN: 1-888451-49-1

"*Headless* is at play in the world. It is fearless, fun, and sometimes filthy. Weissman invites you into an alphabet soup of delight in language. Eat up."
> —Alice Sebold, author of *The Lovely Bones*

"Brilliant. Wildly inventive, profane, and hilarious."
> —Bret Easton Ellis, author of *Glamorama*

SOME OF THE PARTS by T Cooper

264 pages, a trade paperback original, $14.95, ISBN: 1-888451-36-X
* A Barnes & Noble Discover Great New Writers selection

"Cooper's scenes have a quirky appeal . . . [S]he deftly captures the seamier motives of her unconventional characters."
> —*Publishers Weekly*

"A strong, fearless writer not afraid to show her characters' most unflinching vulnerability."
> —*Kirkus Reviews*